PRAISE FOR *THE RESCUE*

"Steven Konkoly's new Ryan Decker series is a triumph—an action-thriller master class in spy craft, tension, and suspense. An absolute must-read for fans of Tom Clancy, Vince Flynn, and Brad Thor."

—Blake Crouch, *New York Times* bestselling author

"*The Rescue* by Steven Konkoly has everything I love in a thriller—betrayal, murder, a badass investigator, and a man fueled by revenge."

—T.R. Ragan, *New York Times* bestselling author

"*The Rescue* grabs you like a bear trap and never lets go. No one writes action sequences any better than Steve Konkoly—he drops his heroes into impossible situations and leaves you no option but to keep your head down, follow where they lead, and hope you make it out alive."

—Matthew Fitzsimmons, *Wall Street Journal* bestselling author

"Breakneck twists, political conspiracy, bristling action—*The Rescue* has it all! Steven Konkoly has created a dynamic and powerful character in Ryan Decker."

—Joe Hart, *Wall Street Journal* bestselling author

"If you are a fan of characters like Scot Harvath and Mitch Rapp, this new series is a must-read. Steven Konkoly delivers a refreshingly unique blend of action, espionage, and well-researched realism."

—Andrew Watts, *USA Today* bestselling author

"An excellent source for your daily dose of action, conspiracy, and intrigue."

—Tim Tigner, author of *Betrayal*

THE
MOUNTAIN

ALSO BY STEVEN KONKOLY

RYAN DECKER SERIES

The Rescue

The Raid

THE FRACTURED STATE SERIES

Fractured State

Rogue State

THE PERSEID COLLAPSE SERIES

The Jakarta Pandemic

The Perseid Collapse

Event Horizon

Point of Crisis

Dispatches

THE BLACK FLAGGED SERIES

Alpha

Redux

Apex

Vektor

Omega

THE ZULU VIRUS CHRONICLES

Hot Zone

Kill Box

Fire Storm

THE MOUNTAIN

STEVEN KONKOLY

THOMAS & MERCER

Text copyright © 2020 by Steven Konkoly
All rights reserved.

Published by Thomas & Mercer, Seattle

www.apub.com

Amazon, the Amazon logo, and Thomas & Mercer are trademarks of Amazon.com, Inc., or its affiliates.

ISBN-13: 9781542021869
ISBN-10: 1542021863

Cover design by Rex Bonomelli

Printed in the United States of America

To Kosia, Matthew, and Sophia—the heart and soul of my writing.

PART ONE

PART ONE

CHAPTER ONE

Ryan Decker slid the rickety metal chair across the doughnut shop's grimy linoleum floor, angling for a slightly more expanded view of the street. A guy he recognized from a picture provided with the firm's intelligence packet lurked near a bustling taco stand down the street from the target motel—juxtaposed against the packed lunchtime gaggle. His razor-bald dome and neck tattoo were just part of the reason. The fact that he remained empty-handed was the biggest tip-off.

He ignored the feeding frenzy on the sidewalk in front of him, constantly checking his phone and furtively glancing at the doughnut shop. His most recent peek in Decker's direction had been anything but secretive. It had lasted long enough to leave him feeling uneasy seated next to a floor-to-ceiling plate glass window. *Exposed* might be a better description of how he appeared.

If Decker had been made, and the group working out of the Ritz Motel was serious enough about protecting their kiddie-peddling enterprise, he'd make a nice target for an unannounced drive-by shooting. Then again, a lunchtime shooting in the middle of North Hollywood would bring far more trouble down on their operation than a nosy private investigator.

Of course, this decision-making logic assumed that they hadn't somehow specifically identified Decker. He'd built somewhat of a ruthless reputation in Los Angeles over the past several months, and despite

Harlow's best efforts to keep his connection to the firm under the radar, word had oozed into the deepest, darkest crevasses of the area's human-trafficking underworld. Decker's presence meant one thing for these scumbags. Serious trouble.

Decker loosened his shirt, giving him better access to the concealed pistol on his right hip. The man stepped away from the taco shop crowd and started walking briskly toward the Ritz Motel, his eyes darting from the sidewalk in front of him to the doughnut shop window. *Shit.* Decker took a sip of coffee while tapping a text to Harlow.

DECKER: Taco Nazi OM toward RM. Pretty sure I'm burned.

HARLOW: Motel is hot. I can feel it.

DECKER: He'll probably walk right past if I'm made.

HARLOW: Can't let that happen. We have to find her ASAP if ur burned. They'll kill her and leave.

DECKER: Agree. Need a room number.

HARLOW: How?

He alternated between Taco Nazi and the screen for a few moments, deciding on a fairly reckless course of action. If it didn't work, they'd be no worse off than now.

DECKER: Have an idea. U won't like it.

HARLOW: Shocker. Do it. Where do u need me?

DECKER: Depends on what happens. OM.

Decker pushed away from the table and ran for the door, barely managing to speed-dial Harlow's number on the way. Predictably, Taco Nazi took off the moment Decker burst onto the sidewalk, passing the entrance to the motel.

Shit!

Given the man's speed and the relatively short distance to the intersection beyond the motel, Decker immediately assessed that he'd lose this footrace if he didn't cheat a little. He needed to herd Taco Nazi back to the motel. Ignoring the green lights clearly visible at the intersection less than a hundred feet away, Decker sprinted diagonally across four lanes of traffic on Lankershim Boulevard—screaming the entire way.

Maybe the sight of a raving lunatic gave the drivers pause. Maybe the powers that be finally decided to give Decker a break. Whatever the case, he managed to run full speed—across the entire width of North Hollywood's busiest street—without stopping. Taco Nazi froze his tracks when Decker burst onto the sidewalk thirty feet in front of him.

Horns blared and car tires screeched as the skinhead glared at Decker, who raised the bottom edge of his shirt to expose the concealed holster on his right hip. The move was a calculated gamble. Decker couldn't legally draw the pistol unless the man displayed a firearm first. A scenario with one clear ending. Taco Nazi dead on the sidewalk—and a whole lot of explaining to do. Not to mention that they might lose their primary target. They had no way of finding the girl unless Taco Nazi led them to the room. The man's eyes immediately locked on to Decker's pistol, his brain no doubt running the options.

During the seconds that ticked by while they stared at each other, Decker willed him to turn around and run for the perceived safety of the motel. Everything else would fall into place if the guy just hauled ass for the motel room, where his Nazi buddies presumably held Brooke Miller. After a few tense seconds, the guy turned and ran toward the motel at full speed. *Thank you.* Decker gave chase, cautiously maintaining the distance between them.

"Taco Nazi is heading back to the motel in a hurry," he said into the phone.

"Perfect. I have a concealed spot with a good view of—"

The skinhead stopped in the middle of the motel parking lot entrance and pivoted, firing a fully automatic pistol in Decker's direction. The first few bullets cracked within inches of Decker's face. The rest flew high as successive pistol recoils tugged the shooter's hand farther off target.

Decker slid behind the nearest parked car and instinctively aimed his pistol over the hood at Taco Nazi, who immediately abandoned his effort to reload the pistol and sprinted into the Ritz Motel's parking lot. Decker's brain locked on to a single train of thought as the man vanished from sight. *I shouldn't be alive right now.* If the skinhead had just taken the extra moment to wrap his other hand around the pistol's grip, a very substantial number of the thirty-three nine-millimeter bullets loaded in the pistol's extended magazine would have hit him.

A muffled voice jarred him out of his mental vapor lock. Harlow. He raised the phone still clutched in his left hand and took off running toward the motel.

"Decker. Decker," she repeated frantically.

"I'm fine. He's headed in your direction!" said Decker. "Stay out of sight! ID the room and let the cops deal with this. They'll be here any moment."

"I see him," she whispered. "He's headed up the stairs."

Decker slowed his pace, relieved to hear that Harlow sounded composed—like always—and unlikely to rush into a shitty situation. Like the one he'd carelessly thrust himself into a few seconds ago.

"Observe and report," said Decker, approaching the parking lot entrance. "I'm almost in position."

"Shit. They're moving her. Room on the second floor," she said.

"Harlow! Do not even think about—"

A long burst of automatic fire cut through the car horns and screams on Lankershim Boulevard. Decker stopped in midstride and put the phone to his ear.

"Harlow?"

Two distinctly spaced gunshots answered his question, followed by another burst of automatic fire. He readied his pistol and barreled into the parking lot, determined to draw all their attention—and gunfire—away from Harlow.

CHAPTER TWO

Harlow's ears still rang from the gunfire. The seemingly endless drum-beat of automatic fire against the dumpster had been loud enough, but her own pistol, a compact Sig Sauer, had sounded like a cannon. She'd never fired her handgun without hearing protection. A first for her and—based on the quick glimpse she got of the motel courtyard—very likely to be repeated.

Two men had just exited one of the rooms on the second floor, car-rying between them the limp body of a girl who more or less matched Brooke Miller's description. She had been relieved to see that they hadn't just executed her in the room. Harlow had assumed they would kill any captives before shooting their way out of the motel. Dump the baggage and eliminate witnesses. Given their current predicament, the decision to drag Miller along didn't make a lot of sense.

Desperate for more information, Harlow risked a quick glance, drawing another long burst of gunfire from the skinhead in the parking lot. Taco Nazi. As bullets rattled against the dumpster and the echo of gunshots hit her from every direction, she processed what she'd seen. The two men were running for the stairs, one of them carrying Brooke over his shoulder. They were in a hurry to get out of here with her. A development Harlow had to stop.

With the pistol trembling in her hands, Harlow leaned a few inches beyond the corner of the dumpster and searched for Taco Nazi. She found him standing halfway up the stairs, reloading his pistol. Before she could line up a shot, he pointed at the dumpster and yelled, drawing her attention toward the upper walkway. One of the escaping thugs turned and braced a nasty-looking rifle against the railing—aimed directly at her. Harlow pressed the trigger twice and yanked her head out of sight, unsure whether her bullets had struck Taco Nazi.

The dumpster shuddered from whatever monstrous weapon he had unleashed, one jackhammer strike after another pounding against the side until she started to doubt whether the dumpster could protect her much longer. She backed up a few feet and crouched low, steeling herself for what came next. The moment this onslaught even paused, Harlow fully intended to drill a hole through the middle of the shooter's forehead.

When the gunfire stopped, she didn't hesitate. Her pistol quickly found the bearded face that had been glaring at her over the barrel of a rifle moments earlier. Before she could fire, repeated supersonic cracks forced her back—Taco Nazi was alive and well. She caught a glimpse of him standing in the same place on the open staircase.

She also spotted Decker, who moved cautiously toward the corner of the motel office, which met the bottom of the staircase. If Decker turned that corner blindly or got distracted by the shooter on the second floor—he would walk right into Taco Nazi's onslaught.

She glanced at her phone on the asphalt but dismissed the idea. Decker would be one hundred percent focused on what lay ahead of him. Right now he was in another world. A world he fully understood and could navigate almost perfectly. Her best strategy was to leave Decker alone and let him do what he did best.

The assessment didn't sit well with Harlow. Not only did she resent her seeming inability to make a difference under the circumstances—she worried that Decker was about to walk into a lethal wall of bullets. She'd made the same mistake a few seconds ago, focusing all her attention on the second-floor shooter, while Taco Nazi fired away. She'd been extremely lucky. Any one of those bullets could and should have punctured her skull.

With that cheery thought in mind, Harlow leaned out and fired the rest of her pistol's magazine at Taco Nazi—hoping it might distract him long enough for Decker to work his magic.

CHAPTER THREE

Decker halted a few inches from the corner, paralyzed by the sight of Harlow carelessly exposed next to the dumpster. She fired round after round from her compact pistol at targets he still couldn't see. Based on the volume and variety of gunfire previously leveled at Harlow, he guessed that she had the undivided attention of at least two shooters. One was undoubtedly armed with a high-capacity automatic shotgun. That sound had been unmistakable.

Fortunately for both Harlow and Decker, neither the shotgun nor the modified Glock was very accurate on full auto—particularly in these idiots' hands. Then again, volume very often made up for accuracy when it came to guns, and it took only one bullet to end your day. Harlow had done everything she could up until this point, and she'd done it exceedingly well. It was his turn now. Time to put an end to this Valkyrie nonsense and bring Brooke Miller home.

He peeked around the corner with his pistol, finding Taco Nazi completely focused on Harlow. Decker fired two quick shots, the bullets forming a tight pattern along the skinhead's left temple. Taco Nazi dropped in his peripheral vision like a sack of dirt. His next shot struck the shotgun guy in the face, or so he thought.

The man remained upright, seemingly frozen in place, with no obvious entry or exit wound. He'd seen this before. The bullet may have entered a nostril or his mouth, rattling around inside the skull instead of punching through the other side. Uncertain of the first bullet's true impact on the situation, he lined up another head shot but paused before pressing the trigger. The Valkyrie carrying Brooke Miller over his shoulders took off for the open motel room door they had presumably just exited. If he got inside with her, Decker and Harlow would have no choice but to hand the situation over to the police, who would turn this into a long, drawn-out hostage negotiation—with no guaranteed outcome.

He shifted his aim down and to the right—and fired twice at the fleeing man's legs, dropping him mostly out of sight on the walkway. Decker reacquired the still seemingly immobile shotgun guy and drilled a hole through his forehead. A bright-red spray hit the salmon-colored wall behind his head. His body accordioned over the railing. The man hung there, blood pouring out of the gaping hole in the top of his head, as Decker scrambled up the stairs.

At the top of the staircase, he quick-peeked down the length of walkway, just as the third skinhead crawled out of sight into the room—leaving a thick trail of blood on the concrete deck. Decker kept his pistol pointed at the door as he moved quickly to Brooke Miller, who lay facedown and listless next to the skinhead hanging over the railing. Movement in the direction of the dumpster broke his focus for a moment. Harlow was on the way. Once again carelessly exposed.

A quick analysis of the situation convinced him that she was safe from any conceivable line of fire from the open door—unless the guy in the room somehow managed to prop himself up to a standing position. Decker didn't consider that likely given the amount of blood on the walkway. For now, he could focus on moving the girl away from whatever threat remained in the motel room.

Decker reached Brooke Miller a few nerve-racking seconds later, grasping one of the girl's wrists with his left hand, while keeping the pistol aimed at the door with the other. Once he was certain that his grip was solid, Decker pulled her back until he was satisfied she was safely out of the door's line of fire. The girl moaned most of the way, likely from the pain of her face scraping across the rough concrete. As much as he would have liked to spare her that last insult, he absolutely couldn't afford the time or distraction of repositioning her body with the shooter still active.

He stepped past her and kneeled, placing himself between the girl and the open door. This late-in-the-game thought gave him a jolt. Up until now, he had assumed that the total number of skinheads on the prowl at the motel was three. For all he knew, they had guys in other rooms. That was how he would have done it. Harlow yelled up at him from below, thankfully staying out of sight.

"Status of the primary?"

"No obvious injuries. I can't really make an assessment under the circumstances," he said, remaining laser focused on the door. "Watch yourself down there. There may be more than three of them."

"They would have come at us by now," she said. "Can I come up and get her?"

He gave the angles and trajectories a quick thought. She'd be exposed to possible gunfire for at least half of the trip up the stairs, and there wasn't much he could do about it. Decker's angle of fire was too shallow to hit anyone more than a few inches inside the doorway. His position was good for one thing—protecting the primary and keeping the guy pinned down in the room.

"I'd rather you didn't," he said. "I'm concerned about the stairs."

"Can you bring her down with me covering the door?" said Harlow.

Decker didn't like that idea. For all he knew, the skinheads had left some firepower behind. Harlow wouldn't stand a chance against a rifle.

"I need to stay focused on the shooter," said Decker.

"I'm worried about what's going to happen when the police show up."

For the first time since the shooting kicked off, the concert of police sirens broke through. From the sound of it, the entire North Hollywood police force had responded.

"It'll be fine," said Decker, not really buying his statement.

If skinhead number three decided to go down in a blaze of glory when the police arrived, Decker and the girl stood a good chance of getting shot in the ensuing chaos. Harlow's situation wasn't much better. He briefly considered sending her out front, to defuse the situation with responding LAPD units, but the volume of gunfire reported on the street and from the motel would have every cop on edge. Shoot first and ask questions later.

That left one option as far as he could tell. Send Harlow back the way she'd come. The route she had traveled to get to the motel was a city-block-long twisted maze of dumpsters, barbed-wire-topped brick walls, and dilapidated fences jammed between several businesses. The police wouldn't bother with it. They'd park in the used car lot next door and deploy on foot immediately behind the motel. She'd be long gone by the time the police cut off that route.

"I have something that might help the situation," she said.

"A *Star Wars* transporter?"

"*Star Trek*," she said. "Take a quick look left."

He did what she asked, keeping the gun level. Interesting. This gave them a slightly better option.

"You keep one of those around for emergencies?"

"I swapped out the lipstick and eye shadow," she said.

"Remind me not to go through your purse," he said.

"I shouldn't have to at this point," said Harlow.

"Toss it up and kick in one of the doors below," said Decker. "We'll need somewhere to weather the LAPD storm. This is just going to make it worse."

"Heads up," she said.

A few moments later, a dark-green cylindrical object sailed into his peripheral vision and struck his left thigh, bouncing to the concrete next to him. He picked it up with his left hand and edged forward along the blood-streaked walkway in a low crouch. Somewhere below him, Harlow kicked furiously at a door until he heard it give in.

"Clear on the ground," she yelled up to him.

Decker passed a rectangular red fire extinguisher box, which marked the start of the skinhead's motel room. He was now indirectly exposed to gunfire from inside the room. Bullets would pass right through the thin exterior walls. When he reached the window, he dropped to his elbows and knees to crawl the rest of the way. Despite the excruciating pain of the coarse concrete grinding away at his elbows, he kept the pistol aimed at the door.

Now for the not-so-fun part. The window was too close to the door for him to rise into a crouch without giving his position away, so he'd have to do this from the most awkward position possible. Lying on his stomach. The sirens intensified, reminding him that he was running out of time. Decker looped his gun hand thumb through the grenade's arming ring and pulled it free, before cocking his left arm as far as possible toward the railing and releasing the plastic pop-off lever.

He tossed the grenade inside the moment the lever detached. Unlike the military police–grade M84 stun grenade, the civilian-available M13 flash bang had a notoriously short fuse. He hoped this did the trick. The M13 was also far less potent than the real deal. Not much more than an extremely loud firecracker, coupled with a partially blinding flash.

Automatic gunfire erupted inside the room as soon as the grenade hit the floor. Dozens of bullets passed through the wall and window directly above him. He'd been right about the skinheads leaving some of their hardware behind. Projectiles punctured the doorframe inches from his head when the grenade exploded.

The sharp detonation stopped the gunfire, and Decker took off for the girl sprawled on the walkway. He had already slung her over his shoulder when the automatic gunfire started again. He glanced back as the bullets flew straight out of the room like before. The skinhead was still shooting from a position that didn't threaten the staircase. He hurried down the stairs until he reached the parking lot, where he put all his remaining energy and focus into reaching the open door next to Harlow.

He continued at full speed until he'd crossed the doorway threshold and reached the foot of the closest bed, where he gently lowered the primary down onto a duvet cover that looked like it hadn't been swapped out in over forty years. Decker turned to Harlow, who had just shut the door and thrown the swing lock.

"Pull the curtains, too," he said, surprised when she didn't immediately react.

Instead, she stared past him, shaking her head and muttering.

"What is it?" he said, glancing from Harlow to the girl.

He put it together before she answered.

"That's not her," she said. "That's not Brooke Miller."

A burst of automatic fire cut through the brief silence that ensued, followed by a few isolated pistol gunshots. Decker really hoped the LAPD didn't try to storm the room. They'd lose officers doing that, and he'd feel partly responsible.

"We can't go back out there. The place will be swarming with cops any second," said Decker. "Shut the curtains and help me get her into the bathroom. We hunker down and call nine-one-one. Let them know what they're up against."

"Fuck," muttered Harlow under her breath, staring at the girl.

"Hey! We did good," he said, motioning toward the bed. "We saved this girl from hell knows what else. We can still find Brooke Miller. It just won't be today."

"I doubt it after this," said Harlow, yanking the curtains together and shutting most of the light out of the room. "Those pieces of shit will go to ground—leaving no witnesses behind."

He grabbed her shoulders.

"Harlow," he said, locking eyes with her. "You win some and you lose some in this business. Nobody knows that better than I do."

She took a quick breath, her expression softening a near-imperceptible amount. "I don't like to lose."

"That's because you never do," he said. "But trust me. If you have to lose, there are far worse alternatives. That girl represents a win for somebody out there, which means this is still a win for you."

"I know. I know," she said. "I just don't know what I'm going to tell Brooke's parents."

"Let's get her into the bathroom," said Decker. "We can work on next steps while we wait for the police to secure this mess."

She nodded and helped him carry her to the bathroom, where they struggled in the tight confines to lay her down in the tub without hurting her. Decker had his hands under her armpits, trying to twist her past the sink, when Harlow froze. Stuck in an awkward and extremely uncomfortable position between the toilet and tub, he took a knee.

"We're almost there," he said, heaving the girl up over the side. "Pull her legs up and that's it. I'll do the rest."

"Holy shit. We're truly screwed," she said.

Straining with the weight, he shook his head. "Harlow, we covered this. We're fine."

"No," she said, tossing the girl's legs into the tub like an afterthought. "We're not."

"Hey. Take it easy on her," he said, still holding her up.

"Look at the tattoo on her back," said Harlow. "Her shirt rode up when you lifted her. You couldn't see it."

He twisted her as far as he could without falling over, catching the word NATION tattooed across the bottom of her back, just below a graphic displaying several small skulls inside some kind of boundary line. Most of the tattoo was covered by a long-sleeved black shirt, but he understood right away why Harlow was concerned.

"I don't . . . uh—" he started, until Harlow pulled the shirt up to her bra strap.

"You gotta be shitting me," he said.

He pulled her out of the tub and set her down on the linoleum floor, facedown. Harlow did the honors, yanking her shirt as far up as possible without ripping it. Decker stared down at the full tattoo. It started just above her bra strap with the word WHITE and morphed into a thick, cartoonish SS symbol that extended down most of her back—each of the lightning bolts filled with human skulls.

"She must have been a girlfriend," said Harlow. "No wonder they tried to get her out of here. It didn't make any sense at the time, but I was just glad they hadn't executed our primary. Or so I thought."

She released the shirt to examine one of her arms. Heroin tracks up and down the length of the inside of her forearm.

"That would explain why she's barely responsive," said Harlow.

"What now?" said Decker, before slumping to the floor next to the toilet.

"Slight modification to the plan. My first call goes to Jess," said Harlow. "It's going to take every trick up her fancy suit sleeve to dodge a kidnapping charge. Not to mention the rest of the mess out there."

"Come here," he said, coaxing her next to him on the grimy floor.

Decker put an arm around her shoulder and kissed her cheek.

"This wasn't exactly what I had in mind for our six-month anniversary escape," he said, and waited.

Harlow didn't react at first, and Decker wondered if he'd crossed the humor line, or if she'd redrawn it. She chuckled a few seconds later, but that was the extent of it. She gripped his other hand and squeezed.

"I'm worried about Brooke," she said. "And I'm worried about the firm. This is going to be a rough ride."

"I know," he said, the sirens coming into sharp focus again. "But call nine-one-one first. It'll look pretty bad if the first call goes to the firm's attorney. Especially if we can prevent machine-gun Hitler up there from killing any of the responding officers."

"You're right," she said, taking out her phone. "You're kind of always right."

"Not always," he said. "And you really don't want to be around when I'm wrong."

He had to wonder if this might be one of those times.

Chapter Four

The distant rumble of approaching trucks woke Brett Hale long before their blinding headlights swept across the farm. A quick glance at his watch told Hale everything he needed to know. His situation on the mountain had drastically changed—for better or worse. No middle ground existed between the two out here, especially at three in the morning.

The prospect of a breakthrough deal with the local leadership terrified him as much as it excited him. A sizable fortune was his for the taking on one side of the table. The other side? He didn't want to think about it. The nickname "Murder Mountain" had endured for a reason. This vast, isolated forest region was essentially lawless.

Fiercely defended by the locals, eastern Humboldt County's redwood forests concealed a dark secret. Nearly half of the state's illegal marijuana industry was based in the area. Everyone living on or around the mountain had a hand in the trade—which made it a dangerous place for outsiders. Brett hoped he hadn't pushed the locals too hard.

Car doors slammed shut, followed by footsteps and muted voices. He'd know soon enough. He remained motionless inside his sleeping bag; the silhouettes of several figures broadcast against the long stretch of plyboard wall behind him. When the other occupants of the cabin started to move and grumble, he unzipped the sleeping bag and dangled his feet over the side of the rigid cot, probing the floor for his boots.

"What time is it?" whispered a woman from the other side of the cabin.

"Three," said Brett.

"This can't be good," she said.

"That's what I was thinking," said Brett.

Angie, a five-season veteran of the mountain, slid off her cot and stayed low. Without saying another word, she started putting on her boots.

"Can you see who it is?" said a groggy voice from the cot next to him.

"Why don't you stick your head up and look," said Angie.

"No thanks," he replied. "I'm still crashed out if they ask."

"I'm sure they'll just leave you alone," said Angie sarcastically.

The shadows started to shift a few moments later, followed by loud voices. Brett quickly finished tying his boots as the rest of the cabin's half dozen occupants began to stir. The doorknob rattled, followed by a heavy pounding. Brett stood up, thankful that the chilly fall nights had persuaded him to sleep in his clothes. Unlike most of his cabinmates, he was ready for the trip up the mountain. Not that they would be making the drive with him. Brett was fairly certain they had come for him.

The time he'd spent among small-time growers and patchouli-stinking seasonal workers had been a means to an end. He was a businessman with a serious proposition for the loose confederation of locals that controlled the bulk of the area's cannabis trade. Serious money to invest in their rapidly expanding empire—for a taste of whatever was happening higher up on the mountain.

Without warning, the flimsy wooden door exploded inward and slammed into the plywood wall next to it, loosely bouncing back in place to block the massive figure that filled the doorway. A powerful kick knocked the door off its hinges and sent it sliding across the floor. Brett backed up against the cot and slid a hand under his pillow. The sharp metallic racking sound froze him in place.

"Not the smartest move, dickhead," said the hulk of a man in the doorway, pointing the business end of a shotgun in Brett's direction.

"Just grabbing my wallet," said Brett, not sure if he'd spoken loud enough to be heard.

"If anything other than a wallet appears, I'll remove your head. That goes for the rest of you," said the man, stepping into the room.

Two more men slid inside behind him and formed a tight perimeter around the doorway, their shotguns covering the entire cabin. Brett grabbed the thin leather wallet under the pillow, his hand momentarily brushing against the satellite phone he'd cleverly managed to keep hidden from the owners and his coworkers.

He should have slipped it into one of his cargo pockets the moment he saw the headlights. If something went drastically wrong tonight, the phone could have pinpointed his last known location. Then again, the discovery of a satellite phone would pretty much guarantee a disaster. The people up here took their privacy and secrecy seriously. He slowly removed the wallet, allowing it to be seen by the man aiming a shotgun at his head.

"Put it in your pocket and get outside," said the man, motioning with the shotgun barrel.

"Can I put my boots on?" said the guy next to Brett.

"The trucks leave in thirty seconds," said the leader. "I don't give a shit what you do between now and then, but if you're not on the trucks—you're done here."

"Where are you taking us?" said the same guy.

"A little ride up the hill," he said. "The clock is ticking."

Brett decided to take a gamble. There was no reason for these men to continue with this facade.

"You don't have to take everyone up there on my account," said Brett. "I'm good with a solo trip."

The man walked up to him and pushed the shotgun barrel into his chest.

"You gonna be a problem?"

"No. Wait. What?" said Brett, suddenly feeling disoriented.

They had to be here for him. Why else would they put on this kind of show?

"Get outside!" said the man, grabbing the loose fabric of Brett's shirt and yanking him toward the door.

The sudden violent move nearly pulled Brett off his feet. He pitched forward and caught the doorframe with one of his hands, only to be forcefully shoved out of the cabin and onto the hard-packed dirt. Another brute took over from there, searching him thoroughly before hauling him to his feet and dragging him to the back of the nearest pickup truck. The man opened the tailgate and grunted.

"Get in."

"I think there's been a little—"

"Either get in by yourself, or I'll help you in!" said the man.

Brett hesitated long enough for the guy to start moving toward him.

"I'm good. I'm good," said Brett, turning to face the extended tailgate. "Take it easy."

"Just get in and shut the fuck up," he said. "And don't even think about jumping out. You're done if that happens."

Brett heaved his lean frame into the back of the oversize pickup and scooted along the hard plastic bed until he could lean his back against the cabin. He started to say something but thought twice about it. There was nothing to gain by pissing these guys off. He'd play whatever game they wanted if this was what it took to make his pitch to the big shots up the hill. For all he knew, these goons had no idea why they'd been sent on this little task.

The last of his cabinmates had barely taken a seat before the truck backed into a three-point turn and sped away from the farm.

Whatever this crew was up to, they sure as hell weren't messing around. If he had run a stopwatch, he wouldn't be surprised to learn that the trucks had taken off precisely at the thirty-second mark. The men sent to retrieve him worked like a military unit. Another sign that he was being taken seriously.

As the cabin receded into the distance and the forest thickened, an uneasy feeling replaced the confidence he had mustered. One of the trucks had remained behind, its headlights still illuminating the cabin. Brett's entire mental focus suddenly narrowed to a single unshakable question. *What happens to me if they find the satellite phone?*

Chapter Five

Carl Trenkor waited just inside the construction trailer for the convoy carrying Brett Hale to arrive. The dingy Spartan structure had served as his office and living quarters for the past several months, while his team of mercenaries carved a multibillion-dollar empire out of the mountain. An empire he had no intention of losing before the harvest ended in a few weeks—even if it meant killing a federal agent. Or whatever Hale turned out to be.

The satellite phone–clipped tactical vest buzzed. He opened the screen door and stepped into the cool night air before taking the call.

"Anything useful?" said Trenkor.

"Nothing obvious. Most calls matched mobile numbers for his parents," said Mike Loftis, his second-in-command on the mountain.

"If those are his real parents," said Trenkor.

"This would be one hell of an undercover penetration if they were fake," said Loftis. "Beyond that we have several calls to contacts saved on the phone. All Indiana area codes. On the surface the phone looks clean."

"Something's off with this guy. I know it."

"Should we have tech support check it out?" said Loftis. "He could be using a decoy app or ghost interface."

"Negative. We'll know everything there is to know about Brett Hale soon enough," said Trenkor. "Destroy the phone at the cabin, before you head up."

"What about the rest of their stuff?"

"Clean it out," said Trenkor. "We'll bury everything with them later."

"Copy that," said Loftis. "We should be Oscar Mike in twenty."

Distant headlights winked through the trees.

"With any luck, we'll know more about Brett Hale's true identity by the time you get back," said Trenkor.

"My money is on CBI," said Loftis.

"I hope you're wrong," said Trenkor, disconnecting the call.

As crazy as it sounded, Trenkor hoped Hale was a federal agent and not an undercover cop with the California Bureau of Investigation or the Humboldt County Sheriff's Department. Especially not the county sheriff. Hale's disappearance would trigger a response, no matter who he turned out to be. Trenkor had already come to terms with that. But if Hale turned out to be a state or local undercover law enforcement officer (LEO), which he strongly suspected, the operation was screwed.

Given the mountain's long history of friction with the Humboldt County Sheriff's Department and the public pressure the sheriff had faced over the past few years to establish some semblance of law and order around "Murder Mountain," he guessed the local response would be swift. A few days at most. This represented the worst-case scenario for Trenkor.

They were roughly three weeks from a full harvest, the bulk of the cutting, bundling, and transportation to start a week from now. An immediate raid represented a catastrophic loss—to the tune of close to two billion dollars. The longer he could delay the inevitable response the better, which was why he hoped that Hale was DEA or FBI.

As much as he didn't relish the idea of deep-sixing any brand of law enforcement officer, Hale's disappearance was likely to go unnoticed longer at the federal level. On top of that, the level of coordination required to clear the red tape and spearhead a federal raid on the mountain could take weeks. Exactly what Trenkor needed to finish the job.

His radio squawked. "Wolfpak One is inbound with our guests."

He triggered the radio transmitter. "Tin Man Actual copies. Tell them to park along the eastern edge of the compound. I want all of those hippies on their knees in a line, facing the trees."

"Copy. Will advise."

"Scarecrow QR. I need you on scene to supervise our Wolfpak friends. They tend to misbehave when they smell blood," said Trenkor.

"Scarecrow QR en route."

He'd just ordered his five-mercenary quick reaction team to the drop-off site. Their presence should guarantee the best possible behavior from their "partners" in the mountain venture. His arrangement with the Wolfpak was a means to an end. An unsavory pact required under the circumstances.

The Wolfpak, a previously obscure white nationalist gang mainly composed of ex-military felons and petty criminals, had served as the public face of EMERALD CITY from the start of the operation. Trenkor's boss at the Athena Corp had insisted on it. The company's presence needed to remain undetectably small—removable at a moment's notice, if necessary, if the operation attracted the wrong kind of attention.

Trenkor hated to think that EMERALD CITY might be a onetime payoff instead of a steady, two-billion-dollar-a-year source of entirely untraceable revenue for Athena Corp. Maybe his instincts had steered him wrong, and Brett Hale wasn't an undercover cop. Perhaps his paranoia had gotten the better of him. Nothing but wishful thinking until he could break Hale.

That was the balancing act the Special Activities Group implicitly trusted him to manage. The money was significant to the Institute but would never eclipse the absolute imperative to insulate Athena Corp from the operation. Everything hinged on dissecting Brett Hale.

He picked up the pace, navigating the shadowy compound to arrive at the vehicle drop-off point just ahead of the quick reaction force.

Hurried footsteps joined him moments later, five heavily armed men in full body armor materializing from the darkness.

"Where do you want us?" said the team leader, pulling up next to him.

Trenkor turned to examine the area. "Back by the trailers. Two of you in the open, where you'll be spotted by headlights. That should keep the Wolves on their best behavior. The rest of you linger near the others, but in the shadows. I don't want to rattle our guests too soon."

"Got it," said the team leader, before withdrawing to the trailers fifty feet back.

The convoy of pickup trucks ferrying Hale and the rest of the farm's unlucky workers broke through the southern tree line, their headlights bouncing up and down as they raced toward him. Trenkor backed up a few feet, putting a little more distance between himself and the dirt road. The last thing he needed was for one of these skinhead idiots to put him in the hospital three weeks from the finish line.

A few moments later, the lead truck skidded to a stop, kicking up a thick storm of dust, which enveloped him. Charles Bowen's massive frame appeared in the cloud, headed in his direction.

"Nice job. Police scanners are quiet. No problems at the farm?" whispered Trenkor, setting the tone for their conversation.

"None. Easy as shit," said Bowen, speaking quietly. "They don't suspect a fucking thing."

"Trust me. They know this isn't a friendly tour of the mountain," said Trenkor. "Which is why we need to go easy on them until it's absolutely necessary to start pressing hard. Especially Hale."

"I don't see why you don't just get right to the point with that pig," said Bowen. "Start on his face with a pair of tin snips. Bring the blowtorch out after he understands you ain't fucking around."

"A little hope goes a long way in my experience," said Trenkor. "And I'm not blowtorching Hale. No matter how stubborn he turns out to be."

"Suit yourself," said Bowen. "In my experience, if you pull someone's pants down and light a blowtorch in front of them—they sing like a bitch."

Trenkor kept a neutral face, deciding to placate this moron instead of swimming against the tide. "Let's get them down and standing in a line just off the road next to the trucks."

"Whatever you say, boss. You're paying the bills," said Bowen. "But if you need my help, just say the word. I'll have Hale singing soprano before you know it."

"I'll keep that in mind," said Trenkor, as Bowen took off to fetch the prisoners.

He couldn't wait to get rid of these idiots. Bowen and his fanatic disciples couldn't be trusted to keep EMERALD CITY out of the public's eye. Eventually, they would fuck up. Big-time. Trenkor had no intention of either keeping them around long enough to let that happen or being here when it did. No matter what Hale turned out to be, the Wolfpak's days were numbered. All their days were numbered up here. The only difference being that nobody outside of Trenkor's Athena Corp detachment would leave the mountain alive.

CHAPTER SIX

Brett Hale began to grasp his mistake the moment the pickup trucks raced through the farm's outer perimeter. The sentries guarding the reinforced vehicle gate looked more like Special Forces operators than local muscle. Serious dudes sporting military-style rifles, full body armor, and night-vision-equipped helmets. The kind of security you could afford if money wasn't an issue and you wanted to keep it that way.

The full scope of his epic miscalculation crystalized shortly after the trucks emerged from the forest. They passed row after row of mature marijuana plants—more than he'd ever seen in one place—before rapidly decelerating next to a neatly arranged cluster of newish-looking construction trailers. To make matters worse, shadowy netting hung several feet above the small city of trailers, presumably hiding it from aerial observation. Whoever put this together hadn't been messing around. It looked more like a military base than a grow farm.

Once the pickup truck came to a firm stop, Hale spotted two heavily armed guards standing in front of the closest trailer. Movement in the darkness behind them led Hale to believe that more of them lurked in the shadows. He couldn't comprehend why anyone would need this level of security for a marijuana farm, regardless of the scope or size of the operation.

Trouble between growers out here wasn't a new concept, but from what he'd witnessed and been told, it rarely escalated beyond vandalism or a shouting match. Fistfights could erupt when tempers really flared, and on rare occasion—a shooting or stabbing. The locals played rough, but they mostly left each other alone. They reserved the serious treatment for outsiders. People buying land and trying to break into the business. The area's nickname had been built on their murders.

Up until a few seconds ago, Hale had assumed he didn't fall into that category. He wasn't trying to steal anyone's profits. Quite the opposite. He'd come here to help them expand, for a stake in the extra earnings. But a quick look around told him that they didn't need the money. Lights from the trailers cast just enough illumination for Brett to determine that another field of plants lay on the other side of the compound. No doubt equally as massive as the one he had just witnessed.

If that turned out to be true, Hale was quite possibly staring at the single largest illegal cannabis farm in California. Maybe the United States. And he had a gut feeling that this was just the tip of the iceberg. Whatever this crew was running on the mountain, they hadn't roused him from bed at three in the morning to hear a business proposal. Angie grabbed his arm and whispered.

"I've never seen anything like this before. We need to get out of here."

He knew she was right, but part of him wanted her to be wrong. He desperately hated the thought of blowing the opportunity he'd spent the past several months putting together.

"Everything will be fine," he said, not really believing his own words.

"I've been working farms up here for close to a decade. This didn't exist a year ago. I know that for a fact. This is something entirely different. Something these people put a lot of effort into hiding. What are the chances they're going to let us go after seeing it?"

"I don't know. They can't get rid of—"

Verbal chaos cut him off, as the brutish men that had brought them here hopped out of the trucks and started to bark orders.

"We won't get another chance," she said. "Not if they move us away from the trees."

Hale stared into the forest bordering the road, the truck's blazing headlights barely penetrating the thick underbrush. He couldn't see how they'd stand a chance out there. A loud jolt startled him. A quick look at the three bruisers standing a few feet beyond the lowered tailgate was all it took for him to make a decision. He stood no chance of surviving the night if he went with them.

"We're out of here. Jump on three?" he whispered.

"Forget the count," she said, pulling him to his feet.

They shuffled with the farm crew before Angie turned toward the forest and jumped over the side. Hale leaped after her, his feet scraping the top of the pickup bed. Hitting the ground off-balance, he tumbled out of control and pitched headfirst through the dense forest scrub—coming to an abrupt halt when his shoulder connected with an unmovable tree trunk. Stunned but still well aware of his desperate situation, he looked around for Angie, spotting her on the ground next to the truck, grasping her ankle.

They locked eyes for a moment. Long enough for Hale to figure out she wasn't going anywhere. He used the tree to pull himself up and plunged haphazardly through the bushes, probing the darkness with his hands to avoid another collision. If he could rapidly open the distance from the road, he might be able to slip away.

Angry voices echoed off the trees, punctuated by Angie's panic-stricken voice—and a single gunshot. *Shit.* They'd executed her. Hale ducked behind the nearest tree and listened for signs of pursuit. Maybe they hadn't seen him jump with her? Branches snapped and bushes rustled before he could form another ridiculously optimistic thought. He bolted into the forest with the same plan as before. Move fast and try not to smash his head on a tree.

A series of gunshots exploded, followed almost instantly by dozens of sharp cracks and wooden thunks all around him. The gunfire stopped just as quickly as it started, but Hale kept sprinting, until he found himself headed downhill. With no bullets chasing him, he slowed to a jog and descended more carefully. An unplanned tumble at this point would be the end of his escape attempt.

The slope steepened rapidly, and he started to career out of control. Before Hale picked up too much downhill speed, he grabbed a smaller tree trunk to halt his forward momentum. Pressed against the tree, he remained still long enough to determine that the men at the farm hadn't continued their pursuit. Yelling and swearing still bellowed through the shadowy forest above, but the voices sounded farther away, and he couldn't detect any movement in the trees. It couldn't be that easy.

Hale took a moment to catch his breath before quietly and cautiously continuing his downhill journey. A few minutes later, convinced that he'd given the men from the trucks the slip—at least temporarily—he picked up the pace, mouthing the word *distance* over and over again. The more distance the better. Eventually they'd pick up his trail again, and he was no match for the skinheads or the soldier types he'd seen by the trailers. A significant head start would spell the difference between life and death.

CHAPTER SEVEN

Carl Trenkor squatted on the road next to the pickup truck, scanning the forest with night-vision goggles. The green-scale image gave him nothing. He'd lost sight of Hale.

"Does anyone still have him?" he said over the radio net, before standing up.

"This is Krueger. I got him moving downhill pretty fast," said one of his QRF snipers. "I might be able to pull off a shot if he stops again. Say the word."

"I have him, too," said Clark. "Close to zero chance at hitting him from this angle."

"Krueger. How long before he's out of sight?" said Trenkor.

"He's about a minute from reaching the next significant terrain drop. By the time the line of sight opens again, I won't be able to hit him—unless I get lucky."

"I'm not staking anything on luck," said Trenkor. "Stay on him as long as possible. We'll send a team to grab him at the bottom of the mountain."

"Copy that," said Krueger.

Bowen sidled in next to him. "I thought your guys were snipers?"

"I thought most of your people did hard time—prisoner transfer security should have come second nature," said Trenkor.

Trenkor felt the man bristle next to him. Normally he went out of his way to avoid pushing Bowen's buttons, but Trenkor needed to shut Bowen's shit down immediately. The last thing he needed right now was this skinhead idiot's macho posturing as a distraction. Bowen's crew had screwed up a basic detainee transfer, putting Trenkor in a really bad spot.

If Hale somehow evaded capture, they'd have to shut down the California side of the operation immediately. Possibly before the sun rose. That was the obvious worst-case scenario. The best case put Hale back in their hands for interrogation in a few hours.

"I'll haul his ass back up here," said Bowen. "Won't take more than ten minutes."

"You're gonna follow Hale down that hill?" said Trenkor.

Bowen didn't answer right away, which was a good sign. The guy might actually be thinking for once.

"I almost forgot about all that bullshit you put out there," said Bowen.

"That bullshit is the only reason we sleep a little easier at night," said Trenkor.

"Maybe we shouldn't if someone can just run right through it," said Bowen.

He considered Bowen's comment and decided not to respond. The guy had a point. If someone could sprint through a thick array of antipersonnel devices, a cautious and deliberate intruder could make their way into the compound. He made a mental note to have a fence installed around the primary farm zone if EMERALD CITY continued beyond this fall's harvest.

Jason Watts, the compound's security chief, approached them from the trailers, followed by a fully kitted squad of mercenaries.

"Make sure the rest of the prisoners are secure," he said to Bowen, before dismissing him.

Bowen mumbled something under his breath and left, patting one of his skinhead compatriots on the shoulder on the way out. Watts slipped past Bowen without acknowledging him and made his way to Trenkor.

"Where do you want us?" said Watts, activating the ruggedized tablet in his hand.

Trenkor examined the map on the tablet and pointed. "His current track will funnel him down this draw, but we have to assume he'll get his shit together at some point and figure out that this is the most likely place for us to wait for him."

"We'll put a few drones up with thermal imaging capability. We should be able to track him, even through the thick canopy. I'll cover the two adjacent draws, just in case he evades detection and gets crafty with his route."

"Grab everyone you can and cover—"

A crunching explosion cut him off. Bowen and a few of the skinheads hooted and hollered.

"Krueger?" he said over the radio net.

"You can call off the hounds," said Krueger. "Hale is gone."

"As in dead or immobilized?"

"Thermal scope shows bits and pieces of him on several trees," said Krueger. "I'd say he's dead."

"Fuck," muttered Trenkor.

Watts lowered the tablet and chuckled. "At least we know the APDs are effective."

"I wish I could laugh at that," said Trenkor. "This complicates things."

"Just slightly," said Watts, with just the right touch of sarcasm.

Trenkor stifled a laugh and shook his head. "I need you to start thinking about shutting down EMERALD CITY. We'll need air support on standby. One hour from call to pickup."

He lowered his voice. "And I really need you to come up with a plan to sweep the Wolfpak under the rug. I know it may not be logistically possible to do a clean sweep if we're pressed for time, but we have to do as thorough a job as possible."

"Understood," said Watts. "I've given it a lot of thought and have some ideas."

"I'd love to hear them—later. Right now, I need you to deep-six the rest of our guests."

"I'm sure Bowen would love to take care of that," said Watts.

Trenkor sensed some hesitation, which he expected from Watts. Most of the Athena Corp's missions revolved around unsavory and morally questionable undertakings, but the murder of innocent civilians was usually avoided. Few of the company's domestic mercenaries had ever been asked to cross that line. Unfortunately, the current circumstances required it. The fewer pliable witnesses to the scope of the operation—the better.

"That's why I need you to do it," said Trenkor. "I can't reward Bowen for this screwup."

"It's hardly a reward."

"To him it is," said Trenkor. "Send Bowen _my_ way after you relieve him of the detainees."

"Sure thing," said Watts, before heading off.

When Bowen returned, Trenkor lit into him before he had a chance to open his irreverent mouth.

"I'm going to talk, and you're going to listen. We have a serious fucking situation on our hands, and you're going to fix it."

"Hey. I don't need you—"

"Do you want to get paid? Do you want to get off this hill without getting arrested?" said Trenkor, not waiting for an answer. "Then shut the fuck up and listen for once. If Hale is—was—working undercover, this whole thing will implode. The only question is _when_. That's where you come in. I need the Wolfpak acting as our eyes and ears in

Alderpoint and the surrounding towns. All the way to Eureka. We need to know when the cops or feds show up to look into Hale's disappearance. That'll mark the beginning of the end for us."

"I'll need to bring in more of the Wolfpak to cover that big an area," said Bowen. "Maybe outsource a little."

Trenkor couldn't imagine what outsourcing might look like—and didn't want to. Then again, he really didn't have a choice. Whatever Bowen managed to scrounge together would have to work.

"Do whatever you need to do to make it happen, but whoever you bring in at this point stays off the mountain. In fact, don't say a word to them about the mountain. Keep them as far away from here as possible. The fewer people that know about the operation, the better," said Trenkor. "With any luck, we can keep this place a secret long enough to finish the harvest. Everyone's a winner."

"I like the sound of that," said Bowen.

Everyone but you, that is.

Chapter Eight

At the end of her "perp" walk through the North Hollywood Community Police Station, Harlow was met by Jessica Arnay. Despite Jess's best efforts, Harlow had spent a long, sleepless night among the dregs of North Hollywood's streets. The holding cell shrank throughout the night, a seemingly endless procession of prostitutes, drunks, and other shifty characters joining the rogue's gallery she had started late in the afternoon. All of them animated and gabby creatures of the night—except for her—which made for a few awkward moments. Fortunately, none of them escalated into anything more than a one-way swearing match.

She had done everything possible to defuse each situation, just in case one of the LAPD officers assigned to the station was looking for a reason to keep her locked up. The firm's activities and investigations had implicated several officers over the past few years in human-trafficking rings. Most had been kicked off the force, but a few managed to slide by—somehow. Harlow suspected that they were protected by some fairly senior police officers, who had a direct stake in the same rings. She wasn't about to give one of them an excuse to bury her deeper in the system, where she might not emerge.

Harlow started to speak, but Jessica cut her off. "Not a word inside this station."

"Right," said Harlow, before following her out the station's front doors.

Decker sat on an angled concrete block next to the wheelchair-accessible ramp that led to Burbank Boulevard.

"Dammit, Decker. I told you to wait in the car," Jessica said, glancing at a black-and-white squad car pulling past them—both officers' eyes locked on Decker. "They saw your handiwork at the motel. You scare the shit out of them."

"Sorry," he said. "I wanted to be here when Harlow checked out of the North Hollywood spa. Make sure she drank enough water after her massage."

Harlow shook her head and smiled at the same time. She'd never been happier to see him. She gave him a quick hug and a kiss, mindful of their situation in front of the station. The sooner they got out of here the better.

"How was your night?" she said.

"Dark and full of—vomit. I think a few of the drunks crapped themselves, too. It was great," he said. "You?"

"Fell asleep and woke up about three thousand times," said Harlow. "A few verbal altercations. Nothing big."

"Verbal altercations?" said Decker. "Sounds exciting."

"You didn't have any problems?"

"Nope. Around ten last night, I kindly informed my fellow cellmates that I would murder, or cause to be murdered, anyone that fucked with me in any way. Told them to pass the word to anyone that showed up after that."

"Jesus, Decker," said Jessica. "I'm sure that got recorded."

"Hey. I got close to eight hours of uninterrupted sleep. Nobody came within five feet of me," he said.

Harlow laughed out loud—almost uncontrollably. She was definitely slaphappy from the sleepless night.

"I didn't actually say that," said Decker. "It was a long, zero-sleep night."

"Can we go now?" said Jessica. "I don't want them changing their minds."

"Where's the car?" said Harlow.

"About two blocks away. You'd think they'd have a parking lot next to this station, given the volume. Probably make a couple hundred thousand dollars a month," said Jessica.

"Anywhere to eat?" said Decker.

"There's a nice little Cuban coffee shop on the way, unless it's a Denny's morning. There's a Denny's on the corner of Burbank and Lankershim," said Jessica.

Harlow looked at Decker, and they both spoke at the same time. "It's a Denny's morning."

"It'll be full of cops," said Jessica.

"I don't really care," said Harlow. "We can go over what we need to know before we get there. The rest can wait."

"Fair enough," said Jessica, leading them east on Burbank. "Let's just get a little further away from the station."

When the foot traffic inbound for the station died down, Harlow threw out the big question.

"How bad is it?"

"Not as bad as you made it sound," said Jessica. "You have a lot of friends in the LAPD—"

"And a few well-connected enemies," said Harlow.

"A few, but I shut them down right away," said Jessica. "Put it this way, you have far more friends than enemies. Decker, on the other hand . . ."

"What have I done?" he said.

"Just messing with you, Decker," said Jessica. "The firm—even including you—is well regarded, especially up here in North Hollywood.

We've done a lot of good work for the community and helped the LAPD put some bad dudes away."

"That's a relief to hear," said Harlow.

Jessica grimaced. *Here comes the bad news.* The motel fiasco presented several layers of problems, each a little stickier than the next. Harlow hadn't expected them to walk away from this without taking a few hits.

"It was enough to get you released without any charges or conditions—but they're going to investigate. They have to, given the circumstances," said Jessica.

"By circumstances you mean the two dead Nazis?" said Decker.

"Three, actually."

"I only killed two of them," said Decker.

"But you shot all three—in self-defense," said Jessica. "Each shooting will be dissected, among other things."

"What other things?" said Harlow. "This is pretty clear-cut. Right? The Nazi on the street lost his shit and fired on Decker, who was well within his rights to be exactly where he was—when he was."

Jessica threw up her hands. "I agree, but a witness in one of the cars saw Decker put his hand on his weapon, before the guy started firing."

"This isn't a 'stand your ground' state," said Harlow. "It still doesn't justify the guy spraying the street with bullets."

"Which is one of the many reasons the two of you are about to enjoy a breakfast at Denny's right now, instead of mystery meat and canned green beans on a Styrofoam tray," said Jessica. "You did everything by the book as far as they could tell—with me feeding them what they needed to hear. The surveillance was legit. I assured them that we had reasonable suspicion, based on previously reliable intelligence, that Brooke Miller was being trafficked out of the motel."

"*Previously* being the operative term," said Decker.

"They were running something out of that motel. That much is clear," said Harlow. "The source is still valid."

"At the end of the day, I see the biggest sticking point being the young woman they found in the bathroom with the two of you. I purposely didn't offer much about that situation. Just said that after everything played out, resulting in the unanticipated deaths of two of the subjects, Decker felt she was in danger from a possible mistaken shooting—by the LAPD. Kind of played on their fears. It worked for now, but when they piece the scene together—they'll have questions."

Jessica had immediately advised both of them to stay silent in custody and to let her answer some basic questions based on the long conversation she'd had with them while they'd waited for the police inside the motel room.

"So we shouldn't mention that we engaged the Valkyries because we thought they were trying to escape with Brooke Miller?" said Harlow.

"We didn't engage them," said Decker. "We were well within our rights as private investigators to be there. Harlow and I should have been able to walk right up to them at the motel, without finding ourselves on the receiving end of an automatic shotgun or pistol. They fired first. We responded."

"Yes," said Jessica. "There's really no disputing that right now, which is—once again—why they let you walk. I'd just stick to my version of your story and say that you both acted in self-defense upon arriving at the motel parking lot. When the smoke cleared, Decker determined that the girl, who was unconscious and unable to help herself, would get caught in the inevitable cross fire. And he acted in her best interest. This is why I insisted that none of you speak with the detectives directly."

She had to give Jessica credit for that idea. As unconventional and risky as it had sounded at first, running all LAPD questions through Jessica had been a stroke of genius. Both Harlow and Decker had been far too eager to explain the intricacies of the gun battle they had precipitated at the motel. Intricacies that would have undoubtedly cast enough doubt on the situation and prolonged their stay. Instead, Jessica leaned on the firm's reputation, giving the LAPD enough information to foster the same sense of cooperation the two organizations had shared for years. The trick at this point would be to adequately address some of the outlier aspects.

"What about the flash bang?" said Harlow, looking to get a jump on these explanations.

"That was her idea, by the way," said Decker.

Jessica shook her head. "I'm not letting him talk to the detectives."

"Please don't," said Harlow. "I'd prefer not to spend any more time in jail."

"Funny," said Decker, squeezing her hand.

Jessica stopped at the intersection and pressed the "Walk" button.

"The flash bang won't be a problem, particularly in light of the fact that you felt it was your only recourse when skinhead number three started firing indiscriminately from inside the room—on full automatic," said Jessica.

"You don't think they'll have some kind of audio replay that will tell them differently?" said Decker.

"The gunshots came first, right?"

"By about a second or two," said Decker wryly.

"You have quick reflexes. Special Forces type," said Jessica. "What can I say?"

"Good point," said Decker.

"We're on solid ground here. We just need to let the process play out and cooperate with investigators. Might be a good idea to back off any cases that might lead to Decker provoking a gunfight on the streets."

"Easier said than done," said Harlow.

She ran a quick mental checklist of their active cases—determining that the firm might be better off if Decker spent most of his time in the office until the investigators cleared him. He'd become increasingly more aggressive over the past several months. Although not his fault in any way, the shoot-out at the motel had been in the making for a while now.

When they reached the other side of Lankershim Boulevard, Jessica's hand paused before pressing the button.

"My car is less than a minute away," she said, nodding down Burbank Boulevard. "Sure I can't lure you away to a place that serves something more along the lines of avocado toast and designer coffee? We won't have to travel far."

"Is that where the best attorney in Los Angeles would like to go?" said Decker.

Harlow shook her head. "Oh, brother."

"Maybe he is a catch after all," said Jessica, winking at Decker.

"More like a highly adaptable brownnose," said Harlow.

"At least he's adaptable," said Jessica. "That's kind of a rare trait in guys. You could do a lot worse."

"I guess I'll keep him around a little longer," said Harlow, taking his arm. "Avocado toast it is."

CHAPTER NINE

Sheriff Harvey Long took a quick sip of cold leftover coffee from the mug his daughter, Andrea, had proudly presented to him on his thirty-sixth birthday—ten years ago. The awkwardly painted, slightly mis-shapen fifth-grade ceramics project had been on his desk every day since, after a quick test in the kitchen to make sure it would actually hold liquid. The well-used mug had taken on even more significance over the past month.

A few weeks ago, Long and his wife had moved their daughter into a dorm room at UC Davis to start her freshman year. He thought about her every time he reached for the mug. *Worried about her* might be a more accurate assessment. He'd seen way too much in his twenty-three-year law enforcement career not to feel a low-grade sense of dread. The trick to keeping it under control was to put his fear into perspective.

That was where his wife, Kayla, came in. She constantly reminded him of the very statistics he produced for the county on an annual basis. For every fatal car crash, five thousand drivers safely got from point A to point B. For every murder, ten thousand folks woke up the next day. The list went on, and mostly grounded his anxiety.

Mostly. The one thing that kept him up at night was the county's rate of disappearances. Close to seven hundred per hundred thousand people a year. Nearly double the state average, which earned Humboldt County the nickname "black hole." That said, the county's illegal cannabis industry probably accounted for two-thirds of the missing-person reports, seriously skewing the statistics he'd just contemplated.

A good number of the reports his office handled every year were filed regarding young adults who came to the Emerald Triangle to work on the marijuana farms. Many of them simply fell out of contact with family and friends due to spotty or nonexistent cell phone coverage in the remote areas favored by outlaw farmers. Time passed, the families got worried, and Long's office spent countless hours filling out reports. Then they showed up after the harvest, and most of the families called back and closed out the report. The cycle repeated year after year, some of the kids racking up several disappearances. At times he found it hard to care.

These yahoos came out here looking to score quick cash to fund whatever slacker life they had managed to carve out of society. They showed up to trim mature cannabis buds, a tedious, unskilled job that paid outrageously well for the short-duration stay. Trimmers could make up to two hundred dollars a pound, putting five thousand dollars or more in their pockets during a typical five-week farm stay—assuming they got paid.

Plenty of trimmers found themselves at the business end of a shotgun toward the end of the harvest, falsely accused of stealing and kicked off the property without pay. For every well-intentioned hippie grower, there were two unscrupulous hillbillies willing to take advantage of the trimmers' precarious situation.

Victims couldn't exactly show up at the sheriff's office and file charges against the crooked farmers, for the same reason prostitutes didn't go to the police when a john ripped them off. When your entire industry was illegal, financial recourse wasn't an option without incriminating yourself and putting your life in jeopardy. Of course, not every report filed turned out to be a false alarm. Plenty of seasonal trimmers disappeared each year, never to be seen again.

Kayla pointed out that the disappearance rate was far lower outside of Humboldt, but that fact did little to reassure him. Even half the accurate Humboldt County rate still put California at the top of the nation's list. People—mostly children, teenagers, and young adults—vanished all the time in the state. No matter how he sliced the numbers, they scared the shit out of him. Enough to text or call Andrea several times a day to check on her. Fortunately, his daughter didn't seem to mind. For now.

The coffee left a bitter taste in his mouth, motivating him to seek a refill. On his way in a few minutes ago, he'd seen his secretary fiddling with the coffee machine. Hopefully she'd just started a new pot. He got up, coffee mug in hand, when Sergeant Tabitha Larson appeared in the doorway. By the look on her face, he could tell coffee might have to wait. She glanced at his mug and nodded.

"Sherry just started a new pot. We can walk and talk," she said.

"You sure, Tabby?" he said.

"Yeah. Sorry if I gave you the impression that the world was coming to an end," she said. "Did you see the flagged dispatch call?"

Flagged meant one thing. Murder Mountain. Only three types of calls came into the station. Shit that could wait. Shit that couldn't wait. And more of the same shit on Murder Mountain. Given the unusual situation out there, he wanted input from the sheriff's department leadership before dispatching deputies to respond. That was why he instructed dispatchers to send a flagged email to all commanding sergeants whenever the station received a report related to the Alderpoint area.

"I literally just got back from my meeting with the board of supervisors," he said, rounding the corner of his desk.

"How'd that go?"

"Just peachy—as always," he said, joining her in the common area that connected all the Humboldt County sheriff's offices. "What's up?"

"I don't know. Kind of a strange nine-one-one call about the Alderpoint area," she said.

"About?" he said, finding her wording a little odd. "Not *from* Alderpoint?"

"Perceptive as always," she said, smirking. "Location services put the caller a few blocks from our station."

"Seriously?" he said. "What time?"

"Eleven forty-two—a.m., obviously," she said. "The event reported allegedly occurred around three in the morning."

"Interesting."

What he meant to say was *telling*, and possibly a game changer. He could count the number of 911 calls originating from the area on one hand. For someone to drive two hours to call the sheriff's department indicated that something might have shifted in Alderpoint. Maybe the rumors were true. He really hoped they weren't.

"Interesting? That's it?" she said, raising an eyebrow.

He sighed and shook his head slowly. "You know what I mean. What are we looking at?"

"Male caller. Unregistered phone—most likely a burner," she said. "Caller reported multiple gunshots and a massive explosion."

Gunshots were nothing new up there, but an explosion was unusual. He hated to think one of the growers had decided to break with tradition and try their stoned hand at cooking meth. The county had its share of self-proclaimed meth chefs, so he was entirely too aware of what happened when you mixed low IQs and explosive chemicals.

"Meth lab?" said Long.

"No. I'm guessing some kind of high-order detonation from the description taken by the dispatcher. No flash. No rumble. Just a loud-ass boom. Meth lab explosions are pretty messy."

"Just one explosion?"

She shrugged. "One that he heard. Said it woke him up. Then the gunfire started."

"So the caller was pretty close to the source?" he said.

"Close enough. Definitely on the mountain," she said. "What do you think? Should we follow up?"

"There's really nothing we can do right now," he said. "One big boom and some gunshots? It's not like we have a war on our hands up there."

A look of disappointment crossed her face, which he fully understood. Tabby had led the county's Drug Enforcement Unit for the past three years, taking the helm on the eve of California's landmark decision to legalize the recreational use of marijuana. The entire drug enforcement landscape in the state changed within the first few months of her tenure, sending the whole department back to the drawing board.

At first the decision had come as a big relief. The illegal weed industry was the least of their problems, and the growers mostly policed themselves. Outside of the annual, state-spearheaded raid to satisfy the "reefer madness" holdouts in the state legislature, the Humboldt County Sheriff's Department mostly ignored the pot farmers. Unless they forced the department's hand, which happened from time to time.

He suspected this might be one of those times, especially if this Wolfpak thing was as serious as he suspected, but a relatively new sensation prevented him from jumping into this headfirst. For the first time in years, he had no idea what he was truly up against on the mountain. He was afraid.

"Maybe we should bring in some outside help," she said, echoing a sentiment he had expressed a few months ago, when it had become obvious that the skinheads were here to stay.

"If the mountainside fireworks show continues, we'll look into that."

"What if last night's fireworks were the start of something bigger?" she said. "Something that spirals out of control faster than we can handle."

"We haven't been in control up there since the dawn of time," he said. "Nobody has. Not even the locals."

49

"Things have changed up there over the past year," she said. "I think the Wolfpak has taken more control than we've been led to believe, and everything we've seen and heard so far is just the tip of the iceberg. We have to do something before it's too late."

"You may not want to hear this—actually, I know you won't—but let's give this a little time," he said. "The harvest will be over in a month. This is their most critical time. The entire Alderpoint community joins hands and goes out of their way to avoid stirring up trouble during the harvest. I expect any and all trouble to downshift at this point. When the harvest is over, we can stomp all over the mountain and nobody will give a shit."

"We don't have enough deputies to cover a quarter of that mountain," she said. "Even during the off-season."

Long chuckled at her statement. Tabby wasn't one to hold back, and he appreciated her candor. He folded his hands and cracked his knuckles, a nervous habit his wife had identified years ago.

"I know we have to do something, if there's any truth to this Wolfpak thing," he said. "But right now—this late in the season—we don't have the resources to make a move against them. Not without putting half of the department in the hospital, or in the morgue. This popped up on us unexpectedly. It's going to take some time to unravel."

"It's the first time any organized crime faction has managed to get a foothold up there," she said. "If it's come to the point where the locals have decided to break their code of silence, we have a serious problem out there. Something we haven't dealt with before. That's bad news for the county."

"When the farms empty and there's nothing to protect, we'll take a look," he said. "Do what we can to break up this Wolfpak. Even bring in the feds or the state."

"Maybe we can get a bit of a head start. I can send Ian Santos up to Garberville in plain clothes, to sniff around," she said. "He's new to my unit, and a complete unknown up there. Maybe someone will open up to him. Give us something we don't know, so we can focus our efforts after the harvest."

"Day trips only. Garberville only. No undercover shit," said Long. "Pull him back immediately at the first sniff of trouble."

"He's not exactly a rookie," she said. "Santos has good instincts."

"I wouldn't have approved his transfer to your unit if he didn't, but Murder Mountain is an entirely different beast," he said. "And now with the skinheads running around up there? I'm sure Santos would like to see his family again."

"Fair enough. Daytime. Steer clear of Alderpoint," she said, pausing. "And I'll shadow him."

"Don't spend too much time on this. Either of you," said Long. "Six weeks from now the mountain will be a ghost town. We'll get to the bottom of this skinhead invasion, or whatever it is, before Thanksgiving."

"I hope so," she said. "I have a bad feeling about this."

"Nothing a hot cup of Sherry's county-famous coffee can't ease," he said, fully aware that he was just kicking the can like always when it came to the mountain.

The problem now appeared to be that he'd finally kicked the can into a corner.

PART TWO

PART TWO

Chapter Ten

Sergeant Craig Russell shot up in his chair and snatched the phone off his desk. He hated these interruptions to his afternoon nap, or "admin time," as he liked to call it, but his supervisor at the Eureka station had made it crystal clear that he either answered the phone or joined the other deputies on patrol. And the last thing he wanted to do at this late stage in his career was drive around these hills policing a bunch of hillbilly potheads.

"Garberville Station. Sergeant Russell," he said, leaning back in the chair.

"Hey, Craig. This is Darla McKinney," announced a familiar voice.

He sat back up. "What can we do for you, Detective?"

"I just walked another missing-person report up the chain of command," she said. "Wondering if anything jumped out at you."

"'Tis the season," he said. "What's the name?"

"Brett Hale. Possibly working on the Dunn property," said McKinney.

"Dunn doesn't ring a bell. Must be a small-timer. Let me skim through the master patrol ledger for Brett Hale. Never know," he said, about to put the phone down.

"I already checked the intelligence database," she said.

"We're a few days behind with the entries," he said, getting up. "Shouldn't take me more than a minute."

"No rush," she said. "As you can probably tell, I'm not exactly swamped with critical business."

"You and me both. Hold on."

Russell stepped out of his tiny office, which took up half of the ramshackle station's administrative area, and made his way over to the cubicle complex used by the patrol deputies to complete their post-shift paperwork. A ten-by-ten-foot holding cell, unisex bathroom, and a bunkroom took up the rest of the station's square footage. He pushed an ancient office chair away from one of the desks and grimaced at a wallet-size puddle of water next to the computer keyboard.

A quick look upward confirmed what he had suspected for weeks. The station's roof had finally given up the ghost; the progressively wider patchwork of tarps he'd installed over the months were no longer able to delay the inevitable. Four new stains had formed on the ceiling tiles in the past day alone, one of them almost directly above the workstation. Russell grabbed the ledger and brought it to his office before putting the desk phone on speaker.

"I got you on speaker now. Nobody else is around," he said, starting to thumb through the pages that reflected the last few days' entries.

"Still just you there during the day?" she said.

"Pretty much. The rest of the deputies are scattered around most of the day," he said. "They pop in here and there to keep me from going completely batty."

"Sounds like a pretty laid-back gig," she said.

"Until it isn't—but that only happens a couple times a year," he said, finishing with the log. "Detective, I'm afraid I don't have anything on Brett Hale or Dunn, but that doesn't mean much. At least half of the farms up here are inaccessible to us, and new farms pop up every season."

"Kind of like a big game of whack-a-pothead," she said.

Russell let out a good laugh. "That's exactly right. I'll have to remember that one."

"Consider it yours. Plenty more where that came from," she said. "Let me know if either of those names surfaces. I couldn't find any references on my end."

"Will do, Detective," said Russell.

After hanging up the phone, he drummed his fingers for several seconds before opening the top drawer and retrieving an old flip phone hidden inside an empty staple box. He powered the ancient-looking device and dialed the only preset number stored in its memory. Four rings later, a gruff voice answered.

"What do you have for me, Sergeant?"

"Missing-person report for Brett Hale. Possibly working on the Dunn property," said Russell.

"That's it?"

"That's it," said Russell.

"All righty then," the voice said, and the call ended.

Russell powered down the phone and returned it to its hiding place. He wasn't proud of what he'd just done. Not by a long shot. But he hadn't seen any way out of this. They had cornered him in the bathroom at Newburg Park, during one of his son's Little League games. Four mean-as-hell-looking skinhead dudes packing concealed holsters. Scary as hell, too, the implication of their visit not lost on him. Family wasn't off limits.

He'd agreed to their simple request on the spot, hoping that would be the end of it. So far it had. He provided names and information for any Alderpoint-related missing-person reports. That was it. No harm. No foul. At least that was what he told himself.

Chapter Eleven

Seth Harding, director of the APEX Institute's Special Activities Group, contemplated Carl Trenkor's statement. Something about his assessment of the Hale situation didn't sit well with him, especially with two billion dollars hanging in the balance. Time to switch into interrogation mode.

"Tell me again how you think you're being overly cautious?" said Harding, known only as OZ to Trenkor. "I had never considered an overabundance of caution to be detrimental to one of our operations, especially EMERALD CITY—until you suggested the possibility."

"I apologize, sir," said Trenkor. "I certainly didn't mean to suggest that I didn't believe in the value of caution."

"No apology required. I'm just intrigued by your choice of words," said Harding, pausing long enough to see if Trenkor would jump in to defend himself.

When the silence went unanswered, as he'd hoped, Harding continued. "So walk me through what you've uncovered."

"Yesterday, our contact in the Humboldt County Sheriff's Department revealed that a missing-person report had been filed."

"This is the deputy in charge of the Garberville station?" said Harding, forming his question from the wealth of data displayed on the curved, ultrawide monitor in front of him.

"Yes. He's proven to be reliable," said Trenkor. "In addition to Hale's name, he referenced the Dunns."

"The brothers that own the farm where Hale worked," said Harding.

"Yes," said Trenkor.

"I assume the Dunn brothers are no longer in the picture?" said Harding.

"Correct. Less than an hour after the deputy reached out to us, the Wolfpak paid them a visit," said Trenkor. "Their bodies will never be found."

"You don't think disappearing an entire farm will come back to bite us?"

"Not this farm. One—it's small. Barely a blip on the radar. Two—the Dunn farm wasn't the kind of endearing mom-and-pop shop that tugs at the local heartstrings. Quite the opposite. Floyd and Wilbur Dunn are the kind of people that won't be missed in the community."

"Very well," said Harding, entering this previously unreported assessment of the Dunn farm into the system. "What else?"

"I just heard from our associates in Indianapolis. They initiated contact with Meredith and Jonathan Hale," said Trenkor.

Harding didn't have any information related to this aspect of the operation, other than the mission of the visit. To determine whether Brett Hale was an undercover law enforcement agent or the blundering twentysomething loser that Trenkor now suspected him to be.

"Proceed," said Harding.

"Two of our people, posing as local FBI agents, met with the Hales at their home in Indianapolis to probe for information," said Trenkor. "The Hales had already contacted the FBI and were told that the agency couldn't get involved. Our team effectively closed that loop, asking that the family contact them with any new information. They feel confident that the family has been effectively severed from any further federal contact."

"That's good to hear," said Harding.

Trenkor continued. "Unless the feds have perfected their under-cover game to the point where they're hiring actors to play parents, complete with fully staged homes and family portraits, I feel confident with the assessment that Brett Hale has no connection to law enforcement. He was an odd outlier that raised my hackles. End of story."

"Let's just make sure this story doesn't have a surprise epilogue," said Harding. "Keep an eye out for any local irregularities."

"Understood. The Wolfpak's expanded presence will remain in place until the harvest is finished," said Trenkor. "They're watching everything from here to Eureka."

"And . . . how is that going?" said Harding.

"They're a rough crowd, but Bowen has kept them under control," said Trenkor. "We haven't had any problems."

"I'm getting ahead of myself here, but Bowen's services won't be necessary next year, if the situation stabilizes enough to pursue a second season on the mountain."

"I was hoping you'd say that," said Trenkor. "I'd love to personally supervise his retirement."

"I figured you would—when the time comes," said Harding. "So what do you need from me right now?"

"Nothing. We have everything under control."

Harding liked to hear that.

"If that changes in any way, I need to know immediately," said Harding. "I can't possibly stress how important the next few weeks are. We're counting on EMERALD CITY's yield to permanently secure a strategic partnership critical to our future. Critical to the nation's future."

"I understand the stakes," said Trenkor. "And we're not taking any chances."

"In other words—you're being overly cautious," said Harding.

"Touché, sir," said Trenkor.

"We're in the home stretch, Carl," said Harding. "Once the product is moved off-site, we can relax a little. We'll reduce our footprint on the mountain at that point and investigate green-lighting another season. You'll be integrally involved in that process, as a stakeholder in the operation. That's a bump up in pay grade and status at APEX—assuming all goes well."

"I feel good about the prospects of a repeat season," said Trenkor.

"So do I," said Harding. "But we'll cross that bridge in a month or so."

He disconnected the call and shook his head. Trenkor could and would never truly understand EMERALD CITY's importance to APEX. Hell, Trenkor didn't even know Athena Corp was connected to the Institute in the first place. A meticulously preserved cutout APEX had maintained from the start of Athena Corp a few decades ago. The ultimate destination of Athena Corp's profits was one of the Institute's most guarded secrets.

The kind of secret that could flush what little trust remained between the people and their government right down the toilet. The kind that could topple a less sturdy administration and scuttle the legitimacy of key government agencies. Most important, it could destroy the Institute. Wipe it completely off the DC influence map, leaving nothing but a glowing radioactive hole that no one would approach—and that nobody associated with the Institute could ever climb out of.

Unknown to everyone outside of an elite circle with APEX and their trusted government proxies, the APEX Institute did far more than research the country's national security and foreign policy strategies. They created them. The Institute had exclusively financed the Beltway's "ghost budget" for decades, with the understanding that the entirely untraceable "deep black projects" funded by APEX's money would align with their clients' financial or political objectives. All the government's intelligence agencies, along with several specialized Department of Defense entities, had gladly accepted the money over the years—along with the unspoken terms—to avoid oversight of their most sensitive programs.

By design, the interests of APEX's clients and the "deep black projects" rarely diverged. Exhaustive and wide-ranging research went into identifying opportunities where the interests of the client and the responsible agency were aligned. The Institute's ghost budget program had emerged nearly two decades ago as a win-win scenario for everyone involved—and had grown accordingly, to the tune of nearly five billion dollars in untraceable funding each year. EMERALD CITY represented the most significant expansion of available ghost budget funding since the program's inception, nearly doubling the available budget.

Most of that money had already been earmarked for a relatively obscure, but up-and-coming, department in the Pentagon. Counterterrorism would be APEX's new focus. Specifically, a series of targeted counterterrorism efforts focused against their clients' rivals at home and abroad—while simultaneously safeguarding American security interests.

"Win-win," he muttered, opening an encrypted application on the screen in front of him.

He took a few minutes to compose a concise and assertive message to the members of the APEX Institute's governing board.

EMERALD CITY STATUS UPDATE: ON-SITE ATHENA PRINCIPAL REPORTS WITH EXTREMELY HIGH CONFIDENCE THAT BRETT HALE IS NOT AN UNDERCOVER LEO, AND THAT HIS DISAPPEARANCE, ALONG WITH THE OTHERS, WILL HAVE NO BEARING ON THE OUTCOME OF EVENTS. I'VE REVIEWED THE EVIDENCE LEADING TO THE PRINCIPAL'S CONCLUSION AND CONCUR WITH HIS ASSESSMENT. THE ADDITIONAL LOCAL AREA SURVEILLANCE

PROVIDED BY THE WOLFPAK WILL REMAIN IN PLACE UNTIL THE PRODUCT HAS BEEN MOVED OFF-SITE. NO FURTHER ALTERATIONS TO THE CURRENT SECURITY AND SURVEILLANCE POSTURE ARE REQUIRED.

Satisfied that the message should alleviate any concern regarding the Brett Hale situation, he sent it to APEX's board of overseers. Within a minute, he had curt, but affirming, responses from all eleven current members. Barring any unforeseen circumstances, the twelfth seat would be his by the end of the year. There was no way the board could deny him the vacant seat, in light of what he was poised to deliver for the Institute.

CHAPTER TWELVE

Senator Margaret Steele filled her delicate wineglass with a liberal pour of the Shea Valley Vineyard Pinot Noir she'd just recently discovered on a trip to the Willamette Valley. An entire week of wine tastings, spa treatments, and exquisite meals—and no distractions. That had been the most luxurious part of the trip for her. A week off from the madness of the Beltway, but her trip had ended far too soon. She took in the sweeping view of the Severn River, accompanied by a generous sip of wine, before scrolling through her phone.

Meredith Hale, her law school roommate and closest friend, had left a message late in the afternoon while Steele had been stuck in a meeting. A few messages, actually. She'd called the office and her cell phone twice in an hour, asking only that Steele call her as soon as possible. No details accompanied the eerily detached tone. All very unlike the Meredith Hale she'd known for close to three decades.

She dialed Meredith's number and took another healthy sip, letting the warm rush of a perfectly balanced red wine bring her down a few notches. Something told her she'd need it.

"Hey, Maggie," her friend answered flatly.

Meredith was one of two people who had called her by that name. Her sister, Ellen, had been the other, much to the chagrin of their parents. She could still remember the dismay they'd voiced when Ellen had started using that nickname in public. *Maggie* was apparently too pedestrian for the elder daughter of Robert and Caroline Steele, an irony given that the nickname had persisted in the Steele family for over a century and a half—until her parents put an end to it.

"Sorry I couldn't get back to you earlier," said Steele. "I just walked in the door, and your call didn't sound like the kind I should take in the car. What's going on?"

"Brett might be missing," said Meredith.

"Might be missing?" said Steele. "He's in California for an internship, right?"

"We called it an internship to avoid awkward questions," said Meredith. "He . . . uh . . . took the money he'd saved by living at home for the past five years and decided to invest in California's marijuana industry."

"Sounds like a decent plan, especially if you can get in on the bottom floor. It's only a matter of time before they legalize marijuana everywhere. There's too much money in it for the states to ignore," said Steele.

"Brett wasn't headed out there to invest in the legal side of the California industry. At least that's not the impression we got," said Meredith. "He was supposedly making inroads with some small-time outlaw growers, who he hoped would introduce him to some of the bigger players in the area. Are you familiar with the Alderpoint area? That's where he ended up."

Steele was familiar enough with the name to know that Meredith was right to worry about her suburban-raised, less-than-street-savvy son. Murder Mountain had a reputation for swallowing people whole.

"Jesus," said Steele. "Why do you think he's missing?"

"We haven't heard from him in six days," said Meredith.

"That's not terribly long," said Steele.

"Brett checked in with us every other day," said Meredith. "We bought him a satellite phone, figuring that cell phone coverage would be unreliable out there. It's a pretty isolated spot. He never went more than two days without calling. Brett may be a little reckless, but he really seemed to understand the importance of checking in with us. I know something is wrong."

"I assume you've already reached out to the local police?" said Steele.

"And got the brush-off," said Meredith. "The Humboldt County Sheriff's Department wasn't concerned at all. Said this kind of thing happened all the time, and almost all of them pop up again right after the harvest. We filed a missing-person report, anyway, for what it's worth. The deputy that took the report told us to call back in a month, and if he hasn't resurfaced by then, they'd look into opening an active investigation."

"A month?" said Steele. "That's entirely too long. Have you considered contacting the FBI?"

"We called the field office in Indianapolis and the satellite office in Eureka, California. That's the closest to Alderpoint. The FBI was even more noncommittal. Since Brett is an adult and there's no interstate angle to his disappearance, they won't get involved outside of providing the locals with laboratory and forensics assistance," she said, starting to say something else but stopping.

Steele knew where this call was headed and had no intention of making it any harder on Meredith than it had already been. Brett had been a handful over the years, barely graduating from high school and struggling with drugs and alcohol at the only community college in the state that would take him. Through all of it, Meredith and her husband had stood by their son, pouring money they didn't really have and time they could barely muster into launching him into the world on a solid footing. It had almost worked.

"I know someone pretty high up in the FBI out in California," said Steele. "I'll give him a call as soon as we hang up. Maybe they can call the sheriff's office and apply a little pressure. Let them know someone somewhere is watching how they handle Brett's disappearance."

"Maggie, I don't know what to say. This means so much to us," she said. "We don't know where else to turn. My husband mentioned flying out to California to look for our son, and the deputy said it was futile—the locals don't talk to outsiders. He also said it could turn ugly if we press too hard on our own."

"I can't make any promises regarding the FBI," said Steele, her voice trailing off.

She'd just thought of something. An idea almost guaranteed to produce results.

"I'm sorry. I didn't catch the last part," said Meredith.

"I have a better idea," said Steele. "Something a little less official, but a lot more effective."

"Private investigator?"

"Something like that," said Steele.

"I don't know. We ran the idea past the deputy, and he didn't paint a very optimistic picture. It's the same problem as Jon showing up and driving around. Nobody will talk to outsiders," said Meredith. "And stomping around the woods isn't really a viable option for anyone during the harvest, including the sheriff's deputies. Lots of itchy trigger fingers and booby traps—he said."

"The group I have in mind can handle just about anything," said Steele. "I'd like to reach out to them and see what they think about the situation."

"I don't know," said Meredith. "I . . . uh . . . maybe we should just let the sheriff handle it for now, and see what they can do."

She hated this part. The two of them had followed distinctly different career paths after law school. Steele clerking for the most prestigious DC-area judges her parents could arrange, followed by increasingly influential appointments within the Beltway's public policy law sphere, and Meredith jumping headfirst into the world of nonprofits, barely making a living as she crisscrossed the nation from one job to the next. Money had always been the only barrier between them, though they had tried pretty successfully to pretend otherwise. It was time to quit pretending. Brett's life likely depended on it.

"This group owes me a huge favor," said Steele.

"It's not the money. I'd sell everything we own and move into a homeless shelter if I thought it would make a difference," said Meredith. "We did a lot of research into the Murder Mountain area. Studied Google Maps. Even spoke to a reporter in Eureka who has written dozens of articles about the Emerald Triangle. Murder Mountain in particular. It's like the Wild West out there. Unless someone familiar with Brett's situation talks, finding our son isn't going to happen."

"That's assuming something happened to him," said Steele.

"Something happened to him. I can feel it."

"Then I'm calling in a favor," said Steele. "And there's nothing you can do to stop me."

"I miss you, Maggie," said Meredith. "I especially miss that unstoppable attitude. I need more of that in my life."

"I think you have me confused with yourself," said Steele. "You've been a motivating force in my life since law school. My family's money can buy a lot, but it can't buy the kind of inspiration you've given me over the years."

"Brett's self-destructive behavior has taken its toll on us. We've been in survival mode here for the past ten years," said Meredith. "I was just starting to feel like we'd turned a corner with him, and now we're back to square one—or worse."

"We'll figure this out," said Steele. "Together. Give me a few hours, and I'll have something for you."

"Thank you, Maggie," said Meredith, continuing a few moments later in a cracked voice. "I didn't want to call and bother you with this mess. After what you've been through—it didn't feel right, but I had to."

Steele started to talk but stopped to fight back the gathering tears.

"Meredith, you probably don't realize this, but you're the only reason I'm not buried with my daughter and husband right now. And I'm not exaggerating. You got me through the worst of the worst of times. Please let me help you find Brett," she said. "Not that you really have a choice."

Meredith laughed. "You were always the more stubborn one."

"Guilty as charged," said Steele. "Let me make a few calls and get back to you."

"All right. I'll tell Jon he can stop planning his commando raid," said Meredith.

"I'm picturing him wandering through an Army Navy store, filling his cart with gear he doesn't know how to use," said Steele.

Meredith broke out into a full laugh. "It's worse than that. He's sharpening knives and oiling up his father's service pistol. Not joking."

"You can blame it on me, but we're going to outsource this one," said Steele. "How's he taking this beyond going full Rambo?"

"He's crushed," said Meredith, leaving it there.

Steele understood this better than anyone. Her husband never pulled out of the nosedive that was triggered by Meghan's murder. She'd buried herself in her work to ease the pain—as best she could. David had crawled under the deck and blew his brains out to stop it—permanently.

"Tell Jon he has nothing to worry about," said Steele. "And let him know I said that."

"Do you really believe it?" said Meredith.

Steele found herself caught off guard by the blunt question. She hadn't expected it—but should have. Meredith rarely pulled punches.

"No. Nothing is guaranteed. I know that better than anybody," said Steele. "But the group I'm going to contact is Brett's best hope—if he's still alive."

CHAPTER THIRTEEN

Decker rested his head on the SUV's rear door armrest and stretched the rest of his body across the back row of seats. Harlow glanced disapprovingly between the front headrests and almost imperceptibly shook her head.

"You're literally going to lie down on the job," she said.

"Pretty much," said Decker. "Unless you want me to run across the street and grab some snacks."

"We're not supposed to leave the vehicle," said Harlow.

"Then I better stay right where I am. In case we get the call," he said mockingly.

"You're a barrel of monkeys today," she said.

"Sorry. I just hate being sidelined. More like flatlined," said Decker.

"At least you're out of the office," said Harlow. "And having you as backup gives the team peace of mind."

"Puts me to sleep," said Decker.

"Enjoy the break," she said. "Once you're—we're—cleared, it's back to work."

"How long can it possibly take them?" said Decker.

"It's barely been a week, Decker," she said. "Jessica told us this could take up to a month."

The thought of sitting in the office or the back of this SUV for the next three weeks didn't sit well with Decker. He logically understood why it was necessary, but it felt more like an unfair punishment than anything else. And it was extremely boring. That bothered him more than anything, though he'd never admit it. It was one thing to express resentment about his situation in the face of logic. It was another thing entirely to add a childish declaration of boredom to his list of grievances. Maybe he'd take some time off to visit his daughter.

"I wonder if I'd be better off spending some of that month with Riley up in Idaho," he said, testing the waters.

"Am I that bad company?" said Harlow. "I've been enjoying the slower pace with you."

Decker sensed by her tone that he needed to tread carefully here, or back away from his suggestion entirely. Despite the sidelining, the two of them had spent more time together over the past week than they had the entire previous month. He'd even say their relationship had taken a step forward in that short span of time. Harlow had finally spent the night at his apartment, something she'd dodged since they'd become more physically involved over the past few months. They weren't ready to move in together—nowhere close, by his estimation—but it had been nice to wake up holding her in the morning.

Decker could barely remember the last time he'd felt that secure and grounded. He'd shared the same bond with his wife, Marley, probably multiplied by a hundred, but those pillars of support had long been ripped away by Jacob Harcourt when he'd murdered her four years ago. He was slipping further and further into the present, a frightening sensation. Decker feared that if he released too much of the past, it would slip away forever—but if he didn't let enough of it go, he could never move forward. No wonder his therapist booked him for two hours at a time.

"What are you thinking on?" she said, smiling at him between the seats.

"How much I've enjoyed the downtime with you, too. Sorry to go all sullen on you."

"No biggie," said Harlow. "I think I'll take you up on the snack idea."

"Are you bending the rules for me, or is this backup assignment as phony as I suspected?" said Decker.

"A little of both," said Harlow. "Katie's running the stakeout."

"In that case, we could grab an early dinner. Everything is in good hands," said Decker. "Diet Coke and . . . ?"

Harlow looked deep in thought. "Hmm. I don't think I've had Cheetos in a while."

"In the unlikely event that Pam does need us, I think we should avoid any snacks that will leave orange fingerprints. That eliminates Doritos, too."

"Seriously?" said Harlow. "That was my second choice. I suppose number three is out of the question?"

"Number three? Are you testing my knowledge of Harlow Mackenzie's junk food favorites?"

"Just checking to see if you've been paying attention," she said.

"I think the residue left behind by Chili Cheese Fritos falls into the acceptable range," said Decker.

"That might be the most romantic thing you've—"

His phone cut her off. For a brief moment, he thought it might be Pam. A quick look at the phone, and Decker shot upright in the back row.

Harlow turned in her seat. "Pam?"

"Better," he said, taking the call. "Senator Steele. How are you?"

"Same old. Same old. For me," she said. "You?"

"We had a little incident in North Hollywood last week," said Decker. "Harlow grounded me until the LAPD investigates."

"Reeves filled me in. Sounded like more than a little incident," said Steele. "Harlow's a smart woman. I'd follow her instructions."

"She's with me right now. Do you mind if I put us on speakerphone?"

"Not at all. I actually wanted to speak with her as well," said Steele. "I have a favor to ask."

"I like the sound of that," said Decker, activating the speakerphone and nodding at Harlow.

"Senator, it's Harlow," she said.

"Always good to hear your voice, Harlow," said Steele. "Is Decker generally behaving himself—outside of work?"

"I really can't complain," said Harlow. "Though I hadn't expected to spend our six-month anniversary in the North Hollywood holding tank."

"Sounds like the two of you make a good pair," said Steele. "In and out of work."

"We do," said Decker, winking at Harlow. "So. Tell us about this favor. Do I need to make a few calls? Update my life insurance policy?"

"No. Nothing like that," said Steele. "I just spoke with a good friend. Actually, my best friend. We roomed together for all three years of law school. Anyway. Her son has gone missing in California, and I am willing to do whatever it takes to find him."

He looked to Harlow, who quickly nodded her approval.

"As it happens, I'm available," said Decker. "Not that I wouldn't have cleared my schedule for this. Where in California?"

"Have you ever heard of Alderpoint?" said Steele.

"Murder Mountain?" said Harlow.

Decker had heard of it but didn't know more than the basics. Murder Mountain was the alleged epicenter of California's illegal marijuana business, a several-billion-dollar-a-year industry. People disappeared all the time up there.

"Exactly," said Steele, before briefly explaining what she knew about her friend's son.

"You said he brought a satellite phone with him?" said Decker.

"Yes. Calls go right to voice mail," said Steele. "I know it's only been a week or so, but she was adamant that her son wouldn't go this long without contact."

"No. It sounds like she has reason to be worried," said Decker. "Do you know if he purchased the phone?"

He shared a knowing look with Harlow, who already knew what he was after.

"She said that they bought it for him," said Steele. "Is that a bad thing?"

"No. It's actually a very good thing. As the phone's owners, they can get the GPS tracking data immediately, without involving law enforcement," said Decker. "That saves us a few days and starts us at his last known location. Unless he got separated from his phone. Either way, we can get a pretty good picture of where he's been, and—if we get lucky—where he is right now."

"That's very good news," said Steele. "If it's all right, I'd like to give Meredith your number so you can walk her through that process and start the investigation. When do you think you can be up in Alderpoint?"

Harlow took over at this point. She seemed to know every flight and every distance between cities in California.

"Flights leave LAX for Eureka regularly. At this point in the afternoon, I'd say we could get Decker in place by early evening, ready to start investigating Brett's GPS track tomorrow morning. I don't think it would be a good idea to head to Alderpoint tonight."

"Just Decker?" said Steele. "I don't like the sound of this Murder Mountain."

"I'll send Pam along," said Harlow. "I'm due in court tomorrow. Something unrelated to last week's little mess."

"Pam's scarier than I am," said Decker.

"Do yourself a favor, Decker, and don't tell her that," said Steele.

"He's told her worse," said Harlow. "Decker's still learning how to deal with women that can kick his ass."

"Sounds like he's in the right place to learn," said Steele. "I can't tell you how much this means to me, and especially to Meredith and her husband."

"I'm glad we can help," said Harlow. "I do have to ask a delicate question, if that's all right."

"Of course," said Steele.

"Does Meredith understand the dynamic out on Murder Mountain? It'll be a tough nut to crack if the GPS trail has gone cold. Even for Decker. I don't want to give her false hope, but I don't want to discourage her. It's a fine line."

"You can speak your mind with her. Meredith is a straight shooter. She's worked in the salt mines of the nonprofit world for as long as I've been playing the DC game. She'll cut right through the bullshit if you give her any," said Steele. "Just do me a favor and don't mention cost, time, or anything that might remotely give her the idea that this could turn out to be an expensive venture. I don't care what it costs to find her son. I'm footing the bill."

"We deal with this all the time. Not all of our clients can afford to pay the true cost of getting their kids back."

"You guys are incredible. Thank you," said Steele. "I'll let her know you're on the case and that she should contact you immediately."

"We'll be ready to talk to her," said Harlow. "With some luck we might have some answers by tomorrow afternoon."

"One more thing," said Steele. "If you uncover evidence that points toward a bad outcome, I ask that you pass it to me first. I should be the one to break the bad news."

"Absolutely," said Harlow. "Decker will update you regularly, good or bad, and we'll contact you immediately with any significant developments."

"I appreciate that," said Steele. "I look forward to hearing from you, Decker. Stay safe."

The call ended, leaving Decker and Harlow silent for a long pause.

"I'm not optimistic about you finding Brett Hale," said Harlow. "The Alderpoint area is notorious for swallowing people up and leaving nothing behind. The satellite phone GPS data should give you a good start, but if you don't find him at the end of that GPS trail, alive or dead, you'll never find him—unless someone talks."

"Doesn't sound like that's going to happen," said Decker.

"Based on the cases I've worked that have a connection to Alderpoint, and every other investigator's experience, it very rarely does," she said. "People up there have a strict code of silence when it comes to outsiders, especially cops and private investigators."

"We'll see about that," said Decker.

Harlow shook her head. "Please don't go rogue up there. We can't afford another police investigation."

"I'll be good. Promise," said Decker.

"I'll get you some flights out around eight tonight," said Harlow.

"Scratch the flights," said Decker. "How long a drive is it?"

"I don't know. Maybe ten hours? You'll want to fly and grab a rental car. Even if you packed up and drove out of here within the next few hours, you won't arrive until the morning," she said. "That'll make tomorrow a very long day."

"I know, but I'd like to bring some specialized gear with me. One of the drones would be nice," said Decker.

"You can check that at the airport along with your handgun and ammunition," said Harlow. "I think you'll have to carry the batteries onto the plane."

Decker tried to think of a way to dodge her suggestion but didn't see how to get around it.

"The drone and some other things," he said.

"Other things?"

"Things I can't easily bring on the flight," said Decker.

"You mean things you shouldn't bring at all?" said Harlow.

"Let's just say I don't want to feel restricted by what I can't or shouldn't bring."

"Am I gonna regret sending you?"

"Not at all," said Decker. "I just want to cover my bases, especially in a place called Murder Mountain."

"I guess I can't blame you," said Harlow. "Wait until you get up there. It's hard to reconcile the natural beauty of the place with the criminal undercurrent—and all of the rumors. Creepy to say the least. Kind of a *Twin Peaks* vibe."

"Sounds like my kind of place," said Decker. "Should I give Pam the heads-up?"

She laughed. "I can almost guarantee that Pam won't be up for an overnight drive."

"I'm sure she'll change her mind when she finds out I'm her travel buddy."

"Somehow I doubt that," she said, offering Decker her hand. "I'll miss you. I really have been enjoying this downtime together."

"Me too," he said, taking her hand. "Hey. If the investigation continues more than a few days, maybe you could take over for Pam?"

"This doesn't count as our six-month getaway," said Harlow. "I'm serious when I say that place is beautiful, but really creepy."

"I just want to spend more alone time with you," he said. "I'm thinking Monterey for our weekend getaway, when all of this business is done."

"I like the sound of Monterey," she said. "Then again, anywhere with you sounds nice—even Murder Mountain."

"I'm not sure how to take that," said Decker.

"As a mildly flippant compliment."

"I'll take what I can get at this point," said Decker, before leaning between the seats to kiss her.

"Yes. You will," she said.

Chapter Fourteen

Ryan Decker rolled into the Humboldt Bay Best Western's parking lot at 6:44 a.m., the exhaustion of an eleven-hour road trip sitting on him like a lead blanket. He stuffed the 4Runner into the nearest parking space and hopped out—afraid he'd fall asleep behind the wheel if he sat there for more than a few seconds.

He'd started to grasp the full scope of his miscalculation when he reached the Bay Area, barely halfway through the trip. The extra equipment he'd deemed mission critical six hours earlier didn't feel as indispensable at one in the morning. He'd spent the next five or so hours downing bad coffee and scorning his decision to drive instead of fly, a pointless exercise that seemed to slow time down even further than he imagined possible. All he wanted to do right now was sleep, a luxury that would have to wait.

He suspected they had a full day ahead of them. Harlow's description of her previous experiences on the mountain hadn't left him optimistic about what they'd encounter. If the GPS data didn't lead them right to Hale, they likely faced a steep uphill battle, both literally and figuratively. There was no telling where they'd find Hale, but Decker's gut told him the search would lead farther up the mountain, where they could expect the locals to be increasingly hostile to their presence.

Decker opened the front passenger seat and removed a cup carrier holding two large drinks from the town's Starbucks. With the badly needed caffeine infusion in hand, he snagged a black nylon briefcase from the passenger footwell and shut the door. He spotted Pam as he walked into the lobby. She popped up from one of the couches and headed in his direction—flannel shirt, cargo pants, hiking boots, and all. Pam was dressed for the hills. No different than any other day.

"You look like shit, Decker."

"Thank you," he said. "You look—fantastic as always."

"Harlow's got you trained well," said Pam, putting a hand to one of her ears. "I think I heard the faint cracking of a whip—all the way from LA."

"Funny," said Decker. "You couldn't find anything a little closer? I passed Garberville on the way in—over an hour ago."

"I'm not sleeping in a dump if I don't have to," said Pam. "Plus I got in kind of late. That whole area turns into junkietown when the sun goes down."

"Fair enough. On both accounts," said Decker, before presenting the coffee tray to his tormentor. "Americanos. Should we grab something to eat?"

"I already ate. Sorry. Been up since five going over the intel package Joshua put together. It took a little longer than expected to get the GPS data from the sat phone company," she said.

Decker stared longingly at the restaurant behind her. With sleep out of the question, he required caffeine and food to function somewhat properly from this point forward today.

"I ordered room service about fifteen minutes ago," said Pam. "You can eat while I walk you through the package."

"Anything jump out at you from the data?" said Decker.

"Yeah. And I don't think it bodes well for Mr. Hale," said Pam.

"That bad? That fast?" he said.

"It's not good. You'll see what I mean in a minute," said Pam.

A few minutes later, his bottom side planted firmly on the couch in Pam's room, Decker studied the information presented on her laptop screen—in between large bites of a rather tasteless breakfast burrito—wishing her assessment had been wrong. GPS pings to Brett Hale's phone had stopped eight days ago, the phone's last location recorded on a patch of land registered to the Dunn family.

Prior to the phone going dead, Hale had established a pattern of regular weekly travel throughout the Alderpoint area and nearby communities. The frequency of his trips suggested that he should have been able to make contact with his parents by now using an alternate means of communication. Cell phone. Borrowed cell phone. Landline. Email. Plenty of options for someone with a car at his disposal.

"Could be a number of explanations," said Decker.

"Like what?" said Pam, taking a sip of coffee.

Decker stared at the screen for a few more seconds, struggling to channel his inner devil's advocate. Other than foul play or an unreported, incapacitating accident, he couldn't conjure a reason why Brett Hale would fall off the grid for this long given the historical GPS data in front of him.

"He's really busy with the harvest, or he's stoned on the harvest," said Decker.

"I couldn't come up with a reasonable explanation, either," said Pam. "Where do you want to start?"

"X marks the spot," said Decker, tapping the screen. "I think we should head straight for the Dunn property. Maybe we'll get lucky. If not, we can swing by the Garberville station and speak with whoever is on duty. See if the deputies can point us in any direction other than driving all over Alderpoint. If anyone might be willing to talk to us, they'll know where we can find them."

"What about the sheriff?" said Pam. "We could swing by on our way out of town. Give him a heads-up that we'll be out there."

Decker shook his head. "I think it would be a waste of time right now. If they haven't opened an investigation into Brett Hale's disappearance, we'll be pretty low on their priority list. That and I'd rather start low and work our way up if we need to liaison with local police. Unless you feel strongly otherwise."

"I don't. I'd just hate for the sheriff to turn this around on us if we need his help a little later. Even if he won't see us, at least we can say we tried. If he has one of those blimp-sized egos some sheriffs haul around, this'll go a long way."

"I'll let you do all of the talking," said Decker.

"Uh . . . you're not getting out of the car," she said. "The last thing we need is for someone to somehow put two and two together to figure out you're the North Hollywood gunslinger."

"Hilarious," said Decker. "Wait. Are you serious?"

"Dead serious. A few calls back to LA and we'll have a freaked-out sheriff on our hands."

Decker hadn't considered that his presence might not be well received given the circumstances of the pending investigation back in Los Angeles. The last thing Decker and Pam needed was a county-appointed babysitter while they tried to shake some information out of the Alderpoint locals.

"I suppose I could catch a quick nap while you wait for the sheriff," said Decker.

"Perfect. You can stretch out in the back seat and snore away," said Pam.

Decker woke to a clicking sound, his right hand instinctively reaching for the concealed holster on his hip. Door locks. False alarm. Still foggy from the deep sleep that had smothered him, he sat up in the back seat of the SUV and immediately spotted a very pissed-off-looking redhead through the front windshield.

Pam stormed across the parking lot, shaking her head the entire way. He checked his watch. Almost nine thirty. She'd been in the Humboldt County Sheriff's Office for nearly two hours. Not good.

Decker got out of the SUV and squinted in the morning sun, his body stiff from the extended nap. He rubbed his eyes and glanced in Pam's direction. Yep. Still pissed off.

As Decker slid into the front passenger seat, he repeated a single imperative over and over in his sleep-hazy mind. More like a survival broadcast. *Whatever you do, Decker, don't tell her I told you so.* She climbed into the driver's seat and started the SUV, cutting him off before he could ask what happened.

"Don't even think about saying it."

"I'll just close my eyes for a little bit," said Decker. "Let me know when it's safe to speak."

She didn't say a word until they had driven about ten minutes south along Route 101, the town of Eureka well behind them.

"The assholes kept me waiting in a conference room," she said. "Stringing me along for two hours. I should have walked out after fifteen minutes."

"Nobody from the department talked to you?" he said.

She shook her head, never taking her eyes off the road ahead.

"So much for the FBI courtesy call," said Decker. "How much did you tell them about the purpose of our visit?"

She gave him a stern look. "This isn't my first investigation."

"I didn't say it was," said Decker.

"I told them I wanted to speak with the sheriff or one of his detectives about a missing person I had been hired to investigate. No name given," said Pam. "Now we know exactly how they feel about private investigators."

"That and the size of the sheriff's ego," said Decker.

The faintest trace of a smile appeared. "Goodyear fucking Blimp sized."

"That doesn't bode well for our future in Humboldt County," said Decker. "I give it twenty-four hours before we have a permanent escort."

"They can't stop us," said Pam.

83

"They can obstruct us at every turn. Scare off the locals," said Decker. "Shit. For all we know, the sheriff and some of his deputies are thick as thieves with the locals. With billions of dollars in illegal marijuana growing in the county, it would be in everyone's best interest to keep outsiders from taking too close a look around. What's the easiest way to do that?"

"Hassle any private investigators," said Pam. "Makes you wonder."

"Seriously. How the hell do you keep a several-billion-dollar-a-year industry alive out here? I know you can't police all of it, or probably even half of it, but from what I read yesterday—the outlaw industry has actually grown since pot was legalized. I mean, I was able to identify at least a hundred farms on the mountain just using Google Maps. You can see the long rows of plants and greenhouses! I couldn't believe it."

"I saw the same thing," said Pam. "Looked like an easy two-week mop-up operation for a few sheriff's department helicopter raid teams."

"The more I think about this, the less enthusiastic I am about stopping by the sheriff's station in Garberville," said Decker. "That'll be ground zero for any corruption in the department."

"Like you said, maybe we'll get lucky and wrap this up at the Dunn farm," said Pam.

"Unfortunately, we both know that isn't happening," said Decker.

CHAPTER FIFTEEN

Decker scanned the seemingly impenetrable wall of pine boughs, steadily losing hope that they'd find a navigable, public shortcut to one of the roads that could take them deeper into Murder Mountain. He had to hand it to the locals. They'd done a thorough job creating the distinct impression that the entire mountainside stretch of Alderpoint Road abutted private property.

Pam and Decker had already driven past three well-traveled dirt roads that had been blocked by cattle gates. Internet satellite maps connected each of those named roads to a dozen or more farms and structures uphill, so Decker was fairly certain they were public. The fact that one of them still had a visible street sign lent more credence to his theory. All that said, they preferred to avoid any ambiguous trespassing situations, if possible. Especially during the first hour of their investigation. The fewer reasons the sheriff had to send them packing, the better.

A light-brown patch flashed between the dark-green curtain.

"Slow down," he said, turning his attention to the weatherproof digital tablet in his lap.

"How slow?" said Pam, bringing their speed down.

Decker scrutinized the satellite map, which was centered on their location along the road. Faint stretches of a dry riverbed or a jeep trail were visible through the forest canopy, running parallel to the road before it turned uphill. If they could find a way through the thick foliage lining the opposite shoulder, the 4Runner should be able to handle the half-mile off-road trek to Madrone Road. From there, they'd have the run of the mountain and a clear shot to the Dunn farm.

"Slow enough to find a way through that mess," he said. "There's a jeep trail or something about thirty feet on the other side."

Pam activated the hazard lights and eased them into a crawl along the far-right side of the road.

"If we stay here too long, I guarantee we'll get rear-ended," she said.

"I'd like to avoid that," said Decker, studying the vegetation for some kind of a break. "You watch the rearview mirror; I'll find us a way through."

"Nothing like watching an accident unfold," she said.

"Funny."

The shoulder on the opposite side widened momentarily, and Decker saw an opportunity.

"Stop right here and cross over," he said, before pointing at what looked like a gap in the pines. "I think we can fit between those two."

"This is not a good idea," she said, stopping the SUV. "Maybe we should just take our chances at one of the roads we passed earlier. Or keep going toward Alderpoint. If we get stuck here, that's a whole day lost, plus any semblance of privacy."

"We can't drive to Alderpoint proper. Not yet," said Decker. "That'll guarantee a visit from one of the sheriff's deputies, which will shut this mountain down hard for us. Just take it easy pushing through. If it looks or feels like we'll get stuck, then that's it. We'll back out and try somewhere else."

"It already looks and feels like we'll get stuck," said Pam.

He shook his head and sighed. "I should probably listen to you."

"You really should," she said, turning the wheel. "But you won't."

"Am I that transparent?"

"Like a see-through shower curtain," said Pam, checking the road in both directions.

"That's kind of a gross image."

"That's why I picked it," she said, before driving them across the opposite lane and into the thick brush.

The 4Runner balked at first, its full-time four-wheel-drive system briefly adjusting to the new terrain. Within a few seconds, the vehicle responded to the challenge and churned forward, seemingly unfazed by the snapping and crackling of the dry bushes. They emerged between the two pines Decker had identified a few minutes earlier to find a mostly overgrown jeep trail. Spotting the path had been pure luck.

Ten bumpy minutes later, Pam stopped them next to a well-packed dirt road. He double-checked the tablet.

"This should be Madrone," said Decker.

"Still taking a right?"

"It looks like the most direct route to the Dunn property—if it crosses Powers Creek. Hard to tell from the satellite photos," said Decker. "If not, we'll have to double back."

Madrone Road dead-ended about twenty minutes later, well short of the creek, and Decker hadn't seen any promising trails along the way. A few of the less traveled turnoffs had potential, but they undoubtedly traversed private land. He desperately wanted to avoid any trouble with the locals, unless it was absolutely necessary. The two of them were effectively in the middle of nowhere, poking into the mountain's dark underbelly. Decker didn't see this ending well if they pushed their luck too far too soon.

"Back the way we came?" said Pam, sounding frustrated.

Decker checked his watch. They were pushing against noon thanks to the sheriff's stunt back in Eureka. Half the day was gone, and the whole mountain was probably on the lookout for a shiny new 4Runner and some strangers who had appeared out of nowhere.

"Yep," he said. "Looks like we're in for a long day."

"We were always in for a long day," said Pam, turning them around. "We're not going to find Brett Hale conveniently waiting for us at the

Dunn farm. It's going to be a long week. Probably longer. This is just the beginning."

"I really hope you're wrong," said Decker, his head buried in the tablet.

Pam nudged his arm. "Take a look at this."

Decker glanced up just as an olive drab–painted Ford Bronco rounded the curve ahead of them. Pam hit the brakes and swerved to the right to make room. Wishful thinking. The Bronco skidded to a halt about five car lengths away, its passengers out of the vehicle and on the road before it fully stopped. Through the thin cloud of dust kicked up by the Bronco, Decker instantly determined that two of the three men carried long guns. Shotguns from the way they held them. The two had jumped down from the bed of the modified relic and followed the seemingly unarmed man who had emerged from the front passenger seat. The group walked nonchalantly toward the 4Runner. Decker sensed less of a threat from them than a casual, almost disinterested menace. He would have preferred that they came across as a threat. Their intentions would have been clearer.

Pam put the SUV in park and discreetly drew her pistol from the holster tucked between the seat and the center console. Decker let go of the tablet before easing his pistol out of the glove box. Like Pam, he had three spare magazines in pockets or concealed magazine pouches. He glanced over his shoulder at the brightly colored serape in the footwell behind Pam. The blanket covered a short-barreled semiautomatic rifle.

"Think we'll need something with a little more punch?" said Decker.

"I don't think so," said Pam. "This looks like our official 'Welcome to Murder Mountain—now get the fuck out of here' pep talk."

"You want to do the talking?" said Decker, keeping his pistol just out of sight.

"I probably should," said Pam. "Then again, if you're talking—you're probably not shooting."

"I don't plan on—"

She started to open her door, but Decker stopped her.

"Just lean your head out of the window," he said. "The less complicated we make this, the less likely I am to shoot anyone."

"For once, we agree."

Pam lowered her window and flashed the 4Runner's headlights, signaling for them to stop. The two shotgun-laden men obliged, while the third kept walking, headed for the driver's side. The dust had settled enough for Decker to better identify their weapons. Run-of-the-mill hunting shotguns. Pump action. Held low. He agreed with Pam's assessment of the situation. The only way this turned deadly was if Decker insisted on that outcome.

He took a deep inhale and let the air slowly leave through his nose. She shook her head, keeping her eyes on the man approaching the vehicle.

"What? It's a relaxation technique," said Decker.

"It's annoying," she said. "And you're holding a gun. I don't think it works with a gun in your hands."

"Maybe not," he said, before nodding at the guy in front of them.

Pam leaned her head out the window. "That's close enough!"

The man raised his hands and took a few more steps before stopping—a forced smile plastered across his face.

"Just checking to see if you need any help," he said. "We don't get a lot of visitors up here. Especially this far down the road. Thought you might be lost."

"Definitely not lost. Just didn't find what we were looking for," she said. "We're headed back."

"Headed back the way you came or headed home?" said the man.

"Does it matter?" she said.

"It does to me," he said, before glancing over his shoulder at the rest of his crew. "And them. And everyone else on the mountain. Nothing good will come from you poking around up here."

Decker had been studying the guy during the short verbal exchange. Underneath the filthy clothes, dirty ball cap, and generally rough exterior, the guy didn't look mean or threatening at all. Mostly tired. Exhausted, actually. And worried. Definitely on edge, and not in an "I'm about to pick a fight" kind of way. Decker wondered if he'd misread them entirely. The casual menace he'd previously guessed washed away in an instant. Something was up with them, but he couldn't put his finger on it. He nudged Pam and whispered. "Give them something to work with."

"Maybe you could help us find what we're looking for. Who we're looking for," she said. "That would be the fastest way to get us off the mountain."

The man shook his head and grinned nervously. "That's not how it works for us."

"We're not cops," she said. "If that's what you're worried about. And we wouldn't be asking you to give anything up on your law-abiding neighbors. I have a job to do, and I'm not going away until it's done."

Decker tapped her thigh. "Don't go overboard."

She whispered back. "I know what I'm doing."

The man turned to the men behind him, who glanced at each other before nodding at him.

"Who are you looking for?" he said.

"Brett Hale. Mid to late twenties. This is his first season up here," said Pam.

The men spoke quickly and quietly. Decker didn't catch any of it.

"We've never heard the name," he said, a look of genuine relief on his face. "But that's not unusual up here. Unless you draw attention to yourself."

"We strongly suspect that he was trying to draw attention from the people in charge up here," said Pam. "That's not you? He had access to investment-level money."

"Nobody's in charge up here," he said. "Unless he came to one of us directly. We'd never know who he was. My guess is he disappeared with money he was given."

"I never said he disappeared," said Pam. "Just that we're looking for him."

One of the shotgun guys started muttering obscenities at them, his shotgun slowly rising. Decker inched his pistol a little higher, wishing he had opted for the rifle lying useless in the back seat. This was about to go sideways.

The man backed up. "You're fucking bounty hunters?"

"Time for some diplomacy," whispered Decker, laying the pistol across his thighs and raising his hands.

Pam did the same, putting her now-empty hands in plain sight.

"We're not bounty hunters," she said. "We're private investigators hired by Brett Hale's parents. They haven't heard from him in a while. He was working at the Dunn property. That's where we're headed."

Instead of defusing the situation, her words instigated chaos. One of the shotgun guys ran back to the Bronco and hopped into the cab without saying a word. The other got into a heated, face-to-face argument with the man who had just been talking with Pam. The blistery squabble ended with the man shoving the second shotgun guy toward the Bronco, before turning his attention to the 4Runner. Decker's recently revised presumptions about this man's capacity for violence evaporated the moment they locked eyes. The man stared at him for a second before launching into a tirade.

"You have no idea what you're messing with!" he screamed. "Do yourself a fucking favor and drive straight out of here. Do not even think about going further up the mountain. That'll end badly for everyone involved!"

This time Decker stuck his head out of the window. "Who's involved? What do you know about Brett Hale and the Dunns?"

"I've never heard of Brett Hale!" he said, stabbing a finger at Decker.

"But you've heard of the Dunns?" said Decker.

The man paused, like he might break the mountain's code of silence.

"You need to get out of here right now. Brett Hale will show up eventually. They always do!"

"Not always," said Decker. "There's a reason they call this Murder Mountain!"

"That's right! Don't forget that!" said the man.

"Is that a threat?" said Decker, feeling his temper rising into the danger zone. He did not like being threatened.

"I'm just saying! Bad shit happens to people who go poking around up here. Especially outsiders. It's always been that way!"

"Well, that's about to change," yelled Decker.

"Decker. You might want to disengage," said Pam, who had shifted the 4Runner into drive, ready to run this little blockade at a moment's notice.

The Bronco revved, and the man took off. Before he reached the vehicle, Decker blurted a threat that he instantly regretted.

"If you pull this shit again—anywhere out here—you're a dead man. Same goes for everyone else!"

The man paused again, a conflicted look blanketing his face. Decker leaned left and reached into the footwell behind Pam, finding the rifle's polymer pistol grip. He'd seen that look before. The man was weighing his options, and Decker knew that at least one of them meant a gunfight.

"Decker, don't," said Pam.

Before he could protest, the man climbed into the Bronco, which promptly turned around and raced away. When the speeding truck disappeared around a curve, Decker repositioned the blanket over the rifle, making sure the weapon couldn't be seen from any of the SUV's windows. They had the proper paperwork for their gear. Most of it, anyway. The last thing they needed was a sheriff's deputy digging through the rest of their stuff.

Decker shook his head. "This is definitely going to be a long day."

"That's an understatement," she said. "You sure you want to try the other approach? I don't think your threat is going to sit well with them. Maybe we should use the drone instead. Snap a few pictures of Hale crashed out in a hammock and send them back to the senator."

"It's tempting. Really tempting," said Decker. "But we need to pay the Dunns a face-to-face visit and figure out what happened to Brett Hale."

"I didn't get the sense any of them were lying about Hale," said Pam.

"Neither did I," said Decker. "But they certainly didn't want to talk about the Dunns. I couldn't tell if it was a code-of-silence stand or something else."

"He looked like he might break for a second. Not much chance of that now," said Pam.

"I probably shouldn't have threatened them," said Decker. "I just didn't like his less-than-subtle threat. I needed to make it clear we weren't messing around."

"They were far more scared of us than we were of them, for some reason," said Pam. "You could see it."

Decker nodded. "Yeah. That's why I'm thinking there's something else at play here. I didn't get the impression these people scared easily. Especially on their own turf."

"If we hit any more trouble like this, we're backing off until we can arrange reinforcements, or come up with a less intrusive plan," said Pam. "If we've somehow touched a raw nerve, I don't think it would be too difficult for them to disappear us."

"That would be the worst thing they could do," said Decker. "Harlow and Senator Steele would turn this place inside out looking for us."

"I agree, but those fools in the Bronco don't know that," said Pam. "People make really bad decisions when they don't have the full picture.

We need to remember that ourselves. We don't have anywhere close to the full picture."

Decker gave her warning some serious consideration. She was right. They were pretty much flying blind up here. No picture at all, which put them at a severe disadvantage.

"We'll head back and try the Rancho Sequoia Drive approach," said Decker. "If things get tense, we'll wave the white flag and leave."

"I hope that's enough to get us out of a jam."

"It really should be. Killing us has to be their last option," he said, hoping he hadn't misread their situation.

Chapter Sixteen

The first ATV started following them long before Pam turned onto a side road that Decker hoped would take them farther up the mountain. The appearance of a second ATV, a few minutes after the turn, convinced him they were headed in the right direction. The locals planned to keep an eye on them, and that was fine—as long as they kept their distance.

"How much farther?" said Pam.

"As the crow flies, ten minutes," said Decker. "Out here? Who knows? My guess is we'll have to snake around for a while. Might even have to backtrack to Sequoia and try a different road."

"What are our friends up to?"

Decker turned in the seat and raised his binoculars. The dust kicked up by the 4Runner kept him from gleaning any details. All he could accurately determine was the number of ATVs and their general distance.

"Doesn't look like anything—" he started, squinting into the binoculars.

He could have sworn he'd spotted a third ATV. Now everything looked the same. He peered through the rear window, waiting.

"What's up?" said Pam.

"Thought I spotted another ATV," said Decker. "I don't—"

Pam braked the 4Runner hard enough to jam Decker against the tightened seat belt, which he'd slipped under his arm to fully twist in the seat. The impact folded him over the misaligned shoulder belt, his head grazing the corner of the display console, before slamming back into the headrest. When he opened his eyes, an uneven layer of dirt covered the windshield, mostly obscuring the silhouettes of two ATVs directly ahead of them.

"They sped out of fucking nowhere!" said Pam.

Decker grunted. "Keep your speed."

"I'll do better than that," said Pam, slowly accelerating.

The ATVs immediately matched their speed, maintaining their position less than twenty feet in front of the 4Runner. Decker didn't need to glance over his shoulder to confirm that the other ATVs had done the same thing behind them, but he looked anyway.

"We're boxed in," said Decker. "Three right behind us."

"You got that white flag ready?"

"I have the next best thing," said Decker, laying the short-barreled rifle across his lap.

"Normally I would protest," said Pam. "But right now?"

Decker did the math. Five targets. All completely exposed. He'd hit the ATVs in back first. Two rounds each. Three seconds tops and they'd be gone. By the time the front ATV drivers realized what happened, one of them would be dead. The next would die before the other could react. Local problem solved—for about an hour. Their problems, both on and off the mountain, would multiply by a thousand after that, with every local and law enforcement standing in their way. End of story for them on the "mountain." Investigation blocked.

For a moment, he wondered how much they could get done in that hour. Would it be enough time to determine Brett Hale's fate? He doubted it, which meant that if they ever wanted to figure out what happened to Hale, they had to roll with whatever these idiots had arranged on this very isolated and unmarked road. He pulled the rifle's charging handle back and shrugged.

"Let's see where this takes us first," said Decker. "I can clear a way out if absolutely necessary."

"Check your three o'clock," she said.

Decker turned his head in time to catch a glimpse of an ATV speeding down the passenger side. The driver briefly met Decker's glance, his face hidden behind a black flat-brim hat, reflective sunglasses, and a skull bandanna mask. The whole getup nowhere near as intimidating as the tricked-out AK-style rifle slung across the guy's back.

"Fucking gangbangers," said Pam. "Probably one of the Mexican cartels or MS-13."

Decker wasn't so sure about her assessment. As the ATV driver passed his window, he caught a glimpse of a tattoo on the back of the guy's head. A skull surrounding the number "88." *Shit.* Skinheads? He'd never seen a tattoo like that before. It really didn't matter right now. The locals that had stopped them earlier had nothing to do with this. Something bigger was going on up here, as they had guessed.

"Hit the brakes," he said.

"I thought you didn't want to stop," said Pam.

"Hit the brakes and turn us around," said Decker. "We're done here—for now."

Pam slammed on the brakes, forcing the two ATVs behind them to swerve off the dirt road. Before he could reorient himself, she'd turned them around and accelerated back the way they'd come. Decker stared through the rear window, studying the dust cloud they had left behind. The ATVs didn't emerge from the dust.

"No wonder the locals are scared," said Decker. "They aren't running the show up here."

"Then who the hell is?" said Pam.

"I don't know, but I say we drive back down to Sequoia and turn onto one of those private roads we saw. Hide for a while, unless they

97

follow us down," said Decker. "We can launch the drone and see what they're hiding up here."

"Our primary job is finding Brett Hale," said Pam.

"Absolutely. We'll send the drone to the Dunn farm first, then poke around uphill," said Decker.

"I don't think poking around is a good idea right now."

"Of course it isn't," said Decker. "That's why we're going to do it."

CHAPTER SEVENTEEN

Decker raised the WASP III above his head and glanced at Pam, who gave him a quick nod. The propeller sprang to life a moment later, nearly tugging the lightweight drone out of his hand.

"Everything looks good," she said. "You sure you want to put thirty thousand dollars in the sky above this shithole?"

"What choice do we have?"

"Uh. We can call Harlow and ask her to send us a five-hundred-dollar drone?" said Pam. "I'm still trying to wrap my head around your decision to bring the most expensive item in our inventory on a preliminary investigation."

"This baby can cover the entire mountain," said Decker. "Unlike one of those quadcopter things."

"We don't need to cover the entire mountain," said Pam. "The Dunn farm is three-point-three kilometers away. Straight line. And it's covered with trees. I can't bring this *baby* close enough to peek through the canopy."

"We can use the thermal camera to pick out targets," said Decker. "Then slave the main camera to take pictures. It's better than trying to maneuver one of those quadcopters through a dense canopy."

Pam grimaced and squinted, a facial tell that Decker had seen on the rare occasion that she gave him credit for a valid argument.

"Launch the drone, Decker," she said dismissively.

"That's what I thought," he said, before throwing the drone.

The WASP III flew parallel to the road for a few seconds before speeding skyward with a loud buzz. It banked left and disappeared beyond the trees before Decker lowered his hand.

"It's fast," said Decker. "You can't deny that."

"Too fast for me to fly and take pictures at the same time," said Pam. "I'm putting it in a slow, autonomous racetrack pattern over the Dunn farm."

"You're the pilot," said Decker, raising a pair of binoculars.

He scanned the trees and foliage along both sides of the jeep trail, searching for anomalies. Satisfied that they were still alone, he made his way to the 4Runner's open tailgate, where Pam sat on a folding chair, clutching the drone's handheld, ground-control tablet like someone might steal it.

"That's quite a death grip you have there," said Decker.

"Thirty-thousand-dollar death grip," she said. "Does Harlow know you brought this?"

"She knows I brought—a drone," said Decker.

"That's what I thought," said Pam, her thumbs maneuvering the tablet's Xbox-like controller.

Decker took a seat next to her on the bumper and leaned in to get a better view of the screen.

"Do you mind?" said Pam, angling the tablet away from him. "The drone is flying close to thirty miles per hour, and you're making me nervous. Not a good combination. You can look all you want when it's on station over the Dunn property."

"Sorry," he said, still trying to catch a peek.

"Don't you have something better to do? Like make sure none of those gangbangers sneak up on us?"

"Nobody is sneaking up on us," said Decker, hopping down from the 4Runner.

He stepped to the side of the SUV and gave the road another quick look through the binoculars, in both directions. Nothing. They'd parked about three hundred yards down the same jeep trail they'd discovered earlier, facing downhill—away from the perceived threat axis. If a bunch of ATVs turned off Rancho Sequoia Drive, Decker would remote deploy the spike strip Pam had placed about a hundred yards back along the trail.

Flat tires and the smoke grenades he'd chuck in their direction should buy them enough time to pack up and drive to Alderpoint Road. They could retrieve the drone later. That was one of the benefits of choosing the WASP over an off-the-shelf drone. It could stay in the air for close to forty-five minutes.

"All clear on my end," said Decker. "What are you seeing?"

"Gaining altitude for the initial pass," said Pam. "Once I get a feel for the property, I'll put her in a nice racetrack pattern so we can make the best use of the cameras. I'm not too hopeful. The tree canopy is thick."

"They need sunlight to grow the plants, right?" said Decker. "Maybe we'll get lucky and get a usable side view into the compound through their field."

"Oh. Sure. Because lady luck has been shining down on us all day," said Pam.

"I feel the odds shifting in our favor, even as I speak," he said, leaning his head against the side of the SUV and closing his eyes.

He really wished they had grabbed coffee in Garberville. After the ridiculous delay imposed on them by the county sheriff in Eureka, they'd decided against stopping. It had been the right call at the time, but three hours later, he could really use a cup of coffee—even shitty, middle-of-nowhere gas station coffee. Anything at this point.

"Decker?" said Pam.

"Yep?" he said, turning in her direction.

"I lost the drone feed," she said, remaining remarkably calm given the implications of her statement.

He glanced at the compact ground-control antenna rigged to the top of the 4Runner, finding it intact.

"The antenna looks fine," said Decker. "Loose connection?"

"No. I triple-checked everything," she said, turning the tablet in his direction. "I have full connectivity between the tablet and antenna."

"I know the drone is charged," said Decker. "I checked that before I left the office."

"And I reconfirmed the battery's status," said Pam. "Everything checked out prior to launch."

"Bad camera?" said Decker.

"I don't think so," said Pam. "I'm not receiving any flight data from the drone. If the problem was isolated to the camera, I'd still be getting that data."

Two ATVs skidded to a halt at the top of the jeep trail, their buzzing engines echoing down the road. Decker grabbed the short-barreled rifle from the back of the SUV, just in case.

"Pack up," said Decker. "Their arrival isn't a coincidence. They took out our drone somehow."

"It's nearly impossible to shoot one of those down. You know that," said Pam, scooting off the bumper. "Especially at five hundred feet and climbing."

"They didn't shoot it down," said Decker. "They either jammed our signal or hacked it."

"Jesus. I'd feel better knowing they did it the old-fashioned way," said Pam.

"Yeah. Me too," said Decker. "There's more than meets the eye out here."

While Pam broke down the antenna, he armed the spike strip trigger mechanism and prepped two military-grade smoke grenades. The ATVs remained in place on Rancho Sequoia Drive, their drivers revving the engines. He turned his attention south, in the opposite direction, relieved to find their escape route clear. Decker kept an eye on the ATVs until Pam finished.

"Ready to roll," said Pam.

"I'll grab the spike strip," said Decker.

Pam grabbed his arm. "Leave it. Just in case. We've already lost thirty thousand dollars. What's another three thousand?"

Decker shook his head and muttered a few choice words.

"Harlow is gonna be really pissed," he said.

"It's an operational loss. Nobody's fault except the bad guys," said Pam. "That's it."

"Except for the part where Harlow specifically told me not to bring the WASP," said Decker.

"She didn't."

"She did," said Decker. "Something about it being too expensive?"

"Jesus, Decker," said Pam. "Maybe we should grab the spike strip. Defray the cost of our morning foray by ten percent."

"Funny," he said.

"What now?" she said.

"We go door to door with pictures of Brett Hale—downhill a bit. Maybe double back through here later or try to find a different way in," said Decker, nodding at the ATVs in the distance. "They didn't seem to bother us until we ventured uphill from Rancho Sequoia."

"This is going to be a long afternoon," said Pam, before disappearing behind the 4Runner.

"Tell me about it," muttered Decker, shutting the 4Runner's rear hatch.

Chapter Eighteen

From a seat at her kitchen table, Harlow absorbed everything Decker and Pam had relayed, compartmentalizing the loss of the WASP for a separate discussion. She didn't want to get into it with Senator Steele on the line. The senator would no doubt graciously compensate them for the exorbitant loss, but that wasn't the issue. Harlow had very specifically asked Decker not to take the thirty-thousand-dollar drone with him to Murder Mountain. Several entirely mission-suitable, and far less expensive, surveillance drones sat untouched in their operations storeroom.

"Don't worry about the drone," said Senator Steele. "I'll cover it. Along with any and all expenses incurred."

Dammit. Harlow really wished the senator hadn't said that. Two years later and Decker still hadn't adjusted to his new reality. Steele's financial assurances just exacerbated the problem. Decker treated every operation like he was still the CEO of World Recovery Group—with millions of dollars at his ready disposal.

Before Jacob Harcourt destroyed WRG and murdered most of its stakeholders, Decker's VIP rescue-and-investigation operation had risen to the top of the industry, running on the seemingly unlimited budget enabled by their exclusive clientele. Her firm wasn't struggling by any stretch of the imagination, but in the real world, where wealthy senators didn't foot the bill, a thirty-thousand-dollar loss was a big fucking deal.

"Thank you, Senator Steele, but we can submit an insurance claim for the drone. Heaven knows we've paid far more in premiums over the years. Let them pay for it," said Harlow.

"Well, if they give you any hassle over the claim or refuse to pay it, don't hesitate to let me know," said Steele.

"I appreciate that," said Harlow, not wanting to sound ungracious.

"It's the least I can do, given the hostile circumstances I've imposed on you with this favor," said Steele.

"With all due respect, Senator Steele, this has been the least hostile situation you've imposed on us to date," said Decker, extracting a round of laughter from everyone on the teleconference.

"Well, I'd like to keep it that way for once—which raises the question," said Steele. "How do you continue the investigation without aggravating the situation?"

"I'm not sure we can. At least not from the ground," said Pam. "We're thinking about hiring a pilot to fly us over the area, so we can get some updated, high-resolution imagery of the area. The satellite pictures we assembled from internet sources haven't been very helpful. There's an unmapped network of jeep trails and dirt roads up there—we just don't know where to look."

"Are you looking for a different way in?" said Steele. "My guess is that the locals or whoever is in charge have the place locked down pretty tightly. I'm not opposed to the idea, Pam. I just wonder if the result will be the same, or possibly put you and Decker in more danger."

"I believe it's worth trying," said Decker. "The main challenge we faced today was time."

"Not the heavily armed guys riding ATVs?" said Harlow.

"There's that, too," said Decker, laughing. "But I think we'd have a good shot at bypassing these mobile roadblocks if we could identify a new route to the Dunn farm. Something unlikely to be watched. The less time we spend en route, the less time they'll have to react if they do somehow detect us."

"And if that doesn't work?" said Steele.

"I could hike in," said Decker. "It might take me a day or two to do it right, but I'd arrive completely undetected at the Dunn property."

"Alone?" said Steele.

Harlow was glad Steele beat her to the question. Coming from the senator, nobody would read anything into it. Coming from her, it would have sounded overly personal.

"Pam's welcome to come along," said Decker.

"That's quite all right," said Pam. "Besides, you're uniquely qualified for that kind of ground surveillance."

"I'm not sure whether that's a compliment or a dig," said Decker.

"A little bit of both," said Pam.

"That's what I thought," said Decker.

"I like the idea of hiring a pilot and trying to plot a quick route to the Dunn property," said Steele. "But I'm not keen on sending anyone on foot. I've done more reading about the Emerald Triangle and illegal marijuana farms over the past twenty-four hours than I'd care to admit, and I don't think trekking through that mountain is a good idea. Lots of booby traps and trigger-happy farmers. I know you're good at what you do, Decker, but I have to draw a line here. I can't endanger any of you on behalf of Meredith Hale's son. To be honest, I'm not sure letting you drive back up the mountain is safe at this point."

"I'd like to give the back roads a try," said Decker.

"I'm good with that," said Pam. "Those ATV fools were scary—but they know we're here on official business. They can't disappear us without bringing a shitstorm down on their heads, and the last thing they probably want this far into the harvest season is a police shitstorm."

"Yeah. But do they know that?" said Harlow. "For all they know, you're just two bumbling private investigators hired to look into Brett Hale's disappearance. Nobodies in the grand scheme of things."

"I have a feeling they know exactly who we are right now, and what we're capable of," said Decker. "Downing a WASP drone indicates a certain level of sophistication. Enough to determine that taking us out would create more problems than it would solve."

"Or it could very well go the other way," said Harlow. "Knowing that our firm is behind this investigation might trigger an overreaction. It's not like we haven't been on the receiving end of that kind of response before."

"Harlow makes a very good point," said Steele. "I'm not comfortable sending you back up there."

"How about this?" said Decker. "If we can identify a promising back road to the Dunn property from the air, we give it a onetime try—turning back immediately if we run into trouble."

"I don't know," said Steele.

You and me both, thought Harlow.

"What if I'm the voice of reason," said Pam. "It's my call whether we try and when we turn back, if necessary."

She leaned back in her office chair and took a deep breath. Pam had always been one of the firm's more reasonable voices when it came to operational risk management. She didn't see any way, or a particular reason, to rationally override her assurances.

"As long as we have an adult in charge, I'm fine with giving it another try," said Harlow, instantly regretting her words.

"I'll do my best to keep Pam in line," said Decker. "But she can be a handful. Just so you're aware of what I'm dealing with."

"I can't believe I agreed to come up here with him," said Pam. "You owe me, Harlow. Big-time."

"I know. I do appreciate your patience. Just keep him out of trouble for another day," said Harlow. "My flight lands tomorrow night."

"I think I can hold it together until then," said Pam.

"We'll see about that," said Decker.

"Decker," said Harlow.

"It's all good. We'll probably spend most of our day trying to find a pilot, anyway," said Pam. "We got a late start calling around and haven't heard back from any of the nearby airfields."

"And I'm not exactly hopeful about finding a pilot around here willing to fly over this mountain. Not if an organized gang is running the show now," said Decker. "My guess is we'll need to look in Redding or Chico to charter a flight. We'll start making those calls first thing in the morning. At the earliest, we're looking at an afternoon flight, so no driving around the mountain tomorrow. The day after at the earliest."

"Sounds like a plan," said Steele. "I'll update the Hales on your progress. And . . . if you can't find a pilot willing to fly over the mountain, I'm not opposed to using your pilot friend to do the job."

"I don't recommend that, Senator," said Decker. "He's extremely expensive, as you well know, especially for a job like this. It would be overkill."

"Maybe. But we'd get about as accurate an assessment of the area as possible. Right?" said Steele.

"Correct. With the combination of sensors he could configure on one of his aircraft, we could create a detailed map of the entire area. Roads. Trails. Paths. Structures. Vehicles. People. Everything."

"Sounds pretty useful," said Steele. "And worth the price."

Harlow liked the prospect of using one of Harry Bernstein's planes to fly the surveillance mission instead of a local charter, mainly because it would drastically improve their situational awareness and safety on any future trips up the mountain or into the general Alderpoint community. She was also fully aware that her support of the idea would completely undermine any lecture she planned to give Decker about taking the WASP drone against her wishes. The cost of Bernstein's services would dwarf the loss of the drone.

"It's your call, Senator. And your money," said Harlow. "I can't think of a downside."

"How soon could we arrange this more expensive surveillance package?" said Steele.

"I'll get back to you within the hour with an answer," said Decker. "I think it's safe to say that it won't happen tomorrow. It all depends on his fleet's current tasking."

"Understood," said Steele. "If he's booked out more than three days, schedule him anyway, but let's still pursue a local charter for tomorrow. I'm eager to make progress."

"Same here. Today was frustrating to say the least," said Decker. "One way or the other, we'll figure out a way to reach the Dunn property and move the investigation forward."

"I want to thank all of you again. Please stay safe," said Steele.

"Safe is my middle name," said Pam, mocking Decker. "Sorry. I couldn't resist. Spending the entire day in a car with Decker will do that to you."

"We'll be in touch shortly, Senator Steele," said Harlow, and the senator left the call. "Do I need to break the two of you up?"

"Yes," said Pam.

"Don't listen to her," said Decker. "She's having the time of her life. We're about to grab a pizza and a six-pack before *Jeopardy* comes on."

"Please. Save me."

"Hang in there until tomorrow night," said Harlow.

"As long as he sticks to cheese pizza," said Pam.

"I can live with that," said Decker. "If I have to."

"I'm afraid you do," said Harlow. "Let me know what Harry says."

"I'll call him as soon as I hang up," said Decker.

"Miss you," said Harlow, holding back with Pam on the line.

"Miss you, too," said Decker.

"Oh for the love of—" said Pam.

"I'll call you later," said Decker. "After I ditch my shadow."

"Harlow, the sooner you get here, the better," said Pam, and they all laughed.

Harlow ended the teleconference and closed her eyes, taking a few slow, deep breaths to consolidate her thoughts. When she opened them, all she could think about was a long soak in a tub, accompanied by a full glass of red wine.

On top of worrying about Decker and Pam, Harlow had spent the better part of the day waiting to testify in juvenile dependency court on behalf of Hailey Cooper, a sixteen-year-old girl who had been rescued from a North Hollywood drug den several months ago by the firm and delivered to a Los Angeles–based rescue home.

Hailey's parents—an abusive, substance-addicted mother and her shiny new two-time-felony-convicted husband—had petitioned the court to return her to their custody. Presumably to put her back to work selling drugs, which had proved quite profitable for the two of them before Hailey had disappeared.

Jessica Arnay represented Hailey on behalf of the rescue organization, fighting tooth and nail to keep the vulnerable, still-drug-addicted teen out of her parents' slimy grasp. Not exactly the easiest job, given the lack of hard evidence supporting Hailey's assertion that they had forced her to peddle drugs for several months before she fled. Jessica faced a "he said, she said" battle in front of the judge.

Thankfully, Hailey's mother hadn't exactly shined in court today, appearing intoxicated and reinforcing that possibility by acting belligerent. Her stepfather had come across as downright scary. "Serial killer scary" had been Jessica's exact words. She felt pretty confident that the judge was leaning toward keeping Hailey in the recovery home. They wouldn't know until the final hearing, three weeks from now.

Tomorrow would be a repeat. Another long day waiting for a short, but important, appearance. At some point in the afternoon, she'd try to convince a judge at the juvenile delinquency court that a severely abused fifteen-year-old kidnap victim had acted completely in self-defense when he attacked Harlow—immediately after she kicked in the door to his basement cell.

Katie would testify in the same hearing. Her quick reaction time and unfortunate deployment of a Taser had kept the panicked boy from doing more damage than a few deep bruises to her arms and ribs. LAPD had arrived moments later, their timing unfortunate, since there was no way to immediately explain away the appearance of an assault. Officers arrested the boy, who landed in juvenile detention after being booked. Jessica would try to get him transferred into a court-approved recovery center before the system swallowed him up. The kid's parents still hadn't been identified.

When Harlow walked out of the court facility tomorrow afternoon, she will have spent close to ten hours waiting to give ten minutes of testimony. During the firm's early years, she viewed court as an entirely inefficient use of her time. Always impatient to get back out on the streets, where she felt she was making a bigger difference—until she finally got it. Until she saw the bigger picture, and how everything they had previously risked to get the kids off the streets hinged on those few minutes in court.

The constant threat to life and limb. The long, exhausting hours in the field. The legal and financial liability to the firm. Not to mention the emotional toll taken on the partners. All of it meaningless if they lost this final battle. Not to mention what would happen to the kids if the firm didn't follow through. Court had morphed into her most important battleground. One she took just as seriously as fieldwork, if not a little more seriously.

All that said, Harlow really wished she didn't have to spend most of tomorrow in juvenile detention court. Circumstances up north suggested that Decker and Pam had stumbled onto something bigger than Brett Hale's disappearance, and she didn't like the idea of them poking around the mountain without backup. Especially if Decker's suspicion about the neck tattoos proved correct.

CHAPTER NINETEEN

Carl Trenkor paused at the door to his trailer, glancing toward the rising inferno at the far end of the compound's trailer park. He shook his head, still not sure how a bonfire, soon to be visible from miles away, fit his order to maintain a "low profile" on the mountain. A quick look at his watch told him he still had a few minutes before the scheduled call. He triggered the radio button on his vest, intending to send someone from the security team to put an end to the night's Wolfpak festivities.

"TIN MAN Ops. This is TIN MAN Actual."

"This is Ops."

He recognized the voice. Exactly who he was looking for.

"Mike, switch over to Bravo Zulu."

"Switching," said Mike Loftis, his second-in-command.

Trenkor opened his radio pouch and changed to an encrypted frequency only known to Loftis and Watts.

"You there, Mike?"

"I'm here. What's up?"

"Our hillbilly friends are at it again with the fucking bonfire," said Trenkor.

A bright flash lit up half the compound, illuminating the treetops.

"Jesus. Did they just blow themselves up?" said Loftis, sounding hopeful.

"Unfortunately, I can still hear them hooting and hollering," said Trenkor.

"I'll head right over," said Loftis. "Are they drinking?"

"They sure as fuck better not be. They might have work to do later tonight," said Trenkor. "When you're done putting out that fire, bring Bowen over to my trailer. Wait with him outside until I call you in."

"I'm on it," said Loftis. "Good luck with the call."

"Yeah. Sounds like I might need it," said Trenkor. "And, Mike?"

"Yes?"

"Take it easy on Bowen. We need to keep him happy for now," said Trenkor.

"I'll be happy when we're done with that guy and his clown car," said Loftis.

"You and me both," said Trenkor. "I'll let you know when I'm ready for Bowen."

He stepped inside and flipped the light switch. His satellite phone buzzed before the harsh fluorescent overhead lights stopped flickering. OZ was early. He removed the satellite phone from his vest and took a seat at the folding table that served as a desk. As with the wizard in the movie, before the curtain was pulled, he'd never met the man he was talking to.

"Good evening, sir," he said, opening his laptop.

"Are you at your computer?"

The fact that OZ had skipped any pretense of small talk didn't bode well. Not surprising given the afternoon's events. Shortly after a rather persistent two-person team of investigators had been physically blocked from approaching the Dunn property, the electronic counter-measures team detected an unusually sophisticated radio frequency—immediately identifying it as a drone-control frequency. The team had scrambled to hack the encrypted signal, barely managing to hijack and crash the drone before it could record and transmit detailed images of the primary mountaintop grow site.

The size of the EMERALD CITY operation entirely dwarfed every illegal grow site on or around Murder Mountain. In fact, its vast scope rivaled most industry-funded, state-regulated farm enterprises. Anyone with any modicum of cannabis industry–related understanding would instantly recognize the unique scope of Athena Corp's operation.

If the Humboldt County sheriff even caught a single glimpse of what they were up to, he'd undoubtedly trigger a rapid series of events that would destroy EMERALD CITY, possibly dragging the company down with it. Which is why Trenkor had been momentarily relieved when they'd discovered that the drone was a thirty-thousand-dollar, military-grade UAV. Humboldt County's board of supervisors kept the sheriff's department on a shoestring budget. The drone didn't belong to the county.

A quick internet search yielded an equally threatening scenario. Federal law enforcement agencies like the ATF, DEA, and Customs and Border Protection frequently worked with US military drone units to conduct surveillance over difficult or vast stretches of terrain. The FBI had their own unmanned aerial vehicle division, employing a wide variety of military-style drones, including the WASP.

Now they faced the possibility that Brett Hale had been an undercover federal agent after all, and he had passed along enough information before his disappearance to justify taking an aerial look at Murder Mountain.

"I just opened it," said Trenkor. "I'll be logged in to the secure network in less than ten seconds."

"You knew the time for our call, right?"

"I did. Some Wolfpak business came up a few minutes ago," said Trenkor.

"They're going to earn their money tonight," he said. "We have a serious problem on our hands."

"Which agency?"

"It's worse than that."

"I don't see how," said Trenkor.

"Let me rephrase that. It will be worse if we don't take immediate action," said OZ. "We identified both of the individuals that have taken a sudden interest in the Alderpoint area. They're private investigators associated with an unnamed investigative firm based out of Los Angeles."

"I'm obviously missing something," said Trenkor. "This sounds like good news to me. No law enforcement."

"Have you ever heard the name Ryan Decker?"

"Rings a bell," said Trenkor, giving it a quick thought. "Wasn't he involved in the botched rescue attempt that killed Senator Steele's daughter?"

"That pretty much sums it up. He was sent to prison for mishandling the rescue attempt. Steele held him personally responsible for her daughter's death—and made sure he paid for it."

"Then what the hell is he doing here?" said Trenkor.

Trenkor accessed his secure email and clicked on the intelligence packet, bringing two pictures up on his screen. The woman looked like more trouble than Decker.

"That appears to be the root of the problem. Decker was inexplicably released from prison two years ago with his conviction erased—apparently at Senator Steele's request."

"Why the change of heart?" said Trenkor.

"That's the million-dollar question," said OZ. "What we do know for certain is that Senator Steele is not a friend of ours. Since Decker's release, she's taken an unhealthy interest in some of our more important initiatives. That's really all I can divulge at this point."

"So he works for her?" said Trenkor.

"We don't know the exact nature of their relationship, but the two of them are definitely connected. And Decker represents a clear and present danger to EMERALD CITY, especially if Steele sent him to investigate Brett Hale's disappearance."

"How is Steele connected to Brett Hale?" said Trenkor.

"Margaret Steele and Meredith Hale, Brett's mother, graduated the same year from Georgetown University Law School. That's all we know right now," said OZ. "Which is where the Wolfpak comes in. We need to determine why Ryan Decker has graced the mountain with his presence today, asking about Brett Hale. If Hale's family hired Decker's firm coincidentally, outside of any connection to Senator Steele, we're in the clear, but if Senator Steele sent Decker or recommended him to the Hales, we'll have to shut down the operation. The combination of Ryan Decker and Senator Steele represents a risk we are not willing to take."

Trenkor shook his head. "I don't see how Decker's connection here is a coincidence."

"Neither do I. But we have to be absolutely sure," he said. "I don't want to shut down a two-billion-dollar operation if I don't have to. Not when we're this close to finishing the harvest."

"I completely understand," said Trenkor. "But I think we should use Athena Corp operators for the takedown. Decker and this Pam Stack woman don't look like they'll go easy."

"Your concerns are noted, but we can't risk the exposure," said OZ. "Send as many of Bowen's skinheads as you see fit. I don't care if you send them all. Just bring Decker and Stack back to the mountain for interrogation."

"Fail-safe protocol?" said Trenkor, pretty sure he knew the answer.

Every mission was assigned a streamlined outcome to be executed if things went far enough sideways to jeopardize full mission accomplishment.

"Terminate and retrieve corpses. Do not lead anyone back to the compound. Eliminate Wolfpak," he said. "Once the Wolfpak initiates contact at the motel, they bring Decker and Stack back dead or alive. Preferably alive."

"I'll make that abundantly clear," said Trenkor. "I'd feel more comfortable if I could send at least one operator to accompany Bowen."

"Too risky. For all we know, Decker and Stack are bait."

"Good point," said Trenkor, a little embarrassed he hadn't thought of that himself.

"Call me the moment you have them back at the compound," said OZ. "And, Carl?"

"Yes, sir?"

"Prepare all harvested product for transport," he said. "If we're forced to abandon EMERALD CITY tonight, I want to take as much of it with us as possible."

"Copy that," said Trenkor to an already disconnected call.

He took a few minutes to read through Decker's and Stack's dossiers. Athena Corp had an unusually comprehensive file on Decker, which led Trenkor to believe that he had either recently tangled with an Athena affiliate or had been hired by the Institute prior to the debacle with Senator Steele's daughter. His guess was the former. It didn't take a lot of reading between the lines to connect the dots.

If Steele had become an enemy of the company over the past few years, as OZ had suggested, and the combined team of Decker and Steele could shut down a two-billion-dollar operation overnight—the conclusion was unavoidable. Decker was one of the senator's wrecking balls, and he had very recently demolished something very dear to Athena Corp on her behalf.

OZ had given him enough hints to make this connection, without directly saying it. Was that an unspoken green light to send a few of his operators to babysit the Wolfpak? Probably not. But why would he say anything about Steele's recent meddling in APEX business?

He could have simply ordered him to send the Wolfpak to capture or kill the two investigators, and Trenkor wouldn't have thought twice about it. Did he want him to send backup but couldn't openly say it? If Decker was so dangerous to Athena Corp, why trust this to the same bunch of idiots who had managed to lose Brett Hale and bring this down on them in the first place?

The only way this backfired on him was if Decker's mountain escapade had indeed been designed to lure them into a trap at the motel. All the more reason for Trenkor to send a small team of highly skilled operators. A little insurance policy would go a long way tonight if things went sideways.

Chapter Twenty

Seth Harding shut the laptop and turned to his late-night visitor, who had already emerged from the deep recesses of an oversize leather couch to set his empty Glencairn whiskey glass on the restored wood coffee table. Instead of leaning back into the well-worn leather, Samuel Quinn stood up and made his way around the table.

"I think you told him too much," said Quinn.

"He's not that intuitive, and he follows orders—almost religiously. That's why I picked him for the job," said Harding. "Can I recharge your glass?"

"Tempting. But no," said Quinn, pausing by the table like he might reconsider his answer. "This Decker guy keeps showing up in the wrong place at the worst possible time."

"So does Senator Steele."

Quinn approached the wide mahogany desk, resting both hands on the surface directly in front of him. He briefly took in the array of photos, awards, and commemorative plaques neatly arranged on the wall behind Harding before resuming eye contact. A tiresome and oft-repeated power play had just unfolded—the fading alpha dog casually sizing up its inevitable replacement.

"Yeah. She's been a bit of an impediment lately. A costly impediment," said Quinn.

"How long do we continue to let that fester?" said Harding.

"We?" said Quinn, the single word delivering a stinging rebuke.

"I didn't mean to suggest I was—"

"Don't go there, Seth, and for God's sake I hope you don't use the *we* word while talking to other members of the board. We—and that's an appropriate use of the word—can't afford to give any of the other members a reason to dislike you. Do yourself a favor for now and strike the word *we* from your vocabulary."

"Understood," said Harding peevishly.

He had just as much at stake as the board of directors. Unlike too many here, he had spent eighteen long years working his way up the Institute's ladder. A few of the directors had spent less than five years in the building, having been poached from other think tanks to boost the Institute's credibility in times of crisis or to kneecap a competitor. They collected a paycheck, occasionally weighing in on top-level decisions. Harding had earned a place on the board, which was the only way he'd ever advance beyond his current position at the Institute.

Director of the Special Activities Group was one of the most important positions at the Institute, but the role didn't influence Institute strategy or direction. Harding basically executed sensitive operations handed down by APEX's opportunity directors with one of their proxy groups, like Athena Corp—the real power brokers of the Beltway, whom he had every intention of soon joining. His appointment to the board of directors came with that promotion.

"And taking out a US senator or any government officeholder is an absolute last resort," said Quinn. "Steele would have to be directly targeting APEX for that to be considered. The senator's previous clashes against APEX interests have been indirect, and from what we can tell, coincidental. It's entirely possible that she did an old friend a favor and asked Decker to look into Hale's disappearance."

"It's the most logical scenario," said Harding. "But I find it hard to believe coincidence dropped Decker on our doorstep again. Especially this doorstep."

"Which is why we need to have a serious chat with him and this Stack woman," said Quinn. "We have to be sure. There's far more than two billion dollars at stake."

"The entire helicopter fleet at KANSAS is on fifteen-minute standby," said Harding. "APEX personnel and any transport-ready product can be airborne in about two hours. Worst-case scenario, we pull the plug tonight and fly away with about five hundred million dollars' worth of product."

"Worst-case scenario, we don't have time to load up the product," said Quinn.

"In that case, ninety minutes from call to personnel evacuation," said Harding. "The assault helicopters are significantly faster than the Skycranes. Trenkor's plan is to send all of the helicopters to the mountain at their best speeds—and determine en route if we have the time to wait for the cargo transports."

"I'll leave those details to you," said Quinn, heading toward the door. "Just make sure there's no way this comes back at APEX."

"I will," said Harding. "And just so I'm clear, Decker and Stack get deep-sixed, regardless of why Steele sent them?"

"I see no upside to keeping them around after they're abducted," said Quinn. "Even if this whole thing turns out to be another unfortunate coincidence, there's no way to unring that bell. They'd go right to Steele."

"I wish there was another way to do this," said Harding. "EMERALD CITY's clock starts ticking the moment the Wolfpak grabs them."

"The clock started ticking the moment we grabbed Brett Hale. We just didn't know it," said Quinn, before letting himself out.

At least Quinn still used the word *we* to describe the Hale situation. The moment he began to say *you*, the clock would start counting down on Harding's career.

CHAPTER
TWENTY-ONE

Decker woke to a sharp chirping noise, his hand instinctively touching the earpiece in his right ear. Something had triggered the motion detector he'd attached to the bumper of the sedan parked between his and Pam's room. He instinctively glanced at the window, catching a glimpse of movement on the side closest to the door. Gone just as fast. Another motel guest walking by?

A quick look at the clock on the nightstand suggested something otherwise: 3:10. The persistent chirping confirmed it. Whoever had set off the motion detector hadn't moved on.

He activated his phone and pressed "Send" on a text he'd readied before closing his eyes a few hours earlier.

DECKER: Possible threat outside.

Pam's response arrived a few seconds later as he slid to the carpet behind his bed.

PAM: Yep. Lots of movement. Cops?

Possible. But he doubted it. He'd kept the short-barreled rifle concealed when he transferred the bulk of their gear from the SUV to his room. The rifle was licensed and legal, but it would draw the wrong kind of attention if spotted by the public—or the police. This was California, not Texas, so he'd been careful.

Decker couldn't think of a legitimate reason why the sheriff's department would raid their rooms at three in the morning. *Legitimate* being the key term. If the department had been infiltrated by whoever ran the show in Alderpoint, as he loosely suspected, the reason would be supplied later. The prospect of this being a police raid vastly complicated things.

DECKER: Not likely. But possible.

He grabbed the rifle leaning against the wall next to the bed, along with the two spare magazines on the nightstand. After tucking the magazines into his pockets, Decker squirmed on his stomach to the foot of the bed, where he pointed the rifle at the door.

PAM: That didn't help. ROE?

Rules of engagement? Good question. They couldn't shoot at sheriff's deputies regardless of who pulled the deputies' strings. This constraint put Decker and Pam in a really difficult position. If the criminals who controlled the mountain stood outside of these doors, ready to permanently purge them from existence, the precious few seconds they wasted trying to identify their intruders could spell the difference between life and death. Still. Decker couldn't justify firing blindly. They'd have to identify their targets as hostile before engaging.

DECKER: Weapons tight.

PAM: Agreed.

DECKER: Door bar in place?

PAM: What do u think?

He'd thrown the portable security bars into the 4Runner as an afterthought, mostly because they'd sat in plain sight on one of the shelves toward the front of the storage area, and he'd had room to spare. Why not? He had to give sheer luck its due. That seemingly impulsive decision might end up saving their lives. The security bars should hold long enough for them to identify their attackers.

A wide shadow appeared in the rightmost window, its form fidgeting for a few moments before going dead still. Decker typed BREACH before dropping the phone on the carpet and settling in behind his rifle. He hoped Pam had done the same with her shotgun.

Despite knowing exactly what was about to happen, Decker still flinched when the door buckled inward with an earsplitting boom. Battering ram. There was no mistaking the sound, yet somehow the security bar withstood the impact, and the door remained in place—dislodged from the doorframe by only a few inches. The next hit would knock the door clean out of the way, unleashing chaos.

As he steeled himself for that inevitable madness, the boom of a shotgun reverberated through the wall in front of him. Had Pam already engaged? How could she have identified them as hostile that quickly? A second boom removed any doubt. The shots came from deep inside Pam's room, where she presumably lay in a similar position on the floor. Decker thumbed the selector switch to FIRE and quickly adjusted his hand on the foregrip to activate the rifle light.

The moment his thumb found the pressure switch, the door exploded inward, revealing two figures. Decker triggered the overpowered beam, instantly blinding the razor-bald, neck-tattooed monsters who rushed into the breach. The lead skinhead halted in the doorway, immediately raising one hand to block the retina-searing light while firing his rifle aimlessly into the room.

As a vortex of steel snapped overhead, Decker fired a single bullet, which simultaneously punched a tiny hole through the palm of the skinhead's hand and the bridge of his nose. The man immediately dropped to the floor, leaving the guy behind him covered in a dark-red, lumpy sheen. Decker shifted the rifle a few inches to the right and pressed the trigger again, whiplashing the skinhead's gore-covered dome backward. He killed the rifle light, plunging the room into the kind of quiet darkness that dared his attackers to step inside.

Bursts of automatic gunfire erupted from the doorway and window, brightly illuminating the room in a dizzying array of muzzle flashes. Bullets thumped into the bed and pounded the wall far above him, convincing Decker that the shooters hadn't discovered his position on the floor.

He aimed just above the muzzle flashes in the doorway, snapping off two quick shots at the partially visible silhouette of a head. Without pausing to evaluate the impact of those bullets, he shifted aim and fired a tight salvo at the wall next to the window—where he guessed the remaining shooter stood. A long burst of fire from the window tore through the bed just above his head, clanging against the metal frame and shredding the mattress. He'd guessed wrong.

Decker fired short bursts at different points along the wall, below and beside the window, hoping to suppress the shooter long enough to assess the situation. The moment gunfire in the window stopped, a thigh-high string of bullets punched through the wall from Pam's room, showering Decker with pieces of drywall—and forcing him into a reckless course of action. The only way they would survive the next several seconds was to change the dynamic of this gunfight.

Without giving it any more thought, he rose and sprinted for the door.

CHAPTER TWENTY-TWO

Charles Bowen peered over the hood of his pickup truck at the scene unfolding in front of the two motel rooms—painfully aware that he was now the proud owner of a complete and utter disaster. Six of the ten men he'd sent to breach the rooms were down. Of the five assigned to grab Decker, only one remained. McNulty. The rest had fallen within the first few seconds of gunfire. Head shots—from what Bowen could tell—which was why he'd decided to stay put and keep a low profile.

At least the team trading shots with the woman was still in the game. Sort of. The first two Wolves through her door had taken point-blank shotgun blasts; one of them was lifted clean off his feet and dropped onto the hood of the sedan behind him. The team leader had smartly pulled the rest of his Wolves back into the parking lot, where they crouched between vehicles and fired repeated bursts of automatic fire at the room. That bitch was probably full of holes by now.

"STORM One. What's your status?" he yelled into his radio.

A shotgun blast punched through the wall, peppering the windshield next to the team leader he'd just contacted.

"She's still fucking at it! STORM Two is wiped out. McNulty looks like he took a hit. He's trying to crawl—"

Two rapid rifle shots cut across the parking lot.

"McNulty's gone! Flat-out dead! What the fuck just happened?" said the team leader. "Is there another shooter out here?"

"Another shooter?" said Bowen, catching movement in his peripheral vision. "Hold on."

The two operators sent to babysit him had piled out of their bulletproof Suburban, headed in his direction between parked vehicles.

"Hey. You're not supposed—"

"Decker's in the parking lot, you fucking idiot!" said the lead operator.

They barreled past him and crouched at the edge of the hood, barely pausing long enough to shoulder their rifles—before rounding the bumper. Both of them dropped from head shots before they got past the pickup truck.

Jesus!

Bowen ducked out of sheer panic, the involuntary reflex saving his life. A single bullet snapped inches over his head, shattering the car window behind him. Who the fuck was this Decker guy?

More single gunshots, followed by panicked yelling and automatic fire from the eight-man reserve team hiding behind the last row of parked cars. He had to do something fast or Decker would kill them all.

"Storm One. Shift your fire to the right side of the parking lot. Decker slipped out of the room. Full auto. Just pound the shit out of everything," he said. "I'll cover the room."

"Copy that," said the team leader.

Bowen scooted toward the front of the pickup truck, where he could lay down suppressive fire on the woman's room. Once he was in position, Storm One's team leader repositioned the remains of his team to face Decker.

"Storm Three. Same orders. Level the parking lot in front of Storm One. Full auto."

"You want me to sweep it with the SAW?" said the team leader.

"Affirmative," said Bowen. "I want the right side of the parking lot uninhabitable."

"Roger," said the reserve team leader.

The bitch's shotgun boomed again, blasting several thumb-size holes through the wall a few feet behind STORM One's team leader.

"I'm done with this shit," said Bowen, nestling the AK-47's stock into his shoulder and aiming at the most recent shotgun hole.

He fired several long, controlled bursts on full automatic, sweeping the barrel back and forth across the front of the room until he had expended the entire seventy-five-round drum. The rest of his men started firing at the same time, the crackle of their rifles barely noticeable above the deafening racket created by his own weapon. When his rifle finally stopped, only the M249 Squad Automatic Weapon (SAW) kept going, its two-hundred-round ammunition box still feeding the military-grade light machine gun.

He waited until the rest of the Wolfpak reloaded and rejoined the battle before he poked his head around the pickup's front bumper. Red tracers from the SAW ricocheted off the vehicles, flying in every direction. Tires flattened. Windows shattered. Bullet holes stitched metal. Hoods and trunks sparked. Some of the tracers passed right through the cars, briefly illuminating their interiors.

He felt equally exhilarated and terrified. Bowen had never seen anything like that. Nothing could have survived the hell they'd just unleashed. He didn't even want to think about the guests in the rooms on that side of the motel. When the SAW went quiet, he ordered a withdrawal. There was no reason to lose any more of his men. The mission was about as fucked as it could get at this point.

"STORM Three. Reload the SAW to cover our departure. Then get the rest of your team to their trucks. We needed to be out of here like thirty seconds ago," he said. "STORM One. Exfil in my truck when the SAW is ready."

"Did we nail Decker?" said Bowen. "No way we didn't get him, right?"

"I didn't see anyone down on the pavement when the SAW was going," said STORM Three. "And I ain't gonna poke my head out to check when it's not firing. That fucker nailed three of my guys with head shots."

"Gotcha," said Bowen, reconsidering his exfiltration plan.

If Decker was still combat effective, he'd give them hell on the way out.

"The SAW is reloaded," said STORM Three.

"STORM One, hold up," he said.

"Holding."

"Hey, Ron?" said Bowen.

"Yep?" said STORM Three.

"Light up the parking lot. Another two hundred rounds," said Bowen. "I don't want to take any chances."

"The barrel's already red hot," said the team leader.

"It'll cool off on the ride back," said Bowen.

"We're on it," said the team leader—and the SAW ripped through the night.

CHAPTER TWENTY-THREE

Decker lay curled in a fetal ball on the back seat floor of the bullet-riddled SUV, listening intently for any out-of-place sounds. The roar of the skinheads' overpowered vehicles had faded to nothing by this point, replaced by several out-of-synch car alarms. Still. He wasn't taking any chances. A few inches above him, the front seatback sizzled from a tracer that had passed right through during one of the longer machine-gun bursts.

A man started wailing in one of the nearby rooms, joined by the distant sound of a police siren. Decker couldn't wait any longer. He needed to get to Pam's room before the sheriff's department found them. If she was in bad shape, the emergency first aid he administered now might be the only medical treatment she received for a long time. Authorities would have their hands full here when they discovered the full scope of the shoot-out.

He opened the car door and crawled out with his rifle, dragging a thick pile of shattered glass with him onto the pavement. A quick glance up at the side of the SUV confirmed that luck had probably played more of a role in his survival than anything else. No fewer than a dozen holes had been punched through the unexposed side, which meant the bullets had passed through the entire vehicle.

Decker pushed himself off the ground with the help of the rifle, his left leg feeling a little unstable. Something had grazed his thigh when all of the skinheads started firing together on full automatic. He should have been cut down during those first few seconds but had somehow made it to the far corner of the lot, where he'd ducked behind the SUV. When bullets started skipping off the pavement around him, he grabbed the door handle, finding it open. Pure luck.

The police sirens grew louder, prompting him to keep moving. He tried to run but found himself fast-limping down the concrete sidewalk instead. Decker scanned the parking lot as he moved. From what he could tell, their attackers had left all their dead behind, a shortsighted decision they would regret. Enough investigative leads lay among the dozen or so bodies strewn around the motel to close this case and shut down whatever criminal organization had set up shop in the Alderpoint area.

He slowed as he approached the cluster of men lying in front of his room, unsure of their status. As Decker slipped past the flattened man he'd shot while dashing into the parking lot, the guy feebly reached for his ankle.

"Help," he whispered, before managing to turn his head far enough to the side to make eye contact. "You?"

His hand drifted toward the rifle that lay well out of his reach on the sidewalk. As much as Decker wanted to stomp on this guy's neck and violently end his life, he couldn't justify it. Judging by the rapidly expanding pool of blood underneath the man, he no longer posed a threat to anyone. He took a moment to kick the man's rifle farther down the walkway before moving on. By the time he arrived outside Pam's door, blue and red lights illuminated the trees in front of the motel.

"Pam! It's Decker! I'm coming in," he said, giving her a few seconds to process his words before slipping inside. "The skinheads are gone. You scared them off."

Red and blue lights penetrated the dark, dust-filled room, giving him just enough light to see.

"Ah . . . Shit."

A wide blood trail led from the floor behind the bed to the bathroom, where he found Pam seated on the floor against the bathtub, her right arm hung over the edge of the tub.

"Pam!"

Decker rushed in and immediately slipped on the blood-slicked linoleum, landing hard on the toilet. A stifled laugh broke out the moment he settled on the floor.

"Pam?"

"It really hurts to laugh," she croaked. "But at least I'm gonna die laughing."

"You're not going to die," said Decker, before sitting up and flipping on the bathroom light.

He stared at her wounds a little too long. A thumb-size hole in her outer right thigh actively pumped blood onto the linoleum. A massive bloodstain covered most of her left abdomen, a hole in her T-shirt evident below the rib cage. Her left shoulder was soaked with blood to the armpit.

"That's what I thought," she said, staring at him glassy eyed.

"Where's your med kit?"

She shook her head. "Don't bother—"

"Where's your fucking med kit, Pam?"

"Backpack behind the bed," she said.

"First things first," he said, taking his shirt off.

"Jesus, Decker. What the fuck?" she said, laughing painfully.

"Tourniquet."

Decker jammed the shirt between her legs and worked it underneath her upper thigh. When the shirt appeared on the other side, he pulled it through and stretched both sides as far as possible, sliding it down her leg until it sat a few inches above the bullet hole.

"This is going to hurt," he said, before pulling the shirt tight across the top of her thigh and tying it off.

Pam grimaced but didn't make a sound. She knew the worst was yet to come. He glanced around the shabby bathroom, looking for anything he could use to tighten the tourniquet. A few seconds later, Decker slid the metal toilet paper roll holder under the tied shirt and twisted it. Pam tensed, drawing air through her teeth. When the blood flowing from her leg wound slowed to a trickle, he stuffed one end of the metal tube under the tightened shirt to keep it in place until he got back. She stifled a scream when he put that final touch on the tourniquet.

"How are you doing?" he said.

"How do you think?"

"Be right back," said Decker, standing up.

"I'm not going anywhere."

Decker grabbed the pack, careful to stay low. From what he could see through the door, at least two police cars had parked on Red Wood Drive, near the motel office. He shut the bathroom door and locked it on the way back in to buy some time, in case the police had already spotted the light.

"Stay with me, Pam," said Decker, setting the backpack down in the tub on top of her shotgun.

"Okay," she murmured.

He opened the backpack and pulled the football-size med kit onto the floor next to her. With the heaviest bleeding stopped, he'd move on to the next life-threatening wound, which appeared to be the hole in her abdomen. Decker turned her over far enough to check for another hole, suspecting a through-and-through wound. He hadn't bothered checking her leg, since he'd planned on a tourniquet from the start.

Finding no additional bullet holes, Decker went to work stuffing the wound with hemostatic gauze to slow the bleeding. With Pam grunting at him, he taped the gauze in place and moved on to her shoulder, which mercifully turned out to be nothing more than a deep bullet graze. A thick surface layer of hemostatic gauze and a few lines of medical tape fixed that for now.

"Pam, I think you're good to—" he started, before noticing that her head had slumped backward against the edge of the tub. "Shit."

He checked her pulse, barely finding one. Pam was fading fast. She needed an EMT crew with an ambulance immediately, or she'd die.

"Hang on for a second," he said. "I'm getting you some real help."

Decker limped out of the bathroom, brainstorming a way to do this without getting himself killed. The responding officers had to be scared out of their minds right now. He gave them a lot of credit for showing up after what had gone down here less than five minutes ago. The southern tip of Garberville must have sounded like a war zone from the sheriff's station. They would no doubt be in a "shoot first and ask questions after shooting again" frame of mind.

He paused halfway across the room, wondering if he shouldn't go back and bring Pam with him. Maybe the sight of him carrying a bloodied casualty out of this mess would take some pressure off those triggers. As he staggered back to get her, his foot kicked something. A bluish glow lit the carpet under the bed. Pam's phone. Even better. He'd let them know he was coming out with a critical gunshot victim.

Decker lowered himself to the carpet and looked under the bed, finding the phone just out of reach. He pushed his arm and shoulder as far as possible, his fingertips touching the phone. A sound at the doorway stopped him. *Shit.* He'd been in too much of a hurry to reach Pam to clear the lot for survivors. Before he could react, his muscles started contracting involuntarily, essentially trapping him under the bed. Decker didn't try to fight it. He'd been Tasered and would be out of commission for at least five seconds.

"I got one in here!" yelled a woman.

"Hostile?" said a male voice.

"I can't tell. He was reaching for something under the bed," she said. "Sergeant Russell said to assume that anyone in one-oh-eight or one-oh-nine was hostile—but I don't know."

Someone activated a flashlight, sweeping it across the room.

"Holy mother," said the male voice. "Looks like he was on the receiving end of whatever hit this place."

"I'm not taking any chances until I can see his other hand," she said.

"I have a blood trail leading to the bathroom."

"This guy has a leg wound," she said.

"No. This is too much blood for that."

Decker's muscles relaxed.

"My partner was shot. She's in the bathroom," said Decker, fully expecting another jolt from the Taser.

A pair of boots approached the bathroom, stepping around the blood.

"You a cop?" said the woman.

"Private investigator," said Decker. "We were investigating the maniacs that shot this place up."

"Jesus," said her partner from the other side of the room. "Dispatch. This is Deputy Horton at the Red Wood Motel. I have a civilian in room one-oh-eight with a critical gunshot wound to the stomach and leg. Leg is in a tourniquet. Request immediate medical assistance."

"An ambulance is pulling up to the motel right now," replied dispatch.

"They need to send everything they have," said Decker. "I heard people moaning inside some of the rooms along the southern end of the parking lot."

"Dispatch. Send everything available. Possible mass casualty situation," said the deputy. "Looks like someone started a war down here."

A new voice joined the other two.

"I'll keep an eye on the suspect while you go room to room looking for other wounded."

"Sergeant, I found a serious-looking rifle in the bathroom. Something's up with these two," said the other deputy.

"You sure, Sergeant?" said the woman. "We can all wait for backup."

"Yeah. I got this. There may be other people dying," said the sergeant.

While the two deputies shuffled out of the room, Decker grabbed the phone and pressed the only button available to him without Pam's passcode. The room went deathly quiet after that.

"Sergeant?"

No response.

"Sergeant, I dialed nine-one-one," said Decker. "Room one-oh-eight."

"Yep. We're already here," said the sergeant.

"No. I dialed nine-one-one with the phone I'm holding under the bed."

"You what?" he said, and Decker's muscles convulsed uncontrollably.

The sergeant's mustached face appeared next to his, staring at the phone he had tossed well out of reach after connecting to 911.

"Hello. Hello," said a frantic voice over the phone. "The police and EMTs are on the scene, sir. Stay in your room and an officer will assist you. I'm sending them right to you."

The sergeant's radio crackled. "Responding units. This is dispatch. I just got a mobile phone call from one-oh-eight. The call is still live. Sergeant Russell, aren't your people already in that room?"

Decker's world went dark right after that.

CHAPTER
TWENTY-FOUR

Carl Trenkor paced the entrance to the compound's parking area, his brain still bouncing between several solutions to the new crisis Bowen had just created. Nearly all of them resulted in Bowen and his crew disappearing forever. He just wasn't sure when he should pull the trigger on that. Trenkor still needed the Wolfpak's network of informants and watchers—or had the motel fiasco pushed everything past the point of no return? If that turned out to be the case, Bowen's continued existence was nothing but a liability.

Instinct told him he should ambush Bowen's convoy the moment they parked. Get it over with before the Nazi put two and two together for himself. The guy wasn't entirely stupid, and the last thing Trenkor needed to worry about right now was Bowen and his band of ill-behaved fanatics. The compound's survival from this moment forward would depend on unquestioning loyalty and the ability to precisely follow orders. Two concepts Bowen had struggled with from the very outset of their relationship.

Jason Watts, compound security chief, emerged from the path leading to the trailers.

"Everyone is in place, prepared for a twenty-four-hour marathon. Perimeter security is doubled. The entire quick reaction force has been reorganized and redeployed. Half on patrol along the periphery of the fields and labor tents. The rest watching the trailer park—with a focus on containing our skinhead friends."

"I'm worried our friends might be the biggest challenge," said Trenkor.

"How bad was it in Garberville?"

"Bad enough that I'm thinking about terminating their contract as soon as they return."

"I can have the entire QRF here in under a minute," said Watts.

Trenkor gave the idea another spin, deciding against it for now. An imminent raid against the compound was unlikely for a number of reasons, the biggest one being the mess Bowen had made at the motel. Unless he had some kind of a death wish, the Humboldt County sheriff would take one look at the carnage and accurately conclude that he didn't have the resources to face off with whoever had hit the motel. They'd call Sacramento.

State investigators would survey the parking lot and kick a few spent shell casings before drawing the same conclusion. The feds might get involved, but nobody would come knocking at their door for a few weeks. Not without a serious plan and significant resources. In an unexpected way, Bowen may have unwittingly bought them more time than they had before—not that this revelation would significantly extend his life span. Bowen had signed his own death warrant when he drove into EMERALD CITY.

"Tin Man Actual, this is Sentinel."

Trenkor grabbed his radio. "Go ahead, Sentinel."

"Wolfpak is inbound. Two vehicles."

Two? They'd left the compound with five! The situation was obviously worse than Bowen had originally reported. He turned to Watts.

"Get the QRF over here immediately."

"Copy that," said Watts, before issuing a single order over the security team channel. "Ten are already in position. Another twenty are on the way."

"I like the way you think," said Trenkor. "Let me know when they're ready."

Watts just nodded and melted away into the brush in front of them. He triggered his radio.

"Wolfpak reentry authorized. Give me a personnel count."

"Counting," said the team leader in charge of the only gate leading into the compound.

The bushes rustled nearby, the QRF team taking positions around the vehicle park. A minute later, SENTINEL reported.

"Wolfpak just passed through. Two vehicles. Six survivors identified visually. Thermal scope confirms six live bodies. They aren't hiding anything."

Six survivors! He'd sent twenty-one heavily armed men down to the motel!

"What's the status of their company-provided escort?" said Trenkor.

"Unknown. Our Suburban is not one of the four returning vehicles."

"Say again?"

"The Suburban that Hicks and Ramirez drove out of the compound did not return," said the team leader at the gate. "I don't know if they're included in the six survivors."

Trenkor didn't respond. If the two men he'd sent to oversee Bowen's operation had been left behind—dead or alive—everything was truly fucked. He triggered his radio.

"Watts, what's your status?" said Trenkor.

"QRF is mostly in position," said Watts. "A few still trickling in."

"Copy that. The Wolfpak is returning with two vehicles and six survivors," said Trenkor.

"That's not good."

"Not good at all," said Trenkor. "Kill them all when I give you the signal."

"Got it," said Watts. "I have more than enough shooters in place right now to make that happen."

"Then that's that," said Trenkor.

Headlights poked through the trees, headed in his direction. Bowen's black F-250 barreled full speed into the grassy field, skidding to a halt about five yards in front of Trenkor. The second pickup truck pulled alongside and stopped. Trenkor raised a hand to shield his eyes from the headlights.

"We have all of them covered," said Watts. "No need to duck."

Trenkor nodded, secretly acknowledging the report without alerting Bowen—who had already jumped down from the F-250's front passenger seat and started toward him. The Wolfpak's leader scanned the parked vehicles behind Trenkor before crossing his arms and shaking his head. He could barely see Bowen because of the glare created by the headlights.

"Do you mind killing the lights?"

"Funny choice of words," said Bowen, before issuing an order through his shoulder mic.

The field plunged into darkness a moment later, replaced by the soft glow of the nearest trailer's porch light.

"Before you have your people gun me down—I need you to know that I've taken out a little insurance policy."

"Hicks and Ramirez?" said Trenkor.

As much as Trenkor despised the thought of Bowen taking his people hostage, a big part of him hoped it was true. Anything was better than leaving their bodies behind—to be identified and linked back to Athena Corp. The Suburban would be nearly impossible for authorities to trace, but its presence on the scene would suggest something a little more complicated than a skinhead kidnap scheme gone wrong.

"No. They both got zapped by Decker. Should have stayed in their bulletproof hideout," said Bowen.

"The Suburban is still back at the motel?" he said.

"I didn't exactly have time to fish the keys off their corpses," said Bowen. "Decker was pulling off head shots like it was his primary fucking job in life. Would've been nice to know we were up against John Wick."

Trenkor wanted to be done with this guy right now, but he needed to make sure Bowen didn't hold anything substantial over his head.

"What's this insurance policy?"

"I sent one of the trucks away with three of my guys—the one with the SAW," said Bowen. "If I don't check in with them by sunrise and every hour after that, they're gonna make an anonymous call to the sheriff's department, FBI, and DEA. Give them the rundown on what you've been up to out here, along with the coordinates."

"For fuck's sake, Bowen. We have a deal. You get paid the same regardless of what we manage to harvest," said Trenkor. "I don't have any incentive to get rid of you."

"Look, Carl. Let's cut the bullshit. I'm not as dumb as you think. I understood from the start that you might consider this whole thing a one-way ticket for the Wolfpak. Use us and lose us," said Bowen. "Given everything that's happened over the past week, I pretty much figured it was guaranteed. I just didn't know when you'd pull the trigger. Tonight's shit show pretty much answered that."

Trenkor didn't have anything to lose by coming clean at this point. Bowen hadn't left him much wiggle room.

"The thought had crossed my mind lately. More than once, to be honest," said Trenkor.

"I bet it has," said Bowen. "Any chance you'd deposit our money now and let us part ways?"

141

"I'll deposit your money, but I can't let you leave the compound until we shut everything down," said Trenkor. "You're too much of a liability out there right now. We'll helicopter you out when we evacuate."

"Fuck that," said Bowen. "Once you close up shop here, my insurance policy doesn't mean shit. You must really think I'm stupid."

"What assurance do I have that you won't take the money and call in our coordinates anyway?"

"My word," said Bowen. "I know that doesn't mean much to you corporate puppet types, but in my world it means everything. You have my word that you'll never hear from me again once we're gone—and paid."

Trenkor had one last card to play. More of a test than anything.

"Or I could just activate the tracker on your guys' truck and send a hunter-killer team after them—with helicopter support."

Bowen smirked. "You think we didn't know about the trackers? Shit. We found those on day one and left them in place so you didn't know we knew. My guys shucked those about a mile down the road from the motel."

"Even the trackers we installed in the bumpers?"

"And the glove box. And the underside of each truck," said Bowen. "My insurance policy is invisible to all of your electronic shenanigans."

"Hmmm. I suppose they found the one we installed inside the dashboard, too?" said Trenkor.

The smirk remained, but his eyes flittered nervously for a moment.

"Yep," said Bowen, rather flatly.

"Both bumpers?"

Bowen turned and ran, knocked flat by a short burst of automatic gunfire. Trenkor immediately dropped to the ground to make himself a difficult target for any Wolfpak shooters who had been slyly targeting him from inside the trucks. Bullets pounded the two trucks mercilessly for several seconds, shattering all the windows and stitching the metal frame. When the fusillade ended, two pairs of body armor–clad Athena

Corp operators materialized from the bushes, each walking alongside one of the trucks and firing down through the windows.

"Clear," the teams shouted, almost simultaneously.

Trenkor rose to his feet and brushed off his pants. Watts joined him in front of the bullet-riddled trucks.

"I'll get a six-man team on the road ASAP," said Watts. "Incognito. I have two junkers just for this kind of operation."

"Sounds good. I'll have coordinates for you in a few minutes," said Trenkor. "I'm also going to bring a Chinook over, loaded with one of the KANSAS assault teams. If Bowen's hillbillies are smart, they'll drive straight through the rest of the night and on into the morning. Your team will never catch up with them in time."

"I don't think they're that smart," said Watts. "But I'll take all the help I can get."

"I'll keep the assault team here to augment security," said Trenkor. "With the Wolfpak gone, we'll have to run our own interference on the local roads and trails up here."

"The more the merrier," said Watts. "How long do you figure we have until it's time to fold up the tents?"

"It really depends. If the county sheriff forgets he's not bulletproof and marches up here at first light, we'll be out of here by lunch—probably sooner. If the sheriff plays it cautious, which I suspect he will after taking a look at the motel, we're realistically looking at anywhere between seventy-two hours to a week before outside surveillance becomes a problem. A week to two weeks before anyone makes a serious move against us."

"Without Bowen's spy network, we won't get a lot of warning when they come," said Watts.

Trenkor sighed. This is where things could get truly ugly out here.

"We'll have to extend our defensive posture with remote measures," he said.

"Command detonated?" said Watts.

"Command activated. Five zones. Progressive damage scheme," said Trenkor.

He'd just authorized Watts to plant a series of remotely armed, motion-triggered roadside bombs along the most likely vehicle approaches to the compound—some extending all the way to Alderpoint. A network of remote-controlled cameras and solar-powered drones would watch the approaches. The outer zone's explosive devices were the smallest, meant to deter or delay. The bombs grew exponentially larger and deadlier after that, posing a serious challenge to any attack force lighter than an armored reconnaissance battalion.

Athena Corp had employed the same tactic with great success at their more vulnerable black sites overseas, where nearby hostile forces posed an immediate threat. Only suicide bombers made it into the final zone—few in their right mind continued after the first. Trenkor sincerely hoped he'd never have to activate any of the zones. Things had already spiraled far enough out of control on his watch.

CHAPTER TWENTY-FIVE

Carl Trenkor huddled around a laptop-strewn table in EMERALD CITY's security operations trailer with Jason Watts and Mike Loftis, waiting for OZ to call. He stared out the window next to him at the velvet-blue sky above the towering redwoods, the first vestiges of what promised to be a long day mocking him. Across the table, Watts's head slowly lowered to the table—eyes closed—before snapping back into place.

"Sorry about that," said Watts, standing up. "Coffee refill?"

"I'll take one," said Trenkor, turning his attention back to the sky.

"Mike?" said Watts.

"Yep," said Loftis. "We might want to consider breaking out the stims at some point today. It's going to take more than coffee to keep the troops alert and focused as the day wears on."

Trenkor absently nodded. "Distribute the stim packs in the late afternoon. They'll start to fade with the sun. We'll have to come up with a dosage regimen based on duty rotation schedules—so the troops can sleep when they're supposed to. Unless we have to maintain a one hundred percent force protection posture until we leave."

"I'll work with our medic team on that," said Loftis.

Watts split the last of the coffeepot between the three mugs. None of them reached for the Tupperware container filled with cream and sugar packets. They were all well past dressing up their caffeine hits.

"Cheers," said Watts, raising his Styrofoam cup.

The satellite-connected conference phone on the table in front of him chirped before Trenkor could take a sip. He set the steaming cup next to the window and accepted the call.

"Sir, I'm here with Jason Watts, my security chief, and Mike Loftis, the operations officer," said Trenkor.

"I'll get right down to business, gentlemen. We've decided to give EMERALD CITY ninety-six hours. I've spoken at length with our buyers, and they can still work with the product. You'll harvest as much of the crop as possible in the given time, prioritizing the more mature plants. Ninety-six hours is a hard-departure deadline."

Loftis nodded before holding up two fingers.

"I'd suggest two runs per night. Both helicopters. That'll give us more than enough leeway to get the second run airborne and out of the state by daybreak," said Trenkor.

"I can move a third Sikorsky to KANSAS by tonight, if that would help," said OZ.

"We'll need to do the math on that, sir," said Trenkor. "I'm not sure the farm crews can cut and prep the product quickly enough to utilize the extra cargo capacity. They'll be working nonstop to meet the current demand—which already has me a little concerned. They're going to know something big is up when we order them to start clear-cutting younger plants."

"Be up-front. Tell them we're shutting down in four days, and pay them each their full salary on the spot," he said. "That should more than motivate them—but make it clear that nobody goes anywhere until the job is done."

"That won't be a problem," said Trenkor. "None of them are keen on wandering off the property. We've seen to that with a Claymore mine demonstration at the start of their employment."

"That would do it," said OZ, chuckling briefly. "It goes without saying that emergency evacuation protocols remain in place. Any serious attempt by law enforcement to breach the compound triggers an immediate evacuation of Athena Corp personnel. Destroy any sensitive equipment you can't fit on the helicopter."

"Understood," said Trenkor.

"Sir, this is Watts. Can you give me specific criteria regarding what constitutes a serious attempt?"

"Mr. Trenkor will make the final call, but I'd say any effort to reach the compound that isn't discouraged by the first and second set of remote-detonated explosives qualifies, regardless of the outcome. Beyond that—any sizable ground incursions detected by remote sensor is bad news. I know your people are good, but we can't afford to get bogged down in a ground battle that might damage your evac helo."

"I assume we're weapons free on inbound helicopters?" said Trenkor.

"Absolutely. Nothing gets near the compound until you're gone," said OZ. "I can't stress that enough. And nice job nailing Bowen's insurance policy. You bought us the time we need to make the best of the situation."

"A shitty situation," said Trenkor, bleakly.

"Keep your head up, Carl," said OZ. "If we can hold on to EMERALD CITY for the next ninety-six hours, we'll come out of this smelling like roses. Hell, even half that long brings in more money than our opportunity analysts originally estimated. Everyone performed exceptionally well and will be rewarded accordingly. I'll make sure of it."

"I like the sound of that," said Trenkor, instantly remembering the time Bowen had spoken those same words.

He just hoped that OZ wasn't on the other side of this call, thinking the same thing Trenkor had thought about Bowen. *Everyone but you.*

CHAPTER TWENTY-SIX

Sheriff Harvey Long ducked under a loose line of yellow police tape held up for him by a tired-looking deputy and headed straight for the small gaggle of uniformed and plainclothes deputies sipping coffee next to the white van stenciled CRIME SCENE UNIT. Several sheriff's department cruisers and SUVs, their roof lights flashing, formed a loose perimeter in front of the motel. The coroner's pickup truck was among them.

He surveyed the parking lot on his short walk down Red Wood Drive, the brutal reality of the reports he'd taken by phone hitting harder than he'd expected. Nothing like this had ever happened in Humboldt County before. Not even close. Whatever happened here last night went way deeper than a local-on-local power play. Someone was at war, and they had no problem bringing it right into the open for everyone to see.

The south side of the motel complex had taken the brunt of the mayhem. Nearly every car window had been shattered or cracked to some degree. Piles of broken glass covered the asphalt between rows of bullet-riddled vehicles. The tight bullet patterns stitched across a few of the windshields suggested sustained, relatively accurate automatic fire.

Definitely not a spray-and-pray gangbanger job. Possibly a belt-fed light machine gun—fired by someone trained to use it. Ex-military? Who the hell used a weapon like that in public? Mexicans? Russians? He didn't want to find out personally. This was as close as he ever wanted to get to the end result of a gun like that.

Several corpses lay strewn across the parking lot, a few rifles visible nearby on the pavement. The latest update he received en route to the motel indicated that all the bodies in the parking lot rested next to some kind of military-style rifle. The skinheads hadn't stood a chance against the weapon that had torn through the vehicles. Same with several of the motel guests.

Damage to the motel appeared to be mostly concentrated on the dozen or so rooms adjacent to the machine-gunned side of the parking lot, where all the dead and wounded civilians had been found. Two killed and eight hospitalized, including the two private investigators who had shown up at his office yesterday morning, asking about Brett Hale.

Now he wished he hadn't blown off their request for a meeting. The two of them clearly had something to do with this mess. A significant amount of gunfire had been fired into one of the two rooms they had checked into—which couldn't be a coincidence. Unfortunately, their role remained a mystery for now. One had been airlifted to the Mercy Medical Center trauma unit in Redding, where doctors didn't sound optimistic about her chances of surviving. The other private investigator had been taken to St. Joseph's in Eureka, knocked out cold by Sergeant Russell while trying to escape his custody. He'd have a chat with that guy as soon as he woke up.

Sergeant Glen Reid, head of their Detective Bureau, broke from the group of deputies as he approached.

"Doesn't look real at first glance, does it?" said Reid, clearly reading the look on his face.

"It's like something you see in a Tarantino movie," said Long.

"Still got some hot coffee if you're interested," said Reid.

"I'm definitely interested."

Long had driven down to UC Davis last night with his wife to deliver some odds and ends to their daughter for her dorm room. He'd taken today off and hoped to spend a long weekend hanging out in Sacramento with his wife and daughter. Instead, he was back on the road less than six hours after checking into their hotel. Four grueling hours later, he was staring at a mass shooting that would soon draw hundreds of news crews to Humboldt County. He'd be mainlining coffee by this time tomorrow.

Sergeant Tabitha Larson greeted him first when they reached the van.

"Welcome back," she said, offering him a lukewarm Styrofoam cup. "Feels like you just left."

"Same here," he said, before downing the entire cup.

"We have some hot coffee on the way," said Ken Hodges, who was donned in full tactical gear and camouflage.

Detective Hodges commanded the Special Enforcement Team (SET), Humboldt County's equivalent of SWAT. They mostly served high-risk warrants and accompanied Larson's Drug Enforcement Unit officers on marijuana field raids. The occasional armed standoff at a convenience store or rural property was about as crazy as things got for his team. The motel shoot-out represented an entirely new level of threat in the county, and from the looks of it, Hodges had responded in kind. A dozen heavily armed, fully kitted officers in camouflage stood guard over the crime scene.

"Good. Looks like we'll all need it," said Long. "So. What are we looking at, Glen?"

Sergeant Reid shook his head. "Not what I originally thought. The skinheads weren't on the receiving end of this shitstorm. I'm pretty sure they caused it."

Long glanced at the parking lot, unable to reconcile Reid's statement with the bodies littering the asphalt.

"Those are all skinheads, right?"

"Most of them," said Reid.

"Wait. I thought everyone dead in the parking lot was a skinhead."

"They are. Except for maybe two of them," said Reid. "They don't look like skinheads, except they're bald."

"Isn't that the definition of a skinhead?" said Long.

Reid chuckled.

"I guess so. But they're different," said Reid. "Come on. Someone back me up here."

"They're different," said Larson.

"Thanks for the boatload of help," said Reid, shaking his head.

"What or who do you think they are?"

Hodges jumped in to help the detective.

"Military contractors or former Special Operations types—if I had to guess. Geared up differently than the skinheads. Plate carriers. Thigh holsters. Tricked-out rifles. IFAKs. Very organized shooting rigs."

"IFAKs?"

"Individual first aid kits. Trauma kits, basically. Standard military issue for ground combat soldiers. All of my team members carry them," said Hodges. "We didn't find them on anyone else."

"So we have a rogue group of ex-commandos fighting it out with a bunch of skinheads out here? Just what we need," said Long. "My fucking head is spinning."

"If that spun your head, you better grab it with both hands," said Reid. "I think the private investigator we transported to St. Joseph's—Ryan Decker—killed all but two of them."

"Wait—how many do we have on the ground in the parking lot?"

"Twelve. Two from shotgun blasts, presumably delivered by the shotgun found in the bathroom with Ms. Pamela Stack. The rest from head shots, except for one of the skinheads near Decker's room. Coroner says the head shot entry wounds look like they came from a point-two-two-three-caliber rifle—same as the one we found near Decker."

"How do you know he didn't grab the rifle from one of the dead guys in all of the chaos?" said Long. "Before rushing off to help his partner."

"We found several spent point-two-two-three shell casings deep inside Decker's room," said Reid. "And everyone in the parking lot carried AK-47s—except for the two ex-military-looking guys. They both had rifles similar to Decker's."

"We need to find out who the two commando types are. Let's prioritize identifying them."

Reid nodded. "We'll do a full workup and send it off to the feds."

"So if Decker did all of the killing," said Long, pointing at the machine-gunned side of the parking lot, "then what the hell happened there?"

"We're still not one hundred percent sure, but we have a working theory," said Reid. "Let's head over to the south side of the parking lot, or the machine-gunned side, as you put it, to get a better look. I'll walk you through it from there."

Long and the rest of the deputies followed the detective to a point in the grass at the edge of the parking lot. A string of yellow tape fluttered in the breeze right in front of them, marking the start of the physical crime scene. Beyond the tape, the first thing he noticed was the thick concentration of spent brass on the asphalt less than fifteen feet away.

"Machine gun must have been in the back of a pickup," said Long.

"Looks like it," said Reid. "We've issued a county-wide APB, warning officers to exercise extreme caution if they stop a pickup truck for any reason. Adjacent counties have been warned as well."

"How many rounds do you think they fired?" said Long, looking from the shiny brass to the destruction in front of them.

"Judging from the pile, I'd say at least three hundred," said Hodges. "Some of the brass may have landed in the pickup bed, so that number could be a lot higher."

"This is bizarre," said Long. "Hundreds of rounds fired but they didn't hit anyone—except for innocent bystanders. What am I missing?"

"The hundred or more bullets fired from that direction. At the same cars," said Reid, pointing toward the southern side of the parking lot. "We found bullet holes facing directly north. No way they came from where we're standing."

"Who were they shooting at?"

The detective winced. "This is kind of a long shot, but my guess is they were shooting at this Decker guy. Actually, I think Decker and his partner were the targets of this whole botched attack."

"Let me hear it," said Long.

"First of all, both rooms had been breached with handheld battering rams."

"I'd say that's pretty conclusive," said Long.

"Right. I think Decker killed the guys trying to get into his room, slipped into the parking lot, and started popping the skinheads in the head, until they decided to turn every gun they had against him at once. We found a ton of spent brass on the north side of the parking lot. All seven-point-six-two millimeter.

"After the surviving skinheads tore out of here, Decker made his way back to his partner's room and patched her up the best he could before the first deputies took him into custody. We found a blood trail leading from the back of an SUV parked in the far corner of the destroyed side of the lot—to the female private investigator's room. Decker was detained in that same room, with a bullet wound to the thigh. A bleeder, but mostly superficial."

Long gave it a quick once-over in his head, finding it plausible.

"All of this for two private investigators?" said Long. "Ms. Stack dropped by the Eureka station yesterday morning but didn't say why."

"Well, whatever they were looking into clearly pissed someone off," said Larson. "And I can almost guarantee that *someone* is sitting at the top of our favorite mountain right now, carving swastikas into the trees."

"Don't get any crazy ideas, Tabby," said Long. "Alderpoint is off limits until we figure this out."

Sergeant Larson shook her head. "Alderpoint is always off limits."

"Take a look around. This is why we tread very lightly up there. We're not equipped to deal with this kind of firepower. No offense, Ken."

"None taken. This isn't a suicide squad," said Hodges.

Long continued. "Look. We're going to get to the bottom of what happened here. If this is the kind of shit we can expect to spill off the mountain from now on, I'll call in enough reinforcements to clean up the entire mess out there. Until then? We take this one step at a time."

"What's the first step?" she said.

"Questioning Decker," said Long. "I swear that name is somehow familiar."

Detective Hodges held out his smartphone. "I didn't want to hit you with everything at once, but here's the other reason we think Decker did most of the precision shooting."

Long took his phone and scrolled through the article on the screen, muttering obscenities the whole time. Now he remembered. The connection couldn't be a coincidence.

"I want a total media blackout on this guy's identity. John Doe. End of story. Make sure everyone on scene understands that I'm not fucking around with this," said Long, handing the phone back. "Media coverage is going to be bad enough as it is. We don't need the extra attention Ryan Decker is guaranteed to deliver. I'll call ahead to Hernandez at the station and have her tighten screws at the hospital. If Decker's stable, I might even move him to the station."

"That bad?" said Hodges. "It's an old article."

"Search RYAN DECKER—NORTH HOLLYWOOD SHOOT-OUT—VALKYRIE," said Long. "You'll see what I mean. Decker has a thing for skinheads, or the other way around, in this case. Either way, the media will run wild with this if they make the connection. John Doe. That's all anyone knows for now."

CHAPTER

TWENTY-SEVEN

Ryan Decker remembered everything about the motel attack, which is why he kept his eyes shut when he woke. Something had been seriously off with Sergeant Russell. He remembered thinking that before dialing 911, but his memory stopped there. If Russell was still there, Decker didn't want him to know he had regained consciousness. Instinct told him his life depended on that. He peeked through his eyelids after carefully listening for any signs of the sergeant. A high-pitched beep sounded somewhere above him, followed by a female voice.

"Dr. Ramirez. Cardiology on line four."

He opened his eyes, finding himself alone in a single-bed hospital room instead of a ramshackle cabin in the woods on Murder Mountain. Decker tried to get out of the bed, but a pair of metal handcuffs attaching his right wrist to the bed rail kept him in place. He sat up and gave the cuffs a solid tug, quickly determining that he wasn't going anywhere in a hurry. Movement in the door caught his eye. Someone had just poked their head inside.

"Hello?" said Decker. "Anyone care to explain why I'm handcuffed to my bed?"

No response. He searched around for the bedside control unit, finding it in a holder attached to the bed rail. Decker pressed the call button several times and waited. When at least a minute had passed, he pressed it again. Nothing. Another look around suggested why. The screen behind him stood blank. The hospital wasn't monitoring his vitals.

"I know you're out there!" said Decker, yanking at the bed rail out of frustration.

A serious-looking face appeared in the doorway. "Cool it, buddy. The sheriff is on the way."

"Am I under arrest?" said Decker.

"Just wait for the sheriff," he said, leaning in a little more.

The deputy wore a tan ballistic vest over his uniform. Decker caught a glimpse of a bulging rifle magazine pouch.

"What happened to my partner?" said Decker. "Did she make it?"

When he hesitated to answer, instead of immediately giving him the sheriff line, Decker's heart sank. She was gone.

"You didn't hear this from me," said the deputy. "They airlifted her to the trauma center in Redding. That's all I can say."

"Is she alive?"

"The sheriff will be here in about five minutes," he said, before disappearing.

The deputy's answer made things worse, turning the next five or so minutes into what felt like an hour. While Decker waited, he assessed the gunshot wound to his thigh. Judging by the light dressing applied by the hospital, it couldn't be that bad. He pulled his knee to his chest, feeling some localized pain at the wound site, but nothing more than that. His thigh would be less of a problem than his head, which ached from the blow presumably delivered by Sergeant Russell.

A loud knock at the door announced the sheriff's arrival. A tall man dressed in jeans and a blue sheriff's department windbreaker stepped inside the room, pausing to look around. Decker recognized him from the internet research he'd done prior to driving up here.

"Mr. Decker. Sheriff Harvey Long. Humboldt County," he said. "Looks like the leg still works?"

Decker didn't bite off on the sheriff's peace offering. His trust of the Humboldt County Sheriff's Department had been reduced to zero by Sergeant Russell's bizarre behavior, not that his level of faith had traveled very far to hit rock bottom. He'd been skeptical of the sheriff's department from the outset. The illegal marijuana industry had somehow continued to flourish and expand right under his nose for years, and now a rogue syndicate was running the show?

"I'd shake your hand, but I'm handcuffed to the bed for some reason," said Decker.

"You tried to flee the motel room," said Long.

"My partner was dying in the bathroom. I wasn't going anywhere."

"That's not what Sergeant Russell reported," said Long.

"Sergeant Russell is lying," said Decker. "You need to take a close look at him."

Sheriff Long crossed his arms. "I have some questions about what happened at the motel."

"Am I under arrest?"

"Not yet."

"Then I need you to unlock these handcuffs. I have some calls to make," said Decker. "The first going to my firm's attorney."

"You're not going anywhere, Mr. Decker. We're processing the fingerprints on a very illegal short-barreled rifle found in Ms. Stack's room," said the sheriff.

"Check the glove compartment of the gray 4Runner directly in front of my room. You'll find all the paperwork regarding the rifle inside," said Decker. "Including a California dangerous weapon license that covers any and all members of my firm."

"I highly doubt the state granted a bunch of private investigators one of those," said Long.

"We had a high-level sponsor," said Decker.

"Regardless. I can hold you without charges for up to forty-eight hours, but I'm sure you already knew that."

Decker was really hoping he wouldn't go there. The clock was ticking on a number of fronts. Most important, Pam's.

"Is Ms. Stack alive?"

"Now you feel like talking?" said Long.

"You're not seriously going to hold that information over my head, are you?"

Long unfolded his arms, a slightly regretful look crossing his face.

"Ms. Stack is alive, but in critical condition," said Long. "We medevaced her to the level-two trauma center in Redding. You definitely saved her life with the tourniquet."

Jessica's voice whispered in his head. *Don't say a word. Not a word. Remain silent.* He'd keep it short.

"What do you want to know about the motel?" said Decker.

Sheriff Long shut the door and walked toward the chair next to the window.

"Don't get too comfortable," said Decker. "I don't plan on telling you my life's story."

Long took a seat anyway. "What were you and Ms. Stack investigating in Alderpoint?"

"Who says we were in Alderpoint?" said Decker.

"Nobody. I just assumed, since that's the proverbial hotbed of fun and games in the county," said Long.

"I can't tell you what we're doing up here without my client's permission," said Decker.

"I need to know what I'm up against here, Mr. Decker," said Long. "I have two dead and six wounded from machine-gun fire at that motel. Not including you and your partner. Machine-gun fire."

"I was there," said Decker. "Definitely an M249 Squad Automatic Weapon. I know that sound."

"We've never seen anything like this before out here, and I sure as hell don't want to see anything like it again," said Long. "I have to know if this is a onetime deal or if I need to call in reinforcements."

"I'd say this was a onetime deal," said Decker. "They were definitely there for us. That's all I can say."

Long examined him for a few moments before nodding. "Fair enough. What about the two guys kitted up like Special Forces types? Shot within feet of each other. How do they fit into this?"

Decker remembered them. Two quick shots had neutralized the most serious threat he'd identified in the parking lot—until the tracers started flying.

"My guess is the two men were sent to oversee the skinheads."

"Why do you think that?"

"They weren't shooting at each other," said Decker. "And they jumped into the mix after I broke out of my room. There was a Suburban parked behind a pickup truck that I'm pretty sure was involved in the attack. The pickup was gone when I returned to help Pam, but the Suburban was still there."

The sheriff looked energized by this information.

"Are we good?" said Decker, raising his cuffed hand as high as possible.

"I need to know who or what you were investigating before I'll even consider letting you go," said Long.

"A phone call?"

Long shook his head slowly. "I have enough distractions right now. I can't afford another."

"How am I a distraction? I just want to get up to Redding to check on my partner."

"I know about the North Hollywood shooting," said Long. "I need some time to figure out what happened in Garberville before someone else makes the connection, and five hundred news crews descend on me."

"What connection?" said Decker.

"You have a thing for mixing it up with skinheads," said Long. "Shooting skinheads, to be precise."

"This was totally unconnected," said Decker. "And for the record, it's the skinheads that have a thing for shooting me."

"The media will have a field day with that," said Long.

"So. You're just going to keep me here for two days without telling anyone?" said Decker. "That's the plan?"

"For now."

"Sheriff Long," said Decker. "Let me give you a phone number. Tell the woman who answers where to find Ms. Stack. She shouldn't be alone right now. Please."

"Not until I have a better handle on what the two of you did to provoke an attack that ferocious," said Long. "I've never seen anything like this in my twenty-plus years wearing a badge."

"We didn't do anything to provoke this other than show up in Humboldt County."

"I kind of doubt that was all the two of you got into yesterday," said Long. "Look. You seem like one of the good guys, Mr. Decker, but you have a bad habit of leaving dead bodies in your wake. I'm going to err on the side of caution until I get a better read on the situation."

"Don't take this the wrong way, Sheriff, but you're going to regret not making that call."

"Hard to take it any other way," said Long.

"Pam is like a sister to them," said Decker.

"Who is them?" said Long.

"Four women who can and will turn your life upside down if anything happens to her in their absence."

"Now you sound like you're threatening me," said Long.

"Just trying to give you fair warning," said Decker.

"I think we're done here."

"Hell hath no fury, Sheriff," said Decker. "Hell hath no fury."

"Last thing I fucking need right now," muttered Long, as he stomped out of the room.

When he was gone, Decker cracked a smile. "You have no idea."

CHAPTER TWENTY-EIGHT

Harlow paced back and forth, cell phone pressed to her ear.

"Dammit, Decker. Where the hell are you?" she said, loud enough to draw a few stares in the courthouse lobby.

She disconnected the call as soon as it went to voice mail, immediately speed-dialing Pam—with the same result. Voice mail. Harlow had already left both of them several increasingly irritated messages. She hadn't heard from either of them since last night. Jessica emerged from an unmarked metal door several feet away, pulling an oversize rolling briefcase behind her.

"Anything?" said Jessica.

"Nothing. I called their sat phones. I even sent them emails," said Harlow.

"Did you call their rooms?" said Jessica.

"They wouldn't be in the rooms," said Harlow.

Jessica gave her that look. "Then call the front desk and ask them to check for the 4Runner. It's not a big place, right?"

"No. It's a one-story deal," said Harlow, already looking up the number on her phone's browser.

"Let's get out of here," said Jessica, checking her watch. "We got lucky with the docket. I didn't expect to get out of here until at least four. You did great, by the way. I can't imagine the judge—you're not listening to a word I'm saying, are you?"

"I'm listening," said Harlow, putting the phone to her ear. "Late lunch? Sushi?"

"Sounds like a plan," said Jessica, before heading for the door.

Harlow trailed her, getting more annoyed with every unanswered ring. What the hell was going on? She stepped outside, shaking her head.

"I can't believe this," said Harlow. "It's like Northern California dropped off the grid."

"Nobody's answering?" said Jessica.

Harlow shrugged and started walking. "It's not even going to a digital directory so I can dial the rooms."

A call came through while she was waiting for someone at the motel to pick up.

"Shit," she muttered.

Jessica mouthed, "What?"

"Hold on," she said, accepting the incoming call. "Senator Steele. Sorry I didn't call earlier. I haven't heard from Decker regarding the surveillance flight yet. I've been trying to reach him most—"

"Harlow. There's been a mass shooting in Garberville."

"Where?" she said, freezing in place.

Jessica put a hand on her shoulder. "What's happening?"

She shook her head at Jessica.

"The Red Wood Motel," said Steele. "It's all over the news. It's really bad."

"Did this just happen?"

"No. It happened around three in the morning your time. Six over here," said Steele. "I didn't catch it until a few minutes ago. I've been in hearings all day."

"How the hell did I miss this?" said Harlow.

She'd watched snippets of the news this morning during breakfast and had been on the internet all morning in her office.

"Sounds like the sheriff sat on this for as long as he could," said Steele. "The story didn't fully break until about noon your time."

"How bad is it?" said Harlow.

"The numbers have fluctuated dramatically. I've heard up to ten dead. There's surprisingly little information flowing for some reason," said Steele. "I'll call Special Agent Reeves. He'll get to the bottom of what happened."

"What's going on?" insisted Jessica.

"Shooting at the Red Wood," she said abruptly.

"Shit," muttered Jessica, along with a few other choice words.

"Harlow, with that many casualties, Decker and Pam have to be fine," said Steele.

She wasn't sure she'd heard the senator correctly. "I'm sorry. I don't think I—"

"Think about it," said Steele. "If someone came after them at the motel, and there's a report of ten casualties—do you think Decker or Pam are among them?"

After a few long seconds, she answered. "They probably caused them."

"That's what I'm assuming, until I'm told otherwise," said Steele.

"They should be answering their phones," said Harlow. "Or at least reaching out to let me know they're okay."

"If they killed that many people," said Steele, "they probably got arrested, or at least detained for questioning. The sheriff up there isn't going to pat them on the back and send them off to get breakfast. I'll get Reeves working on this right away."

The senator was right. Hopefully. Harlow took a long breath and exhaled, clearing some of the fog. She needed to get past the shock of the news and start planning a response.

"I'm going to reach out to Brad Pierce and ask him to put together a team to support the firm's efforts up in Alderpoint."

"Harlow, just focus on Decker and Pam for now. The rest can wait," said Steele. "Let's be honest. If the criminal syndicate up there is willing to come after them in public, Brett Hale is dead. There's nothing more you can do right now, except help your friends."

"Let me know what Reeves finds out," said Harlow. "We'll start there."

"You don't have to do this," said Steele.

"It's what we do," said Harlow.

"I hope Decker and Pam are all right," said Steele. "Please keep me posted, and as always—the rainy day fund is open."

"Thank you, Senator," said Harlow. "I think we're going to need it."

"Good luck," said Steele, ending the call.

Jessica took her hand. "You okay?"

"Not really," said Harlow. "But I have to be right now. We have a ton of work to do."

"So. The entire firm?" said Jessica.

"Everyone, including Josh and his team," said Harlow. "We'll have to drive up."

"You know how I feel about long car trips."

"I do," said Harlow. "Which is why you're flying out as soon as possible. If the sheriff has Pam and Decker in custody, I need you to lean on the DA to get them released."

"I just need about thirty minutes at my apartment to pack a bag," said Jessica. "And a quick stop at the firm to grab one of the 'get out of jail free' binders."

Jessica constantly updated and maintained several accordion binders with copies of every relevant license they might need to provide law enforcement.

"I'll join you later tonight—or I might drive up with the rest of the crew so we can brainstorm a comprehensive plan," said Harlow. "I already have some ideas."

"Well, we have a good thirty minutes to start working through them," said Jessica. "The car's right around the corner."

Harlow didn't have any ideas right now. All she could think about were Decker and Pam—and how she should never have let them stay at that motel after what they ran into on the mountain. Garberville wasn't ground zero, but it was a known drug-trafficking hub for product coming off the mountain. She should have insisted that they stay in Eureka and deal with the drive.

Then again, she would have been wasting her breath. Neither Decker nor Pam would have agreed. Especially Decker. He'd developed a bit of an invincibility complex lately, or maybe he'd always had one. It was hard to tell sometimes, but events of the past two years hadn't helped. He'd survived several brushes with death that could be just as easily attributed to luck as skill. She just hoped his lucky streak remained intact after last night.

CHAPTER TWENTY-NINE

Brad Pierce struggled up the stairs with an oversize cardboard box teeming with his wife's books. Anna had forgotten to mention the floor-to-ceiling bookshelves she'd ordered for the bedroom, or he would have refused to sign the closing documents. Or at least negotiated a different location for the shelves. Who was he kidding? After forcing Anna and the kids to live in exile for the past few years, they could have insisted on a bowling alley in the basement and he would have gladly acquiesced.

"Brad?"

His wife was calling from somewhere downstairs. The house was so much bigger than the last one, he found himself yelling half the time.

"Heading up the stairs with one of your cinder blocks," said Brad.

"Harlow called your cell phone," said Anna. "I heard it from the other room but didn't get to it in time."

"Did she leave a message?" he yelled.

"She might still be leaving it," she said. "Wait. She just texted. URGENT DECKER IN TROUBLE. Sounds important."

Decker in trouble. What else was new?

"Be right down."

Pierce slid the hefty box along the hardwood floor at the top of the stairs and headed back down, finding Anna in the kitchen with his phone. He hadn't heard it ring at all.

"I'm going to buy us all walkie-talkies so we don't have to yell," he said, taking the phone off the kitchen island.

"Or a hearing aid," she said. "For yourself."

Brad laughed. Anna may have been joking, but she was probably right. Years of firing everything from rifles to rocket launchers without hearing protection had done a number on his ears. He just didn't want to surrender to a hearing aid in his forties. It was bad enough that his hair was graying—and thinning. He'd put off the "old man Brad" look as long as he could.

"What do you think he's gotten himself into now?" said Pierce. "He was supposed to lay low after the last incident."

"Maybe they need you to testify on his behalf as a character witness," she said, half jokingly.

"I highly doubt that," said Pierce, before changing his voice. "Mr. Pierce, have you ever worked with Mr. Decker on a job that didn't end with a high casualty count? Not that I recall, Your Honor."

"Just give her a call," said Anna.

Pierce looked around at the boxes stacked in the kitchen and sighed.

"The boxes will be here when you get back," said Anna.

"They will?" he said, raising an eyebrow.

His wife wasn't the type to leave things unsettled.

"Only the ones jam-packed with books."

Harlow answered before he heard the first ringtone. "Hey. What's going on?"

"Have you seen the news?" said Harlow.

"No. We've been moving boxes and unpacking all day," he said. "What happened?"

"There was a huge shoot-out at a motel in Northern California last night. Possibly ten people dead," said Harlow, pausing for a long moment. "Decker and Pam checked into that motel yesterday afternoon. They were investigating a disappearance in the area. I haven't heard from them all day, and I can't get through to them on any of their phones."

"First, I'm sure Decker and Pam are fine. Second, it sounds like they did a number on whoever was sent after them," said Pierce.

"Am I the only one that thinks they could be among the dead?" she said. "You're the second person to tell me this today."

"Ten dead? I guarantee you Decker is not among them."

"What about Pam?" she said, immediately catching his unintentional, but realistic, omission.

"Decker would never let anything happen to her," he said, meeting his wife's doubtful gaze.

"I know, but he's not Superman," said Harlow.

"Just don't tell him that," said Brad. "What can I do to help, Harlow?"

"In full disclosure, there's a little more to all of this than just Decker looking into a disappearance," said Harlow, before briefly explaining the case and what they had discovered so far.

"Steele's favors do have a tendency to take on a life of their own," said Brad.

"They do," said Harlow. "Can you put together a four- to six-operator team to support the firm? I'm bringing everyone up, including the geek squad."

"You plan on going after whoever is behind the attack?" said Brad.

"Yes. And shutting them down for good," said Harlow.

"Any way I can talk you out of this? Maybe settle for backing down and letting the sheriff's department handle it?" said Brad. "There's a shit ton of money at stake in the Emerald Triangle. Billions in profits. I'm not sure what a small team of mercenaries and a private investigative firm can accomplish up there."

"We've fried some pretty big fish together," said Harlow. "I'm sure we'll figure something out."

Pierce looked at his wife, who nodded.

"Anna just gave me the thumbs-up," said Brad.

"Tell her thank you and that our housewarming gift will be along shortly," said Harlow.

"Not the hot tub," said Brad.

"Tell her Decker's idea of a saltwater hot tub is starting to grow on me," said Anna.

"We don't want a hot tub," said Brad.

"Tell her you're getting the hot tub," said Harlow. "It's settled."

"We'll see about that. I'll be on the first available flight to Eureka," said Brad. "I can't say the same for the others I have in mind. It might take a few days to get everyone in place up there, and we're going to need equipment. The usual array of rifles and ammunition. Body armor. Night vision. The kind of stuff most of us would prefer not to check into luggage."

"We're loading the armory into one of the vehicles. You'll have plenty to choose from," said Harlow. "And I need you to contact Harry Bernstein. Decker was in the process of hiring him to conduct a detailed surveillance run over the Murder Mountain area. I have no idea if he ever managed to reach Harry and make an arrangement."

"You still want the surveillance run," said Pierce.

"That—and I want Harry on standby for a few days afterward," said Harlow. "For follow-up jobs based on what we discover."

"That's going to be expensive," said Brad. "Same with the merc team."

"Steele is on board."

"Say no more," said Brad.

"When you get up to Eureka, I need you to find us a base of operations. I'm thinking a small motel within or just outside the Eureka town limits. Take all the rooms."

"What if I can't find a vacant motel?"

"Then offer to put up the occupants in a better place. You have the firm's credit card. Do whatever you need to firmly entrench us in town. I get the feeling the sheriff will not be happy when he finds out we're coming with this many people—to do his job."

"I'm sure he won't," said Brad. "Keep me posted. I'll let you know my flight arrangements when I book the tickets. And, Harlow?"

"I know. They'll be fine," she said.

"I was going to tell you to drive safe, but that, too," said Brad. "See you later tonight or tomorrow."

"Thank you, Brad," said Harlow. "I can't tell you how much this means to me."

"He'd do the same," said Brad.

"I know," said Harlow, ending the call.

Brad stretched his hands out on the granite and shook his head.

"Go hang out with the kids for a little bit," she said. "I'll book the flight."

He kissed her on the forehead. "I really don't want to leave you and the kids here with this mess—or leave any of you at all anymore."

"I know, honey," she said, nuzzling into his chest. "But Decker would do anything to help you. Us. Get him out of this jam. Help Harlow and the senator with whatever is going on up there—and submit your resignation papers when it's over. Everyone will understand. We have a great plan for the security consulting business, and the capital to get it off the ground. It's corporate. It's safe. We can enjoy the kids and this absolutely dreadful suburban, country club life."

"I thought you missed this."

"I did," she said. "I do. But the house in the middle of nowhere grew on me."

"I miss it, too," said Brad. "But the three Starbucks within five minutes of here is kind of nice."

"No argument there," said Anna, pecking his lips. "You better get moving."

"Yep," he said.

"Business class?" she said.

He shrugged. "Hell yeah. We're not paying."

Chapter Thirty

Harlow shifted in her seat, unable to settle in. Five hours had passed since she'd hung up the phone with Senator Steele, and still no word about Decker or Pam. Jessica's flight out of LAX would be on the ground in about fifteen minutes, and she wanted to point her in the right direction—any direction. By the time Jessica grabbed her rental car and got moving, the clock would be pushing 8:00 p.m. on a Friday night. Not exactly "get shit done" time, unless you knew exactly where to go and who to contact.

"How are we doing?" said Sophie. "Bathroom break? Maybe grab some food."

"Probably not a bad idea," said Harlow.

The crew had to be hungry at this point. They'd left the firm around four—just about the worst time possible on a Friday. Or any day in Los Angeles. It had taken them nearly two and a half hours to get clear of the city, most of it spent fighting bumper-to-bumper traffic in San Fernando Valley. Just before departing, she'd suggested grabbing food from the market across the street from the firm, but nobody had shown any interest. Everyone had been laser focused on packing up and getting on the road.

"I'll start looking for an exit," said Sophie.

"In-N-Out coming up in sixteen miles," said Garza, one of the mercenaries Brad had contracted. "Looks like a big-ass rest stop on I-5."

Garza had shown up out of nowhere just before they left the firm. Dressed in sandals, surf shorts, and a well-worn T-shirt, he quickly raided Decker's gear locker, reemerging a few minutes later carrying two large duffel bags. Garza wasn't much of a talker, but Harlow and Sophie had managed to determine that he'd been taking some time off at the beach when Brad called. Harlow suspected that "taking some time off" meant something other than vacation but didn't dig any deeper. She was just glad to have him along. Both Brad and Decker had worked with Garza on the Mexico raid a year ago and spoke highly of him.

"Works for me," said Sophie.

"I'll let the others know," said Harlow.

Before she could pass along the pit stop intentions to the rest of the convoy, her phone rang. The SUV's dashboard screen read SEN STEELE. She paused for a few moments, admittedly nervous about taking the call.

"Garza, I need you to remain entirely silent during this call. We'll be talking with a US senator and possibly a very senior FBI agent, neither of whom will want to go on record with someone they don't know."

"Just finish up before the In-N-Out exit, or you're gonna hear from me," said Garza.

"You really can't say—"

"I'm just kidding," said Garza. "Mostly."

"Don't worry, I'm not missing that exit," said Sophie. "Ready?"

"Yep."

Sophie transferred the call to the vehicle's audio system.

"Senator Steele, this is Harlow. You're on speakerphone with Sophie Woods," she said. "We're on the road north of LA, with about another nine and a half hours to go."

"I have Special Agent Reeves on the call with an update," said Steele.

"Great. Ms. Arnay should be on the ground in Eureka shortly," said Harlow.

"Ms. Mackenzie. Ms. Woods," said Reeves. "I'm just going to come out and say it. Ms. Stack is unconscious and in critical condition at the Mercy Medical Center in Redding. Multiple gunshot wounds."

"Shit," said Harlow.

If Pam was hit, Decker must be hit, too. She couldn't imagine any scenario in which he didn't do everything in his power to protect her.

"It's a level-two trauma center, so she's in good hands," said Reeves. "Ms. Stack was medevaced there from the hospital in Garberville."

"We need to get someone up there to be with her," said Sophie. "She shouldn't be alone."

"One of the special agents from the Redding resident agency is with her for now," said Reeves. "A Humboldt County deputy tried to stop her from entering Ms. Stack's room. She didn't feel comfortable leaving her alone."

"What the hell?" said Harlow. "That's Shasta County."

"That's why the agent is sticking around to keep an eye on her. Something felt odd about the out-of-county deputy arrangement," said Reeves. "The resident agent in charge is doing me a favor and sending a second agent until we can figure out what the Humboldt County sheriff's game is here. His department has been entirely uncooperative with me. Borderline hostile, actually."

"Ms. Arnay should be landing in Eureka shortly. Maybe we should send her to Redding," said Harlow, "in case this asshole sheriff tries to move her, for whatever stupid reason. She can get in touch with the Shasta County district attorney and get her declared off limits or something."

"The resident agent in charge is taking care of that," said Reeves. "The Humboldt County sheriff actually turned his agents away from the Garberville crime scene earlier today. As you can imagine, he was not happy to learn that a Humboldt County deputy was giving one of his agents shit.

"Since Ms. Stack isn't under arrest, I don't know what good it will do to send Ms. Arnay out there right now. By the time she drives through the mountains, which I don't recommend, it'll be close to midnight. One of our agents will be with Ms. Stack all night."

"Thank you. We really appreciate you doing this for her," said Harlow. "I just want Pam to see a familiar face if she wakes up in the middle of the night."

"I completely understand," said Reeves. "I just don't recommend Ms. Arnay make the drive by herself, given everything that's happened today. She'd be passing straight through the Emerald Triangle, and I guarantee the sheriff is keeping a close eye on who comes and goes from the airport."

"Fair enough. We'll get someone there tomorrow morning at the latest. So your agents don't have to spend their weekend on duty, sitting around a hospital," said Harlow.

"What about Decker?" said Sophie.

"I'm a little embarrassed to say that I can't locate him," said Reeves. "The Humboldt County sheriff has very effectively locked down any and all information about the shooting. I got lucky with Ms. Stack. I learned that one patient had been transferred from Garberville to the trauma center in Redding, where we happen to have a resident agency. I asked if they would head over to identify the victim. After she muscled her way past the deputy—bingo. Half of the mystery solved.

"The other half is proving very difficult thanks to the sheriff's information blackout, but I managed to confirm that all of the wounded, except for Ms. Stack, obviously, have been transferred to St. Joseph's Hospital in Eureka. That's good news because St. Joseph's is not where you'd send a critical gunshot victim, so if Decker is among those transferred, he's very likely doing just fine. That being said, I also confirmed that one woman and one man were killed in the shooting—aside from the dozen or more skinheads. Their identities are also being withheld, so there's still a chance Decker didn't survive the attack."

Harlow clenched her fist, releasing it slowly.

"I really can't thank you enough for this, Joe," said Harlow. "Seriously. You should be home with your family right now—not stuck at the office working on our problems."

"Don't worry about me. I'm sipping a cold beer at home," said Reeves. "If anything bubbles up from the Redding office, I'll give you a call. Drive safe."

"Thank you, Joe," said Senator Steele. "We'll let you get back to your beer—and your family. In whichever order you choose."

Reeves laughed. "My wife thanks you."

The moment Reeves disconnected from the call, Steele piped in.

"Pardon my language, but I don't like the sound of this fucking sheriff—at all."

"Ditto," said Sophie. "Gonna kick that shithead in the balls—figuratively speaking."

Steele and someone in the background on her side of the call started laughing.

"I like the way you think, Sophie," she said. "My chief of staff, who you probably heard laughing, just started typing up a letter authorizing you, and whoever you deem appropriate, to act as official representatives of my office—and my preliminary fact-finding mission into the extensive and inexplicably persistent illegal marijuana industry within Humboldt County. This will be signed by me and flown via overnight courier. Ms. Arnay will have this in her hands before you arrive."

"Is this like a legitimate—uhhhh—'do whatever the hell we want' situation?" said Harlow.

"Legally? No. This is entirely a bullshit letter. I'd have to introduce a Senate resolution to initiate a legitimate fact-finding mission, which would take weeks or months to approve, and essentially just authorizes funding to send senators somewhere on the taxpayer's dime."

"Ha! I'd totally fall for that shit," said Sophie.

"That's what we're counting on. There's a reason the sheriff is keeping this under wraps. My guess is he's trying to buy time to cover his ass for reelection or bury any questionable connections to—"

A voice on the other side of the line cut her off.

"Harlow, you haven't met Julie Ragan, my chief of staff. Former fighter pilot and kick-ass all around," said Steele. "She's concerned about Ms. Arnay being up there by herself. I think I agree with her. This sheriff doesn't sound right."

"No need to worry," said Harlow. "Brad Pierce lands in an hour. I'll tell Jessica to stay at the airport until he arrives."

"I feel better hearing that," said Steele. "And don't get me wrong. I know you can handle yourselves, plus some, but Reeves really spooked me with this sheriff crap. Something is not right up there—and hasn't been for a long time. What's the timeline for additional reinforcements?"

"Including Brad, we'll have two on-site when we arrive. Two more by noon. The rest should get here by tomorrow night," said Harlow.

"Is that enough?" said Steele.

"I hope so," said Harlow. "I mean, how corrupt can this sheriff be?"

"That remains to be seen," said Steele. "And he's not your biggest threat. He's most likely covering something up—"

"Yeah. His ass!" said Sophie.

"His ass for sure," said Steele. "But there has to be something else. Has to be. How in the hell can the illegal marijuana industry explode like this after legalization? That's what all of our reports confirm. Despite legalization, the illegal side has grown larger and more profitable than ever. We've all seen the Google Maps images. How hard could it be to crack down on the farms that aren't licensed? You can see them on the internet, for shit's sake."

"It's baffling," said Harlow. "But that's where we're at."

"Here's how I see it. Our number one priority is safeguarding Ms. Stack and Decker. I have zero doubt that he's still alive," said Steele.

"I appreciate your confidence in Decker's survivability," said Harlow.

"Priority number two is figuring out what happened to Brett Hale, without risking any more lives."

"Okay," said Harlow.

"That didn't sound very convincing," said Steele.

"With all due respect, Senator, I plan to get to the bottom of what's going on up there," said Harlow. "No disrespect intended toward your friend's son, but Decker and Pam stumbled on something bigger than a simple murder or disappearance. Something big is going on up there. Big enough to publicly shoot up a motel."

"I hate it when anyone suggests, or in this case proves, that I'm thinking small," said Steele. "When is your air support scheduled to arrive? Assuming he's on board."

"He's most definitely on board," said Harlow. "Apparently, you're one of the few customers he doesn't have to chase down to get paid. He's set to arrive tomorrow evening."

"Perfect," said Steele. "In addition to supporting your immediate efforts, I'd like to pay him to create a comprehensive imagery database of Murder Mountain and the surrounding area. Maybe this bogus fact-finding mission will become a reality—sooner than later."

"I'll pass that along to Brad," said Harlow.

"All right then," said Steele. "Drive safe. Stay in touch."

"Will do," said Harlow, and the call ended.

Sophie piped up immediately. "We should divert to Bakersfield and charter a flight to Redding. I'll fly up and sit with Pam. We have to send someone, and I'm the least useful member of the team when it comes to the kind of fieldwork you'll be engaged in on . . . Murder Mountain. Seriously. I work best in the immediate vicinity of sushi restaurants and Whole Foods."

"I can't guarantee Redding has any of that," said Harlow.

"It does," said Garza.

Harlow glanced over her shoulder at their mostly silent partner, who sat behind Sophie, thumbing through his phone.

"I see five sushi restaurants and a couple of organic grocery places within a few miles of the hospital."

"Then it's settled," said Harlow. "Any commercial flights out of Bakersfield?"

"Not at this time of the night," said Garza. "Looks like there are a few private charter options."

"Do you mind calling around to book one?" said Harlow. "Cost isn't an issue."

"On one condition," said Garza.

"Condition? What are you talking about? That was a rhetorical question. I can make the phone calls," said Harlow, more than a little miffed by the mercenary's talk of "conditions."

"In-N-Out Burger," he said. "We have to stop at In-N-Out Burger. The next one is too damn far away."

"That's it? That's your condition?" said Harlow.

"Yeah. What did you think? I was going to demand double my rate?" said Garza.

"Sorry. I don't know how the mercenary scene works," said Harlow. "I mean, you showed up in shorts and a T-shirt out of nowhere. It was kind of weird."

"I told you I was chilling out at the beach," said Garza. "I'm based out of El Paso, which pretty much sucks, and there's no In-N-Out Burger there—yet. They keep saying it's coming, but they've been saying that shit for years. I come to LA because the beaches rock and—"

"In-N-Out," said Sophie.

"Nailed it," said Garza.

"So. We either turn off at the next exit and get In-N-Out Burger or you refuse to make any calls and brood for the next nine hours," said Harlow, trying not to laugh.

"Pretty much," said Garza.

"I like this guy," said Sophie.

"Me too," said Harlow.

Whether he meant to or not, Garza had given her a brief respite from the seriousness of the situation that lay ahead.

PART THREE

PART THREE

CHAPTER

THIRTY-ONE

Jessica's rental car, a red four-door sedan, pulled into the hospital parking lot with Brad Pierce at the wheel. Harlow flashed the SUV's headlights until Pierce responded and turned in their direction. The two of them had been busy all night paving the way for the firm's arrival.

Jessica managed to track down the Humboldt County district attorney, which proved far easier than expected for a Friday night. She'd started by calling every criminal defense attorney who advertised on the internet for Humboldt County and offering a nonrefundable, ten-thousand-dollar "retainer" for anyone who could put her directly in touch with Laura Swanson or one of her assistant district attorneys.

By 10:00 p.m. she'd secured private numbers for both Swanson and her ADA, along with Swanson's twenty-four-hour "bat phone," as one of the defense attorneys called it—the number the county sheriff and various police chiefs used when they had an emergency. Laura Swanson hadn't been happy to receive a phony call on the "bat phone" line at ten on a Friday night, but agreed to meet Jessica for coffee in the morning to discuss Decker and Pam's situation, and to review Senator Steele's letter, which would be hand delivered by a courier later that night.

While Jessica wrangled a meeting with the DA, Brad secured a suitable base of operations for the firm and their "protective detail." He picked a mom-and-pop-looking twelve-room motel on the south side of town and made the manager-owner an offer she couldn't turn down. Full occupancy for two weeks at double the normal rate, paid in advance. The only catch was that they would have to move the current occupants to a different hotel. Nobody in the three rooms put up an argument when offered a room across the street at the Comfort Inn and a hundred dollars for their troubles.

The motel had seen better days, but its compact layout and single point of entry would be relatively easy to secure against outside threats—like the one that had torn through the Red Wood Motel yesterday morning. Ripley, the most recently arrived mercenary, had stayed behind with Garza and the firm's tech crew to put the final touches on the electronic perimeter that would watch over their new compound.

From what she could tell, their takeover of the motel had gone unnoticed by the sheriff. In fact, all their efforts up to this point had apparently flown under his radar, which made her feel a little uneasy, like a big hammer was about to come down on them. If the sheriff arrived in force and decided to detain everyone for forty-eight hours or longer, not much stood between the sheriff and an extended jail cell visit.

"You ready?" said Katie, opening the front passenger seat door.

"Ready as ever," said Harlow. "I hope this works."

"It'll work," said Sandy from the back seat. "Or we'll all spend some time together in the county jail."

"I really hope that's not where this is headed," said Harlow, getting out of the SUV.

Brad pulled up in front of them, his window down. He gestured toward Jessica with a hand and shook his head.

"I bring you—the miracle worker," he said. "I don't know how the hell she pulled this off."

"The DA is on our side?" said Harlow.

"The sheriff is extremely popular in the county, and the DA has to work with him long after we disappear. She's not going to ruffle his feathers too severely."

"But we're on solid ground?" said Harlow.

"Let's walk and talk," said Jessica. "The clock is ticking. Ms. Swanson went directly to the sheriff's office after our little meeting."

"Oh boy," said Harlow, before patting the roof of the car. "Park and run."

Brad guided the sedan into a spot several spaces down, and they walked together toward the hospital's main entrance.

"How's Pam doing?" said Jessica.

"Still unconscious. Stable, from what the doctors are saying," said Harlow. "Sophie's with her."

"Good," said Jessica. "If we can get the sheriff off our backs and on board, I'll head out and join Sophie."

"You think that'll happen?"

"Senator Steele spoke with the DA for a few minutes, which made a huge difference," said Jessica. "She said she would be happy to speak directly with the sheriff, if necessary."

The sound of screeching tires at the far end of the parking lot put a quick end to their minireunion. A Humboldt County Sheriff's Department SUV roared through the lot, stopping in the middle of the street directly in front of the main entrance.

"Looks like the DA's meeting backfired," said Harlow.

A black Jeep Wrangler turned into the parking lot, headed at a reasonable speed toward the sheriff's department SUV.

"Maybe not," said Jessica. "That's Laura Swanson's Jeep. She didn't strike me as the pushover type."

"We'll see," said Harlow, leading them out of the parking lot and toward the pedestrian walkway blocked by the sheriff's vehicle.

Sheriff Long crossed in front of his SUV and positioned himself in the pedestrian crosswalk, presumably to block them from walking up to the hospital. He held a sheet of paper in one of his hands. The DA's Jeep screeched to a halt a few feet behind the sheriff's vehicle.

"Where's the rest of the department?" said Harlow, stepping into the crosswalk.

"Ms. Arnay, I presume?"

"Ms. Mackenzie," said Harlow, putting her hands on her hips.

Jessica stood next to her. "I'm Ms. Arnay."

"Sheriff Harvey Long," he said, extending his empty hand.

Harlow just stared at his gesture and shook her head. Jessica accepted, clearly not wanting to antagonize him. The DA, a taller-than-average, dark-haired woman, hustled over to the sheriff with one of the firm's "get of out jail free" packets. The sheriff glanced from Harlow to the DA to the piece of paper in his hand. Even from several feet away, Harlow could identify the US Senate letterhead.

"I need this like a hole in the head right now," said the sheriff.

"What? A Senate investigation into your inability to make a dent in the illegal drug trade in your county?" said Harlow.

Jessica nudged her lightly, and the DA did her best to conceal a wince. Surprisingly, Sheriff Harvey Long didn't take the bait. If anything, he looked disappointed.

"Can we all grab a cup of coffee in the hospital cafeteria? My treat," said the sheriff. "I think there's been a big misunderstanding."

"You detained two members of our firm and hid them from us!" said Harlow. "The only misunderstanding that took place here is your misunderstanding of their basic rights. I still don't know where you've stashed Decker, or if he's even alive."

"I can hold a suspect for forty-eight—" started Long.

"Harvey," said the DA. "Don't."

"Mr. Decker is alive and well at our hospital," said Long. "A bullet creased his thigh. He's all patched up."

"Let's go," said Harlow to the small mob behind her, before leading them across the street.

The sheriff stepped out of her way. "I'm serious about that coffee. I've never seen anything like what happened at that motel. I need to know what I'm up against, and I get the feeling you might be able to shed some light on that."

Harlow slowed to let the rest of the group pass. Jessica lingered nearby, sharing a vaguely exasperated look with the district attorney.

"What are you implying?" said Harlow, a little miffed by the last part of his statement.

Long shook his head. "Ms. Mackenzie. Ms. Arnay. We've definitely gotten off on the wrong foot, and that's completely my fault. The shoot-out at the motel has everyone on edge, as you can imagine. I was just suggesting your firm's investigation into Brett Hale might have uncovered information that could help prevent future attacks and get to the bottom of what happened yesterday. The coffee here sucks, but the doughnuts pass muster. What do you say?"

Harlow paid more attention to the delivery than the substance of his offer. As much as she wanted him to come across as an asshole, he actually looked genuine and sounded apologetic.

"I'd like to get Decker out of here and debrief him—before you and I start to share information," said Harlow. "And I mean it when I say *share*. This won't be a one-way street."

"I completely understand," said the sheriff. "How about we meet at my office in a few hours. However long you need."

"How about a more neutral location," said Jessica.

"We can accommodate you at the Travel-Lot Inn—that's a few miles south on Highway 101," said Harlow.

"I know where it is," muttered Long. "That's kind of an odd spot. Not exactly my first, second, or fiftieth choice of places to stay in Eureka."

"Our security team picked it for several reasons," said Harlow. "We have the entire motel for two weeks."

"Two weeks?" said Long, looking deflated. "I was really hoping to hear two days."

"It could be two days," said Harlow. "If that's how long it takes to bring the animals that shot up the motel and my colleagues to justice."

"We really need to talk," said Long. "The Alderpoint area is way more complicated than you think—or any of us knows. It's like another planet, with its own gravity and rules."

"We've taken on bigger challenges," said Harlow.

"I don't know. This one has stymied everyone for decades," said Long. "But there's definitely something different going on up there now. Maybe that'll be our way in."

"Our way?" said Harlow.

"I don't care if you have a letter from the president of the United States. You're not driving around Alderpoint without my deputies," said Long.

"We can hold our own," said Harlow. "And reinforcements are on the way."

"Not to sound like an asshole, but—"

"Because he's never been accused of that," said the DA.

Long rolled his eyes. "I'm more concerned with you upsetting whatever balance remains up there—and exacerbating this new problem."

"You mean you don't want us kicking the hornet's nest?" said Harlow.

"Pretty much," said Long. "If there's a way we can work together, I'd appreciate the chance to try."

"We'll be in touch," said Harlow.

"And I'll be watching," said Long. "Please don't head up to Alderpoint without talking to me first. This isn't a permission thing, or anything like that. Ms. Swanson has assured me that all of your licenses are in order, including the dangerous weapons permit. I can't stop you, and I won't try, but I will send deputies with you or follow you myself if I don't know what you're up to. As sheriff, I don't have a choice."

Harlow glanced at Jessica, who shrugged.

"Fair enough," said Harlow.

"Thank you," said the sheriff, before getting in his vehicle and driving away.

"I don't trust him," said Harlow. "Sorry, Laura, but that seemed too easy."

"What you see is usually what you get with Sheriff Long, and that's about as conciliatory as I've ever seen him. He's done a solid job for the county, but his back is up against the wall after the motel shooting. I know he'll be open to suggestions and lending whatever help he can. That said, I don't blame you for being cautious. Or suspicious."

"We'll take that into consideration," said Jessica. "Thank you again for meeting with me—and running some interference here."

"You made a compelling case," said Swanson. "Glad I could help."

"Thank you," said Harlow. "We'll genuinely try not to create more of a mess up there."

"It'll be hard to beat what happened at that motel," said Swanson.

Harlow and Jessica shared a quick look, each of them trying to keep a neutral face.

"I'll pretend I didn't see that," said Swanson, before getting back in her Jeep.

CHAPTER THIRTY-TWO

Decker sat upright in his hospital bed, inspecting the breakfast on the tray in front of him. A shrunken-looking sausage-and-cheese biscuit sat alone in the middle of a white Styrofoam plate. A small bowl of canned fruit cocktail, half drowned in a sickly sweet liquid. Orange juice cup with the foil top. Plastic utensils—because he'd been caught during his first meal trying to use the tines of a metal fork to unlock his handcuffs. That incident had also earned him a cuffed ankle.

He picked up the biscuit, took a less-than-enthusiastic bite, and tossed it back on the tray. Lukewarm and tasteless like everything else. Decker punched two holes in the top of the orange juice container with the plastic knife. The four ounces of bitter liquid went down before he could officially register his disgust. Another bite of the biscuit rounded out breakfast. He had no intention of touching the fruit cocktail. He hadn't eaten or even seen the stuff since he was a kid.

A radio squawked in the hallway, followed by brief conversation. Deputy Shea popped into the room a moment later, brandishing a set of keys.

"Looks like someone's finally here to claim you," said Shea, before unlocking his ankle cuff.

"Removing the evidence of my incarceration?" said Decker.

"The sheriff told me to tell you *hell hath no fury*," said the deputy. "And no hard feelings."

"He didn't taste this breakfast biscuit," said Decker.

The deputy finally cracked the faintest trace of a smile. "I told you to go with the breakfast burrito. I thought we had established some trust."

"Good point. You never steered me wrong about the food," said Decker. "Just locked me to a hospital bed."

"For your safety," said the deputy. "And my job security."

"No hard feelings," said Decker. "But you better get going. The woman scorned is on her way, and she's not so forgiving."

"In that case, I'm out of here," said Shea, before disappearing into the hallway.

Decker moved the metal tray stand out of the way and swung his feet over the left side of the bed, slowly testing his legs on the floor. His thigh ached around the site of the gunshot but took the weight just fine. He walked back and forth to the door a few times, the pain resulting in a slight limp, which was to be expected. His worst problem right now was a touch of vertigo from lying on the bed for so long.

"Looks like someone hasn't been trying too hard to escape," said a familiar voice. "I expected you to be under guard and cuffed to the bed."

He turned to find Brad Pierce standing in the doorway holding a small backpack.

"Funny," said Decker. "Where's Harlow?"

"Great to see you, too," said Pierce. "She's waiting by the nurses' station with the rest of the entourage. I figured you might need some clothes."

"Good call," said Decker. "The only thing standing between you and my birthday suit is this paper-thin gown."

"No thanks." He tossed Decker the backpack. "Just some basic street clothes and sandals. We'll get you geared up back at the compound."

"Compound?" said Decker, heading straight for the bathroom.

"You'll see," said Pierce.

Decker emerged a minute later dressed in surf shorts, a T-shirt, and rubber sandals.

He gave Pierce a quick hug. "Thanks for coming to my rescue."

"Don't thank me. Thank Harlow," said Pierce. "She called yesterday afternoon when they found out about the shooting. How's the leg?"

Decker shrugged. "It's fine. I'm ninety-eight percent combat effective. What's going on with Pam?"

"Still classified as critical, but the doctors say she's stabilizing," said Pierce. "Sophie's with her. Jessica may be heading out to join her if things have settled down enough around here."

"So. We're in the clear as far as the sheriff is concerned?"

"He basically begged us to meet with him before going back to Alderpoint," said Pierce. "After Harlow refused to be dissuaded."

"Dissuaded from what?" said Decker, a little concerned by what he was implying.

"She plans on heading up to the Dunn property—for starters," said Pierce. "Garza and Ripley are here. Two more will be here by tonight. Solid operators I've known for a while. One of Bernstein's slick surveillance jets will be on station around nightfall to conduct a thorough reconnaissance. The C-123 will be in the area some time tomorrow."

"Sounds like she's about to go to war," said Decker.

"She's a little pissed off," said Pierce.

"That's never a good reason," said Decker. "I know better than anyone."

"We're getting some answers," said Harlow, startling him.

She stood in the doorway, arms crossed and an eyebrow raised.

"Dammit. Don't you people knock?" he said, before rushing past Brad to take her in his arms.

They kissed passionately, but Harlow's body language felt stiff—like he was keeping her from something. He had a pretty good idea what that something might be.

"Pam's doing better?" he whispered in her ear.

"The same," she said. "Which is good."

"I did everything I could," said Decker. "At least I hope I did."

"None of this is your fault," she said. "Nobody is thinking that—at all. It's those assholes on the mountain."

Decker knew this probably wasn't the right time, but he had to try to slow her down a little. He'd felt the same way after waking up handcuffed to the hospital bed. The need for revenge had been black-and-white—with a splatter of red. The handcuffs had probably saved him from a real jail cell, or more likely, the inside of a body bag. Decker had spent the better part of the past twenty-four hours exploring all the reasons why rushing back up Murder Mountain right now was a really bad idea.

"I know. I just—you had to see what they did to that motel to believe it," said Decker. "They're not messing around."

Harlow tensed even more, giving him a sternly surprised look.

"We're getting to the bottom of this," she said.

"The bottom of what? Brett Hale's disappearance or whatever is worth machine-gunning an entire motel filled with civilians to protect?" said Decker.

"They're connected. They have to be, or whoever is calling the shots up there wouldn't risk that much exposure trying to get rid of you and Pam," said Harlow. "If we unravel the Brett Hale thread, the whole thing falls apart."

"Maybe," said Decker. "Or maybe we all get machine-gunned on the ride up."

"I was thinking about that," said Harlow.

"Thinking about getting machine-gunned?"

"I think about it all the time," said Pierce.

195

Harlow gave Pierce a disapproving look.

"She's been giving me that look all morning," said Pierce. "And I've been on my best behavior."

"I decided on a proactive approach to keeping you in line," said Harlow, smirking. "I don't need the two of you driving me batty."

"You picked the right one," said Decker. "I'm never a problem. And he's easily intimidated."

She shook her head, appearing peeved with both of them.

"Anyway—the sheriff made it pretty clear he and his deputies are going to follow us wherever we go, so I was thinking we may as well incorporate them into any obvious forays we make into the Alderpoint area. I can't imagine skinheads, or anyone for that matter, gunning down cops. That would bring the roof down on their heads."

"Normally I would agree, but I'm worried about the two ex-military types that appeared to be watching over these skinheads," said Decker. "And I never got a look at who was working the SAW. Could have been more mercenaries."

"Squad Automatic Weapon?" said Pierce.

"The sound was unmistakable."

"Wow," said Pierce.

"My guess is those mercenaries represent what we're really up against on the mountain," said Decker. "And the skinheads are just what they want us to see."

"Then a police escort might not be a bad idea," said Harlow. "For what it's worth."

"Let's spend some time getting to know the sheriff before we make any decisions," said Decker. "As much as I want to trust him, I don't think it's a good idea—without some conditions. There's no way his department hasn't been compromised on some level. The sergeant that arrested me lied about the circumstances of my arrest, and I swear he was thinking about killing me when the other deputies left."

"We'll invite the sheriff over for a chat," said Harlow. "He seemed reasonable enough."

"The guy had me handcuffed to this bed and kept me under armed guard, while purposefully withholding my location," said Decker. "I feel like I got rendered."

"It's not such a bad place for a rendition," said Pierce, glancing around. "We've seen worse."

"Try some of that biscuit," said Decker, pointing at the tray. "You might reconsider that assessment."

CHAPTER THIRTY-THREE

Decker's first order of business at the motel compound was to change into an outfit that didn't make him feel and look like a Venice Beach tourist. Because the firm's professional licenses and firearms permits had been authenticated and explained to the sheriff by the district attorney, Humboldt County's senior legal authority, Decker went with the same urban-mercenary look the rest of the crew sported.

Drab olive pants with numerous cargo pockets. High-end hiking boots. Dark-blue T-shirt under a basic coyote-brown plate carrier laden with rifle magazine pouches. Nonbranded khaki ball cap. The only thing missing was the drop holster for his pistol. The holster fit snugly against his thigh and would undoubtedly aggravate the hell out of his bullet wound. He'd figure out a way to carry the pistol later, or just tuck it into his belt. A knock at the door startled him.

"Jumpy a bit?" said Harlow, leaning against the doorframe.

"Yeah. Something about motel rooms these days," said Decker.

"How's your leg?" said Harlow.

"Hurts like a mother, but I'll be fine," said Decker. "You sure we wouldn't be better off at a hotel downtown? Fifth floor, maybe. I feel like we're re-creating the Alamo here."

Harlow entered and shut the door behind her. "Brad looked into it, but most of the rooms in the downtown hotels are occupied or have been booked by news crews from around the state—and country. The Garberville shooting has attracted a lot of attention."

"That actually might work in our favor," said Decker, surprised he hadn't thought of it before. "That and working with the sheriff—as long as his department doesn't become a hindrance or liability. Whoever is running the show up in Alderpoint can't afford another public spectacle."

"Are you saying I had a good idea?" said Harlow. "Because it kinda sounds like you might be saying—"

"I always give you credit for a good idea," said Decker, closing the distance between them.

"You do?" she said with a raised eyebrow.

"Yeah. I seem to remember that one time you were right," he said, embracing her.

"Really? When was that?" said Harlow, completely relaxed in his arms.

Decker kissed her. "The time you decided to save my life at the mall and give me a reason to live again."

"That sounds like one major time I was right, which branches out into many more times," said Harlow.

"After that, everything you do is right as far as I'm concerned," said Decker.

She gave him a skeptical look. "Now it sounds like you're messing with me. The sheriff is on his way."

"I hope you're right about this guy," said Decker. "I'd hate to see you break your streak."

Harlow gave him a quick kiss. "Then I'll let you make the final call."

"Touché," he said.

A quick rap at the door detangled them. Their relationship wasn't a secret, but clearly neither one of them thought displaying it in public was appropriate under the circumstances.

"Yeah?" said Decker.

"You guys decent?" said Pierce, before opening the door.

Harlow rolled her eyes.

"Just covering my bases," said Pierce. "Sheriff is here."

"Be right out," said Harlow. "And for the record, I'm reporting your behavior to Anna when this is over."

"What? He's the problem," said Pierce.

"Room three," said Harlow to Decker, before heading for the door.

"I'll wait for you," said Pierce.

Harlow playfully shoved Pierce out of the way as she passed. "Don't be late."

"We won't," said Pierce.

Decker waited until he saw Harlow through the window and could tell she was out of earshot.

"I didn't want to bring this up again in front of Harlow, but what are we really doing about security here?" said Decker. "I understand the hotels in town are booked."

"I figured we're close enough to town and far enough away from Alderpoint to discourage any kind of attack," said Brad.

"I'd normally agree, but there's a small sheriff's station less than a mile down the road from the Red Wood Motel in Garberville, and that didn't deter them."

"Point taken, and the team is aware of it," said Brad. "Our biggest vulnerability at this point, and probably moving forward, is a surprise attack from Highway 101. Four vehicles could easily cluster together as they approach the motel, turn at the last second, and plow through the entrance. We have layers of spike strips and a few other surprises we won't be mentioning to the sheriff, but it's still a significant vulnerability. I'll be sleeping with one eye open."

"I won't be sleeping at all," muttered Decker, catching himself staring at the wall.

"You good?"

"I keep replaying every second of the attack. Running scenario after scenario," said Decker. "I can't think of any way I could have done it differently."

"Dude. Nobody blames you for what happened to Pam. Not even close," said Pierce. "You saved her life. And if you can't think of a better scenario, then it didn't exist."

"I guess," said Decker. "Ready?"

Pierce stopped him in front of the door. "I'm not going to tell you to let it go, because I know how it works. It goes away on its own time, or in some cases, it never does. Just know that everyone has your back. Nobody blames you. In fact, Pam talked with Harlow that night, after the two of you had signed off for the evening, and made fun of you for suggesting that you share rooms for security reasons. She thought you were being paranoid. Mentioned how you were holed up in your room with motion sensors. Door braces. Pretyped texts. The whole team knows you did everything in your power to help her, and ultimately—you did. She would have bled out in that bathroom if you hadn't done what you did."

Decker nodded, his eyes moistening. "I know. This kind of thing just brings me back to a really dark place. I start reliving some ugly stuff that was years in the making, and no alternate scenario could have fixed."

"To be continued," said Pierce. "Harlow is giving me the stink eye."

Decker followed Pierce across the parking lot, trying not to favor his wounded leg—a task easier said than done. It hurt a little more than he'd let on but shouldn't get in the way. At least that was what he told himself. He'd still have to be careful with the stitches. If he popped any of those, bleeding would undoubtedly become a problem. It was something he'd keep an eye on.

Their journey to room three unintentionally coincided with the sheriff's arrival. Garza and Ripley rushed to move the spike strips out of the way, while Decker chuckled to himself at the thought of Sheriff

Long's reaction to the heavily armed, body armor–clad mercenaries in plain sight along the coastal highway.

Through the motel's archway entrance, Decker saw that two of the vehicles in the sheriff's convoy, a sedan and an SUV, had parked in a staggered roadblock pattern about thirty feet from the road. They were either placed there to keep unauthorized vehicles from approaching the motel or to keep Harlow's vehicles from departing. He'd know in a few seconds. Decker waved and smiled as the two SUVs sped through the archway and parked nearby.

"Quit antagonizing them," said Harlow from room three's doorway.

"Just being friendly," said Decker. "Looks like they parked a few vehicles in a barricade pattern near the highway."

"Good. I hope they leave them there," said Harlow. "Do you mind showing them inside? Since you're Mr. Friendly."

"My pleasure," said Decker.

"See you inside," said Pierce, heading for the makeshift command center.

Decker waited for the sheriff's entourage to dismount the SUVs and assemble in the adjacent parking space. Four in total. Sheriff Long. Two plainclothes deputies. And one serious SWAT-looking type dressed in full tactical kit. Actually, they all looked pretty damned serious, and confident—which made Decker feel better about their presence. He wasn't sure why, but if they had come out looking nervous or unsure of themselves, he would have bolted for his room. And his rifle.

"Sheriff Long, good to see you again," said Decker, offering a handshake.

"Likewise. Thank you for taking it easy on Deputy Shea. He reported that you were a complete gentleman and a gracious—"

"Captive," said Decker, shaking his hand. "He didn't mention my escape attempt?"

Long shrugged. "The fork? Didn't sound like much of a problem."

"No. He put it together pretty quickly," said Decker. "I had just bent one of the tines ninety degrees before he popped into the room. He had his shit together. Even did me right with his food recommendations."

One of the SWAT officers stifled a laugh. Long looked over his shoulder and nodded.

"Deputy Shea is one of our SET deputies," said Long, turning his attention to room three. "So. What are we looking at in there?"

"I honestly have no idea," said Decker. "But they're not going to back off. Especially now."

Long rubbed his chin, a deeply contemplative look taking over his face.

"What do you think is going on up there? No bullshit. Just gut feel," said Long.

Decker suddenly felt very vulnerable. He didn't start to understand why until he answered the sheriff's oddly candid question.

"It fits a pattern," said Decker.

"A pattern?" said Long.

"The two mercenaries that somehow happened to be mixed up with a bunch of skinheads."

Long glanced over his shoulder at one of the plainclothes deputies, who raised an eyebrow.

"Why don't we head inside and hash this out," said Long.

He trusted Harvey Long. Maybe Brad, Harlow, or a member of the firm would disagree after this meeting and present a compelling case against him—but for now, he felt like Long was an ally they could count on. Only time would tell.

"Mi casa es su casa," said Decker.

CHAPTER THIRTY-FOUR

Harlow felt a little self-conscious of the dingy, cramped location of the meeting, but the Travel-Lot Inn didn't offer a working ice machine, let alone a conference room. Room three, its furniture replaced with folding tables and chairs purchased at the local Target store less than an hour ago, would serve as their command center for as long as the firm remained in Eureka.

The adjoining room, connected by a decades-old unused door Brad had to "nudge" open with a handheld battering ram, had been similarly converted to house Joshua's electronic support team. Folding tables lined the walls, crowded with flat-screen monitors, keyboards, computer towers, and virtual reality headsets. The wall separating the bathroom from the rest of the unit had been covered with a projector screen that displayed several crystal-clear images provided by security cameras watching the motel compound's perimeter.

Duct-taped wires ran everywhere in both rooms, a few of them snaking out of the windows to pipe in as much digital bandwidth as their array of portable satellite dishes could capture. All the bandwidth fed through an encrypted server sitting in front of the electronics room's air-conditioning vents and out to the various routers—some wireless, most hardwired directly to the computer they served.

One portable, standing air conditioner had been purchased for each room to augment the marginally effective motel unit. The added cooling power was needed to keep the electronics equipment from overheating, and the people stuck inside the rooms all day from killing each other. After stepping inside room three, ahead of the sheriff's team, Harlow wondered if one extra unit per room would be enough. The air felt a little stuffy, as if it could go either way. The addition of a dozen bodies was certain to tip it toward uncomfortable.

Sheriff Long entered first, nodding at Harlow and the rest of her assembled team. Six in total, including Harlow. Katie and Sandy, sporting hip holsters, stood toward the back of the room, near the bathroom, their arms crossed. Jessica sat at one end of the ad hoc conference table they'd created by putting two folding tables side by side. Joshua and Mazzie sat closest to the door between rooms, where Josh could break away, if necessary, to troubleshoot any problems next door. Brad stood next to the portable air conditioner, watching through the window.

"No seat assignments, Sheriff," said Harlow. "Standing is fine, too."

"We'll take you up on the seats," said Long.

As the rest of his team filed into the room and took the seats offered, Sheriff Long poked his head through the connecting door for a few moments before sitting down.

"I'd offer you some space at the station, but it looks like you have . . . a system," said Long.

"We're fairly accustomed to this," said Harlow, nodding at Decker in the doorway.

Decker started to close the door, but Brad stepped behind Harlow to stop him.

"We should probably keep someone in the parking lot," said Brad.

"I can bring one of the deputies from the road over to keep an eye on things if you need to be in here," said the sheriff. "Not to get ahead of myself here, but I'd like to keep two vehicles with two deputies each out front twenty-four hours a day."

"I don't think that'll be necessary," started Decker.

"It's not to babysit you. I think their presence would deter any thought of an attack on your compound, and then maybe you could pull your heavily armed sentries back where they aren't so visible from the street. I've already been getting calls about them."

"I'll keep one of my people on duty at all times. Full tactical kit," said one of the deputies.

Sheriff Long shifted in his seat. "I apologize for jumping ahead of the introductions. The surly-looking gentleman that just offered up one of his deputies is Detective Hodges. Special Enforcement Team commander. That's our less scary term for SWAT.

"To his left is Sergeant Larson. She's our Drug Enforcement Unit lead. Larson has more knowledge than any of us about the Alderpoint area.

"Detective Reid is in charge of the Detective Bureau. He's been processing evidence collected from the motel."

Harlow gave the sheriff and his team a quick rundown of the firm's attendees, eager to get the pleasantries out of the way. In order to move things along, she made a unilateral decision to accept the sheriff's protective detail.

"We'll take you up on the offer to keep your deputies in front of the motel, and pull our people out of public view," said Harlow. "My only rule is that you have to keep your deputies outside the motor court. There's a bathroom in the motel office that's accessible to them from the outside. I think we're good for now, Brad. You can close the door."

"Thank you," said Long, before folding his hands and cracking his knuckles. "So. Where do we start?"

"We'd like to check out the Dunn property," said Harlow. "As you now know, Senator Margaret Steele hired us to locate Brett Hale, and I intend to follow through with that investigation."

She did her best not to glance at Decker, whose subtle look would undoubtedly remind her that she might be misrepresenting her intentions.

"Do you have any additional leads? I assume he worked at the Dunn property?" said Long.

"His parents bought him a satellite phone, which he used regularly to keep in touch," said Harlow. "The last GPS traces put him at the farm, about a week before his parents got in touch with Senator Steele. That's pretty much it."

She left out the part about Hale trying to make some kind of deal with someone bigger than the Dunns. Right now she needed them to think she was laser focused on her only apparent lead.

"Not a very stable family, these Dunns," said Sergeant Larson. "Two hothead brothers that made a lot of enemies up there."

"Has anyone seen or heard from the Dunns recently?" said Katie.

"It's not one of those 'hang out at the local hardware store' kind of communities. There's a little convenience store where people drift in and out to buy booze and cigarettes. That's about it," said Larson.

"I can confirm that," said Decker. "It felt like a ghost town while we drove around."

"And they don't like to stray too far from home this time of the year," said Larson. "Harvest time."

"Then the Dunns should be home," said Harlow. "Ready to shed some light on Brett Hale's whereabouts."

"They won't say a word," said Sergeant Reid. "We've been out to a hundred farms, a thousand trips, even right on the heels of a murder—and they don't say shit."

"I still have to see the property for myself."

"You can't traipse all over their property," said Long. "Even with that fancy letter from Senator Steele."

"That's why we'd like to take you up on your earlier offer to accompany us to Alderpoint," said Harlow.

The sheriff chuckled. "First, that wasn't exactly a negotiable offer. We go where you go. Second, we can't search the Dunn property without a warrant, and I don't care what kind of pull you think you have, Judge Gilliam isn't granting me one on the basis of what you've told me. It's not even worth trying. So. If the Dunns tell us to get off their property, we have to oblige them. You have to oblige them."

"And that's the default position they all take if you don't produce a warrant," said Larson. "They know their rights."

"We have to try," said Harlow, shrugging.

"We'll take you up there," said Long. "But this won't be a free-for-all. I'm willing to push some boundaries and get you a look at the entire farm, but I need you to follow my lead. When I say it's time to go, it's time to go—regardless of what you've discovered. Do we see eye to eye on that?"

Harlow nodded. "Yes."

"Good. I'm ready when you are. I'd rather get this over sooner rather than later," said Long.

"Sheriff Long," said Decker. "We have two more security contractors arriving midafternoon. Given the firepower used during the motel attack, I think we should wait for them to join us."

"I'm not so worried about that anymore," said the sheriff. "We found the truck and the machine gun."

"What?" said Decker. "When?"

"A few hours ago. I found out on the way over here. I didn't want to say anything earlier because details are still a bit sketchy," said Long.

"You could have led with that," said Decker.

"That information hasn't been made available to the public yet, and I had no idea if this meeting would be a success or failure," said Long. "I was kind of hedging my bets."

"Fair enough," said Harlow. "What are we looking at with the pickup truck?"

"Yesterday morning, around five thirty, Trinity County deputies responded to reports of automatic gunfire and helicopters out on Route 36 about ten miles shy of Red Bluff. They spent the better part of yesterday searching the area supported by SWAT—but didn't find anything. A group of Jeep off-roaders spotted the truck in a gulley. Three dead skinheads and an M249 machine gun. The truck was riddled with bullets."

"That's good news," said Harlow.

"How far off road were they found?" said Decker, looking skeptical.

"About four miles north of Route 36," said Long. "The Trinity County sheriff said they hadn't looked up there. It's not a heavily traveled area. Nothing but jeep trails."

"And they were ambushed on one of these obscure off-road trails?" said Decker.

"I don't have all of the details yet. Why?"

"It just seems like an odd place for an ambush," said Decker. "And why wouldn't the skinheads in the pickup just head back up to the mountain? Something doesn't add up. Again."

"The helicopter report is odd," said Brad. "Is it possible someone mistook the gunfire for a helicopter?"

"That's what I thought at first," said Detective Hodges, the SET commander. "I served two tours in Afghanistan and one in Iraq. Sometimes from a distance, for a brief second or so—you could mix the two up. But that's not what happened here. The family that called it in was pretty adamant about hearing both."

"Then this isn't good news at all," said Decker.

"Why?" said Harlow, instantly regretting her question.

She knew why before Decker answered.

"Because whoever's running the show up on Murder Mountain has access to a helicopter capable of shooting trucks off the road in the dark," said Decker.

"They could have been using the helicopter to track the pickup and guide other vehicles in for an ambush," said the sheriff.

"No. The gunfire went on for fifteen minutes. Sporadically," said Detective Hodges.

"Sporadically? You never said sporadically," said Decker. "This is sounding more and more like a helicopter making gun passes."

"I wouldn't go that far," said the sheriff.

"Think about it. The helicopter makes a pass on Route 36 and somehow fails to stop the truck, which then turns into the woods and stumbles onto a trail. With the heavy tree canopy, the helicopter gunner would have a hard time putting rounds on target. They probably made multiple passes until they caught the pickup in the open again or somehow managed to take out the driver—in the fucking dark."

"The gun would have to be mounted," said Brad. "Or at least stabilized with some kind of cross-door strap. Either way, we're not talking about a typical helicopter or crew. Low-level night flying is a military or police skill."

"Wait," said Harlow. "Why would the powers that be on the mountain send a helicopter to gun down the people they sent to kill you and Pam?"

"Good question. An even better one is why did one of the trucks flee the area instead of scooting back to their mountain haven?" said Decker. "Or—how the hell did the helicopter find the truck in the first place? Or who the hell were the two military professional types in the parking lot. Or how did a bunch of skinheads get their hands on an M249 Squad Automatic Weapon?"

"Sounds like you're winding up to something," said Long. "Maybe this is a good time to explain what you meant in the parking lot. What kind of pattern does this fit?"

"I think the skinheads are the least of our problems on the mountain. Actually, I wouldn't be surprised if the skinheads were entirely out of the picture at this point. As in dead and buried. They went through a lot of trouble to take out that pickup truck," said Decker. "Did you ever identify either of those commando types in the parking lot?"

"Nothing yet. We submitted an IAFIS search request to the FBI's Sacramento field office," said Long.

Harlow shook her head. "My guess is you're not very high up on their favors list right now."

"Probably not," said Long.

"We have a contact that can expedite the automated fingerprint analysis," said Harlow.

"That'd be a big help," said Long. "Also, remember that Suburban you saw in the parking lot?"

"Yeah. I almost forgot about that," said Decker. "Totally out of place."

"That's an understatement," said Long. "Armored with bullet-resistant glass and registered to a shell company, from what we can tell."

"I'd like to take a look at the registration. VIN. Any identifying information," said Joshua. "If that's all right."

"We ran it through all of the databases. I'm not sure what you'll be able to find that we couldn't," said Detective Reid.

The room remained quiet for a few awkward seconds, until the sheriff seemed to get what Joshua was suggesting. An illegal hack far deeper than his department could look.

"I suppose it couldn't hurt," said Long. "As long as you share what you find."

"Scouts honor," said Joshua, before looking to Harlow. "Unless she says otherwise."

"We'll share," said Harlow.

The sheriff turned to Decker. "So where does this pattern leave us? What's up there?"

"A paramilitary-style operation at its core, obviously centered around illegal marijuana. The skinheads were the public face of it all, used for local intimidation. They fucked up at the motel and probably got terminated by their employers. My guess is we're looking at a huge farm up there guarded by heavily armed mercenaries. And they have a mean-ass helicopter."

Long didn't look convinced.

"I agree that's something entirely unusual, but I ordered a surveillance flight yesterday and compared the pictures to a month ago. Three months ago. Even a year back. The mountain looks pretty much the same in all four sets of pictures. Little more than a patchwork of mostly smaller farms connected by dirt roads or jeep trails. Nothing grabbed my attention."

"Someone really didn't want us going back up the mountain for another look," said Decker. "Or even taking a look in the first place. They hacked the drone I sent up after we were turned back by a gang of thugs on ATVs. Hacked. Not shot down. And we're talking a thirty-thousand-dollar military-grade drone."

"Don't remind me," said Harlow.

"Well, I got a good look at the mountain yesterday afternoon. High-resolution pictures and video," said the sheriff. "We all did."

"And I've been looking at these aerial shots for years now," said Sergeant Larson. "Nothing stood out. We definitely have more farms than last year, but that's always been the case. Whatever's going on up there has either been very well concealed or it's a forced consolidation of farms by this paramilitary organization. That's always a possibility. Taking over a few dozen of those farms, or even shaking them down for a percentage, represents big money. Millions of dollars."

"I still think they're hiding something big up there," said Decker.

"One step at a time," said the sheriff. "Let's get you up to Brett Hale's last recorded location. Hodges?"

"I'll put together a heavy raid team. Nine officers. Three well-marked sheriff's department vehicles," said Detective Hodges. "We'll be ready to roll in an hour."

Harlow motioned for Decker to chime in regarding their tactical deployment, figuring he already had a plan in mind. Instead of jumping right in, he passed the torch to Pierce. Something was off with him. She'd sensed it earlier but couldn't put her finger on it. It almost felt like he wanted to shut the operation down and go home. Not because he was afraid. It was something else. And that something worried her. She needed him as sharp as ever right now. All their lives depended on it.

"Brad?" said Decker.

Pierce flashed her an almost imperceptible look, but she saw it. He was worried, too.

"We'll deploy in three vehicles. Two SUVs and our electronic support van. I don't know if you saw the van on the way in, but it's a custom-built 4X4, so it can handle the roads up there. I hope," said Brad.

"It can handle it," said Katie. "I'm their chauffeur."

"Three techs go with the van," said Brad. "Your pick."

"Ooh. Me. Me," said Mazzie.

Joshua just shook his head.

"What exactly will their role be?" said Long. "No offense, but it looks like you have your hands full in that room full of monitors and computers."

Before Joshua could respond with an answer that would probably add another ten minutes to the meeting, Decker jumped in.

"Trust me, Sheriff. The electronic support team is worth its weight in gold. I have no idea how they do what they do, but it's pure magic."

"They're not doing anything illegal, right?" said Long.

"Nope," said Decker.

"Never," added Joshua.

"Supporting the geek squad, we have five shooters, which will be split between the SUVs," said Brad. "Sorry, Sheriff, but we're rolling out heavy. Full kits. Rifles. Helmets. Everything."

"The more the merrier, in this case," said Long.

"We'll intersperse your vehicles with ours," said Harlow. "If that's acceptable."

Long turned to Detective Hodges, who nodded.

"That's acceptable. Step off in ninety minutes?" said Long.

"Works for us," said Harlow.

"We'll meet you in the Humboldt Bay National Wildlife Refuge parking lot, about seven miles south of here along 101," said Long. "I plan on staggering our departures from the station. I suggest you do the same. The last thing I need the people of Eureka seeing is a convoy of Humboldt County Sheriff's Department vehicles rolling out of town. We'd attract every damn TV station van in the county."

"Agreed," said Harlow. "We'll be discreet."

"We'll go over the convoy plan and approach to the Dunn property at the parking lot," said Long, standing up. "Sorry to run, but we have a lot of work to get done in ninety minutes."

When the sheriff and his deputies were back in their vehicles, Harlow stepped back into the room and shut the door behind her.

"What's everyone's take?" she said.

"I'm worried that if we don't find anything up there, and it sounds like the Dunns will make sure of that, the sheriff is going to turn to us and say, *There's nothing else you can do without breaking the law. Your investigation is over for now*," said Katie.

"Yeah. He's definitely painted himself into a corner with this trip," said Sandy.

"We really don't have any other options," said Harlow. "This is a relatively easy and safe way to get a look at the property—and maybe get lucky."

"Doubtful," said Brad.

"I know, but we have Bernie's surveillance bird on station this evening. He's going to give us daytime and nighttime imagery. We can draw our own conclusions about what's really going on up there."

"And if we don't find anything?" said Katie. "It's not like we can form a human chain and walk the mountain for evidence."

"That's why I want Joshua's crew out there with us," said Decker. "They can see things we can't. We'll get an electronic signals map on the way up and down—then compare that to digital imagery Bernie sends us. I guarantee we'll find something worth a closer look. On foot. With a small army."

She glanced at Pierce, who gave her a quick wink. The Decker she'd always known was back. The trick would be keeping him here for the rest of the mission.

Chapter Thirty-Five

Carl Trenkor dropped onto one of the folding chairs behind the two surveillance technicians, his eyes never leaving the screens above their heads. A six-vehicle convoy had turned off Alderpoint Road onto Dockweiler Road, a well-concealed private dirt road that fed directly into the heart of the mountain. In theory, if they knew the precise route, these vehicles could be at the compound's main gate in fifteen minutes. Mike Loftis took the seat next to him before signaling for Watts to shut the trailer door.

"What are we looking at?" said Trenkor.

The technician directly in front of him answered.

"Five SUVs. Three of them are clearly marked as Humboldt County Sheriff's Department. Occupants look like SWAT. Maybe three to four per vehicle. The other two SUVs have civilian plates. Three occupants per vehicle. Similarly geared up. I have no idea what the van is. I'm seeing some unusual antennas, so I'm going to guess it's a command vehicle. Mobile command post?"

"Fuck. Should we arm the second zone? They're halfway through the first," said Loftis.

"And blow up three sheriff's department vehicles—that close to Alderpoint Road? No. If they're headed for the compound, we can take care of them at the main gate. We're only talking about six vehicles. That's a thirty-second gun battle after detonating a few Claymores alongside of them. We reserve the big stuff for what comes after they report the attack."

"Roger that," said Loftis. "I'm just a little nervous about our exposure."

"We all are," said Trenkor. "Watts, you may as well prepare the welcoming committee."

"I'll personally supervise the final touches," said Watts. "As soon as you give the order, we'll detonate the mines. Whatever crawls out will go down just as fast. I have three 240s at the gate, along with our snipers. It'll be over quick."

"Don't wait for my order. If they approach the gate, you're weapons free. Concentrate your machine-gun fire on the command van at first. Maybe they won't get an SOS out to Garberville."

"Will do," said Watts, before leaving the trailer.

"How the hell did they find us?" said Loftis.

"My guess is the surveillance pilot had a change of heart," said Trenkor. "Or he fucked up and got caught. Maybe passed along last month's imagery? It doesn't matter."

Trenkor watched as the convoy snaked through the network of farms south of Rancho Sequoia Road, making its way north. Once they hit Rancho Sequoia, their intentions would become clearer.

"I have a positive identification for a few of the occupants," said the technician. "One of them is Ryan Decker. He's in vehicle number two. Civilian plates. The other is Sheriff Harvey Long. He's in the lead vehicle."

"Interesting," said Trenkor. "I know where they're headed."

"Dunn farm?" said Loftis.

"That's my guess," said Trenkor, nodding at the screen.

Less than a minute later, the convoy turned right when it reached Rancho Sequoia, headed away from the compound.

"Definitely the Dunn farm," said Trenkor.

"It's not going to look good when they find the place empty," said Loftis.

"As long as they don't know about the compound, it doesn't matter," said Trenkor. "They can comb through that shithole all day. There's nothing to find."

"True. But it'll pique the sheriff's interest," said Loftis.

"By the time the sheriff even gets a whiff of this place, we'll be long gone," said Trenkor.

"What if he leaves a team in place and they report the helicopters coming in tonight?"

"If he leaves deputies out there tonight, you're going to quietly eliminate them before the helicopters arrive," said Trenkor. "Then make them disappear."

CHAPTER THIRTY-SIX

Decker alternated looking through the windshield and the open window next to him, searching for anything out of place. Feigned watchfulness, for all practical purposes. The chances of spotting a threat among the thick pines and dense brush that lined the dirt road hovered just above zero. Despite this stony assessment of these efforts, he continued the sham vigil for Harlow—who looked one muffler backfire away from pulling a hard right into the bushes.

"This is about where we first saw the ATVs," said Decker.

"So far, so good," said Garza, sliding from one side of the back seat to the other.

Decker's earpiece crackled. "Turning left."

"It got busy about a half a mile after this turn," said Decker.

The convoy turned onto a tight jeep trail, which opened into a hard-packed dirt road a few hundred yards later. Decker bounced up, his elbow slamming down on the door with a painful jolt. Nothing compared to the sharp pain in his leg.

"Dammit. I forgot how shitty this road was."

"There's not a lot of room to maneuver in here," said Garza.

Decker glanced over his shoulder at the former Delta Force operator, who sat in the center of the bench seat, his rifle partially protruding from the right window.

"Sheriff Long didn't want us displaying weapons," said Decker.

Garza deftly shifted his rifle to the left window, keeping the barrel pointed upward when it passed Harlow and Decker.

"Fuck that shit," said Garza. "You got twelve to six."

He nodded before lifting his rifle out of his lap and resting the front vertical grip against the windowsill. Twelve to six, representing the hands and motion of a clock, meant Decker was responsible for covering the sector that started directly ahead of them and extended along the right side of the vehicle to directly behind them. Since Garza couldn't see or shoot at a good portion of the left front sector due to his position behind Harlow, Decker had to cover that as well. More like ten to six.

"We're coming up on the fork in the road where they boxed us in with ATVs," said Decker over the radio.

"Looks clear. Maybe your theory about the skinheads is right," said Long. "Do your computer wizards have anything?"

"Nothing yet," said Decker, sharing a sly look with Harlow. "Just the usual cell phone frequencies."

"Let me know if that changes. We're about three minutes from the Dunn place," said Long. "And please get those rifles out of sight. I guarantee that'll be a showstopper when we reach the farm."

"Copy that," said Decker, nodding at Garza.

Both of them lowered their rifles out of sight.

"Thank you," said Long.

After they passed the split-off without incident a few seconds later, Decker contacted Joshua on a separate handheld radio.

"What are you seeing?"

"Nothing new on this trail," said Joshua. "We definitely had some unusual radio frequency activity at five points along our route from Alderpoint Road to the turnoff of Rancho Sequoia. L-band."

"Satellite," said Decker.

"Substantial, continuous data upload," said Joshua. "I'm guessing remote-controlled, satellite-linked cameras. Cellular is almost nonexistent up here. They could be simple game trail cameras with a shitty image, and no zoom or remote control, or the high-end stuff. We're researching known data profiles to narrow that down. I feel pretty confident saying this is a single network, not a patchwork of local cameras."

"Good work. Anything else?" said Decker.

"You'll be the first to know."

He turned to Harlow. "Joshua is fairly certain we passed several roadside satellite cameras. All part of the same network."

"Someone knows we're here," said Harlow.

"I guess so," said Decker.

"Sounds expensive," said Garza. "No cell coverage up here?"

"Apparently not," said Decker.

He fished his cell phone out of a cargo pocket and checked the signal. Zero bars and about a dozen new voice mails. Decker scrolled through the message notifications, all of them from Harlow's phone— except for one. He recognized the area code immediately: 707. Humboldt County. And it came in this morning when he powered up his phone after the sheriff returned it. Very interesting.

"Eyes up," said Garza, nudging his seat.

"Hold on," said Decker, pressing the message.

Hi. This message is for Decker. I don't know exactly what's going on up on the mountain, but things have been different around here for several months now. Nazis shaking people down. Kicking folks off their property. Nobody wants to talk about it. I think these skinheads have taken over a large part of the Alderpoint area. There's supposedly explosive booby traps up there. Some kind of a compound. I don't know, but it's big. They use helicopters, somehow. Not sure how the skinheads have helicopters. Maybe this is some kind of corporate thing. Like a corporate takeover. That's kind of how they treated it. Buyouts at first, then some real hard-line shit. Started way back in February. Anyway. The helicopters are back. It's been a while since we've heard those, but they're back. Two nights in a row now. Lots of them last night. They came in waves. Once about nine. Then again around three. I don't know if this helps you, but I thought it might. I really hope you didn't get caught up in the motel thing. Bye.

"That changes things a bit," said Decker.

"What's up?" said Harlow.

"Got a voice mail from someone Pam and I must have visited the other day, during the afternoon," said Decker. "I honestly didn't think anyone would get in touch with us. Only a few people opened their doors, and nobody said much more than *get off my property*."

He played the message on speakerphone.

"Sounds like our mountaintop friends have been extra busy since the motel shoot-out," said Harlow. "Packing up and leaving?"

"Packing up as much weed as possible before leaving," said Garza.

"That's what I was thinking," said Decker.

"I don't like the idea of these fuckers packing up in the middle of the night and disappearing like a carnival," said Harlow. "Not after what they did at the motel."

"When we're finished at the Dunn farm, remind me to call Bernie," said Decker. "We're going to need that surveillance bird to stick around a little longer. I'd like to follow those helicopters back to their source. If that's possible, we have a shot at taking this whole operation down without getting too bloody. Maybe take it even further. This entire thing reeks of something bigger."

"I'm glad to hear you excited to kick ass again," said Harlow.

"I've been trying to temper my enthusiasm for your proposed suicide mission," said Decker.

"I don't think I ever proposed anything reckless."

He gave Garza a quick look that suggested otherwise.

"You just ratted me out, bro," said Garza.

"What? I was never serious about anything I said," said Harlow. "I'm not crazy."

"Sounded pretty serious to me," said Decker.

"Back me up here, Garza," said Harlow.

"Uh—you had me pretty worried a few times, maybe," said Garza. "But overall? Yeah. Well. I'm pretty sure you wouldn't have—anyway. We should be watching our sectors."

"Two rats," said Harlow, smirking.

"Overprotective rats," said Decker. "Looks like we're coming up on something."

He grabbed the pair of binoculars on the dashboard and scanned beyond the sheriff's vehicle. Some kind of flimsy metal gate, flanked on both sides by a neglected-looking chain-link fence. The road continued past the gate for maybe fifty yards before emptying into a clearing.

"We're coming up on a gate," said Decker. "I can see a house and a few other structures out there."

"See any people?" said Garza.

"Nope."

Sheriff Long spoke over the radio net.

"We're coming up on a gate marking the property. I'm going to push on through, and we'll all drive up to the edge of the clearing, where my vehicle and Sergeant Reid's will proceed. Everyone else stays put until we've figured out what's what with the Dunns."

"I smell a big nothing burger coming our way," said Garza.

"We won't see a damn thing," said Harlow.

Decker answered Long. "Understood. We'll hold back with your third unit until called forward."

"Thank you," said the sheriff.

"Seriously? No pushback?" said Harlow.

Decker kept scanning the forest ahead of them with binoculars.

"Garza will take a look for us," he said. "You didn't think we were going to leave here empty-handed, did you?" said Decker.

"For a minute there, I wasn't sure," said Harlow.

"Make sure the interior lights are off," said Decker.

While she messed with the light controls, Joshua called him over the handheld.

"I have a strong satellite signal dead ahead. Activated a few seconds ago. Same frequency and data profile as the others. This whole mountain is rigged. We're having a real Rockwell moment here."

A female voice came over the handheld. "I always feel like— somebody's watching me. And I have no privacy."

"Lock it down back there," said Decker, shaking his head. "And find that camera. I need to know if it's a fixed or pannable lens."

The support team's van was capable of three-hundred-and-sixty-degree, high-resolution day and night camera surveillance. A few moments later, the lead vehicle stopped at the gate, and one of the deputies hopped out. He retrieved a pair of bolt cutters from the cargo compartment and disappeared in front of the SUV.

"I'm surprised the sheriff authorized that," said Harlow.

"I get the feeling he's serious about helping us out," said Decker. "To a point."

"Yeah. The sooner he gets this little dog-and-pony show over, the sooner he gets us off his back," said Harlow.

"That's what I'd be thinking," said Decker, triggering the handheld. "Josh. Did you locate the camera? We're almost out of time."

"Got it. We're zoomed in, taking pictures," said Joshua. "It looks fixed, but I can't say for sure unless we identify the model. Shouldn't take long."

"I'd say you have about fifteen seconds," said Decker.

The convoy continued past the gate and stopped about thirty feet from the edge of the clearing, still deep in the trees.

"Joshua?" said Decker. "I need an answer."

"It just stopped transmitting," said Joshua.

"Could they be recording us?"

"Yes."

"Then I still need an answer," said Decker.

On the off chance this whole Dunn farm was a setup, he didn't want whoever might be watching to know they had an ace up their sleeve. Garza's surprise appearance could spell the difference between life and death in a coordinated ambush. After a few seconds of muttered curses over the radio, Joshua gave them his verdict.

"Best guess is pannable—but only within the lens's fixed field of view," said Joshua. "It was placed facing the approach to the gate. They can't see us."

"I hope you're right," said Decker, before nudging Harlow's arm. "Pull as far to the left of the road as you can."

Harlow eased the SUV to the left, and the sheriff's department vehicle directly behind them crept down their right side. Once it had passed them, Sheriff Long's SUV took off for the clearing with the second vehicle in tow. When both SUVs broke out of the forest, he contacted Brad.

"We're ready," said Decker.

"Copy. Waving them through," said Brad.

Decker watched his side mirror as the third sheriff's department SUV pulled around Brad's vehicle and continued down the right side of the dirt road. When they drew even with his window, he stopped them.

"Figured you guys should lead the way if the sheriff gives us the green light," said Decker.

The serious-looking deputy just nodded and pulled forward. Garza was long gone before the sheriff's department SUV came to a stop, racing diagonally away from the road in the direction the sheriff had turned. Decker could barely spot him moving through the trees.

"That was slick," said Harlow.

"Yeah. Not bad," said Decker. "The real trick will be getting him back in the vehicle if the sheriff turns us around."

Decker's handheld crackled.

"This is Josh. A second satellite signal went live a few seconds after the sheriff's vehicles broke into the clearing."

"Bearing?" said Decker.

"Roughly twenty degrees to the right," said Joshua. "Same frequency characteristics."

"Are you getting any other RF activity?"

"Just the two frequencies we're using. Nothing else."

That was good news. They were being watched from an operations center somewhere, or by very disciplined teams in the forest. His guess was the former. There would have been some radio or satellite phone chatter when the sheriff's vehicles broke out of the forest and approached the house.

"Joshua, I figured out who's watching us now," said Decker into the radio.

"Who?"

Harlow elbowed him, shaking her head.

"The IRS."

"Damn," said Joshua.

"That was a good one," said Garza.

Decker lowered the radio. "It's the little victories."

"Like a bunch of teenage boys," said Harlow.

He was about to respond with something decidedly unwitty when Sheriff Long's voice came across the primary radio net.

"Nobody's answering at the house, and I don't see anyone around," said the sheriff. "The place is a ghost town. I don't see any reason you can't have a look around. Pull on up."

"I wasn't expecting that," said Harlow.

"Which? The place being a ghost town or the sheriff letting us take a look?"

"Both," said Harlow. "But maybe it makes perfect sense. If the same people that tried to kill you at the motel are behind Brett Hale's disappearance, which I'm certain is the case, then they wouldn't leave any trace of Hale here, either."

"No witnesses," said Decker.

Harlow nodded. "My guess is that everyone connected to this farm is buried with Brett Hale. We're looking at a literal dead end."

Decker considered what she'd said as they pulled into the clearing, a devilish idea forming.

"Dead end," he muttered, chuckling to himself.

"You have that look," said Harlow.

"What look?"

"Your 'up to no good' look," she said.

He raised the handheld. "Garza. Change of plans. Flank around the clearing to the opposite side. Stay deep in the forest until we know more about that camera. We're up to no good."

CHAPTER THIRTY-SEVEN

Trenkor deliberated over what he was watching on the screen. What the hell was Decker up to? After what appeared to be a comprehensive search of the farm's structures and house, Harlow Mackenzie and her associates very subtly orchestrated a sequence of distractions that allowed Decker to slip into Brett Hale's former bunkroom carrying some kind of padded duffel bag he'd retrieved from the tricked-out 4X4 communications van.

"Zoom in on the bunkroom. I want to know what he's doing in there," said Trenkor.

"We can't see anything with the door shut," said the surveillance tech in front of him. "The curtains on the windows are too thick."

"Just zoom in and center the picture on the front door. Maybe we'll catch something when he opens it."

"I'll prep a team to investigate," said Loftis. "As soon as they leave, we can check it out."

"Do it," said Trenkor. "But make sure they don't get anywhere near the property until the sheriff's posse is long gone."

"They'll take one of the back roads to the Sitwell farm and wait for the word," said Loftis. "Walk in from there."

"I want you with them," said Trenkor. "Turn that bunkroom inside out if you have to."

"We'll be Oscar Mike in five," said Loftis, getting up.

"He just opened one of the windows!" said the tech.

"Hold on, Mike," said Trenkor, focusing all his attention on the live feed.

Decker had opened one of the eastern-facing windows and torn down the curtains. Unfortunately, the shallow angle between the camera and the window prevented them from seeing inside. They still couldn't determine what Decker was doing in the bunkroom. One of Harlow Mackenzie's associates suddenly appeared directly outside the window, looking into the room.

"Who is that?" said Trenkor.

"Joshua Keller. Computer science degree from Purdue University. Hired by Raytheon IIS—Intelligence, Information, and Services—right out of college. Spent at least five years and a few months with Raytheon, from what we can tell. He scrubbed all of his social media profiles at that point. We got the Raytheon information from a cached LinkedIn profile database."

"He left Raytheon to work for this ragtag outfit?" said Loftis.

"Makes me wonder if we're underestimating them somehow," said Trenkor. "They seem to have attracted some decent talent, and they have the backing of an influential US senator."

"Outside of Decker's stunt at the motel, they haven't exactly impressed me," said Loftis.

"I don't know," said Trenkor.

Decker appeared on the other side of the open window. After several seconds of heated back-and-forth conversation, Decker disappeared. Keller looked tense, constantly glancing over his shoulder. They were definitely up to something. Decker reappeared a few moments later, holding a light-gray quadcopter drone with both of his hands. He slowly guided it through the opened window, the sides barely clearing the windowsill by a few inches.

Keller gave him an enthusiastic thumbs-up and disappeared from the screen, presumably headed back to the van. Decker shook his head skeptically and carefully pulled the drone back through the window, vanishing again.

"Pull the camera back," said Trenkor.

"A fucking drone?" said Loftis. "Didn't he learn his lesson the first time? And why launch it from inside the house?"

"Good question," said Trenkor. "I want you down there right away. Ready to pounce on that bunkroom the second they drive out of that gate. I don't like this."

Loftis started for the door.

"We can hack the drone within seconds of detecting a signal," said the surveillance tech. "If this Keller guy somehow managed to hard-encrypt the control signal, we can still jam the frequency and render the drone useless. It won't get out of the clearing. Probably not even the house."

Keller would know this. Same with Decker. Unless they assumed launching it much deeper into enemy territory than before would give the drone enough time to transmit some imagery. A mistaken assumption—or was it something else? Had to be something they had either missed or hadn't considered. A way to avoid electronic interference.

"Shit," said Trenkor. "Can one of those drones operate autonomously? Could it fly a preprogrammed pattern?"

"Yes. But that's—"

"Get out there immediately," said Trenkor, cutting off the technician.

Loftis left in a flash, yelling back into the trailer, "We'll be there in ten minutes!"

The longest ten minutes of Trenkor's career, and potentially the most expensive. The cancellation of this evening's airlift operations would cost Athena Corp five hundred million dollars—and probably torpedo his career.

CHAPTER THIRTY-EIGHT

Harlow excused herself from the small cluster of deputies gathered in front of the Dunns' dilapidated house and poked her head inside the support vehicle. She found Decker standing over Joshua and Mazzie, all of them focused intently on one of the screens.

"Sheriff Long looks like he's about to pull the plug on this," said Decker. "How much more time do you need?"

"I think they took the bait," said Joshua. "I can't triangulate until we're moving, but we identified six encrypted radios to the northwest, slowly increasing in strength. Best guess is they're moving in our direction—on foot. Given the hilly terrain and thick forest, I'd say they're getting close. Five hundred yards or less."

"Didn't take them long to get here," said Harlow.

"Eleven minutes," said Decker. "They definitely took the bait."

"Where's Garza?" said Harlow.

"Making his way around the southeast side of the clearing. It took him a little longer than expected to make his arrangements," said Decker. "He'll be here in five minutes."

"Can I talk to you for a minute?" said Harlow. "While we wait."

"Yeah. What's up?" said Decker, his eyes still glued to the screen.

"Outside," said Harlow.

She guided him around the van to a spot along the tree line, presumably out of earshot from everyone else.

"I don't like it when you keep my team in the dark," said Harlow.

"Your team?" said Decker.

"You don't like the way that sounds?"

"Not particularly," said Decker.

"Then you need to knock it off with the secrets that only *your* team seems to be in the know about," said Harlow. "Like Garza's bolting from the vehicle and God knows whatever he did out in the woods. Your sudden need to get into Brett Hale's bunkroom unobserved by the sheriff. All of it."

The regretful look on Decker's face suggested he not only understood but "got it." Then again, she could never tell with him. He'd proven extremely difficult to read, even after they'd started spending more and more time together. At times Harlow wondered if he'd always been like this, and if this was something she could live with.

"Fair enough," said Decker. "I don't mean to be secretive. I think I like to surprise you. Or impress you. I know that sounds weird."

"It kind of does, coming from you. You're impressive enough without the surprises," said Harlow, not ready to let him off the hook that easy. "But I need to know what's going on around us. Full situational awareness, so I don't make a mistake that gets someone killed. You can't compartmentalize information and plans anymore. Okay?"

"Yes. I won't do it again," said Decker, surprisingly curt with his answer.

"So . . . what was Garza up to?" said Harlow. "I caught a glimpse of him behind the bunkroom, and now Ripley is standing guard in front of the door?"

"You're not going to like it," said Decker.

"That's it? You're really not going to tell me after you just promised you would?" said Harlow. "Try me."

"Technically, I said I won't do it again," said Decker.

She just stared at him, which was all it ever took with him.

"It's for Pam. For Brett Hale. For every life these fuckers have snuffed out or ruined," said Decker. "Just a small preview of what's to come. Do you really want to know the details?"

Harlow really didn't care what happened to these scumbags, but she had made promises to others that extended beyond Decker's "eye for an eye" payback.

"How does this impact the bigger picture?" said Harlow. "Tracing this to the source?"

"No impact at all. In fact, this should pave our way," said Decker. "Trust me."

"No more of this."

"Promise," said Decker, edging closer to her.

"Back in the van," said Harlow. "I'll buy *us* five more minutes."

CHAPTER
THIRTY-NINE

Carl Trenkor paced the crowded trailer, muttering obscenities. Twenty-one minutes had elapsed since Decker had left the bunkroom. Apparently long enough for a Raytheon-trained computer genius to put the final touches on a drone's autonomous flight program.

He'd watched the front of the drone slowly drift back and forth just inside the window, until it finally aligned with the window opening. He half expected it to fly out of the window and immediately put an end to EMERALD CITY, but it floated back out of sight—where it still remained. Taunting him.

"They're leaving," said Watts. "The contractor type by the bunkroom just left."

"Pan the camera back, but keep it focused on that window," said Trenkor.

The picture zoomed out, confirming his security chief's assessment. The sheriff's deputies, along with Harlow Mackenzie's "not so ragtag" crew, hopped back in their respective vehicles. The convoy formed up at the edge of the tree line and waited for the lone mercenary who had been guarding the bunkroom structure. The body armor–clad operator effortlessly sprinted across the dusty clearing. None of the Athena

Corp contractors on this compound could move like that wearing a full armor kit.

"Ragtag my ass," muttered Trenkor.

"TIN MAN Actual. This is OUTREACH," said Loftis, his voice projected through the stuffy trailer.

"Speak freely," said Trenkor, triggering his radio. "What do you have?"

"Waiting at the edge of the tree line," said Loftis. "I have visual contact with the convoy. I can take out the communications van right now."

"Negative. You do that and we'll have the National Guard here tonight," said Trenkor.

"That wouldn't be good," said Loftis. "We're ready to pounce."

The convoy started rolling a few seconds later, quickly disappearing from the screen.

"They're on the move. We don't have them on camera anymore," said Trenkor. "What are you seeing?"

"That's it. The convoy has left the clearing, headed south on the road leading to the main gate."

"Copy that. Get to that fucking window immediately," said Trenkor.

"I already have a guy on the way," said Loftis. "Ten seconds. The rest of us are on his heels."

The ten seconds felt like ten minutes—but nothing flew out of the window before Loftis's point man arrived at the side of the house. The operator tried to shut the window, but it didn't budge.

"Point reports the window is jammed," said Loftis.

"I see that. Tell him to block the window. The drone barely had enough room to slip through the opening," said Trenkor. "Actually . . . if he can see the drone on the floor—just have him shoot it."

"Copy that," said Loftis.

Trenkor breathed a sigh of relief. He had just saved the company a lot of money. No matter what happened from this point forward, the rest of the airlifts could proceed. Outside of another attempt to plant a drone, neither Mackenzie's group nor the sheriff could possibly bring down EMERALD CITY prior to its natural expiration date—three nights from now.

"My point man can't locate the drone from the window," said Loftis. "But the convoy is completely out of sight. We can breach right now."

Shit!

He didn't like that report. The damn drone should be somewhere close to the window.

"Not until they clear the gate," said Trenkor. "Just in case they turn around."

Less than thirty seconds later, one of the technicians pointed to a small picture-in-picture image in the right bottom corner of the screen, which showed a convoy of vehicles moving away from the camera.

"They're past the gate, heading out fast," said the tech.

"Get in there and smash that drone," said Trenkor over the radio net.

"We're moving in," said Loftis.

Trenkor watched as OUTREACH moved into position. Loftis stationed an additional operator at the window, ensuring that the drone couldn't possibly escape the cabin. Two experienced operators should have no problem keeping a slow-moving chunk of unstable plastic from flying out a window. At least that was what he kept telling himself.

"We're ready to breach," said Loftis, giving the camera a quick thumbs-up from his position at the front door.

"Do it," said Trenkor.

Loftis pushed the door halfway open and crouched low, pointing his rifle inside.

"Careful, Mike," said Trenkor. "Never know what they left behind."

"Looks clean. I think I see the drone," said Loftis, leaning his upper body into the doorway. "Southeast corner—sitting on one of the beds."

"Anything else in there?" said Trenkor.

"Doesn't look like it," said Loftis, continuing to lean into the cabin. "I can't see the other side. This stupid fucking door is stuck on something."

Loftis shoved the door with his left hand—and momentarily disappeared in a blast of dust and splintered wood. His mangled, legless torso tumble-wheeled into the three shrapnel-punctured men outside the doorway. The entire four-man entry team collapsed in a tangled, bloody heap.

The entire trailer went deathly still—nobody, including Trenkor, was able to immediately comprehend what had just happened. A crunching boom reached them a few seconds later, jarring everyone back into action.

"Tell them to cease fire and render first aid to any survivors," said Trenkor. "The area is clear of hostiles. Loftis triggered an explosive device."

The two men assigned to the window had dropped to the ground, firing wildly into the structure. They stopped a few seconds later and cautiously moved toward the southeast corner of the structure.

"We might be able to time the activation of the outermost explosive layer to catch the van with the very first charge," said Watts. "Get a little payback."

"It's tempting," said Trenkor, finding it hard to push back against the idea.

He'd known Loftis for close to a decade, working on and off together on a number of projects for Athena Corp and a few of its partners. Trenkor had always appreciated Mike's hands-on style and had specifically requested him for this job. He'd hoped it would give Mike the visibility boost he needed within the Special Activities Group's DC-based leadership to start picking up independent assignments. The first step toward leading something big like EMERALD CITY. One careless move had erased all of that—compliments of Ryan Decker.

"Very tempting," he said. "But even if we could pull it off without injuring the deputies in the second-to-last vehicle, we'd likely be pulling the plug on EMERALD CITY. The sheriff would call in the troops, and who the hell knows what Decker and company might do."

"I know. I just hated seeing Mike and the guys go out like that," said Watts.

"We have to swallow this one for now, and stay focused on the mission," said Trenkor. "When all of this is finished—we can look into a little payback."

Chapter Forty

Decker took Harlow's hand for a moment, squeezing it gently before letting go. The Claymore mine Garza had rigged inside the bunkroom had just exploded. The high-order C-4 detonation had been somewhat dampened by the dense forest and off-road racket created by the jeep trail, but the sound had been unmistakable to Decker—even with the windows closed. On cue, his earpiece crackled.

"This is Sheriff Long. Did anyone else hear that?" he said. "Sounded like an explosion."

He let the reports filter in, softly chuckling at the final tally. The three sheriff's department vehicles confirmed some kind of distant blast. Brad's SUV and the support van claimed they didn't detect anything unusual, citing closed windows and the rough roads as their excuse. In order to make it a little less obvious that the firm may have had a hand in the explosion, Decker broke ranks.

"I had my window open and heard something pretty loud. Sounded like it came from the east. Pretty far away, but definitely there," said Decker, before lowering his window to match the story.

The distant crackle of gunfire filled the SUV. Fortunately, most of the sound would reach the sheriff's people after bouncing off hundreds of trees, rendering it nearly impossible to determine the gunfire's original direction.

"This is Sergeant Larson. I hear gunfire now."

"I confirm that. Same distance as the explosion. A mile away or greater," he said over the radio net, winking at Harlow.

"Mile my ass," whispered Garza.

The shooting stopped a few seconds later, leaving him to wonder how Sheriff Long would ultimately react. The sheriff hadn't slowed his vehicle—which was a good indicator that he wanted to get off the mountain just as badly as Decker.

The absolute worst thing they could do right now was stick around the Dunn property. He felt pretty confident that the group watching them wouldn't retaliate with the sheriff and his deputies present, but he didn't want to push that assumption. Not after what he had just pulled. Every person watching them right now was thinking the same thing. Revenge.

"Now what?" said Harlow.

"Now we wait for Bernie's surveillance," said Decker. "From a safe distance."

"Are you sure we're safe at the motel?" said Harlow. "No offense, Garza."

"None taken, ma'am," he said. "We're spread a little thin, but I agree with Decker. As long as we have the sheriff's people with us, we should be good."

"Maybe we should ask him to beef up their presence," said Harlow. "Or at least put a third vehicle inside the motor court. Even if they only add one deputy to the roster, that would provide a significant deterrent."

"That's a great idea," said Decker. "I can't imagine it'll be a tough sell. That's cushy overtime duty. We can even give the sheriff's department one of the rooms."

"I'll propose it when we get back to the motel," said Harlow. "Or wherever he stops us to stagger everyone's return."

"I have to give him credit," said Decker. "As much as I don't want to like him for handcuffing me to a bed and hiding Pam—he's got his shit together. I mostly trust him."

"I agree," said Harlow. "But he's also keen on getting rid of us. Outside of this very significant problem on the mountain, we're his biggest liability right now. He obviously can't boot us out of Eureka, but I imagine he could make our lives pretty uncomfortable. He definitely won't let us set foot on the mountain again. Our investigation into Brett Hale's disappearance is essentially stalled at this point, and I guarantee he won't buy any bullshit about us launching our own investigation into the motel shooting. I mean, we're well within our rights to investigate as a firm, but I don't see that having legs if he doesn't want us here."

"How do you all see this playing out?" said Garza. "I'm talking endgame."

"Are we holding you up from another job?" said Decker.

"Nope. Just curious," said Garza. "You know I'm in."

"I'm not there yet," said Decker, tapping the side of his head. "But I know we have to get them off the mountain. We don't have the numbers to make a move against them up here. I see this playing out somewhere else. I'm just not sure where. For all we know, those helicopters could end up landing at a fucking Army base."

"Wouldn't surprise me at all, given what we've seen before," said Harlow.

"Seriously," said Decker, staring into the trees.

Decker's thoughts drifted far away, to the city where Jacob Harcourt ran his well-oiled grift machine, buying outcomes that tore apart lives— while he sipped expensive scotch on expensive leather furniture. He couldn't shake the thought that Harcourt was just one of many influence peddlers within the Beltway, and that they were all connected by something bigger. Something he'd smash to fucking pieces given the chance—no matter what the cost.

He lifted his handheld. "Joshua?"

"Yep. Uh. Roger. I'm here."

"I need you to pinpoint the location of the very first camera we encountered on the way in."

"I already have it mapped out," said Joshua.

"Perfect. Let me know when we're thirty seconds out."

Harlow glanced at him. "What are you up to?"

"Making sure they got the message," said Decker. "I need paper and a pen."

Chapter Forty-One

Carl Trenkor watched the wall-mounted split screen. On the right, a second security team led by Jason Watts loaded three body bags into the back of a pickup truck. On the left, the sheriff's convoy drove down the mountain, taking the same route they used when they arrived. He tried to focus on the sheriff's vehicles. The sight of those body bags triggered primal thoughts that had no place in EMERALD CITY.

"Convoy is approaching Alderpoint Road," said one of the techs.

He glanced at the digital map on one of the monitors below the split screen. The convoy had just exited the outermost defensive zone. Good. He could concentrate on the big picture without contemplating the convoy's destruction, a persistent thought he found increasingly difficult to resist while watching Watts's team load Loftis's remains into the body bag—piece by piece.

Trenkor took a seat in the back of the trailer, gathering his thoughts. He had no choice but to report the situation to his boss, sooner than later. OZ would undoubtedly suggest they evacuate immediately, but Trenkor didn't think it was necessary. Not right now. The sheriff's convoy hadn't responded to the explosion or gunfire, which told him that the sheriff was either scared of a confrontation on the mountain or he truly didn't comprehend what was happening. Both scenarios kept him back in Eureka, where he couldn't threaten EMERALD CITY.

Decker and Mackenzie were a different story, but even they had to realize that they faced a hopeless situation. Trenkor had done the math. They had four serious shooters. The rest of the group was composed of private investigators and computer nerds. He didn't expect to see them on the mountain again.

"One of the vehicles just pulled off the road," said one of the techs. "The rest of the convoy stopped."

"Which vehicle?" said Trenkor.

"Decker's," said the tech.

"I can't see shit," said Trenkor. "How far away is the camera?"

"Right on the edge of its range," said the tech.

"What about the next camera?"

"It's right next to them," said the tech. "We won't be able to see the entire convoy. Given their position, we'll be lucky to have two of their vehicles on screen."

"Switch to the other camera," said Trenkor.

He wanted to get a good look at Decker. To commit the man's face to memory—for later.

"Switching."

The left side of the screen went blank for a moment, revealing Ryan Decker when it came back online. Decker held a piece of paper in one hand and pointed to it with the other.

"Zoom in on the paper," said Trenkor, knowing he probably shouldn't.

The handwritten message induced a collective gasp in the trailer.

Sorry about your dumb friends. Rookie ass mistake pushing that door open. Right? Hope your company provides life insurance. You're all going to need it.

Decker's face filled the screen a moment later, flashing a psychotic grin. He winked before giving the camera the middle finger.

"Cut the feed," said Trenkor, glancing at the body bags. "Both sides."

When the screen went blank, he radioed Watts.

"Andy, Decker somehow knows about the cameras. My guess is that his support team is far more sophisticated than we originally suspected. I think they used that knowledge to orchestrate the ambush."

"I think you're right," said Watts. "We found the drone, and there's no battery or control unit."

"That doesn't make sense," said Trenkor. "We saw it float in and out of the window."

"We also found one of the back windows open, and a fresh piss stain against the siding," said Watts. "Someone else was in there with Decker—and stayed after he left. Probably just held the drone and moved it back and forth."

"Hold on," said Trenkor, walking up to the lead surveillance technician. "Show me when the drone was drifting in and out of the window."

A few seconds later, the Dunn farm camera feed took up the entire screen—paused at the point where the drone appeared in the window.

"Play it in slow motion," said Trenkor.

The picture started moving, the drone sluggishly floating around inside the cabin, eventually lining up with the window and partially emerging. He saw it right away. The enclosed rotor blades didn't move.

"Watts, hop on Bravo Zulu," said Trenkor.

"Copy that."

Trenkor left the trailer and switched to their private frequency.

"You there?"

"Yep," said Watts.

"When you get back, I want a surveillance team watching Decker and his friends twenty-four seven," said Trenkor. "And a full assault team to back them up. If the opportunity arises—we'll take it."

"Do we know where they're staying?"

"Not yet," said Trenkor. "I'll contact the surveillance team in Garberville. Highway 101 is the primary route back to Eureka, and it shouldn't be too hard to pick up a six-vehicle convoy passing through."

"I'll start working on this as soon as I get back," said Watts.

"How bad was it down there?" said Trenkor.

"Pretty bad. There wasn't much left of Mike," said Watts. "Cooper was killed instantly. Breene bled out by the time we got there. Mayer should be fine. I really hope that opportunity arises before we leave."

"More and more, I'm starting to think it will," said Trenkor.

PART FOUR

PART FOUR

CHAPTER FORTY-TWO

Ryan Decker studied the high-resolution image on the projection screen, shaking his head. He'd say it was impossible, but pictures didn't lie, unless they were provided by a corrupt source. Sheriff Long wasn't going to be happy to learn that the money his department had spent on aerial surveillance had been pocketed, and that the imagery they'd been fed for the past several months had been faked.

"Joshua, can you sift through these and put together an image deck in the next minute?" said Decker. "Something impactful to show the sheriff?"

"I think that image alone should do the trick," said Harlow.

"Seriously. I mean—this is crazy," said Decker.

"How about this one compared side to side with the image the sheriff gave us?" said Joshua. "And a few more to demonstrate the scale and scope of the operation."

"Perfect. I'll go grab them," said Decker. "Meet you in the other room."

He stepped out of the electronic support room into the crisp night air and jogged over to the sheriff, who sat with a few of his deputies on a picnic table they had dragged into the parking lot.

"The surprise I promised just arrived," he said. "You're not going to believe this."

"This surprise better be good," said Detective Reid. "I'm missing family pizza night for this."

"Trust me. This is going to be worth it," said Decker.

"That's a high bar," said Sergeant Larson. "Sheryl's pizza is hard to beat."

"Impossible to beat," said Sheriff Long, getting up. "But let's take a look at whatever it is that couldn't wait until tomorrow."

When the sheriff and his three sergeants were seated, Harlow signaled for Joshua to start the show. A split image of the mountaintop appeared on the massive flat screen monitor they had mounted to the wall separating the two rooms. Decker waited for Harlow to start talking, but she remained quiet, letting the veteran law enforcement officers puzzle over the image.

"Holy shit," muttered Sergeant Larson, glancing at Harlow. "That can't be right."

"What is this?" said Sheriff Long. "Some kind of CGI rendition of what could happen up there if we let this group run amok?"

"When was this taken?" said Larson.

"Taken? Tabby. This isn't real," said the sheriff, his eyes fixed on the screen. "Right?"

"The picture on the right was taken about twenty minutes ago by a Bombardier Challenger jet retrofitted for medium- to high-altitude surveillance," said Harlow, nodding at Joshua. "And this one."

The next image occupied the entire screen, showing a slightly zoomed-out version of the previous frame.

"This can't be real," said the sheriff. "That's like ten football fields long."

"More like twenty," said Joshua.

"And maybe about half as wide," said Harlow. "We estimate about four hundred to five hundred acres. Most of it used to grow plants."

"That's a lot of pot," said Larson.

"And that's just one part of it," said Harlow. "Take a look at the entire Alderpoint area compared to the imagery provided by your surveillance people."

The screen split, showing fairly similar topographical images. Lush green, forested hills marked by several easily identifiable roads and creeks. Only one noticeable difference really stood out. Nearly every farm within a one-mile radius of the massive plot had been expanded to five times its original size.

"This is insane," said the sheriff, getting up to take a closer look. "And you guys aren't punking me with this?"

Harlow shook her head. "This is real."

"It explains a lot," said Detective Reid.

"Yeah. There's a shit ton more money at stake up there now," said Larson. "At least ten times as much, judging by these pictures."

"How much do you estimate it's all worth?" said Decker.

Larson pulled out her smartphone.

"You got a weed calculator on there?" said Sheriff Long, eliciting a few laughs.

"Yeah. So I know how much to put in the trunk of your car at the end of the day to get you busted for distribution."

"Remind me to check my trunk from now on," said Long.

"You can put it in mine instead," said Detective Reid. "I'll find it a good home."

"The good detective's parents were part of Humboldt County's original hippie migration," said the sheriff. "They're what you might call the Emerald Triangle's pioneers of pot."

"Too bad they sold everything off years ago," said Reid. "I'd be up there raking in the money."

Long shook his head. "Anyway. What's the value of this superfarm?"

Larson broke down the math, which Harlow and Joshua followed on their own phones.

"A professionally run and funded grow site can produce two to three thousand large plants per acre," said Larson. "I think it's fair to assume we're looking at a very well-funded operation, so I'll go big with three thousand. A plant that size, if grown properly, could produce a pound of dried bud. Probably a little less. Then again, if they're using high-end fertilizer—"

"Tabby, let's go with the abbreviated version."

"Street value will be anywhere from fifteen hundred to two thousand dollars. Less if it's shit. More if it's some kind of premium strain," said Larson. "But that's street value, and this is a monster of an operation. They'll wholesale this out to a big corporation or some other kind of major distributor for seven hundred to a thousand dollars."

"Assume one thousand," said Long.

"Okay," said Larson, adding the number to her calculation. "How many acres are we talking?"

"Four hundred and ninety-five, based on the twenty-by-twelve football field estimate," said Joshua.

"Jesus," said Harlow, glancing up at Larson.

"Wow," added Joshua.

"How much?" said Decker and the sheriff at the same time.

"One-point-five billion dollars," said Larson. "And that's just the big kahuna field in the center of it all. The rest of the farms could bring that up to two billion."

"That actually explains everything," said Sheriff Long, suddenly looking lost.

Nobody spoke for the next half minute, each of them obviously plotting the next move, or in Decker's case, several moves down the line.

"That definitely quieted the room," said Harlow.

"We need to call Sacramento," said Larson. "There's no way we can handle this on our own."

"You got that right," said Sheriff Long. "I can't believe we actually went up there this morning. The Dunn farm can't be more than a quarter of a mile from some of those expanded sites."

"They were probably watching us the entire time," said Detective Hodges. "One wrong turn and boom. Maybe that explosion and all that gunfire was some kind of warning."

"They were watching us the whole time," said Decker.

"Why do I feel like I'm about two steps behind you guys?" said Long.

"More like ten," said Larson.

"We detected and visually identified several satellite-enabled cameras along our route to the Dunn property. One was watching over the property, transmitting imagery while we poked around," said Decker. "That's why we brought the van with all of the antennas. My guess is they have the whole area under surveillance."

"Would have been nice to know that my deputies were under surveillance," said Long. "And most likely in danger."

"And have your deputies peeking up at the trees constantly, trying not to act suspicious? That would have tipped them off and potentially created a more dangerous situation," said Decker.

"I'll decide what's safe or unsafe for my deputies, thank you," said Long.

"Fine," said Decker. "We're also being watched right now, from across the street. Assuming you don't have a team spying on us."

"We're spying on you from inside the motor court, at your request," said the sheriff. "So. How long have you known that the motel is under surveillance?"

"Since around two this afternoon?" said Decker, glancing at Joshua.

"The surveillance team showed up first, a little after two," said Joshua. "The rest arrived closer to four."

"How many are over there?"

"We detected a total of nine encrypted P25 radios at the Comfort Inn. Three in a room facing this motel. Second floor. The rest are concentrated in two rooms down the hallway, facing the opposite direction. We're most likely looking at a dedicated, twenty-four-hours surveillance team and an assault team."

"Assault? As in try to take this place down?" said Long.

"I don't think so," said Brad. "They know we have our own security force, plus your deputies. Six sounds more like an opportunity team. Like if we sent one or two of our people on a grocery run, and they decided it presented them with an opportunity to send a message or take a prisoner."

"Do we need more of my deputies here?" said Hodges.

"I have another idea for your SET deputies," said Decker.

"Oh, do you?" said Long. "Am I no longer sheriff?"

"I didn't mean it that way, Sheriff," said Decker. "I have the start of an idea that I think could solve this entire problem. We get to the bottom of why Brett Hale disappeared and strike a blow at the people responsible. You get your mountain back, while delivering some good old-fashioned county justice. But most important, you get rid of us."

"I like the last part," said Long, and they all laughed. "So how do we do this without starting a war?"

"We have reason to believe that the events of the past few days have convinced these new mountaintop overlords that their time has expired," said Decker.

"Damn right it's expired," said the sheriff.

"Has your office fielded any more reports of helicopters in the Alderpoint area?" said Decker.

"They have. But that's nothing new," said the sheriff. "Ever since we started using National Guard helicopters several years back to raid farms, we get a few calls a week just to mess with us."

"Well, I got this call from a onetime informant," said Decker, taking his phone out of his pocket. "I knocked on some doors and left business cards at the few farms we could approach—the same day we were attacked at the motel."

He played the message on speakerphone. Sheriff Long nodded and rubbed his chin.

"You think the helicopters are coming back tonight?" said Long.

"We do," said Decker. "And that surveillance jet up there has six more hours on station. We're going to track those helicopters back to their source."

"Okay. And then what?" said Long.

"I haven't completely worked that out yet," said Decker. "But if you let me buy you all the pizza you can eat—delivered here—I think we can put together a plan that accomplishes everything I mentioned before. And if we can't come up with a relatively safe, workable idea— you still get rid of us. Eventually."

"Pepperoni, green peppers, and onions," said Sheriff Long. "From that place on Third Street."

"Put an order together for all of the deputies," said Decker. "Drinks. Whatever. We'll take care of it."

While the sheriff and his crew debated the pizza order, Harlow motioned for him to step into the other room. He excused himself and followed her through the door.

"What's up?" he said. "You look like I'm in trouble."

"No. I think that went well," she said. "I'm just surprised you didn't show them the helicopter."

"I'm kind of surprised they didn't see it," said Decker, chuckling. "I figured, why spook them even more than they already are? Did you see the looks on their faces when Larson said two billion dollars? Everyone vapor-locked for several seconds."

"To be fair—it kind of knocked the wind out of me, too," said Harlow. "That's an insane amount of money. Individual farmers have killed sheriff's deputies over quarter-acre plots before. This is five hundred acres. In one place."

"You're right," said Decker. "I'll bring up the helicopter after the second set of surveillance images arrive. It'll stand out like a sore thumb in the thermal imagery anyway."

"I'm surprised they'd bring a Chinook to the mountain," said Harlow. "They could have used a helicopter half that size to chase down the skinheads' pickup truck. This seems like overkill."

"That's what I was thinking," said Decker. "There has to be a specific reason they'd have a helicopter that big sitting up there. You can move thirty to fifty people with one of those, depending on how the people are geared up."

"Maybe we shouldn't tell the sheriff," said Harlow, smiling. "He might construe that as a possible invasion threat to Eureka."

"True," he said, forcing a laugh so Harlow wouldn't worry.

Decker considered how easy it would be for that helicopter to offload enough troops behind the motel to wipe out the entire compound. Just sweep their troubles right off the map. That was what he'd do, especially if he knew the megafarm had been discovered. There would be nothing to lose at that point—only a ton of money if the sheriff got the word out. And when the helicopter flew away, and everyone here was dead, it would probably take investigators weeks to figure out what happened, if they ever did. And by then, they'd be gone for good.

"Why don't we hold on to that helicopter information for now," he said quietly. "No point in starting an invasion scare."

CHAPTER FORTY-THREE

The faint echo of helicopter rotors washed through the treetop-level lookout tower. Trenkor switched the sensor input to thermal and quickly located the two inbound Sikorsky 64 Skycranes before he gave the horizon a three-hundred-and-sixty-degree sweep, searching for out-of-place heat signatures. Basically, anything airborne except for the Skycranes represented a threat. Nothing flew over this area at night except for his helicopters.

Satisfied that the pickup was safe from aerial interdiction, he aimed the sensor at the two Sikorskys, which burned bright white in the center of the screen. The helicopters were still a few minutes out. More than enough time to check in with OZ. Since the surveillance team in the trailer below him saw the same screen, there was no reason to contact them. He switched the sensor out of local control so his techs could maintain their vigil over the sky.

He contacted OZ on his satellite phone, taking in the serenity of the pitch-black treetops and sky as he waited for a connection.

"Carl, we've been anticipating your call."

We? He wasn't thrilled to know he had an audience. Especially now—with EMERALD CITY hanging precariously in the balance due to factors mostly out of his control, but undeniably his responsibility. The captain went down with the ship regardless of why it sank.

"Everything is proceeding on schedule—with no complications. Both Skycranes are headed for the landing zone. The cargo containers are packed with product, waiting to be attached. We'll hot refuel while attaching the containers, and both birds will be headed back to KANSAS in less than fifteen minutes."

"Sorry to hear about Mike Loftis, Carl," announced a deep male voice he didn't recognize. "We're all counting on you to see this thing through."

"I will, sir," said Trenkor. "Thank you."

"I'll let the two of you finish your chat," the man said.

Trenkor remained quiet, letting OZ deal with whoever had decided to pay him an unexpected visit.

"Everybody is watching this one," said OZ after several long seconds.

"I've attracted too much attention in the past week," said Trenkor.

"It's been a tough week, but everybody has been watching EMERALD CITY very closely from the start. That's why I picked you to run it," he said. "They're just sweating me unnecessarily at this point. I don't want to hold you up with the helos inbound. How are things looking with Decker and the sheriff?"

"About the same. They've been holed up at the motel all afternoon and evening. Two more mercenaries arrived during the late afternoon, bringing their total number of serious shooters to six, including Decker. The sheriff and a small number of his sergeants showed up about an hour and a half ago. They had a bunch of pizza delivered, so hopefully this is a farewell party."

"Don't count him out," said OZ. "Decker won't let this go that easily."

"He did get his revenge—and some," said Trenkor, clenching a fist. "But I'm not counting him out of this until he's gone."

"Carl, no matter how angry you are about Mike's death, and no matter how tempting circumstances might prove in the next two to three days—do not proactively go after Decker and his crew until we've concluded EMERALD CITY operations in California. I can't stress that enough."

"And if he returns to the mountain?" said Trenkor.

"You apply the same rules of engagement you always have," he said. "This is not the time to attract additional attention. You have less than—what—sixty hours to go? We're almost there, Carl. Stay focused, and we can discuss payback when you're free and clear of this operation. Sound good?"

"Very good," said Trenkor.

"All right. I'll be available at all hours. Keep me posted."

"Will do," said Trenkor, ending the call.

He considered the assault team staged at the Comfort Inn, debating whether he should bring them back to the mountain. Decker was a burning itch he truly couldn't afford to scratch right now. Keeping the team at the hotel might prove too tempting. Then again, they might come in handy if Decker pulled something unexpected. OZ had all but sanctioned the deployment of the team when he said not to count Decker out.

Well aware that he wasn't being entirely honest with himself about the team's true purpose, Trenkor decided to keep them at the hotel as an insurance policy—and just in case a golden opportunity to kill Decker or Ms. Mackenzie materialized.

CHAPTER FORTY-FOUR

Harlow Mackenzie stood in the doorway connecting the two motel rooms, relaying information from Joshua's electronics and surveillance gurus to the most improbable ad hoc task force ever assembled. Career law enforcement officers. Salty private investigators. Top-tier mercenaries. All working together under the same roof, toward the same goal. No wonder the sheriff was so eager to get rid of them. If the true nature of this alliance leaked to the public, he'd probably face a recall election next week.

"NEBULA is off station," she said. "They started taking heat from Reno air traffic control about the military-restricted airspace nearby and figured there was no reason to push their luck any further."

A few groans echoed through the group.

"Because they already got everything they needed," said Harlow.

A collective cheer erupted, followed by a round of high fives. Harlow shook her head. Definitely the most bizarre professional gathering she'd ever been a part of. Paid mercenaries high-fiving sheriff's deputies.

"So? What are we looking at?" said Decker. "Obviously somewhere in Nevada."

"They're putting together some footage," said Harlow. "It didn't look too far over the border."

Joshua yelled out. "They landed at a facility near the southern tip of Pyramid Lake, Nevada."

"A military base?" said Decker.

"Tell them to hold on," said Joshua.

"You started it," said Harlow.

Joshua nodded. "I know. This is just very exciting. Like a Tom Clancy novel."

"It kind of is," she said, leaning into the other room. "They're working on it."

Everyone in the jam-packed room was on their phones, presumably looking up Pyramid Lake.

"That's on the Pyramid Lake Paiute Indian Reservation," said Decker. "Definitely not a military base. I wish they would hurry up. This is killing me."

Mazzie shot up from her station, tapping Joshua on the shoulder.

"Sent you what I have," she said.

A minute later, Joshua stood up. "It's ready."

"Let's go," said Harlow, motioning for Joshua to follow. "This is your show."

"Great," said Joshua, clicking a few final keys before joining her.

Harlow kicked Decker out of his seat and gave it to Joshua. When she and Decker had settled into a spot next to Katie and Sandy on the back wall, he started the presentation. The screen changed to a thermal-scale image of the Alderpoint area, identifiable only by the lines drawn by Joshua around the massive mountaintop farm—and the words drawn in the bottom right corner that read ALDERPOINT 2032 HOURS.

"For quick reference, this is the greater Alderpoint area, to include the mountaintop complex and all farms of interest," said Joshua. "As you can see, there's considerable activity at all of the locations."

He switched to a green-scale night-vision image of the same picture, which looked considerably different but flared brightly in the same locations.

"Night-vision imagery confirms the use of lighting at the same locations," said Joshua, clicking a button on his remote and turning the still image into a video. "Interestingly, we can see several vehicles moving back and forth between the satellite farms and the main complex in the middle. My guess is that they're moving product from the farms to the top for transport. This is a compressed video running from eight thirty-two, when our aircraft started shooting imagery, until the next video."

The screen changed to display a top-down thermal image zoomed into the main compound. MAIN COMPLEX 2120. Seconds later, two helicopters flew in from the right side of the screen. They quickly landed in a staggered column, on the only unused patch of ground in the compound.

"At nine twenty, two Sikorsky 64 Skycranes land in the main complex. Each of them carries a modified shipping container, which is promptly detached and moved out of the landing zone. They are replaced by two presumably prepacked shipping containers waiting nearby."

"Can you estimate how much each container can carry?" said Sergeant Larson.

Joshua paused the video.

"A twenty-foot maritime shipping container, which this resembles, can be packed with close to fifty thousand pounds, but the carrying capacity of the Skycrane is twenty thousand pounds. So twenty thousand."

"They must be jamming the containers with full plants and taking them to the other facility for drying and trimming," said Larson.

"You don't think they're drying any here?" said Decker.

"I doubt it. Grow sites are always limited by space."

"They seem to have cracked the space code," said Decker.

"That would be true if half of the compound was used for drying, but that doesn't appear to be the case. Aside from the little trailer park, I don't see any big structures, which you'd need to dry the plants. Remember the Dunn farm? They had a sizable barn for drying, which would normally be completely filled with hanging plants at the end of the harvest. And that's just for three-quarters of an acre. For a five-hundred-acre farm, plus another hundred acres of scattered farms—you get the picture."

The video started again, showing the helicopters take off and head east, disappearing from the screen at the same spot where they originally appeared.

"Total time on the ground was sixteen minutes, with a refueling," said Joshua.

"That's pretty tight," said Brad. "We're talking veteran pilots and an experienced ground crew."

"Fits that pattern I told you about, Sheriff," said Decker. "Expensive military contractors."

Joshua switched the screen to a digital map of California and Nevada. A line steadily crossed the map, originating in Alderpoint and ending at the Pyramid Lake Paiute Indian Reservation.

"Our surveillance bird, flying a racetrack pattern overhead, tracked the helicopters for the duration of their two-hour-and-eighteen-minute flight to this facility," said Joshua.

A green-scale image appeared, displaying a perfectly spaced, east-to-west line of eight warehouses. The faint outline of a fence line could be detected, forming a near-perfect box around the entire facility. The warehouses sat toward the bottom of the box, in the south, giving the impression that the vast, flat area north of the row of structures served as a landing zone.

Harlow's interpretation of the facility was confirmed when the two helicopters flew in from the west, both of them landing in front of the third warehouse. A flurry of ground vehicles sped out to meet them.

"You probably get the picture at this point," said Joshua. "The containers are detached and replaced, presumably by empty ones to be taken back to Alderpoint to maintain the cycle. Based on what Sergeant Larson said, the product is probably taken into the warehouses and dried."

"Did the surveillance aircraft get a look inside those warehouses? Maybe through one of the doors?" said the sheriff. "I'd love to confirm they were hanging marijuana plants. I think that would be more than enough to get the feds involved—over in Nevada. I'm not going to bullshit any of you. The last thing I need is a full-scale federal or state invasion of Alderpoint. All the better if we can steer the big bust toward our neighboring state. I'd gladly settle for a return to status quo on the mountain, rather than an angry hornet's nest of small-time pot growers and marijuana activists descending on my office."

Harlow liked where this conversation was headed—out of state and bigger picture.

"Unfortunately, in order to avoid detection while flying circles above the target area, the pilots maintained a fifteen-thousand-foot altitude—which presents a look-down profile. Almost entirely a two-dimensional presentation. And they didn't unpack outside. The containers were taken directly into the warehouse," said Joshua. "Back in Alderpoint, we could probably show plants being loaded onto trucks and transported up the mountain. I haven't reviewed the footage in that kind of detail yet."

Sheriff Long stood up. "You put that together, and I'll gladly vouch for what's going on up there. Based on what you've said in passing, I presume you have some high-level contacts at the federal level that could make a raid happen—in Nevada?"

Long's question was music to her ears.

"We'll talk to our contacts tomorrow morning. I think hearing from the experts on Humboldt County's illegal drug industry, plus some recently recorded footage, would seal the deal," said Harlow.

"Ideally, we'd catch them in the act," said Decker. "Deliver the whole operation in one tidy package."

"With half of this paramilitary operation here and the other half over there, it sounds like I'm still going to have a mess in Alderpoint," said the sheriff.

"It all depends on your definition of the word *mess*," said Decker.

"The word *mess* to me means dead or injured deputies. Civilian casualties," said Long. "Basically any kind of confrontation or standoff up in Alderpoint that's going to draw even more attention to the shit show someone brought to our doorstep."

Decker crossed his arms and smiled. "I have a plan that sweeps the dangerous elements away, leaving you with little more than a cleanup."

The sheriff shifted in his chair to face Decker. "That simple, huh?"

"Absolutely not. But I think we can pull it off," said Decker. "It's just going to take a little teamwork—and a boatload of my assumptions working out in our favor."

"A lot of luck, basically," said Long.

"Decker's assumptions have an uncanny way of working out," said Harlow.

CHAPTER
FORTY-FIVE

Supervisory Special Agent Reeves took the teleconference call in his car, on the way to a coworking space his wife, Claire, used on occasion to meet face-to-face with her graphic design clients. Neither of the senior agents felt comfortable discussing his proposal in any more detail over the phone at home, and they especially didn't want any record of the meeting at either of the federal buildings housing their respective agencies. His wife's coworking space membership included access to on-site, private conference rooms, where they'd agreed to meet.

"I apologize for running a little late," said Reeves. "Starbucks was mobbed, and the two agents who so graciously agreed to meet me on a Sunday morning shook me down for every bizarre drink on the menu. I'd never even heard of a flat white before this morning."

"Don't you do the mobile order thing?" said Decker.

"No. I actually walk into the store and interact with people, Decker," said Reeves. "You've been hanging out with that millennial crowd a little too long."

"I think it's Generation Z that does everything by app," said Harlow.

"I use the mobile app all the time," said Senator Steele. "And I'm a boomer, Joe. What's your excuse?"

"I just haven't uploaded it yet," said Reeves, getting some laughs. "Hey. I'm about ten minutes away from the meeting, so we need to make this quick. I don't want to keep them waiting."

"I don't have anything to add," said Steele. "So I'll turn the floor over to Decker and Ms. Mackenzie."

"Before we start—how is Pam doing?" said Reeves.

"She's still unconscious, mostly from the drugs they're pumping through her," said Harlow. "But she's stable. The doctors really didn't want to say that, since she's technically still listed in critical condition. They don't see any reason why she won't make a full recovery."

Reeves exhaled. "That's good news. I've spent time with colleagues in the hospital, and uh . . . yeah. Not comparing notes, but you know what I mean."

"I do," said Harlow. "Thank you."

"We'll have to arrange something special for the resident agency up in Redding," said Decker. "They stepped up when they didn't have to. Maybe we'll throw in a nice bottle of scotch for the agent that made sure that happened."

"Knowing you two, I'm sure this conversation is being recorded," said Reeves.

"I sure hope not," said Steele.

"It's not," said Harlow. "Agent Reeves, did you get a chance to look through the file we sent this morning?"

"I did. Please call me Joe. I think we're past the formalities stage," said Reeves.

"Call me Harlow, then," she said. "Is there anything else you can think of that you might need? We'll have aerial surveillance back on station in about four hours."

"Obviously, it would help immensely if we had images or firsthand reports of what's being stored in those warehouses," said Reeves. "I know the dots are not difficult to connect based on the imagery you've provided and the testimony of the sheriff and his deputies—but we're talking about mobilizing a major joint-agency raid on short notice. And to be entirely frank with you, getting the Joint Drug Task Force to move quickly on anything is difficult enough. Shoving evidence they didn't collect or vet into their faces and asking them to jump is going to be a stretch."

"We're talking at least a billion-dollar bust," said Decker. "More than half of those warehouses will be full tonight. Not to mention the paramilitary, pseudo-corporate group running this whole operation. That's the most interesting aspect, if you ask me. Pulling the mask off the bandits."

"Yeah. Well. Those bandits have lawyers. Usually armies of lawyers. Which is why we tend to move very carefully in these situations. There's nothing more frustrating than pulling the mask off a bank robber and watching them walk free on a technicality. Trust me, I've been there."

"All right. Let me ask you this," said Decker.

Reeves knew he wasn't going to like what was coming next.

"Shoot," said Reeves.

"No shit. What are the chances of the task force pulling off a raid tonight?" said Decker.

"Ten percent. Maybe," said Reeves.

"Shit," said Decker. "Okay. What about the chance of getting someone out to the reservation tonight—to sniff around the fence right around the time the helicopters arrive?"

"I really can't make any promises, Decker," said Reeves. "I wish I could, but once I hand this over and make my pitch, it's in their hands. I think we have a compelling case, and they're very unlikely to brush it aside. I just can't see them rushing into this tonight—unless you think we have more time."

"I don't know if we do," said Decker.

"Not even a few days?" said Reeves. "This base in Nevada doesn't look like the kind of thing you can fold up overnight like a carnival and drive away."

"Joe," said Senator Steele. "Our biggest concern here is losing the big fish. The marijuana isn't going anywhere, from what I gather. It's been transported to the Nevada facility for drying and processing. The only way they're going to make that disappear quickly is by burning it, and there will still be plenty of evidence left behind to file serious charges. But the leadership can disappear into the night, never to be seen again—leaving little behind to connect the operation with the organization responsible. We've seen this before. You could swoop in a week from now and arrest a hundred people at that site, and even the ones willing to cut a deal won't be able to pierce the bigger veil. These paramilitary corporations use proxies and cutouts. The government will get the big drug bust, which is a big win in itself, but the real conspirators and traitors—people like Jacob Harcourt—will write off the loss and get right to work on the next scheme."

"I like her speech better," said Reeves.

"I give speeches for a living, so I would hope that's the case," said Steele.

Reeves had a few minutes left before pulling into the parking lot.

"Decker. Harlow. If I can't pull off this miracle you're proposing, what's your plan?"

"I don't know if I should tell you," said Decker. "Given that you're a sworn federal law enforcement agent."

"Don't give me that shit," said Reeves. "We're past that point in our relationship."

"Fair enough," said Decker. "Here's the bottom line. I have a plan to get everyone of any consequence off that mountain and to the facility in Nevada. Once they arrive, we'll do whatever is necessary to keep them there. That's nonnegotiable. These people will scatter to the wind if given the chance."

"Dammit, Decker. That's in the middle of nowhere! A couple DEA agents and the Pyramid Lake Paiute Tribal Police Department will not be equipped to handle the kind of situation you're describing."

"Then you better start cheerleading for some more support," said Decker. "At least enough to block the road out of there."

"Decker, I'm willing to look the other way for Senator Steele, but I won't let you put those agents and police officers in danger," said Reeves. "Sorry, Senator, but I can't let that happen."

"I don't believe Decker would intentionally do such a thing," said Steele.

"I think what Decker was trying to say, but didn't—because he's Decker," said Harlow, "is that if the task force can't muster a large enough force to safely raid the facility, then you should make sure that the tribal police are warned not to approach the facility. Same with any small groups of agents on the scene."

"That sounds more like what I had in mind," said Decker.

"Amazing how that works when you have smart women around to interpret, a.k.a. fix things, for you," said Reeves.

"I only associate with the best and the brightest women for that very reason," said Decker.

"We're also pretty good at detecting bullshit, Decker," said Steele. "So you might want to quit while you're ahead."

"Good point, Senator," said Decker.

"Final question before I professionally embarrass myself in front of two longtime colleagues on a Sunday morning," said Reeves. "Do I have any leeway regarding the timeline? Does this have to happen tonight?"

Harlow answered, which was a good thing given his impatience at the moment.

"Based on our calculations, they've moved about a billion dollars' worth of product into those warehouses already. They started filling the warehouses shortly after the motel shooting, so it's pretty clear they were nervous about losing everything—and I think it's fair to assume they're still extremely nervous. We don't think it would take much for them to order a complete evacuation."

"And leave the other billion behind?" said Reeves.

"Yes," said Harlow. "The most damning evidence that connects the real puppet masters to this operation is the leadership crew running the show on the mountain. They'll bolt at the first sign of trouble, and we can't guarantee when that'll be or where they'll go. Our aerial surveillance asset is amazing, but it's not capable of twenty-four-hour operations. Decker's plan controls both the when and the where, which is why we want to execute it tonight, while our surveillance bird is topped off and capable of an extended chase. Even if you can't wrangle support from the task force tonight, we think we're better off forcing the evacuation and . . ."

"Working our magic at the facility in Nevada," said Decker.

"I really don't want to know what that means," said Reeves.

"Neither do I," said Senator Steele.

"Is there any way I can talk you out of this?" said Reeves.

"No," said Decker.

"I didn't think so," said Reeves, debating whether to share the only bit of information he'd withheld to this point.

Decker deserved to know, and if there was any connection—the dirtbags on the other end of this mountain mess deserved what was coming.

"Hey, Decker?"

"Yeah?"

"I got a fingerprint hit on one of the two guys that inexplicably died of five-point-fifty-six-millimeter aneurysms in front of your motel room," said Reeves. "Former Constellation Security employee."

"That's a defunct Aegis subsidiary," said Senator Steele.

Aegis had been Jacob Harcourt's military contracting corporation, until Decker put it, along with Harcourt, out of business—after learning the businessman had ordered the murder of his wife and son.

"Yes. Which is why I'm not pushing back any harder against Decker's proposed plan," said Reeves. "If there's even a trace of Jacob Harcourt, or his ilk, in the system, I want it purged just as badly."

CHAPTER FORTY-SIX

Sheriff Long shook Decker's hand, giving him a quick pat on the shoulder.

"I'm not going to miss you and the rest of this motley crew," said Long.

Decker laughed, shaking his head. "We're not going to miss you, either."

"So. You guys really think this'll work?" said Long. "We're not talking about any old hornet's nest up there. This nest can produce quite a sting, from what I've seen."

"It'll work," said Decker. "And I don't anticipate any sting. Just make sure you have enough SWAT officers, or whatever you call them here, on-site to deter those idiots from making a bad decision."

"I have the equivalent of SWAT from Trinity and Mendocino Counties working on this with me. Close to sixty officers," said Long.

"Sounds like you have this locked down," said Decker.

"We do," said Long. "How is your end looking?"

"Like it did when I first came up with the idea," said Decker. "Sketchy at best."

"Hey. As long as the first part works, I'm a happy camper," said Long, followed by a hearty laugh. "Seriously, though. I really do hope you jam these people good. They deserve it."

"One way or the other, someone is getting jammed tonight," said Decker. "I just hope it doesn't turn out to be me."

"Somehow, I very much doubt that," said Long. "You strike me as a survivor."

"That's one of the few things I'm good at," said Decker. "We'll head out fifteen minutes after you leave. I'll call you when we're on the road. It's critical that they see you driving in the opposite direction."

"I know," said Long.

"Let Detective Hodges do his job," said Decker. "The first step toward retaking Humboldt County will be over in less than thirty minutes—without a shot fired."

"Hopefully," said Long.

"Let me rephrase that," said Decker. "Without a single law enforcement casualty."

"I almost like the sound of that better," said Long. "Take care, Decker. Let me know if you're ever up this way again and get a speeding ticket or something."

"Why? So you can lock me up for the night?"

"Funny man," said Long, before taking off for his SUV.

Less than a minute later, the sheriff and all his deputies were gone, headed north up the highway toward downtown Eureka. Decker glanced through the archway leading out of the motor court, his eyes briefly scanning the two-story hotel across the street. The sheriff's departure must be causing a stir up on the mountain. Thoughts of revenge maturing now that the Humboldt County Sheriff's Department was out of the picture. He'd made sure to say goodbye to the sheriff in plain view, to help that along.

Harlow stepped out of the electronic support room and joined him at the edge of the parking lot, out of the hotel's line of sight. She looked exhausted, like everyone else in the compound. They'd managed to catch a few hours of scattered sleep after the sheriff and his deputies had left for the night, waking up early to start planning tonight's mission. Unfortunately, there was little prospect of rest for any of them between now and tomorrow morning.

"The team picked up heavy satellite traffic across the street as soon as the sheriff drove off," said Harlow. "A lot of encrypted radio chatter as well."

"They're probably debating what to do now that we're exposed," said Decker.

Joshua appeared in the doorway, looking concerned.

"Three of the six presumed shooters have started moving toward the lobby," he said.

"That was a quick debate," said Harlow.

"Thanks, Josh. Let us know if they move the other three," said Decker, turning back to Harlow. "They're just shifting assets around. That's common when any major change to a target profile occurs. The sheriff leaving and taking his deputies back to town constitutes a major change."

"Yeah. It's a serious change to our defensive posture," said Harlow. "I'm a little concerned about what happens when you drive away with the rest of it."

"If they don't bite," said Decker, "we'll swing back into town through the neighborhoods to the east and sneak back into the compound. Honestly, nothing would make me happier than ambushing those smug assholes right here—right in front of their surveillance team. The more I think about it, the better it sounds."

"What if they hit us as soon as you drive out of sight?" said Harlow.

"You know how to trigger the Claymores, right?" said Decker.

She nodded.

"Then you have nothing to worry about."

Harlow shook her head. "I'm tossing those in the Pacific when this is over. I can't believe you were keeping them at our office."

"I was holding them for someone," said Decker. "And they're perfectly safe until armed."

"I was more concerned about the possibility of spending the rest of my life in prison if they were ever discovered," said Harlow.

"I'm pretty sure they're covered under our dangerous weapons permit."

"I'm pretty sure they aren't," said Harlow, before putting her arms around his waist. "I wish we didn't have to split up right now."

"We'll be back together in an hour," said Decker. "If you're still insistent on coming to Nevada."

"I'm not missing out on that," said Harlow.

"It could get ugly," said Decker. "Reeves didn't sound too positive about his meeting this morning. We're going into this with the assumption that we'll have to do most of the heavy lifting out there. I'm still not sure what that will entail."

"We talked about this already," she said, before kissing him.

He held her tight, wishing she hadn't insisted on coming with them to the Nevada site. With a billion dollars at stake, the puppet masters running this show would throw everything at their disposal toward saving it, especially when it became painfully obvious that the army laying siege to their fortune was composed of four people.

Brad walked out of the electronic support room.

"Time to gear up," he said. "Still only three on the move at the motel. They're most likely prestaging a tail—in case we bolt without much notice."

Decker gave her a quick kiss before checking his watch.

"Then let's give them what they want. On the road in nine minutes."

CHAPTER
FORTY-SEVEN

Roland McDermott peeked through the hotel room curtains with a pair of binoculars, trying to make sense of the scene unfolding at the motel across the street. The surveillance guys had called him into the room when Decker had stopped in the middle of the motor court and started chatting with Brad Pierce—both of them kitted up like they were headed off to war. Less than fifteen minutes ago, dressed in khaki pants and a gray hoodie, Decker had stood in nearly the same spot shaking Sheriff Long's hand. Something was definitely up.

Two more mercenaries joined them, rifles slung across their magazine pouch–laden ballistic vests. Decker patted a few of them on the shoulder, and they all walked out of view inside the motor court. This didn't look good at all. Several seconds later, his fears were confirmed. Two SUVs backed up into view, each pausing before tearing out of the parking lot and through the archway. Neither vehicle stopped for traffic, which caused a discordance of squealing tires and car horns in front of the motel.

He followed the SUVs as far as he could before the edge of the window cut off his view.

"Call this in to Tin Man Operations immediately and request instructions," said McDermott, sprinting to the door. "Two SUVs just departed the motel in a hurry, headed south on 101. Three shooters per vehicle. Fully kitted. Request instructions."

He was out the door before they responded.

"Stinger One. I need you headed south on 101 immediately," said McDermott. "Decker flew the coop. You're looking for a gray Toyota Land Cruiser and a dark-green Nissan Pathfinder. Three guys per vehicle. Do your best to remain covert. I'll catch up with you as quickly as I can."

"Copy that," said the team leader sitting in the parking lot. "Is the motel compound unguarded?"

"I wouldn't consider it unguarded, but it's a soft target at this point," said McDermott.

"You might want to mention that to Tin Man," he said. "Could be a treasure trove of intelligence waiting for us in there."

"I will," said McDermott, reaching his hotel room door.

He slid his card into the reader and flung the door open when it flashed green. The two remaining members of his Stinger team, Gary and Baker, scrambled to pack one of their oversize black nylon duffel bags. Gary grabbed the tactical vests stacked on the bed, while Baker swiped a second duffel bag off the floor.

"Did you load the spare magazines?" said McDermott, pointing at the packed duffel bag.

"Yep," said Gary. "Four each."

"That's more than enough," said McDermott, taking off. "We need to go now."

McDermott sprinted with his team down the stairwell, barely slowing as they crossed the lobby. They were speeding south on 101 less than three minutes after he'd first observed Decker scooting out of the motel with a convoy of mercenaries.

While Gary unpacked the duffel bag and started readying weapons, McDermott contacted the surveillance team back at the motel.

"OVERLOOK, this is STINGER Actual. Both vehicles in pursuit. Any instructions from TIN MAN?"

"TIN MAN requests that you establish direct contact," said the surveillance tech.

"Copy that. Keep a close eye on the motel. Anything changes over there, and you contact TIN MAN directly. We'll be out of radio range soon. Out," said McDermott. "STINGER One, how are we looking?"

"I'm pretty sure we have the Pathfinder ahead. It'll be another minute before I'm one hundred percent sure. We're driving as fast as we dare," said Chuck.

"Sounds good. Don't push your speed," said McDermott. "The last thing we need is a run-in with one of the sheriff's deputies. Are you running your driver alert system?"

"Affirmative. No hits so far. I think the sheriff's department has bigger concerns than speeders right now."

"I agree, but we can't afford to lose them, so play it safe," said McDermott. "We're going to press our luck a little, since you've already cleared the way. Hopefully."

"Any idea what his game is?" said Chuck.

"My guess is he's headed to the Alderpoint area to try and infiltrate the compound," said McDermott. "TIN MAN identified everyone in their group as former SOCOM or some kind of high-speed shit. Evaluated at Tier Two or better. They're entirely capable of getting inside the EMERALD CITY."

"Shit. No pressure," said Chuck. "See you in a few."

"Yep," said McDermott, removing the satellite phone in one of his cargo pockets.

He dialed TIN MAN Operations, immediately connecting with one of the techs.

"This is Roland McDermott," he said.

"Stand by for Tin Man Actual," said the tech.

McDermott shook his head. Like Trenkor wasn't standing two feet away. "Standing by."

"Stinger, this is Tin Man," said Trenkor, less than a second later. "What's your read of Decker's intentions?"

That seemed to be the question du jour.

"They were kitted up heavy. The four I saw, at least," said McDermott. "More than just weapons and ammo. A few rucksacks, too. I think they're planning on taking a field trip through the woods up in Alderpoint."

"They're good, but not that good," said Trenkor.

"Maybe not," said McDermott. "But Decker's got a screw loose. After that Claymore business, I wouldn't put anything past him."

"Yeah," said Trenkor, sounding distracted.

His radio crackled. "Stinger One confirms both the Pathfinder and the Land Cruiser ahead. We're maintaining our distance."

"Tin Man copied that. Nice work," said Trenkor.

"Thank you, sir."

"Let me know when you've linked up with Stinger One," said Trenkor. "We're going to identify some long stretches of highway between here and Garberville. I want you to take them out before they reach that town. That gives you about an hour."

"Traffic is light, so we should be able to make it happen at the first stretch you pass along," said McDermott.

"Operations will pass the recommended locations along to your tablet," said Trenkor.

Shit. He'd left the tablet back in the hotel room.

"Sir, we rushed out so fast, I left the tablet behind," said McDermott.

"Operations will come up with a work-around. We're tracking your vehicles, so it shouldn't be a problem," said Trenkor. "What's the status of the group at the motel?"

"OVERLOOK reported all quiet at the motel immediately prior to this call," said McDermott. "I told OVERLOOK to contact you directly if anything changes."

"TIN MAN Ops will reach out to them."

"For what it's worth, sir. The motel group is a soft target without Decker and those mercs around."

"Copy that. Let's get rid of Decker first and then turn our attention back to the motel. We'll be in touch shortly," said Trenkor, ending the call.

The more McDermott thought about it, the more he wondered if the better choice would have been taking down the motel. STINGER One could follow Decker until Trenkor sent another covert team down from the mountain. The takedown might not happen until after Garberville, but what did it matter? McDermott, backed up by two of the surveillance guys, could easily slice through the motel. Three private investigators, no matter how experienced, were no match for his team, and the remaining support staff didn't look like it could put up much of a fight.

He glanced at the phone but dismissed the idea just as quickly. He'd basically floated the idea by Trenkor, who summarily rejected it, so there was nothing to gain by bringing it up again. In fact, he had everything to lose by suggesting a plan that leadership hadn't considered.

McDermott hadn't seen it in practice at Athena Corp, but outshining your boss was widely recognized as a bad move, and he'd seen it bite more than a few people in the ass during his time in uniform. No. He'd let this play out as ordered. Plus, he looked forward to wiping these smears out of existence.

He'd become good friends with Mike Loftis over the past couple of years—to the point where their families had rented adjacent homes on the Outer Banks for a rare two-week vacation. What Decker did to him was cowardly and unforgiveable. Fuck the motel idea. Time for payback.

"Why so glum?" said Baker, adjusting his grip on the steering wheel. "Bad news?"

"No," said McDermott. "Just thinking something through. It's nothing."

"This should cheer you up," said Gary, pushing a loaded MP7 submachine gun between the front seats.

"I'm smiling already," said McDermott.

The MP7 was perfect for this job. Compact and easily maneuverable inside their vehicle, it packed an outsize punch for its size—firing an armor-piercing bullet specifically designed for the MP7 by the gun's manufacturer. The bullet could pass through a car door and retain more than enough velocity to pierce soft body armor. They couldn't penetrate ceramic ballistic plates or helmets, but Decker's people hadn't been wearing helmets, and most of the bullets they fired would be aimed at head or neck level.

A few minutes later, he located STINGER One through a spotting scope Gary had tossed in the duffel bag. Traffic was still light, so he had Baker maintain their speed. Anything faster might be noticeable by one of their target vehicles. Decker may not suspect a six-man assault team was trailing him, but he'd be on high alert for a tail. He attached a concealable headset to the radio and contacted Chuck in the lead vehicle.

"STINGER One, we have you in sight," said McDermott. "I think I have a visual on Decker's little convoy. Your spacing looks good. I'm going to have my back seater drop out of sight. Three to a car might look a little off, especially with two vehicles trailing. Traffic is going to seriously thin after Fortuna, leaving us pretty exposed."

"Yeah. Pretty much screams 'kill team,'" said Chuck. "I think it's too late for us to change our configuration. I guarantee they've been looking back. Suddenly going from three to two would be a red flag."

McDermott did a quick mental calculation.

"We should catch up with you in about two minutes," said McDermott. "I'll keep a car or two between us. TIN MAN is going to send us some recommended kill zones along 101. I'm thinking we'll do a drive-by."

"I'll be here," said Chuck.

Fortuna passed by in a flash, its two highway exits removing nearly all the southbound traffic around them, including the two separating STINGER One from STINGER Two. Cars sporadically zipped in the opposite direction. They were too exposed at this point. A quick glance over his shoulder yielded a less-than-optimal solution.

"Baker, slow down and let one of the cars behind us pass by," said McDermott.

"I was thinking the same thing," said Baker, the SUV rapidly decelerating.

McDermott triggered his radio with a remote handpiece.

"STINGER One, we're dropping back to give you some room."

"Wait! The Land Cruiser just put on its turn signal," said Chuck. "Shit. Now the Pathfinder's turn signal is on, and I can see a green exit sign up ahead. Where the fuck are they headed?"

Now he really wished he hadn't left the tablet behind. None of them carried a smartphone. They were strictly prohibited for security reasons. Only Athena Corp–issued electronic devices were permitted. This was about to get really embarrassing.

"It doesn't matter. We have to follow them. I don't have my tablet," said McDermott, pressing "Send" on his satellite phone. "I'm seeking help from TIN MAN. Stand by."

The call connected.

"TIN MAN—"

"This is STINGER Actual. Decker is getting off the highway. We're following him, but I have no idea if this is legit. It could be some kind of countersurveillance move."

"Stand by."

Fuck your standby. His earpiece crackled.

"This is STINGER One. Both vehicles just exited the highway," said Chuck.

"Did you copy that, TIN MAN Operations?" said McDermott, scanning the highway ahead.

The two vehicles had indeed veered off the highway. STINGER One had already activated its turn signal.

"STINGER, this is TIN MAN Ops. Based on your position, this is the exit for Route 36, which connects to the northernmost point of Alderpoint Road in Bridgeville, about twenty-two miles east of the exit. It's an entirely legitimate approach to Alderpoint," said the operations tech. "Maintain your surveillance and stand by for intercept instructions. Intercept will occur prior to Alderpoint Road."

"Got it," said McDermott, ending the call and contacting STINGER One via radio. "Chuck, we're good to go. They're headed east on Route 36. It's an alternate way into Alderpoint. We'll hit them at some point in the next twenty miles."

"All right. I'm backing off a little," said Chuck.

"Same here," said McDermott. "I'll probably stay out of sight on 36. I'm guessing it's a two-laner."

"We'll know in a moment."

Baker followed STINGER One off the highway, each of them coming to a brief stop at the top of the exit, before turning onto the overpass. STINGER One had just started to cross over the highway when McDermott noticed a swarm of SUVs in his side-view mirror. *Shit.* A quick look over his shoulder confirmed they were police vehicles. Before he could activate his radio, Chuck's voice filled his left ear.

"I have some kind of police—fuck, we're cut off to the east."

STINGER One came to a tire-screeching halt halfway across the overpass, a wall of police SUVs skidding to a stop to block them from crossing.

"What are we doing?" said Baker, slowing them down.

McDermott did the math. They couldn't back up or turn around in time before they were trapped on the overpass. His satellite phone buzzed, displaying OVERLOOK COMPROMISED. The hotel team was gone, too. The whole thing had been a setup. Baker repeated his question.

"Stop the vehicle," said McDermott.

He dialed TIN MAN Operations—and the call immediately failed. That was it for them. Disavowed. Disowned. Discarded. Whatever you wanted to call it. If they were lucky, Athena Corp would anonymously provide them with an attorney, mostly to prevent them from taking a deal or leaking sensitive information. Damage control until they could arrange a more permanent solution.

"Are we surrendering?" said Gary, still lying down across the seats.

Gunfire erupted from STINGER One, Chuck's team quickly coming to the same nihilistic conclusion—and answering that question for all of them.

CHAPTER

FORTY-EIGHT

Two miles east of the ambush site, Decker waited in the Hydesville Elementary School parking lot for Detective Hodges. Judging by the level of gunfire he'd heard in the distance as they'd sped east, he guessed they might be here for a while, which is why he was surprised when a Humboldt County Sheriff's Department SUV pulled into the parking lot just a few minutes after they settled into the empty lot, followed by an ancient-looking Chevy Suburban.

"We good with this?" said Nix, a mercenary neither Brad nor Decker had met before yesterday.

"Yeah," said Decker, opening his door. "We're totally good."

Nix came highly recommended by Garza, but she made Decker entirely nervous—almost all the time. He guessed that she had spent most of her contract time in war zones or parts of the world where flashing a weapon worked as one of the raw currencies that kept you alive. She still had a thing or two to learn about subtlety and US laws, not that Decker was the best example.

Less than a half hour ago, he'd seriously tried to argue that the extremely controversial weapons permit Senator Steele had bent over backward to secure for them somehow covered the use of an antipersonnel mine strictly regulated by the 1997 mine ban treaty. Harlow hadn't bought it. He guessed Nix would hold it against him if he tried to regulate her too strictly. Maybe that was why Garza had insisted she should be part of the Nevada team. She wouldn't hesitate to call him out when he desperately needed it.

The sheriff's department vehicle blocked the entrance as the Suburban settled into the space next to them. He wasn't surprised to see Sheriff Long's smiling face in the driver's seat. Decker signaled for Brad and Nix to stay in the SUV.

"Sheriff Long, you sneaky bastard," said Decker, heading around the front of the sheriff's meticulously maintained relic.

"Pays to know the back roads," said the sheriff.

"This is an antique," said Decker.

"Nineteen seventy. So—yeah," said Long. "I spend more time working on her than driving her."

Decker shook his hand, feeling unusually reassured to see him. He could see how the sheriff had been reelected three times.

"The ambush?" said Decker. "Hodges?"

"He's a little busy. Five deputies were transported to St. Joseph's. One might have to be flown to the trauma center in Redding. No fatalities on our side," said Long. "Hodges told me about your little side talk. Good thing he listened."

"Hodges knew what I was talking about. He'd seen them at work during his time in the Army," said Decker. "Miserable fucking losers pining away for whatever combat-zone vacuum they previously inhabited. No way they were surrendering. When he left the motel, I wasn't sure he completely got it."

"The whole thing was over in less than five seconds, so I'd say he did," said Long. "And one of the mercenaries surrendered without firing a shot. They found him in the back seat of one of the vehicles."

"Sole survivor?" said Decker.

"Looks like it," said Long. "The other guy isn't long for this world."

"What about the hotel?" said Decker.

"Three captured. Nothing destroyed," said Long. "They found a bunch of gear in the other two rooms, including some kind of tablet."

"Seriously?" said Decker. "You need to get Laura Swanson involved immediately, and she needs to contact Sacramento and the FBI. You have four direct witnesses to play off each other. That's huge."

"I'm still processing all of this," said Long.

"They need to be put in protective custody. Trust me when I say that the criminal masterminds behind all of this will not be happy to learn of their capture."

Long gave him a skeptical look.

"Sheriff, I spent two years in federal prison—under constant attack by the kind of people you're dealing with here. They'll be dead within a month if they aren't given special protection."

"How did you survive?" said Long.

"Pure spite—and pure fucking luck," said Decker. "I should not be standing here right now."

The sheriff cracked a rare grin. "What now?"

"Same plan. My team is en route to the mountain. They'll get as close as they can without triggering any of the sensors and wait for nightfall. You'll move at dusk and prestage on Alderpoint Road, where we entered yesterday—but you will not go any farther than that."

Long started to form a response.

"Sheriff, I can't stress this enough. You're only there to provoke a response. Same with my team," said Decker. "They'll see you with their remote cameras, and that's good enough. If you send deputies up the mountain, you'll carry more than you care to count back down the mountain—in body bags. Hodges got the jump on those guys, and he still took casualties. My people have the same orders. Provoke from a safe distance."

"What if it doesn't work?"

"It'll work," said Decker.

"That's it?" said Long. "You normally have a lot to say when I ask a question like that."

"Sheriff. Harvey, if I may. I pretty much ran out of bullshit about thirty minutes ago," said Decker. "I'm running on bullshit fumes right now."

Long broke into a prolonged laugh, which dragged Decker along. When the laughter settled, the sheriff shook his hand.

"We'll coordinate with that Garza fellow. He has my number, and I have theirs. No heroics. I promise."

"Nothing wrong with heroics. Just not tonight," said Decker.

"Why do I get the feeling you rarely take your own advice?" said Long.

"Because I don't," said Decker. "We'll be fine."

"Then I'll let you get on with it," said Long. "Watch yourself out there."

"Always do. It just doesn't always help," said Decker.

"We'll see," he said. "Ms. Mackenzie is on her way to the airport with a sheriff's department escort. The rest of your team is packing up at the motel. This may sound rude, but I hope I don't see any of you again for at least a month."

"Likewise. Though I suspect we'll be back," said Decker. "I'm guessing that your coast is one of Northern California's best-kept secrets."

"I don't know what you're talking about, Decker," said Long, before getting back into his vintage beast and departing.

Decker rejoined Brad and Nix in the SUV.

"All good?" said Brad.

"The plan is a go," said Decker. "But I'm a little concerned about what happened at the ambush site. The mercs didn't back down—at all. We might need to rethink our plan for the Nevada site."

"I'll call Bernie. I'm sure he has a trick or two he can arrange to level the playing field," said Brad.

"Or level the facility," said Decker.

"I'm not going there," said Brad.

Decker gripped the steering wheel, thinking about Harlow.

"We may not have a choice."

CHAPTER FORTY-NINE

Trenkor stepped out of the operations trailer with Jason Watts in tow. They were headed to the perimeter of the compound closest to the trailer park. They passed by the vehicle lot, Trenkor taking note of the latest empty spaces, until they reached the one-lane, hard-packed dirt road that ran along the entire perimeter tree line. He stood with Watts in the same spot where their problems had begun, nearly two weeks ago, when Charles Bowen's skinhead idiots had botched a simple prisoner transfer.

He couldn't help but think that if they had learned about Brett Hale's connection to Senator Steele during an interrogation and passed that information along to OZ, they could have figured out a way to prevent the premature collapse of EMERALD CITY. They could have paid the kid off and told him to keep his mouth shut or they'd kill him. Or forced him to check in with his parents and report that he was fine but wouldn't be able to talk to them for another three to four weeks due to the busy harvest.

Hell, they could have booted him off the mountain with a suitcase of cash and threatened to kill his family if he told anyone about what he saw. Athena Corp or one of its partners had the resources to watch Hale closely and put an end to him if he started to act squirrelly. Or just wait until the harvest was finished and run him over with a car. Accidents happen. Instead, pieces of Brett Hale still littered the forested hillside about three hundred yards down this draw.

"I assume we're not out here to take in the fresh air?" said Watts.

"Actually, that sounds like a great idea," said Trenkor, before taking a deep breath and exhaling.

Watts chuckled, shaking his head. "I can't believe we didn't see that coming."

"We underestimated their electronics capabilities. Twice," said Trenkor. "They clearly have the ability to detect, analyze, and track a wide range of radio frequencies and strengths. Do you think they could spoof the motion sensors? We have to assume they can detect them somehow."

Watts stared off into the trees, appearing to be deep in thought.

"I really don't see how. I mean—anything is possible, but we've put this gear through the wringer," said Watts, shaking his head. "I suppose, with a lot of patience, they could locate a sensor. But they'd have to get close enough to detect the device's check-in burst, without setting off the sensor."

"Check-in burst?"

"Each sensor checks in with the sensor network hub, to tell us they're still operating. The hub sets the check-in times, which follow no detectable pattern. If a sensor fails to report, we investigate immediately. We can also change the frequency of that check-in to tighten the window of opportunity an intruder would have if they managed to disable one of the sensors."

"But you don't seem to think that's possible?"

"I see two ways, but they're both highly improbable. One is for them to hack the signal. The other is shoot the sensor and kill it."

"The second option doesn't sound all that difficult," said Trenkor.

"The bullet would have to simultaneously and completely destroy both the outward-facing motion sensor and the antitamper device, which we've never been able to achieve in our tests. The antitamper device is too sensitive, and it's offset from the sensor," said Watts. "On top of that, one of our listening devices would pick up the sound of the bullet smashing the sensor."

"Let's increase the frequency of those check-ins," said Trenkor. "It'll give away the sensor locations, but that's a trade-off I'm willing to accept. Do you agree?"

"I do," said Watts.

"And the hacking option?"

"Even less likely. They'd need to have the hacker and a pretty serious laptop rig in the field with them, in addition to some sophisticated communications gear to interface with the laptop. Even then, there's no guarantee the hack will be successful."

"What about some kind of darknet, black hat, off-the-shelf program specifically designed to hack this brand of sensor?" said Trenkor. "I know that sounds ridiculous."

"Not as ridiculous as you might think," said Watts. "But Athena's security gurus check for that kind of stuff and haven't identified a Bitcoin-buyable hack."

"Then the billion-dollar question—literally—comes down to the six commandos that disappeared from the grid less than an hour ago. Should I be overly concerned?"

"Are you asking me whether I think they can shoot their way inside the perimeter and fuck up the compound?"

"Pretty much," said Trenkor.

"I don't see that happening," said Watts. "They'd be fighting uphill on rough terrain, against a highly trained, well-equipped defense force. And they'd be fighting while moving through a dense layer of antipersonnel mines. I'd be surprised if any of them got as far as this road, where they'd quickly be surrounded and killed. That said, they're definitely planning something."

"Knowing everything you know about EMERALD CITY, what would you do to inflict maximum damage against us?"

"I'd try to take down one of the Sikorskys—right on top of the compound," said Watts, without skipping a beat. "They've been here two nights in a row, at roughly the same times. I'd be racking my brain trying to figure that one out."

"I really don't like you sometimes," said Trenkor.

"I'll take that as a compliment," said Watts.

"So. How do we protect the helicopters?" said Trenkor.

"Well, assuming that Decker does not have access to a surface-to-air missile system, we're talking about a small-arms threat. Rifle or light-machine-gun fire. Possibly fifty-caliber sniper rifle. Because of the thick forest canopy surrounding the compound, they'd have to place themselves directly in the path of the oncoming helicopter and shoot at a very high angle. They'd almost have to shoot directly overhead, which doesn't give them much time to put bullets on a fast-moving target. Half of the bullets would still probably hit the trees.

"They'd have to get extremely lucky to disable one of our helicopters that way. And I don't see how they could hit one of the helicopters while it's directly above the compound. They'd have to fire from the perimeter tree line or inside the perimeter to avoid the same angle issue. The only other way would be for them to climb a tree outside of the sensor line and fire at the helicopters while approaching or departing the landing zone. Actually, that doesn't sound like a bad plan."

Trenkor patted Watts's shoulder. "If you could come up with that on the fly, in thirty seconds, I guarantee they've already thought of it. This is all they've been doing for the past twenty-four hours. I'll contact KANSAS and have the helicopters circle the compound and approach from the west."

"Perfect. I'll post snipers and a two-forty team in the tower above the operation's trailer. If Decker engages our helicopters from the tree-tops, we'll hit them hard and fast," said Watts. "What do you think about using the Chinook as a rapid response asset? We could keep it at a safe altitude and use it to pounce on threats. They can also scan the forest with infrared and night-vision optics."

"I like the idea," said Trenkor.

"The only problem will be fuel. We need to minimize their time in the air, and we can't do this twice a night for two more nights, unless the Sikorskys deliver more fuel. We only budgeted fuel for the evacuation run with the Chinook."

"That won't be a problem," said Trenkor. "OZ moved up the evacuation timeline by a day. We leave with tonight's second transport run."

"When did that order come down?"

"One minute before I pulled you out for this chat," said Trenkor. "The powers that be wanted to evacuate us immediately after learning about what happened to McDermott's team, but I talked OZ into one more night of operations."

"Before you grilled me on our potential vulnerabilities?"

"If you told me Decker could easily breach the perimeter or shoot down one of the helicopters, I would have gone back to OZ and requested permission to evacuate," said Trenkor. "I only had one chance to change his mind. Right then and there. I had to take it. Every Sikorsky run from here to Nevada represents a two-hundred-and-fifty-million-dollar profit for Athena. Every run that doesn't happen repre-sents a two-hundred-and-fifty-million-dollar loss—that they'll more or less blame on us."

"A billion dollars isn't enough for them?" said Watts.

"The way I see it, the bigwigs wanted to cut this off at a billion dollars, and we're going to bring them another five hundred million by the end of tonight. They can't discount that."

"But they're still short five hundred million because Charles Bowen fucked up," said Watts.

Trenkor nodded and grinned. "OZ hired the Wolfpak. I had nothing to do with that, and OZ knows it. Everyone knows it. The collapse of EMERALD CITY is his cross to bear. If we salvage more than everyone expects, both OZ and his masters at Athena Corp will be happy."

"I'm too tired to contradict your logic," said Watts. "But it sounds about right. And I really don't see any way for Decker to shut us down."

"I guarantee he'll try. But we'll be more than ready to greet him—with superior numbers, firepower, and an unexpected trick or two," said Trenkor, not entirely confident in his decision to extend their stay on the mountain.

PART FIVE

Chapter Fifty

Harlow squeezed Decker's hand every time the aircraft jolted, fighting the urge to scream. She was deathly afraid of flying, to the point that she hadn't flown in over thirty years—a secret she'd kept until today. To be precise, she'd let the cat out of the proverbial bag about forty minutes ago, when Harry Bernstein leveled off after his gut-wrenching takeoff from Redding Airport.

She'd hoped that Bernie would continue the wild ride all the way to Pyramid Lake, so she could feign terror at the hands of a crazy pilot. But no. The son of a bitch eased the aircraft into a "comfortable flight," from what she'd been told by—everyone!

"I give you a ton of credit," said Decker.

"For what?"

"Everything you do, for starters," he said. "But the fact that you got on this particular aircraft—which was built in the sixties and refurbished a billion times to keep it flying, by the way—is a true testament to your awesomeness. Why didn't you tell me you were terrified of flying back at the motel? We could have driven you to the site. Maybe."

"It didn't occur to me at the time," she said, her other hand wrapped so hard around the seat netting that it was turning white. "How long until we land?"

"About ten minutes," said Decker, a pained look on his face.

"What?"

"Never mind. It's nothing."

"What!" she demanded, drawing Brad's and Nix's attention.

"The landing is going to be a little rough," said Decker. "We're setting down in the middle of the desert. Some kind of salt flat."

"I wish you hadn't told me that."

"Would it have made a difference?" he said, before kissing her cheek.

"Probably not," she said, burying her head in his shoulder.

Brad tried to make eye contact with Decker, but she caught him. His eyes darted upward.

"I'm embarrassing you," said Harlow. "Sorry."

"Nope," said Decker. "I'm ignoring Brad, and Nix doesn't seem to care one way or the other."

"She's a little scary."

"Just a little," said Decker.

Harry Bernstein emerged from the door leading out of the cockpit, a huge smile on his face. He held two shot glasses filled with clear liquid, one in each hand as he walked effortlessly across the swaying deck.

"I have something that might help," he said, taking a seat next to her.

"Won't that upset her stomach?" said Decker.

"This has nothing to do with her stomach," said Bernie.

"I don't think booze is going to calm her nerves," said Decker. "Not to mention that we actually have a mission ahead of us."

"This has nothing to do with nerves or the mission, either," said Bernie. "This is all about me and Ms. Mackenzie sharing a drink as friends."

"What is going on?" said Harlow.

"Just drink," said Bernie, placing a glass in her hand.

They clinked glasses and she downed the shot. Sambuca. Not so bad going down at all. He offered her the second glass.

"I thought we were drinking as friends?"

"Friends don't let friends drink and fly," said Bernie, taking the empty from her hand and replacing it with the other glass. "We'll have a proper drink in LA. Promise."

She downed the second glass, starting to feel a little more relaxed.

"Who's flying the plane while you're serving drinks?" said Decker.

"Quincy," said Bernie. "I finally lost my mind and trained someone to replace me. I know I'll regret it."

The intercom crackled. "I've already planned your retirement, old man."

"See what I mean?" said Bernie. "Seventy years old and they've already started plotting against me."

Brad laughed. "I hate to break it to you, Bernie, but Quincy has been plotting against you for like ten years."

"More like fifteen," said Quincy over the intercom. "But who's counting?"

Harlow felt a little better. The Sambuca had taken the edge off her anxiety. She just hoped it didn't hit her too hard. They had a long night ahead of them. Bernie took the empty glass.

"I bet you feel a teensy bit better," he said.

"Oddly enough, I do," she said, her grip on the cargo netting between them easing.

Bernie turned to Brad and Nix. "Quick briefing before we land."

The two operatives crossed the C-123's spacious cargo bay and crowded in next to the veteran pilot.

"We've uploaded all of the approach routes to the GPS units on your ATVs. I'm eighty percent sure we'll be able to drop you off at the northern end of Pyramid Lake, about twenty-three miles from your target. It's a hard-packed, flat-sand area, from what I can tell. We'll fly over a few times and let some very expensive equipment make the final call. If that spot is no good, you have two options. I know for a fact I can land in the Smoke Creek Desert, about twenty-five miles northwest of the primary location—"

"That's close to fifty miles off road on the ATVs," said Brad.

"Yep. Two hours, probably less. Aerial reconnaissance shows a good trail extending down the eastern side of the lake," said Bernie. "You'll be vibrating at the same frequency as the engine by the time you get to the target, but you'll get there."

"What's the other option?" said Decker.

"I land on Route 447, which runs north–south to the east of Pyramid Lake," said Bernie. "I assume traffic is light out here. I just need a thirty-second window to land and kick you out of the back. I could drop you ten miles north of the target, so they don't hear us. You can follow the road south and cut west into the hills a few miles away from your proposed observation point. I see all kind of trails on the aerial surveillance maps, which have been uploaded to your tablets."

"The best approach is from the landing at the northern tip of the lake?" said Decker.

"I think so," said Bernie. "The ATV trails down the eastern side of the lake are well defined and easy to follow at night. You keep the lake to your right. Doesn't get easier than that."

"We'll try that first and go with Route 447 as our backup. Fifty miles on ATVs—at night. I don't like the sound of that," said Decker. "Unless anyone disagrees."

"Good to go," said Brad, turning to Nix.

She shrugged.

"I'll take that as a yes all around," said Bernie. "Going once. Gone. We don't go around twice here."

They all laughed, except for Nix, who momentarily displayed a crooked grin before going back to deadpan.

"Last but not least," said Bernie. "You mentioned possibly needing more than surveillance?"

"I don't know if we're going to have any outside help once the helicopters reach the facility," said Decker. "There's only so much the four of us can do. We can't let the key players escape."

Harlow felt her death grip return, the stress of Decker's plan instantly negating the effects of the alcohol.

"I can follow them anywhere," said Bernie. "Doesn't matter if they take off in one of the helicopters or drive off in a chauffeured limo."

"But you can't watch them forever," said Decker. "And we won't be able to follow them if they leave the Pyramid Lake facility. Not if we're on the ground. We have to hit them when they land. Disable the helicopters and any vehicles that try to leave. I'm betting that if we create enough of a stir out there, the DEA-FBI task force will respond. At the very least, they'll call for reinforcements to cut off the roads leading out of there. Create some kind of formidable-enough obstacle for anything that gets out."

"Reeves's latest update didn't sound too promising. Three agents—one DEA and two FBI—from the Reno office," said Brad. "And they're keeping their distance."

"How in the hell did these people manage to build something like this on tribal land?" said Bernie.

"That question explains why we only have three agents—watching from a standoff range," said Brad. "Task force leadership recommended leaving the tribal police department out of this. We're probably talking about a legitimate business lease between the Paiute and whoever is running that facility, but you never know if a few pockets were lined in the process. If that's the case, they might tip off the facility owners."

"We have enough firepower to put this place out of business," said Decker.

Even Nix almost rolled her eyes at that one.

"I have a few tricks up my sleeve," said Bernie. "But if I use them—I gotta skedaddle right away. We're talking big trouble for me if I don't become a ghost in this airspace. I won't be able to pick you up."

"Then we'll hitch a ride home with the task force agents," said Decker, looking around for a few laughs. "Maybe we should pack a few MREs and some extra water. Just in case."

"Still not funny," said Harlow.

"I wasn't kidding," said Decker.

Harlow shook her head. She was starting to seriously question whether she would be more of a hindrance than a help on this mission. It had sounded a lot better before the prospect of federal involvement more or less evaporated. Maybe she'd let her thirst for revenge get the better of her judgment. Then again, if she didn't go, Decker might not be able to walk away if the odds shifted significantly against them. He seemed hell-bent on making sure that the mountaintop's leadership didn't escape. It wasn't enough to strip them of two billion dollars and send them packing.

"What's the plan if the whole thing starts to unravel?" said Harlow. "At any point during the attack."

"We'll be engaging the compound from elevated positions outside the fence," said Decker. "Assuming the helicopters are out of the picture, we'll fall back to the ATVs and head north along the lake. My guess is they won't follow us. They'll have their hands full with the mess we create. If they do send people after us, it'll be a small group we can handle."

"And there's always the spoilsport option," said Bernie. "But that means you'll be walking home. The ATVs carry enough fuel to get you from the Pyramid Lake drop point to the target and back—plus another fifteen to twenty miles with the extra gas cans. You might want to have your friends start driving in this direction."

Bernie's copilot interrupted them with an announcement.

"Three minutes!"

"I better get back up there," said Bernie. "Strap in. I may or may not put us down on the first pass."

"What about using that equipment to test the ground first?" said Harlow.

Bernie laughed. "The test equipment is our lights and landing gear."

"What?" she said, turning to Decker, who was also laughing.

"Don't worry. I've done this a few times before," said Bernie. "Need another drink?"

"Yes. But I'll pass," said Harlow.

"She's a keeper. Just make sure you keep 'er alive down there," said Bernie, giving her a wink before climbing the short set of stairs and disappearing through the cockpit door.

"How rough is this going to be?" said Harlow.

"Like medium turbulence," said Brad, heading back to his spot on the other side of the fuselage.

"I haven't flown in thirtysomething years!" she yelled over the engine noise.

Brad started to answer, but Decker cut him off with a hand wave and a shake of his head. Nix wore a shit-eating grin that Harlow recognized well. She could be staring in a mirror—on the ground. Not flying around in this ancient artifact. Brad fastened his harness and pulled it tight. Harlow instinctively checked hers, finding it exactly how she'd left it prior to takeoff. Snugly uncomfortable.

"Hang on back there!" said Bernie.

A few seconds later, the aircraft fell out of the sky. At least that was how it felt. Harlow closed her eyes and grabbed the nylon netting next to her thighs, gripping as tightly as possible. Decker squeezed her hand, a small act of reassurance that had no effect on her. In her mind, the plane was headed nose-first into the desert. In reality, it had already steadied a few hundred feet above the dry lake bed at the northern tip of Pyramid Lake, its landing gear edging toward the ground below.

A few seconds later, she got the sense that they were floating. As if the engine had quit propelling them forward. Harlow was about to scream when the aircraft jolted underneath her and rumbled for a few seconds, before floating back up. She tried to form words but couldn't. Decker squeezed her hand harder, just before the plane dropped and started shaking—the vibrations easing up as the aircraft slowed to a crawl.

"Please remain seated until the aircraft has come to a complete stop," said Bernie. "I just want to get into position for a quick departure. About twenty more seconds."

"Twenty seconds too long," said Harlow, finding that her voice worked again. "I'll gladly walk back to California."

"Careful what you ask for," said Decker. "Hey. You did awesome. That wasn't exactly what I had in mind for your thirty-year inaugural flight."

"You had other flights in mind for me?" said Harlow, the mere thought of getting back into the air again panicking her.

"No. No flights," said Decker. "Just a short ATV trip."

Harlow glanced toward the back of the cargo hold at the three equipment-laden ATVs strapped to the deck. What the hell had she gotten herself into?

Chapter

Fifty-One

Garza raised a closed fist, halting the team in a thicker-than-usual stand of trees. He shouldered his rifle and scanned uphill through the attached scope. Nothing. He'd thought he'd caught some movement up there, which freaked him out a little. According to the detailed aerial surveillance provided by Bernie's aircraft, he didn't think they'd come into visual contact with sentries at any point in their mission, unless the mountain's occupants hadn't installed a sensor barrier. If that turned out to be the case, they'd initiate a long-distance gunfight and quickly pull back to safety.

He signaled for the team to continue. They slowly and quietly walked single file through the thick forest scrub, gentle with every footfall and careful how they moved through the brush. Their passage generated the occasional low-grade rustle. Essentially silent beyond a few hundred feet. Possibly closer. More than quiet enough for this mission.

They could go quieter, but it would slow them down significantly, and they were already on a bit of a self-compressed timeline. It had taken them longer than expected to get here, mostly due to the Eel River, which flowed a lot stronger than any of them had anticipated. Safely crossing the river had cost them close to two hours. The forest's thick shadows and deepening hues would soon blend together, leaving them in near pitch darkness. An hour at most before they switched to night optics.

Ripley clicked his tongue a few times, a practiced sound barely audible outside of their formation. Garza glanced over his shoulder. The former SEAL signaled that they needed to talk. He crouched behind a sizable tree trunk and waited for Ripley to silently cross the twenty-foot gap between them. They had decided against using radios until it was absolutely necessary. The electronics voodoo Decker's support team had demonstrated over the past few days had convinced them it wasn't a smart idea. Ripley kneeled next to him and showed him the RF detector. The screen indicated three extremely faint, brief signal spikes. One almost directly ahead. The others offset from the first by about fifteen degrees on each side.

"How far?" whispered Garza.

"Impossible to say," said Ripley. "Decker's people said to stop and call it good when we first pick up a signal. Any further and we might stray into sensor range."

Garza removed a digital tablet from one of his cargo pockets, activating the map function. Decker's electronics wizards had created a GPS interactive overlay using the surveillance photos taken by Bernie's pilots. The tablet locked on to a few weak satellite signals penetrating the forest canopy, identifying their position on the map. He zoomed out to view the compound. They were roughly three-quarters of a mile away from the perimeter road surrounding the compound.

"Can you guess the spacing of the sensors?" said Garza.

"I can always guess," said Ripley. "But without knowing the sensor's range, it's an educated guess. Based on the directional shifts from the one dead ahead of us, I'd say fifty yards, maximum."

"That sounds about right, given the ranges I've seen before and the need for overlap coverage out here," said Garza.

"They could be spaced even tighter," said Ripley. "This is going to be easier than we thought."

"Don't say that," said Garza. "You trying to jinx us?"

He signaled for Max, a Marine-trained sniper quieter and faster than either Garza or Ripley, to join them. A few minutes later, Max and Ripley crept in opposite directions along the parallel axis of the sensor field, until the rapidly dimming forest almost swallowed them. Garza watched the radio frequency meter's digital display closely for any changes. Nothing. If either of them had triggered a sensor, the display would have showed a serious data spike in the same frequency range detected earlier.

Garza gave each of them a thumbs-up before hunkering down behind an enormous sequoia trunk, where he'd patiently wait for nightfall.

CHAPTER FIFTY-TWO

Carl Trenkor paced the darkened operations trailer, scanning the bright screens for any signs of trouble. So far, so good. The two Sikorskys had landed eight minutes and thirty-three seconds ago, according to the green digital timer mounted on one of the walls. Their empty metal storage boxes had been quickly swapped with the jam-packed containers while the refueling teams went to work. He expected them to be back in the air by the fifteen-minute mark.

About five hours later, they'd repeat the process, except all three helicopters would leave that time—taking any and all identifying pieces of EMERALD CITY with them. Trenkor couldn't wait. The past ten months had been shitty enough stuck up here, but the last week or so had been a living nightmare. Everything he'd worked so hard to achieve at Athena Corp had nearly been flushed down the toilet by a random political connection. He hoped they'd send him back to a fucking war zone next—so he could relax.

One of the screens changed while Trenkor watched, launching Watts out of his seat.

"Five sensors in the northwest sector just registered movement," said the operations tech in front of the screen.

"At the same time?" said Watts.

"Pretty much," said the tech.

Trenkor nearly pushed the guy out of his seat, trying to get a closer look at the sensor network diagram displayed on the screen. He didn't like what he saw. The breaches were spread out, skipping sensors in between. Watts immediately picked up on the same observation.

"Looks like three separate teams testing that sector for a weak point," said Watts. "Though I'm not sure what three teams of two could possibly hope to accomplish."

"Maybe they were reinforced along the way. Nothing would surprise me at this point," said Trenkor.

"I'm on it," said Watts, raising his radio to start coordinating a response.

The screen in front of them changed again, the word OFF-LINE blinking everywhere.

"The sensor network is down!" said the tech. "It's showing no connection."

Watts turned to Trenkor with a look of disbelief. "I'm getting nothing but a warbled tone when I try to talk on my radio. I think we're being jammed somehow."

"Jammed? By what? They don't have that capability," said Trenkor. "What about the cameras?"

"Still functional," said one of the other techs. "Same with the remote explosives. All of our satellite-based gear still functions."

"Take one of the Jeeps and alert the perimeter," said Trenkor. "Grab a sat phone and keep me posted."

Watts took a sat phone from the charging station and headed for the door. "I'll scramble the QRF to the northwest sector."

"Weapons free on the perimeter," said Trenkor. "Anything that moves out there is a hostile target."

"Got it."

"Sir! We have vehicles approaching the Dockweiler Road turnoff."

Watts paused in the doorway. "What am I doing?"

Trenkor thought it over quickly. The vehicles would never make it past the remote-triggered roadside bombs. The perimeter intrusion was the more pressing threat. If the hostiles got close enough to the helicopter landing zone to fire on the Sikorskys while refueling, they could blow the whole place sky high.

"Get the perimeter ready. Start with the sector closest to the helicopters. Don't say anything about evacuation," said Trenkor, turning his attention back to the screen. "What are we dealing with?"

"Law enforcement vehicles. About ten of them. All SUVs," said the tech. "I can read a few of their markings. Humboldt County and Trinity County."

"Wonderful. A multicounty effort," said Trenkor.

"Should I activate the remote zones?" said the tech.

Trenkor glanced at the digital clock: 10:31 and counting. It would take the sheriff's vehicles at least fifteen minutes to get up here, and that didn't take into account the various remote-activated spike strips he could deploy along the way to slow them down. The Sikorskys would be gone in five minutes, making room for the Chinook to land and start loading all Athena Corp personnel.

Everyone in the air and gone by the thirty-minute mark if everything went smoothly—but what were the chances of that? Especially with the radios jammed. He needed to buy them more time.

"Jeff, detonate the first three explosive devices on Dockweiler Road. That should make them think twice about heading up here," said Trenkor. "I'm headed over to the air operations trailer to let them know what's going on. Call me with any changes to the perimeter situation."

"Understood," said the tech. "Sir? What if the sheriff's convoy tears up the road, despite the warning?"

"If they start moving, activate zones one and two. Whatever survives those zones won't pose any serious threat to our perimeter. And,

Jeff?" said Trenkor. "Start preparing for an on-site scrub. We're not going to have time to take anything with us on the helicopter."

"So we're evacuating?" he said.

"Yes. As soon as the Sikorskys leave," said Trenkor. "Remember. We'll be the last to board that helicopter, no matter what happens. This place absolutely must be sanitized of anything that could lead back to Athena Corp."

The technicians nodded their understanding before Trenkor took off running. Dust kicked up by the helicopters' powerful rotors washed through the dark trailer park, stinging his eyes and making it difficult to see more than twenty feet in front of him. Two distant explosions echoed between the trailers, barely audible above the helicopter rotor chop. He really hoped those were the roadside bombs he'd ordered operations to detonate. If not, they were in serious trouble. When no additional blasts cut through the night, he dialed OZ.

"Right on time. Your crew doesn't mess around," said OZ.

"Are you alone right now?" said Trenkor.

"Yes. What's wrong?"

"I've ordered an immediate evacuation," said Trenkor.

"Did the helicopters—"

Of course that was all he cared about.

"The shipment should be on the way in a few minutes," said Trenkor, cutting him off. "But we've had an outer perimeter breach. Several motion sensors—"

"Have you identified—"

"Sir, I need you to listen right now," said Trenkor, fully aware that OZ hated to be interrupted. "We also have a convoy of ten sheriff's department vehicles lined up on Alderpoint Road—and our radios have been jammed."

"Jesus. I guess this is really it, then," said OZ, pausing for a moment. "You did a great job, Carl. Pack up the crew and get them out of there. I assume you'll be scrubbing the site in a hurry?"

"On-site protocols. We'll destroy the sensitive gear and burn down the operations trailers," said Carl. "Weapons, minimized ammunition load, radios, and night vision only on the helicopter. Everything else stays behind."

The scene would be surreal—a line of Athena Corp contractors tossing their ballistic plates, helmets, and excess ammunition into a pile before boarding the helicopter.

"Call me when you're in the air."

"I will," said Trenkor, ending the call that probably just ended his career.

CHAPTER FIFTY-THREE

Garza lay flat on the damp, spongy forest floor, most of his body hidden from the mountaintop behind a thick redwood trunk. The RF meter had stopped pinging, since everyone on the team had taken cover and gone still, but the increased activity along the perimeter verified that their mission had been successful—along with Harry Bernstein's confirmation from above.

He expected to back out of their position shortly. Sheriff Long's convoy should have pulled up on Alderpoint Road at this point, convincing whoever was in charge up there that the compound was under imminent threat and triggering a full evacuation.

Since his team had obviously triggered the motion detectors, Garza didn't see any reason to maintain radio silence.

"Rip. Max. What are you seeing up there?" said Garza over the radio.

"Looks about the same," said Ripley. "Maybe twenty heat signatures compressed into a hundred-yard space along the perimeter. Nothing moving in our direction, as far as I can tell. But it's kind of hard to say with all of the trees in the way."

"Max?" said Garza.

"I concur with Rip's assessment. Doesn't look like they're leaving the perimeter."

Garza was having some trouble hearing them over the constant drumbeat of the helicopters inside the compound.

"Say again?" said Garza.

Ripley repeated what he had said.

"Copy that, Rip," said Garza. "Has anyone heard the Chinook lately?"

"Negative," said Ripley.

"Same here," said Max. "With all that racket up there, I don't think we'd hear it until it was right on top of us."

"I agree," said Garza. "Stay sharp."

He was nervous about the Chinook, which had overflown them a few times while they waited for the green light to advance on the sensors. His team was wrapped up pretty tightly in thermal protective clothing, but there was no way to completely conceal their infrared signatures, especially against the kind of sophisticated optics the helicopter would employ.

If the mountaintop commander sent the Chinook after them, they'd have a problem on their hands. Coordinated rifle fire from his team might initially discourage the pilot, but once the helicopter gunner got his shit together—game over. They'd be outgunned from above. A worst-case scenario. Garza didn't think they'd risk sending the Chinook into a fight, since it looked to be their primary method of evacuation, but the thought of bullets raining down on the team left him feeling uneasy.

"Copy that. I'm going to check in with our eye in the sky," said Garza.

Harry's C-123, circling high above, was the only reason he'd agreed to approach the compound on foot. Garza had been assured by his friend that if things went completely sideways down here, he'd throw him a lifeline. He removed the satellite phone from his vest and dialed Harry's number.

"You getting nervous down there?" said Harry, after answering on the first ring.

"Just a little."

"You're good to go, from what I can see," said Harry. "Nobody has left the perimeter, and the Chinook appears to be in a holding pattern about three miles to the west. Feel better?"

"I'll feel better when we're out of here," said Garza.

"You're clear to start heading back," said Harry. "If anything changes, I'll let you know right away."

"I'm counting on it," said Garza.

"You can always count on me," said Harry, before ending the call.

Garza tucked the phone away and radioed the team.

"We're moving out. Rally point will be on me—roughly five hundred meters northwest. Keep a thick tree behind you at all times. If we can see their heat signatures, they can see ours. No point in tempting one of their snipers."

Ripley and Max acknowledged the order and took off down the hill. Garza stepped off a moment later, moving tree to tree along the exfiltration route. A few minutes into the trek, the two Sikorsky helicopters took off, leaving the compound deathly silent. He halted his team, knowing the Chinook would likely return to base shortly. His satellite phone buzzed twice, indicating he had a message.

HARRY: Chinook inbound. Expect it to land asap for evac. Got u covered.

He left a quick reply and waited, growing more anxious as the sound of helicopter rotors grew louder. Less than thirty seconds later, the Chinook roared over the compound and seemed to hover in place. He couldn't tell if it had landed or remained airborne above the mountain. His phone buzzed again.

HARRY: Told you. Safe travels.

GARZA: Thx. Nevada should be fun.

HARRY: You drew the right straw. Out.

He was probably right. Every firefight had the potential to be your last, and the one about to go down at Pyramid Lake promised to be a big one.

CHAPTER FIFTY-FOUR

Decker slowed his ATV as they approached the final GPS waypoint entered into the system. From here, they'd have to decide whether to drive closer to the facility or hike the rest of the way in. Given the way his leg felt after the torturous drive, no amount of hiking appealed to him. But that wasn't an option tonight. One way or the other, he was in for a painful journey through the hills. The only question was how far.

Bringing the ATVs closer would expedite their inevitable, rapid exfiltration of the area, an attractive proposition given what was about to go down, while at the same time, they risked possible detection by driving any closer to the facility. They'd all taken in the absolute silence and stillness of the lake area after Bernie had disappeared into the night sky. Even coming this close carried some risk. For all they knew, regular patrols scoured the rocky hills overlooking the compound. If that were the case, they might have already attracted some unwanted attention.

He eased their pack of four-wheel-drive machines as close to the rocky outcroppings to their left as possible, until the nearly full moon high in the eastern sky disappeared. The moment the moon vanished, his night-vision goggles became nearly useless. The ambient light provided by the moon to this point had been more than enough to navigate the well-defined trail. He activated the ATV's low-intensity infrared headlights, reilluminating the area through the goggles attached to his helmet.

Decker edged forward, nudging against the rock wall towering above him. The spot was as good as any to conceal them from a casual observer or nosy local. They'd passed the still-smoldering remains of a few campfires along their lakeside journey. Decker turned off his ATV and hopped down. The rest of the group joined him on a long flat rock overlooking the glass-smooth lake.

"I think we should walk it in from here," he said.

"How far?" said Harlow.

"A little over a mile," said Decker.

"Are you going to be okay with that?" said Harlow.

"I've done more in worse shape than this," said Decker, seeing she wasn't convinced. "Seriously."

"You don't think we could push it a little farther?" said Brad. "It'll be one hell of a sprint back here—in the dark, over shitty terrain."

"The hills dogleg left about a hundred yards up," said Decker. "Opening to the target. I think the sound will carry."

"We've heard other ATVs out here," said Nix.

"I know," said Decker. "But I'm worried about patrols. One look at us from the hills up there and the show is over. I'd rather take the last mile carefully."

"How much time do we have?" said Harlow.

"Hold on," said Decker, taking out his satellite phone.

They'd stopped twice on the way down to rest, hydrate, and check for messages. The last stop had been about twenty minutes ago. He found four new messages on the phone.

KILLERBEE (Sent 2113): Skycranes on the way back. ETA 2330. Chinook delayed by evac. Site scrambling.

KILLERBEE (Sent 2129): Chinook airborne. Faster than Skycranes. Predict will catch up. Same ETA.

SHERIFF (Sent 2133): Good luck. All good here. EOD inbound. Asshole planted roadside bombs.

GARZA (Sent 2135): Worked like a charm. Place emptied out fast. Headed back to—where the fuck am I going?

He passed the phone around instead of reading the messages out loud.

"Wow. That's great news," said Harlow.

"This is going to be epic," said Nix.

"Maybe a little too epic. We should probably have Garza start driving our way?" said Brad. "Just in case."

"Good point," said Decker, starting to type a message. "What's the nearest town we could reach with the ATVs?"

Nix already had her tablet out. "There isn't one. Our best bet is to follow the lake around to the west and hide out along . . . Surprise Valley Road. We can guide Garza to our location from there."

"There's really no other town within driving range?" said Decker.

"There's always Nixon," she said. "But that would mean driving south or trying to cut through these hills somehow and backtracking down Route 447. And dealing with the tribal police."

"Yeah. That won't work," said Decker. "Give me a town for Garza to aim for. We'll guide him in as we get closer."

"Reno. Or Spanish Springs, just north of Reno," said Nix. "It's about an hour trip from there to where we should run out of gas."

"Reno's that close?" said Harlow.

"Crazy—right?" said Nix.

"If things go well, we'll rest up in Reno," said Decker. "Cheap buffets, spa treatments, suites. The works."

"Sounds good to me," said Harlow.

"I'm in," said Nix.

"I could use a pedicure," said Brad.

"I don't even know what that means," said Decker.

"I can confirm that," said Harlow, getting a quiet laugh out of the group.

Decker finished typing his message to Garza and pressed "Send," getting an immediate reply.

"They're on the way," he said.

"With enough room for all of us?" said Brad. "Garza is hard-core, but he needs a little guidance now and then."

Decker typed another message. The reply came back a second later. He handed the phone to Brad.

Tell Brad to piss off.

"I'm guessing we'll be fine," said Decker.

"Sounds like it," said Brad. "So what now?"

"Gear up and head out," said Decker. "Assault load. Max ammo. Water. That's it. Everyone good?"

Nix yanked the Milkor M32 multiple grenade launcher out of her ATV's cargo netting, cradling it in the crook of her arm. The M32 featured a six-round drum enabling semiautomatic fire at a rate of two to three grenades per second.

"I've never used one of these before," she said.

"Seriously?" said Decker.

"IDF used the M203 exclusively," she said.

"IDF?" said Harlow.

"Israeli Defense Force," said Brad. "And don't let her fool you. She was Shayetet 13. Jewish SEALs, basically."

"She doesn't sound Israeli," said Harlow.

Nix shook her head. "You guys like to chatter. I know how a grenade launcher works. I've just never used this particular system. Just a little disclaimer. It might take me a few tries to start landing rounds on target."

"I'm actually glad you brought it up," said Decker. "The forty-millimeter grenades you'll use are extended-range munitions. Double the range."

"Seriously?" said Nix. "Okay. I'll definitely need a few rounds to get used to this."

"You have a total of seventy-two rounds. Twelve reloads," said Decker. "And not to pile on the pressure, but we'll be relying on you to take out the helicopters—and to suppress any counterattacks."

"Is that all?" said Nix. "What are the rest of you going to be doing? By the way, I grew up in Brooklyn. Moved back to Israel when I was old enough to serve."

"Respect for Brooklyn," said Brad. "I grew up in Long Island."

"Good for you," said Nix.

"To answer your question, Brooklyn—which is your new nickname, by the way—" started Decker.

"No it's not," said Nix.

"Yes it is. Nix is too quirky. More like some hacker's name than a former Shayetet 13 mercenary," said Decker.

When she didn't continue arguing, he went on. "I'll be on the light fifty finishing off whatever you miss, and Brad will be on a light machine gun, keeping heads down."

"And her?" said Brooklyn.

"She's our eyes and ears," said Decker. "And our link to the spoilsport option."

"What exactly is this spoilsport option?" said Harlow.

Decker hated the thought of resorting to the "nuclear option," because without a miracle, it effectively cut them off from the real puppet masters behind the mountain operation. But without any help from the feds, he didn't see any other alternative. The four of them couldn't hope to force the facility to surrender. Ergo . . .

"We basically burn down the entire house," said Decker.

CHAPTER FIFTY-FIVE

Decker lowered the thermal scope and crawled across the rocky stretch of hillside to Harlow, who lay flat on her back—both hands under her head. In the bright moonlight, he could tell by her face she was annoyed. His leg burned from the awkward crawl. He'd have to put this out of his mind from this point forward.

"Did I miss anything?" she said.

"No," he said, sliding next to her.

"Can I have the scope back?" she said. "Or do you want to have Brad check my work, too?"

"Sorry. It's normal to double-check this kind of stuff," said Decker. "You just happened to be the one that started out with the scope, and I just happened to be the one stuck with you."

"I really don't know how to interpret the last part of that sentence," she said, turning over on her side. "And I don't believe your double-check story for a second."

"How many combat surveillance missions have you been on lately?" said Decker, instantly regretting the question.

"None," she said wryly.

"Well, you're doing an exceptional job for someone who's never done something quite like this before," said Decker. "I needed to make sure you didn't miss anything. Just like with street work, there are subtleties in this type of environment that can only be learned from hard experience. I learn lessons from you and your team every day."

"And fight those lessons tooth and nail," said Harlow.

"Fair enough. But I always come around—mostly," he said, and they both chuckled.

"Almost time?" said Harlow.

Decker had just checked his watch before crawling over.

"Anytime now."

"Looks like any other day down there," said Harlow. "You'd think after the stunt we pulled back at the mountain, they'd have the place locked down like Area 51."

"Unless we're missing something, I truly don't think they suspect a thing. And why would they? The helicopters were the only link between this facility and the mountain, and how could someone follow a helicopter—at night?" said Decker.

"I guess unless you have the right contacts and a few hundred thousand dollars at your disposal to hire the best private aerial surveillance on the market, you can't," said Harlow.

"That's what I was thinking," said Decker. "The trick will be keeping them here."

"And if we can't?" said Harlow.

"We'll burn the whole thing down," they said simultaneously.

"What does that even mean?" said Harlow.

"Literally what it sounds like," said Decker. "As a last resort, we can burn that entire facility to the ground and deprive whoever is running this shit show of more than a billion dollars."

"Why don't we just start with that?" said Harlow.

"Are you just saying that because you don't want to fly back?"

"Yes and no," said Harlow, smiling. "Seriously, though. Why not just burn the place to the ground before the helicopters arrive? It's not like they have the fuel to go anywhere else."

"The Chinook has nearly twice the range of the Sikorskys," said Decker. "If we burn down the facility, they may not be able to divert the shipment, but I guarantee you they'll send the Chinook elsewhere, with close to fifty heavily armed mercenaries on board to protect it wherever it lands. Even if Bernie followed them, there's nothing we could do once they landed. At least here we have a shot at keeping them in one place long enough for the federal task force and police to respond."

"And get killed," said Harlow.

"Reeves talked with the agents about that," said Decker. "Once the shooting starts, the federal agents watching over this will immediately coordinate with the department and keep them from driving into trouble. Reeves also said they'd call the Reno PD and report a massive gun battle north of Nixon. Their job is to get as many cops or federal agents out here as quickly as possible. Force a surrender."

"It'll take them too long," said Harlow.

"These people can't move the marijuana—not without more helicopters or a convoy of trucks—which leaves them with one hell of a liability sitting out there. And they have to know the gunfire and grenade explosions will draw law enforcement attention eventually. That leaves them with a few choices.

"One, stay and fight until they can haul off the product. I don't see that happening. They'll draw every cop within five hundred miles to the battle. Two, throw as much product as they can into whatever vehicles they have and bolt. They won't get more than fifty miles away before they're shooting it out with hundreds of cops, thanks to the federal agents that will follow them. The other option is to sneak the leadership away and hope for the best back at the compound. Trust me, an organization big enough to pull off this kind of an operation will walk away from the money before implicating themselves. They'll get the remaining leadership out of there."

His phone buzzed with a message from Bernie. FIVE MINUTES. He typed a quick reply before handing her the scope.

"Stay completely under the blanket until I tell you it's safe," said Decker. "The Chinook has thermal imaging capability. Same capability as this scope, except they can automatically scan wide areas. It's pretty scary."

"And this blanket is really going to help?"

"More or less," said Decker. "If they hover above us and scour the hillside, we're screwed."

"A wonderful thought," she said, before giving him a quick kiss. "Shoot straight, Decker."

Decker returned the kiss, pressing his lips and hers a little longer than he expected. Long enough to question why he'd let her pressure him into bringing her out here. This mission could go to shit so fast, in so many ways—he didn't want to think about it. Right now, they all needed to focus on the task in front of them. He pulled back a little too abruptly.

"Keep your head buried in the night-vision scope. If we start taking fire and nobody can figure out where it's coming from, you'll switch back to the thermal scope and look for someone we missed. Keep us informed of any significant movement or developments. Any personnel or vehicles moving outside of the fence line qualifies as very significant, since we'll be dealing with them up close. If you see any fixed or crew-served weapons, report those immediately."

"I don't even know what that means," said Harlow.

"Big shit. Machine guns or rocket launchers," said Decker.

"Got it," said Harlow.

"If we start taking fire, stay as low profile as possible," said Decker. "Like tilt your head and rest the scope on a rock."

"Don't you have a blanket to hide under?" said Harlow.

"Funny," said Decker, squeezing her hand before crawling back into position.

He activated his throat microphone, which broadcast anything he spoke or whispered—without the need to press a transmitter button. A useful feature in a focused, hands-on gunfight.

"Going hands-free. All gunfighters check in," said Decker, pulling his thermal blanket most of the way over him.

"Pierce up."

"The mercenary formerly known as Nix is up."

"You're Brooklyn now. End of discussion," said Decker.

"Just fucking with you. Brooklyn up."

"Harlow up."

"Time to pull the blankets up tight over your heads. Helicopters are about four minutes out. Bernie will let me know when the Chinook is on final approach. We'll unmask at that point and start the show."

"What if the Chinook takes an unhealthy interest in our location?" said Brad.

"Then Brooklyn is going to make it go away with six forty-millimeter grenades," said Decker.

"You serious about these grenades going out to two thousand feet?" said Brooklyn.

"Start with a forty-five-degree angle and adjust from there," said Brad. "The rounds are easy to overshoot, so if you land short, don't make a big adjustment."

While the two of them went back and forth about how to effectively fire the grenade launcher, Decker cocked his head, squinting at the night sky.

"You hear that?" said Harlow.

He glanced in her direction, almost forgetting that everything they said would be transmitted over the radio net from this point forward.

"I do. Just the faintest sound," said Decker. "Tuck yourselves in, people."

"Are you and Harlow sharing a blanket?" said Brad.

"Funny," said Decker, the rotor chop now echoing off the hillside.

He pulled the top of the blanket over his head, making sure he was completely wrapped like a burrito. Convinced he was as invisible as possible to the Chinook's thermal camera, Decker wiggled his satellite phone up to his face and waited for Bernie's message.

A few minutes later, the rotor sounds intensified to the point that he swore they must be right overhead. His phone illuminated with a new message. ALL CLEAR. He didn't move for a few seconds, convinced Bernie had miscalculated or was watching from a bad angle. The rotor chop sounded so damn close. Another message came through. YOU GUYS ASLEEP?

Decker squirmed out of the blanket, taking a quick peek over the flat rock that would serve as his shooting platform. The Sikorskys were on final approach, a few hundred yards in front of the fifth warehouse from the right. Exterior lights mounted just below the warehouse roof bathed the landing zone in a ghastly orange glow. The Chinook hovered above and behind the transport helicopters, like a protective mother. They'd have to wait until the Chinook landed and started offloading its human cargo.

"We're clear," said Decker, lifting the Barrett M82 .50-caliber semi-automatic sniper rifle onto the flat rock in front of him. "Move into position and start identifying targets."

As the rest of the team acknowledged his order, Decker unzipped a backpack filled with ten-round .50-caliber magazines, removing a few and laying them on the rock next to the rifle for quick access. He glanced to his left along the moonlit hillside; Pierce and Brooklyn were settling into their positions.

Decker pushed the "light fifty's" oversize stock into his right shoulder and flipped up the rear scope cover, revealing a green night-vision image. He eased into the eyepiece, quickly finding one of the Sikorskys, which had just landed. With the scope already adjusted for the distance between his perch and the landing zone, he shifted the reticle onto the Sikorsky's rear rotor assembly.

"Harlow, let me know when the Chinook lands and people start walking down the ramp," he said.

"The Chinook has drifted into the landing zone," said Harlow. "Looks like it's spinning in place to face north."

He took his eye out of the scope to confirm what she had said. It didn't change their plan, but it indicated that the Chinook pilot was vigilant enough to point the helicopter in a direction it could move quickly and safely if trouble developed. They could expect the Chinook to try for a rapid escape when all hell broke loose.

"Brooklyn, that Chinook won't stick around for long when we start shooting," said Decker.

"No pressure," she said.

"Harlow, the moment you see anyone coming out—"

"The ramp is down. They're offloading," said Harlow.

That was fast. The Chinook pilot might be a problem. He shifted his scope reticle to the Chinook's cockpit but decided against putting a bullet through the pilot. It shouldn't be necessary. With the reticle back on the Sikorsky's tail rotor, he started applying pressure to the trigger.

"Weapons free," said Decker.

CHAPTER FIFTY-SIX

A mentally weary Carl Trenkor jogged down the helicopter's rear-facing ramp. It wasn't just the final panicky hours or the ups and downs of this insane past week that fatigued him, but the ordeal of the entire EMERALD CITY experience. Running a nearly yearlong, touch-and-go operation, with so much on the line, had taken its toll. When his feet hit the hard-packed ground, it finally hit him. He'd never see Alderpoint, California, again. He felt better already.

As the last of EMERALD CITY's team emptied out the helicopter, Jason Watts came up beside Trenkor and patted him on the shoulder.

"We did it," said Watts. "They'll be scratching their heads back in Alderpoint for years to come."

Trenkor hoped he was right. They still didn't have a complete grasp of the exposure left behind in the aftermath of McDermott's ambush, but OZ had all but assured him it would be minimal. A few of the dead or captured operators would be traced back to Athena Corp, a problem the company was well versed in handling.

The tablet and surveillance equipment seized in the Comfort Inn had been remotely scrubbed the moment the surveillance operative sent out the distress signal, not that they ever contained any information implicating Athena Corp.

As long as Trenkor's team properly destroyed the proprietary electronics, authorities would only get a whiff of Athena Corp here or there, but not enough to launch an investigation with teeth. Or as OZ had put it: "Nothing a small fraction of that one and a quarter billion dollars can't put to rest."

"I'll feel better when this is entirely out of my hands," said Trenkor, nodding at the transport helicopters a few hundred feet away.

Ground crews twice the size of the mountaintop team scurried to detach the product-stuffed containers and slide them onto low-profile trailer beds, to be towed by tractors into a warehouse where the plants would be hung upside down to dry.

"Who would have ever guessed one of those containers could be worth—"

A sharp metallic bang cut him off. Both of them crouched instinctively. Trenkor thought he had caught a few sparks flying off the tail of the nearest Sikorsky. Watts spoke into his radio.

"Possible incoming fire. Single shot. Heavy caliber," said Watts. "Rivera. Move your squad about twenty meters north of the helicopters. I want you to—"

A flash of light drew Trenkor's attention north, followed immediately by a crunching boom. A compact cloud of dust rose in the distant glow of the warehouse lights.

"That was a grenade," said Watts, edging closer to the helicopter ramp before pointing at the lights mounted above the warehouse bay doors. "They need to kill those lights!"

Trenkor turned and searched for the nearest member of the KANSAS security team, finding one already headed his way. A stocky, bearded guy in a dark-green uniform. From what he remembered, this was the facility's security head. He also recalled that the concept of security around here meant something entirely different than it did on the mountain.

The warehouse compound sat unthreatened on Paiute tribal land, its safety and privacy secured by a lucrative deal, while EMERALD CITY had been carved out of hostile territory, constantly probed and threatened by locals, cops, and private investigators. Pulling duty here versus Alderpoint was like the difference between serving at a major military base outside of Kabul and a firebase in the Korangal Valley. Night and day.

"Kill the lights!" said Trenkor.

The security chief barked an order over his radio, and the landing zone went dark, except for the fluorescent light spilling out of the hangar bay next to the two Sikorskys. A second grenade struck much closer than the first, the blast louder and the concussion stronger. Shrapnel fragments pinged off the Chinook and kicked up dirt in front of Trenkor. He scanned the dark hills to the north, unable to locate the source of fire.

"You might want to take cover," said Watts, beckoning him over to the helicopter ramp. "The next grenade will be on target."

The nearest Sikorsky's tail rotor broke apart, shredding the tail rudder. Trenkor and the security chief sprinted for the ramp, following Watts just inside the helicopter.

"This feels like the last place we should be seeking cover," said Trenkor.

A third grenade landed next to the Chinook, peppering the starboard fuselage with fragments. They all lay flat on the metal deck.

"Better than out there, but we should move behind the warehouses the first chance we get," said Watts, reaching up and grabbing a pair of night-vision goggles from the bench seat next to them. "My guess is we have hostiles in the hills to the north. It's the only cover for miles around."

"What's your name?" said Trenkor, grabbing the security chief's shoulder.

"Caleb."

"Caleb, get your quick reaction force moving toward the hills," said Trenkor. "Focus your sharpshooters on the hostiles while QRF approaches."

"We don't have a formal QRF, but I can put together a few four-by-fours with guards," said Caleb. "As far as sharpshooters go, your team is far better trained."

Trenkor scanned the area beyond the ramp, spotting members of the EMERALD CITY team lying prone next to the warehouse corner directly behind the helicopter. A few peeked out of the small access hatch next to the massive bay door.

"All right. Get your QRF moving. We'll set up shooters inside and between the warehouses," he said before turning to Watts. "Make sure everyone is talking on the same radio frequency. We'll need to coordinate the shooters and QRF."

The top right corner of the warehouse bay door exploded in a shower of sparks and aluminum metal fragments that produced an ear-piercing detonation. Bits and pieces of the warehouse rained down on the back of the helicopter, a brief staccato series of mini-explosions and sparks erupting when the debris hit the spinning rotor. Trenkor lay flat, expecting the rotors to shatter and spray thick metal shards in every direction.

"That's nothing. I've seen these things take way worse," said Watts. "Caleb, do you have a few extra vehicles?"

"Yes. About a dozen," said Caleb, visibly shaking at this point.

"I'll send two teams of four with your QRF. I think you're going to need the help," said Watts, glancing at Trenkor. "We should probably all get moving."

The three of them got up and started down the ramp.

"Mr. Trenkor!" called out one of the pilots from the cockpit door.

Trenkor grabbed Watts halfway down the ramp. Caleb kept sprinting for the open doorway to the warehouse.

"We've still got the door guns rigged from the mountain overwatch mission!" he yelled over the engine whine. "I'd like to get this bird airborne and put the guns to work!"

He remembered that they also had a FLIR (forward-looking infrared radar) pod mounted to the helicopter's nose. They'd be able to locate hostile positions and suppress them with gun runs while the QRF moved in to mop them up.

"Do it! Coordinate with Watts over the secondary security frequency," said Trenkor.

An explosion behind him sprayed the back of the helicopter with rocks that rattled around the cargo hold. Trenkor turned his head away from the pilot in time to see Caleb drop to the ground in a violent twist of dust and debris.

"I'll get the QRF together," said Watts. "But we need to start laying down some suppressive fire, or these helicopters aren't going anywhere."

The pilot appeared next to Trenkor, signaling for his crew to return. Two figures darted out of the warehouse, passing Caleb's crumpled form halfway to the helicopter. Watts started issuing orders as he edged toward the side of the ramp.

"Rivera, have everyone switch over to night vision. I'm going to mark some targets with my IR laser," said Watts, waiting for an answer. "I need you to start laying down suppressive fire as soon as I start marking. I'll catch up with you inside the hangar in a minute. We need to organize a hunter-killer team to head up into those hills."

The engine sounds deepened, and the helicopter started rattling as the crew members dashed up the ramp. Watts crouched on the ramp, peeking around the edge of the fuselage through night-vision goggles he held up to his face with one hand. An intense metallic crack pierced the crescendoing rotor sounds. The pilot yelled back before disappearing into the cockpit.

"They shot out the other Skycrane's tail rotor! We're out of here!"

Trenkor grabbed Watts. "Jason, we need to go."

Watts shook his grip. "I got 'em! Two. Maybe three of them in the rocks."

"The helicopter is leaving!" said Trenkor.

"Give me five seconds!" said Watts, raising his rifle and speaking into his radio. "Rivera, marking targets for suppressive fire."

A crew member readying one of the guns yelled at Trenkor. "The pilot needs to know if you're staying or going?"

"Watts! We're sitting ducks—" started Trenkor, as a warm spray doused his face.

Jason Watts flew backward, his legs backpedaling down the ramp until his feet hit the dirt—where he toppled onto his back like a discarded rag doll. Half-blind from the blood that drenched his face, Trenkor wiped his eyes with the back of a hand until he could finally see again. His still-blurry vision shifted from Watts to Caleb, who lay equally dead on the ground. Without giving it a second thought, he yelled over his shoulder.

"I'm going! Get me the fuck out of here!"

CHAPTER
FIFTY-SEVEN

Decker kept the rifle reticle sighted on the corner of the Chinook's ramp, unable to confirm that his bullet had neutralized the man marking their hillside positions with a laser. He supposed it didn't ultimately matter. The damage had already been done. Bullets snapped overhead and chipped at nearby boulders. The mercenaries hiding in and around the warehouses knew generally where to find Decker's team. It wouldn't be long until they identified their exact positions.

"The Chinook is leaving," said Harlow.

He glanced over the scope. The Chinook kicked up a dust storm, indicating that the pilot had just tilted the rotors and increased rotor RPMs. It would be gone in less than ten seconds—raining bullets down on their heads soon after that. Decker shifted his aim to the cockpit.

"Brooklyn!" said Decker.

"I think I got the hang of this thing now," she said. "Watch this."

A hollow-sounding thump filled the air, competing with the crackle of distant gunfire and zips of incoming bullets.

"That's it?" said Decker. "One shot?"

"Last shot in the cylinder," she said. "Reloading."

"Brad, get ready to light up the Chinook," said Decker.

He tracked the helicopter through the scope as the grenade followed a lazy, invisible arc toward the landing zone. If the grenade missed, they'd have to do this the messy way. The helicopter was about twenty feet in the air and rising.

"Splash. Out," said Brooklyn.

Splash. An artillery term meaning rounds are close to impact. He highly doubted that she'd clocked her shots' previous times of flight. Decker's view through the scope whited out for a moment, followed by an explosive crunch in the distance.

"Direct hit to the forward rotor assembly," said Brad. "It's going down."

Decker pulled his face out of the scope in time to see the helicopter drop like a rock to the ground about fifty yards from where it had originally landed. The forward and aft rotor arcs bowed downward from the impact, the forward rotor arc hitting the ground in front of the cockpit and throwing the entire assembly out of synch. Within the span of a few seconds, both the forward and aft rotors chewed each other to pieces, launching chunks of shattered rotor in every direction.

As the mostly stripped rotor assemblies continued to spin, the helicopter rolled onto its left side, exposing its crumpled underbelly.

"Never doubted you for a second," said Decker, glancing over to Harlow thirty feet away and shaking his head.

"We have more lasers," said Harlow.

Decker lowered his night-vision goggles and scanned the scene. Several bright-green lines shot out of the doors or gaps between the warehouses, mostly focused on his and Brooklyn's positions. Dozens of muzzle flashes joined in a moment later. Bullets immediately pounded the rock ledge in front of Decker, forcing him off the rock.

"Brad, I think it's time you joined the fun," said Decker, slinging the ammunition backpack over his shoulder. "I'm repositioning."

"Yep," said Pierce, immediately followed by a long burst of automatic gunfire.

Pierce fired several more bursts, stitching the warehouses with bullets as Decker searched for a new location. The volume of incoming bullets noticeably slackened halfway through Pierce's return fire.

"Harlow, what's happening down there?" said Decker, climbing down onto an oblong boulder he'd picked to hide behind.

"They're targeting Pierce now," said Harlow.

The gunfire intensified, chipping away at the rocks around him. Pierce's automatic rifle barked a few more times before he got on the radio.

"I'm looking for a secondary position. Incoming is too fucking intense," said Pierce. "Must be twenty rifles pounding away at us."

"Probably forty," said Decker. "Brooklyn, how's that reload coming along?"

Six tightly spaced, consecutive thumps from her grenade launcher answered his question.

"Reloading," said Brooklyn.

Decker crouched behind the boulder, inching his head up to see where the grenades landed. If Brooklyn managed to suppress the security crew on the ground long enough for Decker and Pierce to start poking holes in people again, they might be back in business. The six grenades struck in rapid succession, exploding near the most active gunfire points along the line of warehouses. The level of incoming gunfire nearly stopped.

"I have someone running from the helicopter toward the warehouses," said Harlow.

He heaved his rifle onto the rock and found the fleeing target with the riflescope. Looked like a pilot. There had to be more survivors. The helicopter had gone down hard, but it was still structurally intact. Maybe he was going for help? He'd keep that in mind for later. He suspected that one of the high-value targets had boarded the helicopter at the last moment. If they were trapped, that might work to Decker's advantage later. But first things first.

"Brad, reengage immediately. We might not get another chance."

"I'm not in position yet," said Pierce.

"Shit," said Decker, already picking out a new target.

A head and rifle poked around the corner of the warehouse directly behind the damaged Chinook. Decker placed the reticle at chest level on the front-facing corrugated metal wall, about six inches from the corner—and pressed the trigger. The .50-caliber projectile punched through the building and removed the man from sight.

Sporadic gunfire erupted from the warehouses again as he settled in on an M240 machine gun inside one of the doorways. The moon provided sufficient ambient light for his scope to see far enough into the warehouse to identify the distinctive bipod and front sight. If the gun crew had set it up a few feet deeper into the building, he would have missed it.

"Two-forty in the third warehouse from the left. Inside the door. Engaging," said Decker. "Harlow. Switch to the thermal scope and start scanning those doorways for warm bodies."

Decker fired three evenly spaced shots through the doorway at the barrel of the machine gun, hoping for the best.

"Can't tell if I hit them," said Decker, moving on to the closest muzzle flash.

"Trust me. You hit them," she said. "Looked like someone exploded a can of white paint inside."

Red tracers exploded from another doorway, racing in his direction. Decker dropped behind the rock a moment before a hail of bullets and tracers tore overhead. The tracers flew erratically after striking the boulder, some bouncing skyward—most deflecting into the hillside behind him. During a short pause in the mayhem, he pulled the sniper rifle down, immediately noticing that the eyepiece wasn't glowing green. A quick inspection revealed the problem. The front lens was cracked. He instinctively reached for his primary rifle, which he'd left at his last position.

"The fifty is down," said Decker.

"I'm almost in position here," said Pierce. "Should give me better cover. We'll have to do this with rifles and a grenade launcher. Brooklyn, you almost ready?"

"A few more seconds," she said.

Incoming tracer fire intensified, the hillside infested with red flashes.

"Harlow, what's going on?"

"They have three machine guns going. All from the doorways," she said. "Second, third, and fifth warehouses from the right."

"You copy that, Brooklyn?"

"Affirmative. Rounds out," she said.

"Harlow, spot those rounds for us, please."

Three two-round salvos of grenades left the hillside, sailing toward the warehouses. Decker could have sworn he heard a grunt over the radio at one point while Brooklyn was firing. He'd follow up with that in a minute. Six explosions rang out, significantly slowing the tracer party going on around him.

"Direct hits on all three buildings, but mostly exterior damage," said Harlow. "One of the grenades exploded inside warehouse number five. Blew the bay door halfway off."

"Copy that," said Decker. "Is anyone hit?"

"I'm good," said Harlow.

"Pierce up."

A short pause ensued.

"Brooklyn?"

"I'm down," she said.

Shit!

That was the last thing they needed right now. With her grenade launcher out of action, they were in trouble.

"How bad?" said Decker.

"Not that bad," she said. "Fucking tracer round bounced out of nowhere and zipped through my knee—while I was kneeling. Looked like a laser went through it. Weirdest fucking thing ever."

"Sounds bad," said Decker.

"It's not," she said. "Really. But I can't put any weight on it."

"Do I need to micromanage your first aid?" said Decker.

"Negative! I got it under control," she said. "I'll just need a little help getting the hell out of here."

"Speaking of getting out of here," said Brad. "What's the plan now that the fifty and the grenade launcher are out of the picture?"

The return gunfire picked up again quicker than he expected, accompanied by the fire hose of tracers.

"Harlow, do you see any change to the situation?" said Decker. "Any improvement?"

"One of the machine guns is still down, but beyond that," she said, "I'd say they have close to fifty—hold on. A group of six just emerged from warehouse three, headed for the Chinook."

"Must be someone important on board," said Decker. "We saw two leadership types standing in the open right before we started lighting up the compound."

"I'm on it," said Pierce.

"Don't get yourself killed," said Decker. "I'm about to pull the plug on this."

Pierce fired five tightly spaced bursts—ten rounds each if he had to guess—before his gun went quiet.

"Pierce?"

"I'm still here—kinda wishing I was somewhere else," he said. "Harlow, how'd I do?"

"All six are down," she said. "A few still moving."

"The return gunfire is too much. I'm not doing that again," said Pierce. "Time to burn this place down."

"Agreed. I'm making the call," said Decker, fishing the satellite phone out of his pocket.

A new message waited for him from Bernie, sent a minute ago. Ur still at it down there?

DECKER: Slow learner. Time to burn it down.

KILLER BEE: Already inbound. Figured you'd come to ur senses. Tot 1 minute.

DECKER: Owe u one.

KILLER BEE: One million . . . just kidding. Restock fee only. Hope you arranged a ride.

DECKER: All good. Drinks in la?

KILLER BEE: On u.

DECKER: As always. Fly safe.

"Time on target one minute," said Decker. "Everyone stay down until Bernie's done with his pass."

"How will we know that?" said Harlow.

"You'll know," said Decker.

CHAPTER

FIFTY-EIGHT

Carl Trenkor rolled onto his back and found himself staring straight up through a circular window—half of the moon visible through its thick glass. It took him a moment to figure out why he was looking at the cargo hold's windows. *Jesus.* The Chinook had rolled after crashing. He was lying on the opposite side of the fuselage.

He hadn't remembered that part of the experience. All he could recall was taking a seat on the bench next to the starboard-side gunner, thinking he'd escaped whatever hell had erupted on the ground. The Chinook dropped out from under him at that point, its sudden fall preceded by an overhead explosion.

A streak of red tracers flew past the window, briefly illuminating the cargo. A pitched battle raged outside the helicopter—exchanges of machine-gun fire punctuated by a heavy-caliber sniper rifle and a rapid series of forty-millimeter-grenade explosions. The entire helicopter vibrated from the nearby detonations, bringing a thin layer of dirt down onto him. He coughed and wiped his face with a soaking-wet sleeve, tasting blood on his lips. Watts.

"Fuck!" he muttered, reaching for the flashlight in one of his vest pouches.

"Sir. Don't do that," said a voice next to him. "They'll see the light through the windows. They've left us alone so far."

"How far did we get before crashing?" said Trenkor.

"About fifty yards."

At least they hadn't traveled too far away from friendly lines.

"Do you know what we're up against?" said Trenkor, his senses starting to reboot. "How many are out there?"

"I have no idea. Everything happened so fast, we were focused on getting the bird out of here."

Another line of tracers tore past the window, giving him enough light to see the man next to him. He wore a flight suit and an aircrew survival vest. A night-vision-equipped flight helmet sat in his lap.

"Are you one of the pilots?"

"Jim Cook. Copilot. One of the gunners survived, too. Ramirez. He's guarding the ramp. We don't know what happened to the crew chief. He was on the portside gun. My guess is he fell out and was crushed when we rolled."

"What happened to the pilot?"

"Went for help," said Cook.

"Did he make it?"

"We're pretty sure he did," said Cook. "He disappeared between two of the warehouses."

"Then we need to make a run for the warehouses," said Trenkor. "We'll order up some cover fire and make it happen."

"Your guys already tried to send a squad over to help us. They were cut down before they made it halfway. We're stuck here for now," said Cook. "Actually, we're in a pretty good spot. Far enough away that we're not caught in the cross fire."

A thick kerosene smell hung in the air. He wasn't sure if the odor had just arrived or if it had been there all along.

"I smell JP8. A lot of it," said Trenkor. "We need to get out of here."

"It's safe," said Cook. "You can hold a blowtorch to a puddle of JP8 and it won't catch fire. It only burns when it's run through one of our turboshaft engines."

"I'd rather not test your theory," said Trenkor, starting to get up—but quickly lying back down.

"Just take it easy for a minute," said Cook. "I couldn't find any obvious injuries, but it's possible you broke something. Ramirez has a broken leg—the thing is bent sideways—and one of his arms isn't really working."

"And he's guarding us?"

"He insisted," said Cook.

"What about you?" said Trenkor.

"I'm fine. Bruised up good but fine."

"We should at least get outside and hide behind the helicopter. Put a few more layers of metal or an engine between us and the hills," said Trenkor. "And I need to regain tactical and situational awareness."

"Yeah. Not much awareness going on in here," said Cook. "The only way out is to squeeze through the ramp. Its hydraulics got smashed when we hit the ground, and it pinched mostly shut when we rolled—so it's a tight fit. The rest of the usable exits expose us directly to the hillside."

"We'll go with the ramp," said Trenkor. "Help me up."

Cook helped him to his feet, where it became painfully obvious, literally, that something was drastically wrong with his left hip. He couldn't put any weight on the leg at all without agonizing pain.

"Motherfuhhh—I think my left hip is broken," said Trenkor.

The copilot moved over to Trenkor's left side to take the weight off his hip. While a small-scale war continued outside of the helicopter, they slowly made their way to the ramp.

"How are we looking out there?" said Cook.

"I think the tide is turning. I'm not detecting as much return fire from the hills," said Ramirez. "But when they hit us—they hit us hard."

"Mr. Trenkor wants us behind the helicopter," said Cook. "Where he can direct a counterattack."

"It's kind of shitty out there," said Ramirez.

"We'll be fine. The helicopter fuselage should stop anything coming from the hills, and the grenades are hitting the warehouse area. That's well out of fragmentation range."

"You'll have to pull me through and set me up, Cookie," said Ramirez, leaning toward Trenkor. "I'm basically a gun turret at this point, sir. Just plop me down and face me in whatever direction you want to cover."

"That's about all I'm good for, too," said Trenkor with a chuckle.

After Cook eased Ramirez through the gap between the fuselage and ramp, at the very back of the helicopter, Trenkor edged closer to the opening and waited for the copilot to return. The battle outside had definitely changed. All he heard at this point was automatic fire from EMERALD CITY's M240 machine guns. Maybe it was over.

"Ready for you, sir," said Cook, extending his hands through the gap.

Trenkor rolled onto his right side and grabbed Cook's hands. "This is going to hurt."

"A little," said the copilot.

Trenkor groaned as Cook pulled him through the tight opening and dragged him over the hardscrabble ground to a covered position behind the engine pylon. Ramirez sat with his back against the pylon, pointing a compact rifle into the darkness beyond the front of the helicopter. Trenkor pushed himself into a seated position next to Ramirez, scanning the facility.

The enemy grenade launcher had left several jagged, scorch-marked holes strewn across the building fronts, but overall hadn't done nearly as much damage as he'd anticipated. Tracers poured out of two warehouse doors, racing toward the hillside, while dozens of muzzle flashes erupted from multiple points between the structures.

At first glance it appeared that his people had the situation mostly under control—until you considered the loss of three helicopters within the span of a minute. Hardly optimal, but under the circumstances, hardly a disaster. As long as the harvest remained intact, OZ wouldn't care if every Athena Corp asset at the site had been destroyed, including Trenkor. A fact he should never forget. They were all expendable assets to Athena Corp.

"You hear that?" said Cook.

"Yeah. No return fire, from what I can tell," said Trenkor. "I think this is over."

"No. I hear an aircraft approaching," said Cook.

"Helicopters?" said Trenkor, stiffening.

He was unaware of any support assets in KANSAS's vicinity. Then again, OZ had an incredible amount of power at his fingertips, and he wasn't the kind of person to take chances. This could very well be a quick-reaction force he'd prepositioned somewhere close by during the transport phase of the operation, to protect the harvest.

"Negative. Fixed-wing propeller type. Big, like a C-130," said Cook. "Coming in low from the west. It's almost right on top of us."

Now he heard it. *Damn.* It did sound low in the sky.

"There it is!" said Cook, pointing toward the rightmost warehouse.

The moment Trenkor's eyes spotted the enormous dark mass racing toward the facility at near treetop level he knew this wasn't a rescue and started crawling away from the kerosene bomb behind him. He didn't care if Cook felt comfortable enough to take a bath in JP8 while someone tossed matches at the tub. The farther away he could get from this thing, the better. That inbound aircraft wasn't about to drop leaflets on them. He got about fifteen feet before night turned to day.

And he caught fire.

Chapter

Fifty-Nine

Against Decker's advice, Harlow watched the entire scene unfold with a morbid fascination. At first she wasn't sure what was happening, but by the time Bernie's C-123 had sped halfway across the row of warehouses, she had a pretty good idea based on something Decker had been watching on the American Heroes Channel a few months back.

For reasons she couldn't possibly conceive, Bernie's aircraft was equipped with a military-grade missile countermeasure system capable of launching hundreds of flares in a wide pattern underneath the aircraft. In a wartime environment, at a much higher altitude, the flares would drift below and behind the aircraft, hopefully spoofing infrared homing missiles.

Fired a hundred feet or so above the ground over the compound, the magnesium flares, burning at close to four thousand degrees Fahrenheit, blanketed the warehouses and helicopters—lighting everything on fire. All three helicopters exploded before the aircraft had cleared the site, and fires broke out inside every warehouse—the white-hot flares almost instantly burning right through the thin metal rooftops and falling into the dried marijuana plants.

Incoming gunfire stopped abruptly, as compound security personnel scrambled to get clear of the rising inferno.

"I think it's safe to take a look," said Harlow.

A few seconds passed before the team reacted.

"Holy shit," said Pierce. "That redefines Cheech and Chong's *Up in Smoke*. What direction is the wind blowing?"

"Why? You plan on sticking around if it's headed our way?" said Harlow.

"Not tonight," said Brad. "I don't want to drive my ATV into the lake."

Everyone laughed.

"Looks like the wind is a nonissue," said Decker. "The smoke is lingering."

"That's a good thing," said Brooklyn. "They'll be too stoned to come after us."

"I think they've come to the same realization," said Harlow. "They're backing up from the smoke."

"Brad, put a few bursts over their heads, and force them back into the smoke," said Decker.

"I like that idea," said Pierce, his automatic rifle crackling a moment later.

The men scrambled for cover the moment Pierce started firing, nearly all of them vanishing in the smoke. Return fire was sporadic and inaccurate.

"Fire a few more bursts to keep them—happy," said Decker.

"Is this all for real?" said Brooklyn.

"I've seen weirder, but this might be the winner," said Pierce. "Welcome to the team."

Harlow spotted movement at the far-right edge of her scope's field of vision. Something really bright. She centered on the object, immediately feeling repulsed. A figure crawled away from the Chinook—burning alive.

"Pierce, I have a lone target crawling away from the Chinook. Headed west. They're on fire," said Harlow. "I'm thinking a mercy kill?"

"Copy that," said Pierce.

"Hold on," said Decker.

A few seconds passed before Decker came back over the radio net.

"I'm headed back to the ATVs."

"What?" said Harlow.

"That's a possible high-value target. I want it," said Decker.

"That's fucking suicide," said Harlow.

"Where are the bolt cutters?" said Decker, ignoring her.

"My ATV," said Brooklyn.

"Decker, this is reckless," said Harlow.

"Welcome to the team," he said. "Make your way down to Brooklyn and help her back to the ATVs. Brad, you're my cover while I'm down there. I suggest repositioning closer to the ATVs."

"This is reckless and stupid," said Pierce.

"Yep. Let me know when you're in position," said Decker.

Harlow walked over to Decker's rifle, blocking him when he arrived. She shook her head, not wanting to transmit over the voice-activated net. Decker rushed in and kissed her passionately before backing up a few feet and mouthing, "All good." She shook her head and threw the rifle at him, which he caught as if he expected it. He winked and mouthed, "I love you," before vanishing from sight.

"Is this normal for him on one of these operations?" said Harlow, breaking her silence.

Pierce replied immediately. "This is why I let his calls go to voice mail."

CHAPTER SIXTY

Brad Pierce scaled the largest boulder accessible to him without climbing gear and crawled into position, overlooking the facility. With the bipod firmly planted against the rock, and a fresh sixty-round drum ready to go, he scanned the area around the flaming warehouses through his automatic rifle's 3X Squad Day Optic.

Nobody had ventured into the open, leading him to guess the security team had retreated behind the warehouses—as far away from the "toxic" haze billowing out of the buildings as possible without exposing themselves to the hillside. Judging from the pungent skunky odor that had already reached the hills, Pierce couldn't imagine any of them were in any condition to fight.

"Brad, you in position?" said Decker.

"Foolishly. Yes."

"How is our target doing?"

"He's no longer on fire," said Pierce. "Still crawling. I think one of his legs is busted. He's almost entirely using his arms."

"Fuck. That's hard-core," said Decker. "Nobody is coming to help him?"

"I don't have any hostiles on scope. They're all hiding somewhere behind the warehouses. Probably fighting over a bag of Doritos," said Pierce.

"Funny," said Decker.

"Where are you?" said Pierce.

"At the ATVs," he said. "I'll be Oscar Mike in thirty seconds. Give me two minutes to get to the fence. Another two to cut through. Probably—"

"We need to rethink that part of the plan. Brooklyn is way more fucked up than she admitted," said Pierce. "She'll be lucky to keep anything below her knee."

"Dammit," said Decker. "I knew she was downplaying this."

"I'm still on the radio net," said Brooklyn.

"I know," said Decker.

"You forgot," said Brooklyn.

"Maybe," said Decker.

"Jesus," said Harlow. "Is she really going to lose her leg? It looks pretty bad."

"If she doesn't get to a surgeon soon," said Pierce.

"Then we forget grabbing the guy and head south along the lake. Link up with the federal agents near Nixon," said Harlow. "That's what . . . ten miles from here? They can have an ambulance waiting to take her to the nearest trauma center."

"We need to really think this one through," said Decker.

"What is there to think about?" said Harlow. "We can't do both."

"Forget the guy," said Decker. "I'm talking about what happens when Brooklyn is admitted to a hospital with a gunshot wound," said Decker. "The police usually get involved in stuff like that."

"Then call Reeves and figure something out," said Harlow. "He can smooth this over."

"You know that's not exactly how it works," said Decker. "Once she's out of our hands, anything goes."

"Well, we have to try and save her leg," said Harlow.

"Brooklyn, are you okay with rolling the dice?" said Decker.

"If you're asking me if I want to save my leg, the answer is yes," said Brooklyn. "I can't imagine I'll get invited back with only one leg."

"You actually want to work with this crew again?" said Pierce.

"I'd sign with you permanently if I could," said Brooklyn. "This has been an insane ride."

"We don't do this all the time," said Decker.

"Just once a year, it seems," said Pierce.

"Make sure you call me when it happens again," she said.

"I might have some work for you on a more permanent basis," said Harlow. "But it doesn't involve grenade launchers."

They all laughed before Pierce got some bad news.

"Brad?"

"Yes?"

"Hate to do this to you, but I need you to stay in position and cover our transit south," said Decker. "We'll veer away from the facility and skirt the lake until we're clear, but they'll have a small window of opportunity to intercept us—if they somehow manage to get their shit together."

"So I'm walking home," said Pierce.

"ATV ride for most of it," said Decker. "Either we'll pick you up or Garza will. I have no idea how this'll go down with the feds and police in Nixon. We might all end up answering some questions."

"Can I make a suggestion?" said Pierce.

"Can I stop you?" said Decker.

"We really don't have time for this, guys," said Harlow.

"He started it," said Pierce. "Anyway. You guys should change into the civilian clothes we brought for the anticipated walk back, and ditch everything else in the lake. Except the ATVs—obviously. That'll give the feds some leeway with the local police when you show up out of nowhere. You can say you were passing by when the whole place turned into a shooting gallery, and Brooklyn took a stray bullet. Something like that. Tell Reeves to have the federal agents claim jurisdiction over you as witnesses to their investigation."

"I think it's a solid idea," said Harlow.

"Bernie won't be happy about losing a grenade launcher," said Decker. "That's kind of an irreplaceable item."

"I'll haul the grenade launcher with me," said Pierce.

"And the fifty cal?"

"Don't push it," said Pierce.

"Harlow, I'm headed up to help you get Brooklyn down," said Decker. "We have some work to do before we start driving south."

Pierce scanned the warehouses again, still seeing no signs of the security force. A long look at the road leading out of the compound's gate similarly showed zero activity. They hadn't bolted yet, which led him to believe they'd wait until the fire burned out—and then check for any surviving product. Judging by the flames and smoke rising from the four packed warehouses and pouring out of the two metal containers still sitting on the landing zone, it looked like the full one-point-two-five billion would go up in smoke.

"I don't see any activity on the compound right now," said Pierce. "And the fires are still burning bright. I'll keep you posted."

"Don't breathe too much of that in, Brad," said Harlow. "At a minimum, you need to be able to drive and operate a GPS at the same time."

"If you don't hear from me in the next twenty-four hours, you know where to find me," he said.

Pierce checked on the man crawling west across the landing zone. Still going, but he'd definitely slowed down. If Decker worked fast, he could probably cut through the fence, grab the guy, and catch up with Harlow. That said—the ATV's engine noise might draw some unwanted attention.

A quick flanking maneuver around the western side of the complex, supported by vehicles, would be on top of Decker before Pierce could do anything about it. The risk wasn't worth the reward. Maybe none of this was worth the risk anymore. He needed to have a serious talk with Decker when they got back. His days of taking outsize risks and depending more on luck than skill were over. The time to rebuild a normal life with his family was way overdue.

CHAPTER SIXTY-ONE

Decker approached the GPS location given to him by Reeves, with his hands raised above his head. Harlow and Brooklyn waited about fifty yards back along the shoreline, their hands similarly raised as a show of good faith. Ahead of him, a five-foot-high rock wall grew out of a raised sand berm that extended as far as he could see across the moonlit desert floor. He caught some movement on the rock wall.

"Ryan Decker?" said a female voice.

"Yes. Supervisory Special Agent Reeves sent me," said Decker.

"Is anyone in your party armed?" she said.

He really hoped this was one of the special agents. "Aren't you supposed to say some kind of code word?"

"Shit. Sorry. He said he still wants to know how you ditched him at LAX."

Decker relaxed. Reeves bugged him about that trick every time they got together. It had become a bit of a running joke, and a secret they continued to hold over his head.

"We're unarmed. We were out for a ride, when all hell—"

"Yeah. Yeah," said the agent, standing up on the wall. "We've been briefed on the situation by Reeves."

"Can we put our hands down?"

"Sorry. Yes," she said. "I have a vehicle on the other side of that berm that'll take your colleague to the nearest trauma center. Actually, we'll arrange for an ambulance to meet them en route. The closest facility is in Reno."

"That far?" said Decker.

"There's not much of anything out this way," she said. "There's a footbridge that crosses this about twenty feet down the berm. Leave the ATVs. We need to get this show on the road, before we have visitors."

Decker signaled Harlow, and the ATV started up.

"What is this?"

"I don't know. Some kind of irrigation ditch," said the agent. "We really do need to hurry. The police chief wasn't happy to hear from us. There's no telling what kind of arrangement his department had with the folks out at that compound. We kind of vanished on him after that."

"I bet he wasn't happy," said Decker. "Did you see what happened out there?"

"As far as anyone outside of this group is concerned, we didn't see shit," she said. "But that was one hell of a show."

"I just wish we didn't have to burn all of your evidence," said Decker.

"Trust me. We'll have more than enough residual to work with," she said. "This isn't the first time drug harvesters have tried to burn themselves out of a conviction."

The ATV pulled up next to Decker, and the agent directed them to the footbridge. Two other agents remained at a safe distance in the dark, watching over the transfer. He appreciated their caution and made sure to stay as far away from the special agent handling the situation as was feasible. A minute later, they had a partially sedated Brooklyn loaded into the back seat of a Tahoe, with one of the shadow agents at the wheel.

"Who's going with her?" said the lead agent.

"All of us," said Decker.

"I like that answer," she said. "Agent Blue will take you as far as the ambulance transfer."

"How far away is the transfer?" said Harlow.

"Probably twenty minutes," she said. "The ambulance is already on the way from Reno. They're sending a trauma team, so she'll be in good hands."

"I assume they won't let us ride with her?" said Harlow, climbing into the seat next to Brooklyn.

The agent shook her head. "No. We booked you a room under Ryan Decker at the Comfort Suites in Fernley. That's at the junction of 447 and Interstate 80. My guess is the transfer will either happen just before or just after that junction. You're on your own from there. Fair enough?"

"Thank you," said Harlow. "Good luck with all of this."

"Yeah. Thank you," said Decker.

"Don't thank me. Thank Reeves. You owe him one," she said. "Probably that LAX story."

"You're probably right," said Decker, helping get Harlow situated with Brooklyn across her lap. "But I have something that might even up the score. Right here. Right now."

"I'm listening," she said.

"How close do you think you could get to the facility's western fence line?" said Decker.

CHAPTER
SIXTY-TWO

Carl Trenkor clenched the chain-link metal in his right hand, thankful KANSAS's security chief hadn't insisted on installing an electric fence. He glanced over his shoulder at the burning Chinook, somewhat impressed that he'd managed to crawl this far without the use of his legs. His right leg worked but he found the pain in his left was far more manageable when he didn't use his legs at all.

He pulled himself up far enough to turn and sit with his back against the fence. Decker was long gone by this point. He'd heard a number of ATVs speed off—headed south. He was convinced it had been Decker. He had no idea how, but it was the only scenario that made sense. Decker had essentially disappeared after McDermott's ambush, several hours ago. More than enough time to make his way out here.

But why? Especially when they had the means to just burn this place to the ground in an instant. Why attack them with machine guns and grenades first? What did it matter? He was done. His career had been on thin ice all week. Now it was iced—permanently. A noise outside the fence line drew Trenkor's attention. He glanced over his shoulder in time to see two dark figures just feet away, moving rapidly in his direction.

Trenkor reached for the pistol on his right thigh, but his hand never made it. His muscles locked for a brief moment before a repetitive series of involuntary convulsions struck. He'd been Tasered in the back. Now he understood why Decker had made the trip—to capture him. And thanks to Trenkor's single-minded focus on getting to the fence, a pointless goal he was now convinced had been trauma induced, Decker would succeed against all odds.

He couldn't tell what they were doing behind him, but the moment he regained muscle control, he was yanked through the fence, which had been cut in a pattern that matched his upright profile. A woman dressed in jeans and a dark long-sleeve shirt tossed a pair of bolt cutters to the ground, while the person who had dragged him through the fence stripped the pistol from his holster. Before he could contemplate a plan to escape, the two of them flipped him on his stomach and yanked his hands behind his back.

"You have the right to remain silent," said the woman, covering his mouth with an ear-to-ear piece of duct tape. "We'll get to the rest of your rights later."

One of the agents kneeled next to his head before shoving his face into the rough desert floor. When they lifted his head a few inches, one of them slid a badge holder in front of his eyes. He read Drug Enforcement Agency before the badge was pulled away, and he knew that was the end of him.

OZ would immediately declare him "black flagged," a sentence that would be mercilessly carried out while he was in federal custody. At least with Decker, he had a chance to work out a deal and actually escape with his life. Nobody could protect him now. Trenkor was as dead as Mike Loftis and Jason Watts, except his end wouldn't come quickly or painlessly. He'd be tortured until OZ's cutthroats were convinced he had nothing left to give them—except his life.

PART SIX

Chapter

Sixty-Three

Seth Harding sat in an antique bow-back Windsor chair in the anteroom to the APEX Institute's board of directors chamber. He'd always assumed the chair was an antique, because it actually looked like it had been used for centuries. With its seat worn around the edges and legs scratched, it stood out in the exquisitely furnished, deep mahogany–paneled room. It was almost an eyesore, yet he felt drawn to sit in it every time he was summoned to speak to the board.

Under the circumstances, perhaps he should have chosen one of the Victorian red velvet chairs—and poured a brandy from the small bar tucked away into the built-in shelves. It would very likely be his last luxury at this job, or any job, for that matter. The board of directors would make sure he never worked in the Beltway again, or in any job connected to it.

The right half of the double door opened to reveal Samuel Quinn, wearing a somber face. Yep. He should have gone for the brandy.

"The board is ready for you," said Quinn, without a hint of friendliness.

Harding knew it would be bad, but getting the cold shoulder from Quinn stung a little. Then again, what did he expect? EMERALD

CITY had sunk with Harding at the helm, taking two billion dollars down with it. He felt somewhat fortunate that his car hadn't exploded in the garage when he'd started it this morning. Or maybe that would have been the easier way. He nodded and passed over the threshold into one of the most powerful chambers in Washington, DC.

A rectangular, polished wood table long enough to seat ten sat in the middle of the room, which was paneled in mahogany with a massive flat screen television mounted on the far wall. No windows or shelves. A simple space with a simple purpose. To finalize decisions that would shape the course of our nation's affairs—to the benefit of the Institute's clients.

He stood behind the two empty chairs at the end of the table closest to the door and waited for Quinn to sit down. He'd either be asked to remain standing or to take a seat. Harding didn't suppose it mattered which option he was offered. The result would be the same. The rest of the board looked especially aloof today. He glanced at the empty seat between Sloane Pruitt and Allan Kline, two of the most junior members of the board, allowing himself to briefly yearn for what should have been his as soon as Garrison Keeler's corpulent body had signed off with a massive heart attack seven months and eighteen days ago. Not that he was counting.

Harold Abbott, a balding, gray-haired man in his early seventies, and the senior member of the board, leaned forward from his seat on the far-left side. Nobody sat at the other head of the table. Traditionally, board members held coequal power, even if that wasn't exactly true.

"Mr. Harding, would you please take your seat," said Abbott.

Harding started to pull out the chair in front of him.

"Not that seat," said Abbott.

Seriously. They're going to fuck with him like a child? Whatever. He grabbed the other chair at the top of the table and started to pull it back.

"Not that seat, either."

He stood there for a moment, keeping any type of reaction completely in check. No eye rolling, head shaking, squinting, fist clenching. Nothing. Harding wouldn't give them the satisfaction.

Abbott motioned toward the empty chair on the right side of the table.

"Your seat," he said.

"I don't understand," said Harding, cocking his head slightly.

"We'll explain," said Abbott.

He met Samuel Quinn's gaze, which registered the faintest trace of a grin, while the rest of the board maintained their stony facade. Once he'd taken *his* seat, Abbott began.

"Just so we're clear. This was a unanimous decision, and your appointment to the board is provisional. Actually, a better description would be—conditional."

"Thank you," said Harding, trying his best not to show how taken aback he felt. "All of you."

Ezra Dalton, one of the founding members of the Institute, chuckled along with most of the other members.

"That's it?" she said. "Thank you?"

"I apologize, ma'am," said Harding. "I'm kind of at a loss for words."

"Well, that's a first for you," said Dalton. "And you don't call us sir or ma'am. First names."

"Thank you, Ezra," said Harding, still not quite sure this was happening.

"Since the Special Activities Group has brought you together with everyone in this room on dozens of occasions, we'll skip formal introductions," said Abbott.

Harding nodded before glancing around the table at slightly less distant, but perceivably skeptical, faces.

"Don't you want to know what the condition is?" said Abbott.

"Very much so," said Harding, feeling a little more grounded. "But first I have to ask about EMERALD CITY."

"What about it?" said Vernon Franklin, another Institute plank owner.

"I mean, it was—"

"A disaster?" said Pruitt, seated next to him.

"In the end," said Harding. "Yes."

"'In the end' being the key phrase," said Abbott. "By all accounts, EMERALD CITY should have succeeded. For a high-risk, extreme-value opportunity, things settled down quickly under your guidance, and we felt confident that the operation would produce an unmatched amount of revenue—even if it only lasted one season. Nobody here was overly optimistic about a repeat run, given the peculiarities of the Alderpoint area and the overall dynamic in the Emerald Triangle. But you understood that."

Harding nodded. That had been the assessment he'd presented to the board midway through the harvest season, long before they'd grabbed Brett Hale. Abbott sat back in his chair.

"What or who do you blame for the downfall of EMERALD CITY?" said Abbott. "And don't say yourself. We don't play that game around here, unless it truly is your fault."

Harding thought about the many factors contributing to the uncanny series of events that had toppled the operation, settling on the one uncontrollable factor that—if removed—would have changed everything.

"Senator Margaret Steele," said Harding.

Ezra Dalton started clapping. "Bravo, Seth. We agree."

"She's been a thorn in our side for a number of years now," said Harding. "A two-billion-dollar thorn as of a few days ago."

"What are you suggesting?" said Dalton.

"Nothing. Just pointing out what I'm certain you've already analyzed from a hundred different directions," said Harding.

"There certainly is no easy way to harness or steer her," said Abbott. "She's proven quite resistant to pressure, but I think her time has finally come. Coincidentally, or not, she's put a serious dent into our ghost budget funding projects over the past few years. We'd prefer there be no more coincidences."

He glanced furtively across the table at Samuel Quinn, who subtly shook his head. Assassination was still off the table.

Dalton leaned forward in her seat. "We need to come to an agreement with Senator Steele."

"Then I think it's time we sent someone to pay her another visit," said Abbott, leveling a stern gaze at Harding.

Harding hadn't expected the board to trust him with such a critical task right out of the gate, though it made sense to him. Handling Senator Steele would be the perfect test of his worthiness to sit at this table, particularly in light of the role the senator had played in destroying EMERALD CITY. It would be his redemption.

"I assume this doesn't just involve me waltzing into her office and asking her to quit sticking her nose where it doesn't belong?" said Harding, wondering if he'd gotten a little too comfortable, too quickly.

Ezra Dalton chuckled and shook her head, followed by everyone else in the room except for Samuel Quinn, who avoided eye contact and maintained a neutral face. Harding suddenly understood what had just happened, the abject cruelty of their charade leaving him speechless. Donovan Mayhew, who hadn't said a word yet, excused himself from the table and opened the boardroom door, admitting four serious-looking men dressed in suits. Dalton stood up.

"Ezra will handle the senator," said Abbott. "Your services are no longer required. These gentlemen will escort you out of the building. You can expect to receive your separation package shortly."

Harding knew what that meant. They'd escort him right into the back of a van, and he'd never be seen again. The men split up into two groups and quickly made their way down both sides of the table. He thought about the metal pen in his suit coat jacket, wondering if he could plunge it into Ezra Dalton's neck before they stopped him. What was the point? He got out of his seat and waited for the men to surround him.

"Any last questions?" said Abbott.

"The Windsor chair outside. Does it have a special significance?" said Harding. "It looks out of place."

"It was used by the Founding Fathers during the drafting of the Declaration of Independence," said Abbott. "We're just not sure who sat in it. Maybe all of them at one point."

Harding was blown away by the revelation. "I'd like to sit in it one more time."

Abbott shook his head. "I can think of two billion reasons why you'll never sit in that chair again."

Now he regretted not trying to stab Abbott. As the security team guided him out of the room, he came up with a different idea. Not exactly a better one, but possibly just as satisfying. He gave Samuel Quinn a last look before exiting the room, which was met by the same stoic face. Betrayed and discarded—but at least he would go out in style.

The moment Harding stepped through the door, he burst forward, breaking free of his guards, two of whom were still inside the boardroom. A quick sprint across the anteroom brought him to the historical bow-back Windsor chair, which he lifted above his head and crashed to the marble floor, moments before a guard body-slammed him against the wood-paneled wall.

Harding laughed hysterically as the board members spilled into the anteroom, a broken, splintered piece of history greeting their shocked faces.

"You can take that out of my severance," said Harding, before his world went dark.

Chapter Sixty-Four

Senator Steele yawned and stretched her arms before glancing at the brass Tiffany clock on her desk. Four thirty. She should have heeded Julie's advice and taken the day off, but the thought of sitting around the house by herself sounded like a bad idea. Especially today. She'd returned late last night from several long days in Indianapolis, where she'd spent nearly every waking hour with the Hales—from receiving their son's remains at the airport to committing him to the earth.

At several times during the somber process, Steele hadn't been sure who exactly was holding up whom, but she'd fought through her own resurfaced memories and stayed strong for her friend—knowing it made all the difference. Meredith had done the same for her during her darkest days. Steele's husband had been there, too, but he'd been little more than a fragile shell waiting to shatter at that point.

Meredith had been the rock that kept her from joining him. She intended to be the same for her, just in case Jon started to crumble. He seemed fine right now, showing none of the vacant signs she'd seen in her own husband, but their tragedies shared too much in common. It was the revelation of details leading up to and the questions after her daughter's death that had finally consumed her husband. The bizarre circumstances surrounding Brett Hale's untimely and brutal death had the potential to do the same.

After several days of tense work by dozens of explosives ordnance disposal teams brought in from around the country, the forest around the mountain compound had finally been cleared for forensics work. The Humboldt County Sheriff's Department found Brett's remains buried in a long, shallow ditch outside the compound's western perimeter—along with nearly three dozen other bodies, in various states of decay. Investigators were still working to determine cause and time of death, as far as the Hales knew. The truth would be too much for them right now.

Investigators had found Brett in several pieces, concluding that he'd been killed by a tree-mounted antipersonnel mine. They found the half-exploded tree a few hundred yards southeast of the compound perimeter, matching DNA scraped from the surrounding trees to his. He'd either tripped the mine trying to escape the compound or attempting to sneak in.

Given that the Dunn brothers had been found in the same pit, along with several other corpses in the same state of decay as Brett, investigators felt comfortable concluding that the entire Dunn farm had been rounded up one night and executed. Brett had almost escaped the massacre, a fact that Steele knew would torment the Hales even more. Eventually, they'd see the full report, but the longer that took, the better equipped they'd be to handle something that made so little sense.

They'd ask questions that would never be answered. To the local and federal law enforcement agencies involved, Brett Hale's case was essentially closed, and justice would never be served within official channels. At best, they might be notified months or years later if the perpetrators had been identified, even though Steele knew that call would never come. Athena Corp, the entity she was certain had been responsible for the Alderpoint operation, had covered its tracks well enough to reasonably avoid prosecution—for now.

The DEA and FBI special agents sent by Reeves to "watch" the Nevada facility the night Decker attacked it had somehow walked away with Carl Trenkor, a known Athena Corp mercenary, and quite possibly the leader of the entire drug operation. The challenge now was keeping him alive long enough to give up the next link in the chain. Athena Corp, like every other DC-connected "military contractor" mercenary outfit, had a particular way of burning loose ends. Of course, the Hales would never learn any of this.

When she sensed the time was right, Steele would let Meredith and Jon know that their son's death had been avenged, and that was the best they could hope for in terms of any closure. Knowing that her daughter and husband had been avenged was the only thing that closed the wound enough for her to carry on. For that, she would be eternally grateful to Decker, Harlow, Reeves—and a whole host of others connected to them. She hoped the same knowledge would help the Hales.

A quick look at the clock told her she had been staring off into space for nearly five minutes. What was she trying to prove by sitting here like a paperweight? Time to wrap it up for the day. She'd DoorDash something on the way home and be in bed by eight—hopefully feeling somewhat recharged by tomorrow. She pressed the intercom button on her office phone.

"Julie? I think I'm calling it a day."

"I think that's a good idea," said her chief of staff. "I'll call for your driver."

"Thank you, Julie," she said. "We'll skip today's debrief if you don't mind."

Normally she met with Julie at the end of the day to recap significant events and go over the next day's schedule.

"I guessed as much," said Julie.

A few minutes later, after Steele had assembled everything she planned on taking home for the night, her intercom chimed.

"Senator, I don't know what to make of this, but we've had a drop-in visitor that insists on meeting with you."

"Is this a security situation?"

"I . . . don't think so?"

"You don't sound so sure," said Steele.

"She says she's with the APEX Institute. Ezra Dalton?" said Julie.

Steele shrugged and shook her head. Interesting first name, with a hefty biblical significance—but she'd never come across Ezra Dalton in her decades of work in the Senate.

"She said she's a colleague of Harold Abbott."

Now what was Abbott trying to sell? A US-led peacekeeping mission to the Arctic Circle to secure oil rights for another one of the Institute's clients? She really wasn't in the mood for this right now. APEX, like the vast majority of "think tanks" that had infected Washington, DC, over the past few decades, was nothing more than a lobbying firm for the filthy rich and well connected—both here in the US and abroad. In a way, they were worse than the obviously partisan think tanks. At least with the others, you knew where you stood when they walked in the door. With APEX, you had no idea who they represented.

"Tell her to email her proposal, and we'll get back to them."

The classic "don't call us, we'll call you." They were used to it. She hadn't taken a meeting with APEX since Harold Abbott had suggested she support a bill loosening oversight of the private prison industry—an industry already woefully undersupervised at the time of the bill's proposal. Predictably, even without her help, the bill had passed both the House and Senate, and a company associated with the Brown River military contracting company had immediately announced that it was getting into the private prison business.

"Sounds good," said Julie. "Your car is on the way. Maybe three minutes."

"Thank you, Julie."

A minute later, Julie appeared in her office doorway.

"Sorry to bug you with this," she said. "On the way out she said that the two of you had a good friend in common. Carl Trenkor."

Steele tried not to show her surprise, but Julie had worked for her long enough to know better.

"Security?" she said.

"No. Is she still around?"

Julie called their receptionist and spoke with her briefly.

"She's out in the hallway, thumbing through her phone," said Julie.

"I'll see her in my office," said Steele. "Alone."

"Are you sure?"

She nodded reluctantly. "Yes. Just make sure she's scanned for any kind of electronic devices. Nothing comes back here."

After the thumb drive incident with Senator Duncan last year, when the senator had tried to slip a backdoor virus into Steele's office computer network, they'd installed a proprietary scanner system capable of identifying electronics gear as small as a hidden hearing aid. Joshua Keller, Mackenzie's security guru, had walked them through the various threats, both active and passive, that could compromise their digital security, quickly convincing them that the scanner was necessary—in addition to several software and hardware system upgrades to their wireless network.

"Got it," said Julie.

Julie returned with a tall, elegant woman dressed in an impeccably tailored pantsuit. She introduced herself with a feigned smile and extended a hand. Steele declined.

"Thank you, Julie," said Steele.

When the door closed, she leaned back in her chair. "What can I do for the APEX Institute today?"

"Mind if I take a seat?" said Dalton.

"I'd prefer you didn't get comfortable," she said, before checking her watch. "It's been a long day, and a long weekend thanks to the second associate you mentioned—so if you don't mind getting to the point?"

"I heard about what happened. A very unfortunate happenstance."

"That's one way to put it," she said, glaring at her.

Carl Trenkor had been found dead in his cell a few hours ago at the Nevada Southern Detention Center. Cardiac arrest—no doubt induced by a foreign substance that would remain undetectable to pathologists.

"What do you want?"

"I want to avoid anything like this from happening again," said Dalton.

"Then don't run a two-billion-dollar drug operation on US soil again. Or any kind of illegal enterprise," said Steele. "Pretty simple."

"It's never that simple," said Dalton. "But to avoid any future complications, perhaps you could check in with us—before you dispatch your private black ops team to do your illegal bidding?"

"Illegal?" said Steele.

"Well, that's a matter of judicial opinion, or a Senate ethics committee opinion," said Harding, removing several spine-bound folders from a brown leather satchel and placing them on her desk. "And I'm sure the extensive research conducted and evidence collected by APEX, on behalf of a concerned patriot, will convince either that you've strayed pretty far outside of your job description as a US senator over the past few years."

She started to respond, but Dalton cut her off.

"Look. You've been doing admirable work with the best of intentions. Extremely impressive work when viewed objectively. The motley crew you've assembled functions with surprising efficiency. Decker. Mackenzie and company. Pierce. Reeves. The guy with the airplanes. None of this has to stop, as long as it doesn't create another setback for us. And the only way to ensure that is for you to run your proposed off-the-books stuff through us. Who knows? We might even be able to offer our assistance."

"And if there's a conflict of interest?" said Steele.

"Then we'll work something out," said Dalton.

"How would we have worked out the fact that your surrogates murdered my friend's son?" said Steele.

Dalton considered her question, her face coming nowhere close to expressing the requisite amount of emotion she might require to be deemed sincere.

"We would have worked it out somehow," said Dalton, delivering the nonanswer Steele had anticipated.

"I just asked a few friends to look into a disappearance out in the middle of nowhere," said Steele. "How was I supposed to know what they'd find?"

"You couldn't, unless you came to us first," said Dalton. "Which is what I suggest moving forward."

"And that's all?" said Steele, placing her hands on the folders. "Seems like you guys have been watching me for a while."

"Harold Abbott made it very clear that you weren't fond of the Institute, so I strongly recommended that we secure this agreement and call it good," said Dalton. "Just because we can't be friends doesn't mean we have to be enemies."

She opened the folders and scanned their contents, while Dalton just smiled pleasantly. *Damn.* They really had done their homework, particularly with regard to Southern Cross, the conspiracy Decker and Harlow had helped her unravel last year. The level of detail suggested that APEX might have been more than just an observer in Jacob Harcourt's border scheme.

The same could also be said about their summary of what happened a year before that, at Jacob Harcourt's estate. The possible connection left her wondering exactly how far back APEX and Harcourt's relationship extended. Far enough back to ensnare her daughter? Her heart rate started to rise, and she suddenly felt cold. Steele's body was preparing her for a fight—that wouldn't happen here. She'd take her time with this one.

"I'll have to think this over," she said.

"Time is one luxury we can't afford at the moment," said Dalton. "And the arrangement is very simple and very fair in my opinion. For everyone involved."

The threat was subtle. *Everyone involved.* Steele didn't see a downside to sending her on her way with good news. It truly didn't impact the course of action she'd decided on the moment she'd connected Harcourt to APEX.

She nodded. "I'll get back to you in a few days."

"I'll be sure to pass that on," she said, before opening her satchel and removing more folders.

"I'm just going to leave some additional reading material with you. Dossiers for all your coconspirators, their vulnerabilities and questionable activities highlighted. The folders already on the table outline your involvement, as well as theirs, in a number of unsanctioned operations that caused considerable loss of life and damage across several states and at least one foreign country. I highly advise that you contact these individuals and ask them to cease and desist any current inquiries related to the most recent operation."

"I'll take that under advisement," said Steele.

"I hope you do," said Dalton, placing her business card on the table and departing.

After she had been escorted out of the office, Julie stepped inside.

"How bad is it?" said Julie.

"Not so bad," said Steele. "But not so good. I'm going to need to speak with the group you hired last year to examine the thumb drive Senator Duncan tried to slip past us. How connected are they to the Beltway scene?"

"Not at all," said Julie, filling the glasses. "That's why I used them. Why?"

"Because this whole miserable place is more corrupt than I ever thought possible," said Steele.

CHAPTER
SIXTY-FIVE

Decker limped toward the home's gated entry, taking in the cool sea breeze rustling through the palms. He loved the late fall in Southern California. Still shorts and T-shirt weather, but chilly enough at night to throw on a hoodie. The juxtaposition of day and night temperatures was about the only sign of seasonal change you got out here, which was probably why this was his favorite time of the year.

He checked his phone and entered the code given to him by Harlow into the keypad next to the gate—a code separate from the discreet parking entrance—and the gate clicked, opening several inches. Once he passed through, the gate automatically closed, shutting out the parking area behind it.

A gray slate walkway bordered by lush green bushes led him to the front door, where he entered a third code into the biometric scanner. This place was definitely not designed for the memory challenged. A pleasant, unobtrusive chime announced his arrival, as the door swung silently and smoothly inward to reveal what Senator Steele had generously arranged for Pam's recovery. Definitely not for the wallet challenged, either.

"We're in here, Decker!" said Pam, sounding remarkably recovered.

Decker followed the direction of her voice through the white, polished marble grand entry to a vast room of open floor-to-ceiling window sliders overlooking the Pacific Ocean; the same breeze he'd felt earlier washed through the room. Pam lay in a hospital bed next to a sectional couch and table arrangement, which hosted the rest of the firm—and two half-empty pitchers of margaritas.

Pam raised a salt-rimmed margarita glass. "Welcome to the party, Decker!"

A woman he barely recognized out of tactical gear wheeled herself out of the kitchen, a bottle of expensive-looking tequila in her lap. Brooklyn?

He shook his head. "Looks like it pays to get shot."

"You just didn't get shot bad enough," said Pam. "Get over here and give me a 'get well' hug. I missed you at the hospital up in Redding."

Decker glanced at Harlow and the rest of the crew like he might be at the wrong address.

"She's been like this since she woke up at the hospital," said Sophie. "I think they somehow switched her with someone else."

He gave her more of an air hug than a real one, mindful of her wounds, which he knew from experience could flare up with the smallest muscle contraction. While he hovered over her, she whispered in his ear.

"Thank you for saving my life," she said. "If you tell anyone I said that, I'll deny it and punish you when I'm better."

"Got it. Glad you pulled through," said Decker, standing up and addressing the group. "I can say with full confidence that she did not get switched at the hospital."

"Good. Because we were starting to get worried," said Harlow, making room for him on the couch next to her.

"So. What are we celebrating?" said Decker, giving Harlow a quick kiss before sinking into the couch. "And what is Brooklyn doing here?"

Harlow gave him that look.

"Sorry. I just wasn't expecting to see you," said Decker.

Decker hadn't seen her since EMTs had loaded her into the back of an ambulance and transported her to a level-two trauma center in Reno, where doctors had managed to save the leg. She'd regain full use of her knee after several months of intensive physical therapy, but doctors made it clear that Brooklyn's days of parachuting into hot spots and hopping off the backs of moving trucks into combat were probably over. They didn't put it that way, of course, because they had no idea what she did for a living.

"No offense taken," she said, stopping next to the opposite side of the couch, where Sophie took the bottle. "Harlow very kindly offered me a place to recover, and Pam very graciously agreed. Thank you, again."

Maybe this wasn't Pam after all.

"There's plenty of room," said Harlow. "And we're kind of looking at this as a job interview. If Pam doesn't roll her off the balcony at some point in the next few weeks, I'd like to offer her an interim position at the firm."

"How am I supposed to do that from this bed?" said Pam, getting a round of laughs.

"The first twenty-four hours have gone smoothly enough," said Harlow.

"I was asleep for half of them," said Pam, taking a long sip from her glass.

"I was pretending to be asleep for the rest," said Brooklyn, pulling up to the table.

"I think you can hire her right away," said Decker. "She's already figured out the safest way to spend time with Pam. So what are we calling you? I don't want to give any trade secrets away."

"Brooklyn," she said. "The name grew on me."

Sophie busied herself pouring shots of tequila into glasses she had pulled from a tray under the table. Menacingly large–looking shots, and he didn't see any salt or limes around.

"What's this all about?" said Decker.

"Celebrating," said Jessica, taking one of the shot glasses.

The rest of them took glasses, leaving Decker's alone on the table.

"Can we celebrate with beer?" he said. "I'm really not a fan of tequila."

"Jesus, Decker," said Pam. "Just grab your glass."

"Is she even supposed to be drinking?" said Decker, taking his drink. "I'm pretty sure tequila shots are not recommended a few days after major surgery."

"We're cutting her off after this," said Harlow.

"What is this about?" said Decker quietly.

"I honestly don't know."

Jessica raised her glass. "First, to pulling off the impossible in Humboldt County and then again in Nevada."

They clinked glasses, and Jessica continued. "Second, to Decker and Harlow. The Los Angeles Police Department and district attorney's office cleared both of them in the shooting. Interestingly enough, I was told that Sheriff Harvey Long called down to vouch for your professionalism and handling of the shooting at the motel in Garberville."

"Damn. How many shootings are you involved in on a regular basis?" said Brooklyn.

"It's been an unusually busy month," said Decker, getting a round of laughs.

"To the firm," said Jessica, downing her shot.

They all followed her immediately, including Decker, who felt instantly nauseous. A hazy memory about drinking from a bottle of tequila after an Army-Navy game had ruined that particular spirit for him. He winced and waited for the feeling to pass—relieved that nobody seemed interested in a second round after the cheers died down.

He turned to Harlow. "Can I talk to you outside?"

"Sure," she said, a skeptical look on her face.

She took his hand and they walked onto the sweeping terrace overlooking the Pacific.

"Must be nice to own a place like this," said Decker, the tequila hitting his head a little.

"One of these days," said Harlow. "But not until I retire. Nothing but empty second homes, celebrities, and retired rich people out here."

"Very rich people," said Decker.

"Plus, the whole place is going to burn to the ground within the next five years. It's just a matter of time. I'll buy in after that," said Harlow. "What's up?"

"Pierce is off the roster," said Decker. "That's why I was late. He rescheduled his flight and grabbed me for a drink back in Santa Monica."

"What exactly does 'off the roster' mean?" said Harlow. "It's not like this kind of stuff comes up very often, and we certainly don't seek it out."

"That's not what it means. He'll always be available in a pinch, but he's starting a security consulting business out of Denver," said Decker. "He plans on devoting all of his 'bail Decker out of trouble' time to getting that off the ground."

"He really stuck his neck out this time—every time, actually," said Harlow. "I'll miss having him around."

"Me too," said Decker. "I told him I'll do my best to stay out of trouble, so he has a chance of getting his business off the ground before having to fly out of town again at a moment's notice."

"Trouble seems to find you," said Harlow.

"Yeah. It kinda does," said Decker, staring out at the ocean's horizon.

"What are you thinking?" she said, putting an arm around him.

"I need to be more careful," he said. "Back off from the field work for a while and simmer down."

"Sounds like there's more on your mind than just hanging back at the office or running surveillance support," said Harlow. "What's really going on?"

"I don't know. Pierce got me thinking about things. Priorities," he said, turning to her. "Don't worry. This isn't what you think."

"We'll see about that," said Harlow.

"Basically, I want to spend more time with Riley," he said, her face somehow remaining unbiased. "But not at the expense of spending less time with you."

She visibly relaxed and squeezed his hand.

"I thought you might be breaking up with me," she said.

"No. Your probationary period expired a long time ago," said Decker.

"Really?" she said. "Because you're always on probation. I expect your best behavior at all times."

He kissed her. "I think I can live under those conditions."

"Good," she said. "So. Since I'm not relocating the firm to Idaho, what's your plan?"

"I haven't exactly worked that out yet," said Decker. "I could offer to move Riley and my parents down here. Maybe Orange County, where it's a little less crazy? I don't know. What do you think?"

"About Orange County or having them living closer?"

"Sorry. I kind of went out of order," said Decker. "How do you feel about having Riley and my parents living a lot closer."

"I think it would be great," said Harlow. "As much as I enjoy monopolizing your time, you need more of them in your life. Not just more. You need them *in* your life. Frankly, I need them, too, if we're going to take this to the next level."

"We're taking this to the next level?" said Decker, holding her.

"I sure hope so," she said, kissing him.

"What's the next level?" he said.

She shrugged. "Whatever comes next for us."

Pam's piercing voice cut through the sea breeze.

"Do the two of you mind!" said Pam. "You're blocking my view—thereby hindering my recovery. Join the party or get a room!"

"She was like this the entire time up north," said Decker.

"I give you a lot of credit for saving her," said Harlow, and they both laughed.

Decker's phone buzzed in his pocket, and he almost ignored it. The off chance that it was Brad convinced him to check the caller ID. For all he knew, his friend could have gotten into a fender bender on the way to the airport.

"Go ahead. I'll be right behind you," said Decker, taking out his phone.

After a quick glance at its screen, he was glad he hadn't blown off the call.

"Everything okay?" said Harlow.

"It's the senator."

She squeezed his hand. "I'll let the two of you talk."

Decker answered the phone as Harlow walked back inside.

"Senator, good timing. We were just about—" said Decker.

"We need to talk," said Steele.

About the Author

Steven Konkoly is a *Wall Street Journal* and *USA Today* bestselling author. A graduate of the US Naval Academy and veteran of several elite US Navy and Marine Corps units, Konkoly has brought his in-depth military experience to bear in his fiction. His novels include *The Rescue* and *The Raid* in the Ryan Decker series; the Black Flagged conspiracy saga; and the speculative postapocalyptic thrillers *The Jakarta Pandemic*, *The Perseid Collapse*, and the Fractured State series. Konkoly lives in central Indiana with his family. For more information, visit www.stevenkonkoly.com.